SKYJACK

SKYJACK

K.J. HOWE

A Thea Paris Novel

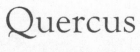

New York • London

Quercus

New York • London

Copyright © 2018 by Kimberley Howe
First published in the United States by Quercus in 2018

ISBN 978-1-68-144301-0
e-ISBN 978-1-68-144299-0

Library of Congress Control Number: 2018931641

Distributed in the United States and Canada by
Hachette Book Group
1290 Avenue of the Americas
New York, NY 10104

Manufactured in the United States

10 9 8 7 6 5 4 3 2 1

www.quercus.com

SKYJACK

K.J. HOWE

A Thea Paris Novel

Quercus

New York • London

Quercus

New York • London

ISBN 978-1-68-144301-0
e-ISBN 978-1-68-144299-0

Library of Congress Control Number: 2018931641

Distributed in the United States and Canada by
Hachette Book Group
1290 Avenue of the Americas
New York, NY 10104

Manufactured in the United States

10 9 8 7 6 5 4 3 2 1

www.quercus.com

For Rambo's Daddy, David Morrell:
inspiration, mentor, friend

There must always be a struggle between a father and son, while one aims at power and one at independence.

—Samuel Johnson

Prologue

March 10, 1956
37,000 feet above the Mediterranean Sea

Captain Earl Johnson had never felt so alive.

The B-47's lightning speed and unparalleled maneuverability set his senses ablaze. But even the jet's six engines couldn't keep his crew warm today. Plummeting temperatures had shrouded the plane in an icy shell. He concentrated, his frozen fingers caressing the throttle, careful to keep his plane in formation with the three other Stratojets.

Earl shifted in the cramped space, his breath exiting in crystallized puffs. The plane's beefy manual rested under his feet, protecting his toes from frostbite. His copilot's and engineer's teeth chattered, but they'd never utter a word of complaint. Cold, stiff, uncomfortable—and all as happy as prize pigs slathered in mud. Earl couldn't imagine a more perfect moment than this: rocketing along at 37,000 feet, the altitude at which they had optimum fuel consumption but where the difference between overspeed and stall speed was only a few knots. By pushing the forward edge of this narrow speed range, Earl risked a shockwave that could strip the air from his wings and pitch him into an unrecoverable dive; at the slow end, the aircraft could stall and fall out of the sky. A little turbulence could mean the difference between the two. Dangerous but efficient, it was the sweet spot known among pilots as "coffin corner," a place where Earl felt right at home. Riding the edge kept him sharp and provided a good distraction from the icy temperatures and the financial pressures of a new baby on the way.

They'd left MacDill Air Force Base in Florida over eight hours ago, destination Ben Guerir in Morocco. The four planes torpedoed through the sky, headed for their rendezvous with the aircraft tankers so they could execute their second refueling. Each B-47 held two containers of uranium 235, enough fissile material to construct two nuclear bombs, each a hundred times more powerful than the one that had pancaked Hiroshima.

Earl's radio buzzed on the encrypted frequency.

"Bluebird Three, visibility's socked in from 28,500 to 14,500 feet. We'll need to descend to 14,000 for refueling. Stand by." Earl's best friend, Slow Joe—as he was ironically called due to his need for speed—piloted the fourth plane.

"Roger." Earl pushed the throttle up to 275 knots, a roaring 557 mph across the ground 37,000 feet below, and let the engines howl for a few seconds before they had to dive deep into the clouds to make the rendezvous. Joe's hand would undoubtedly be twitching as Earl's bomber took the lead.

"You're forty-seven screams louder than your wife after a five-day layover." Slow Joe's voice was playful over the radio. "Yessiree, she told the squadron commander that no way could she handle you for three hours, let alone five days."

Earl's copilot and engineer laughed at Joe's poke, used to the two of them carrying on. The tight space inside the bubble canopy offered zero privacy.

"Y'all think you're funny, but no one's cooking grits for you at home," Earl replied. The single men weren't subtle about envying his married status. He took his ribbing with a dash of humility—until the guys got too rambunctious and he had to tamp them down.

He checked the time and pressed the radio button. The tankers should be waiting for them under the clouds. "Trail formation on the way down," he said, commanding one plane to follow the next. "Thicker than corn syrup today. Try not to get lost, Joe." Okay, maybe he wasn't oozing with humility, but any pilot worth his salt had to have a pair.

"Roger. You're buying the beer when we get to Morocco. It's the least you can do for making me refuel last." Slow Joe might be full of sass, but there was no more reliable captain.

"I bought last time. Nice try. Over and out." Earl dove through the thick clouds, keeping an eye on his altimeter. The cloud cover was impenetrable, like a kettle billowing steam straight at the windscreen.

He followed Bluebird Two in trail formation, as planned. His eyes darted back and forth, and his knees quivered—from the cold or pressure, he wasn't sure. Damn, he could barely see the tail of the plane in front of him. Good thing the precise power control made formation flying relatively simple.

He blocked all distractions, his world narrowing to a pinpoint focus. Ragged, wispy clouds whipped by the canopy, then disappeared as the B-47 shot into the clear. A quick glance at the altimeter. Yep, fourteen thousand feet and out of the goo, just as the weather guessers had advertised. Earl eased the control wheel aft to arrest the bird's descent and nudged a handful of throttles forward to hold altitude. He exhaled a long, steady breath.

Three tankers hovered below. Bluebird One and Two were already starting the process of connecting with two of them. Behind each tanker was an imaginary cone-shaped segment of space known as the envelope. Inside that zone, the boomer could transfer the fuel.

The third tanker loomed in front of him, a huge mother ship. Connecting with the tubby KC-97s always presented a challenge.

Two planes linking up midair to deliver highly combustible fuel—what could possibly go wrong?

Earl's attention sharpened, his speed dropping to a pedestrian 200 knots to match the tanker's shallow dive. Slow Joe had a phenomenal track record of first-shot contacts; he was an air-refueling ace. Earl didn't want any glitches, or he'd take more razzing tonight over drinks. Bottom line: wind, weather, and just about anything else could mess with the process.

He opened the small refueling door in the nose and maneuvered the B-47 up and a little to the left. The boomer placed the receiver in the receptacle, connecting the bomber with the KC-97.

"Fill 'er up, and get that windscreen cleaned, sir?" the KC-97 engineer asked.

Earl shook his head with a smile. "Why is everyone a comedian today? Let's just get this done." It had been a long, grueling flight.

The "connected" signal lit up, and the engineer initiated the fuel transfer. A thirsty B-47 could suck in six hundred gallons per minute during refueling—even faster than Slow Joe's beer intake on a good night.

Earl concentrated on keeping the B-47 steady, trying to adjust for the burble of air buffeting the plane from the KC-97. Fuel splattered the windscreen, startling him. Dammit, the seal must not be airtight. Slow Joe would have a go at him for this. Looked like an elephant was taking a whiz right on them. He flicked on the bomber's wiper blade and strained to see through the spray and oily film smearing the windscreen.

The tanker sped up slightly as its fuel load decreased. Grateful, Earl increased his speed to keep pace. The B-47 ached to go faster, like a reined-in racehorse.

He fought to stay in position, the control wheel in constant motion as he made small adjustments, but the film of fuel on the windscreen warped his view of the tanker.

Finally, the boomer finished refueling and radioed him. "You're full, sir. Cleared to disconnect."

"Roger, over and out." He smiled. Success, even with a crack in the seal. Let's see if Joe could be this slick.

"We're clear," Earl's engineer said.

Freed from the tanker, Earl pulled alongside the KC-97 so the crew could read his bomber's number. He yearned to return to the thinner air, where the B-47 was more at home.

"Slow Joe, you're up. See if you can beat my time." He waited for a smart-aleck reply.

Silence greeted him.

Unusual. His buddy was never at a loss for words.

"Come in, Bluebird Four." He waited.

Nothing.

"You see him?" Earl asked his copilot.

"No joy, sir."

Earl tried the radio again.

No response.

"Bluebird One and Two, any visual on Four?" Earl asked.

Several seconds passed.

"No, sir."

"Can't see it."

For a moment, Earl thought, even hoped, that Slow Joe might be playing a trick. But he knew better. Joe would never compromise a mission, especially not this one.

Earl tried again and again, but it was as if Joe's plane had vanished. Despite the frigid temperature, a wave of heat radiated down his spine, and sweat soaked his back.

Seconds later, he contacted Strategic Air Command headquarters at MacDill Air Force Base.

"What is it, Captain Johnson?" A duty officer at the command post sounded sleepy, as if he had just woken up. Then again, it was the middle of the night in Florida.

"Sir, it looks like we have a Broken Arrow. I repeat, Broken Arrow."

"Stand by." The officer's voice snapped to attention, no longer groggy.

Broken Arrow. The loss of two containers full of fissile material with a 704-million-year half-life—along with a B-47 and its crew—meant no one in the Strategic Air Command would be sleeping tonight.

Chapter 1

Thea Paris felt as if she were trapped inside a giant cocktail shaker. Up, down, side to side—the turbulence delivered a walloping to the 737. A sheen of sweat dampened her forehead, her vision was blurred, and the world felt slightly off-kilter. Was her blood sugar out of whack? A quick glance at the app on her phone: 110. All under control. Her nerves, not so much. Modern airliners were resilient enough to ride out severe turbulence without coming apart or falling out of the sky, but that knowledge didn't help her feel any better.

She just hated flying.

Maybe it was the lack of control that drove her crazy? Rif Asker—her colleague and longtime friend—was an ace pilot, and he gently chided her about how she was able to remain calm under enormous duress in her job, while the sound of jet engines firing up rattled her to the core. Well, Rif wasn't there today, and air travel was an essential part of being a crisis response consultant, the industry term for a kidnap negotiator.

Most of the time, she could distract herself by focusing on her current case, but it didn't always work. She gritted her teeth and tried to present a brave front to the two boys beside her, both first-time fliers. The African charity her late brother, Nikos, had founded to help recovering child soldiers had started an adoption program, and these two brothers were headed to their new home in London with the Waverton family. Jabari Kuria was twelve, Ayan, nine. After witnessing their parents' beheadings by Boko Haram, they had been forced to invade neighboring villages to abduct other children, soldiers in a war they didn't understand.

The plane dropped suddenly, leaving them weightless for what felt like an endless moment. Then their butts slammed back into their seats as the metal bird hit an updraft. Thea's stomach protested. If the seat-belt light hadn't been on, she'd have been tempted to grab an Ativan from her SINK (survival insurance nightmare kit) in the overhead compartment. The tote contained everything *but* the kitchen sink, including a steel compass, a flashlight, a booster, first-aid supplies, her diabetes medications, and other potentially useful items that, if detected, would cause an airport security officer to escort her to a window-less room for further questioning. As a freedom broker, she traveled undercover to global hot spots and never knew what might be needed. The SINK came with her everywhere.

Jabari smiled and poked her arm. "This is more fun than riding an ostrich."

Only a kid could think of this shaken-not-stirred flight as a good time. Her fingers strangled the armrests. She checked the boys' seat belts for the fourth time. "It sure is." She forced a smile. "And every flight is different. Sometimes there's no shaking at all."

She shouldn't complain about the rocky skies. Getting the boys to their adoptive home was what counted. They'd missed their connection in Nairobi, but with Rif's help, they had been able to secure three seats on a chartered Boeing Business Jet, flying to London in style. The Wavertons and Papa planned to pick them up at Heathrow, bringing Aegis, the Paris family dog, to meet the boys and help put them at ease. The last time they'd been together, Thea and her father had argued about Nikos's memorial; she'd wanted to place it next to her mother's tomb at their house in Martha's Vineyard, but Papa had refused. Yet more fallout from her brother's death. Maybe when she reached London, the two of them could find some time to work on healing their fractured relationship.

Ayan was curled up in his window seat, pointing outside. "Why aren't the wings flapping?"

"It's not a bird, silly. It's a plane, a jet." Jabari enjoyed lording his superior knowledge over his little brother, but if anyone tried to bully Ayan, Jabari would be the first to defend him. Knowing the hell they'd gone through, she hoped this would be a fresh start, a chance to reclaim their childhoods. The boys' situation struck a very personal chord with her, as Nikos had also been kidnapped by an African warlord at twelve and forced to do unspeakable things. He'd never fully recovered from the trauma. And the orphanage was his legacy—now their legacy, as she'd assumed responsibility for the charity with Nikos gone.

Ayan's index finger hammered at the TV screen in the seat back in front of him. "Look, Jabari, it's a story about a lion."

A smile managed to surface through her unease. *The Lion King* was one of the in-flight movies.

"What if I want to watch something else?" Jabari's lower lip jutted forward.

"Then you can play another movie on your own screen. Pick whatever you like. We're very lucky—we can choose anything."

Thea scanned the plane, cataloging the other passengers, an occupational reflex. A stunning middle-aged Asian woman dressed in black, an old man wearing a fedora, a fair-haired beanpole with wire-rimmed glasses and a bow tie who was clutching his computer bag, a slickster dressed in Versace, a strapping guy with a handlebar mustache, a dandy wearing seersucker pants and a panama hat. She couldn't fight an unsettled mood that had nothing to do with the turbulence.

The plane shook again, rattling the overhead bins. An older, barrel-chested gentleman seated near the emergency exit turned and looked in her direction. Sweat drenched his forehead, and he kept crossing and uncrossing his legs. Maybe he felt nervous or nauseated from the turbulence but couldn't use the lavatory because the seat-belt lights were on.

She could relate.

"Do they have many animals in London?" Jabari asked.

"You'll see some dogs and cats and even horses, but the UK is quite different from Africa." She guessed the London Zoo could either be their favorite outing or a thoroughly depressing spectacle. The boys would definitely experience culture shock in London, but they were smart and capable, and the family adopting them would provide opportunities they never would have had at the orphanage.

Another sudden drop.

"Wheee!" Ayan laughed and raised his slender arms in the air.

She swore under her breath, not wanting to challenge the boys' opinion that this aeronautical roller-coaster ride was brilliant fun. Although it felt as if they'd plummeted three thousand feet in two seconds, the plane's altitude had probably only dropped ten or twenty feet. But the turbulence caused the 737 to pitch and roll like a rowboat in a typhoon.

She'd learned everything she could about planes and safety, hoping the knowledge would ease her anxiety. It didn't.

She checked her blood sugar levels again. A little low. She hoped the pummeling would stop soon, so the flight attendants could offer food and beverage service. She needed to eat, and the two boys would gobble any food the second it appeared—a habit learned during their captivity and, no doubt, reinforced at the orphanage.

A few minutes later, the turbulence settled a touch. Had they reached calmer skies, or was it like an earthquake, where aftershocks came rippling in just when you thought it was safe?

Movement at the front of the plane caught her attention. The cockpit door opened, and the copilot stepped out into the cabin. Didn't the seat-belt sign apply to him? Two pilots on the flight deck were better than one, especially in these conditions.

After a quick word with a flight attendant, the copilot slipped into the forward bathroom. Was he in desperate need of relief, ill, or what?

Thea's gaze locked on the lavatory door, waiting for him to reemerge.

One thousand, two thousand, three thousand . . .

A solid thump startled her. The heavyset older man who'd been sweating a couple of rows ahead had slumped over the edge of his seat and was hanging into the aisle. She waited a couple of seconds for him to move.

He didn't.

She held out her little finger to Jabari and Ayan. "Stay here, buckled up. Pinky swear." She'd taught them this ritual during one of her visits to the orphanage.

The plane jolted to the left and dipped.

The boys entwined their pinkies with hers.

"Thanks, guys." She released her seat belt and stood. Bracing herself on the overhead compartments, she clambered forward to where the man had collapsed in his seat. One of the flight attendants met her there.

She placed two fingers on the stocky man's neck. "No pulse."

The plane started shaking again.

The attendant held his wrist. "I'm not getting anything either."

Several passengers leaned forward, trying to get a better look. She snapped open the man's seat belt, looped her arms underneath his shoulders, and pulled him out of the seat. The plane dropped abruptly, and she almost lost her hold on him. She stabilized her footing, yanked him into the aisle, and lowered him to the floor. Not easy. The man was built like a fully loaded washing machine.

The flight attendant knelt beside her, brushing his red hair off his forehead. His name tag read BERNARD.

"You a doctor?" he asked.

"More like a combat medic." Gunshots, puncture wounds, and other side effects of extreme violence were her specialty. Given the man's age, pallor, and physical condition, her first thought was that he'd suffered a heart attack. He needed oxygen. Four to five minutes without it, and he'd be brain dead. "Defibrillator," Thea said.

Bernard hurried off to get it.

She placed the heel of her left hand on the center of his chest, resting her right hand directly on top. Linking her fingers together, she kept her elbows straight and pushed down hard. Queen's "Another One Bites the Dust" ran through her head. During training, they'd played the familiar tune over and over, as it had one hundred beats per minute, the ideal rhythm for compressions. She delivered a quick thirty thrusts to keep his circulation going.

She reached under his neck to ease open his airway and listened for any sign of breathing. He smelled strongly of onions, but there was no hint of air movement from his lungs. Another bout of turbulence thrust her against the nearby seats. She steadied herself, pinched his nostrils shut while pulling his head slightly back, and puffed a breath into the man's mouth, initiating artificial respiration. His chest rose. *Okay, no obstruction.* She gave him another big lungful, then completed thirty more compressions.

Bernard returned with the defibrillator, the copilot at his heels. "Keep going while I get it ready."

"Not looking good?" the copilot asked, concern in his eyes.

"I'd recommend an emergency landing."

"Roger." He sped toward the cockpit.

After she'd finished five rounds of thirty compressions and two breaths, sweat dripped down her back. In the distance, someone was banging at the front of the cabin, but she couldn't worry about that now. She shot a quick glance at the boys. They were in their seats, as promised, but, like the rest of the passengers, they were craning their necks so they could see what she was doing. She gave Ayan and Jabari a reassuring smile. They certainly wouldn't forget their first flight.

Bernard had started the automated external defibrillator. He ripped the man's shirt open and applied the electrode pads to the upper right and lower left chest.

"Analyzing rhythm, clear," Bernard warned.

She moved aside, letting the AED complete its analysis.

"Shock advised. Remain clear."

"Got it."

Bernard pressed the shock button.

Waited.

The AED advised him to shock again.

And again.

Dammit. The man's heart wasn't responding. She started the compressions again, replaying the throbbing beats of "Another One Bites the Dust" in her mind.

Come on, Freddie, help me out here.

Bernard felt for a pulse. He shook his head.

She wouldn't give up.

Thea completed another round of compressions and looked up to see the copilot, who had returned from the front of the plane. "Are we landing somewhere soon?" she asked. "This man needs immediate medical intervention."

The copilot lowered his voice. "Bit of an issue. The pilot has locked the door and won't let me back in."

Chapter 2

Sicily, Italy

The pungent scent of chlorine clung to Prospero Salvatore's skin even though it had been two hours since he'd completed his 150 laps. Swimming wasn't his first choice to stay in fighting shape, just his only one right now. He ambled up the church steps, trying not to wince. His left hip ached with every step these days. So much so that he'd booked a flight to New York in ten days so he could visit an orthopedic specialist without his contacts in Sicily being any the wiser.

Prospero would never show vulnerability around the sharks who worked for him. Fifty-four wasn't old, but he'd been hard on his body, and the hip had finally blasted a hearty *fuck you* at him. Even a handful of pain meds and a couple of acrobatic mistresses couldn't fix it. Every morning, the agony of his first steps brought back memories of his father's slow and excruciating demise from bone cancer. Stefano Salvatore had fought like a son of a bitch to eke out every single minute he had left, and Prospero took inspiration from the old man's grit and determination.

Still, a quick stab of envy shot through him as his twenty-three-year-old nephew, Luciano Baggio, leapt up the steps and opened the door for him.

"H-h-here you go, *signore*."

Prospero cringed inside every time he heard that stutter, but family was family, so he'd taken Luciano under his wing. The kid was a good earner—better than expected, actually, given his handicap. But his nephew also had a dark side. Prospero had witnessed Luciano's barely contained zeal when making forcible collections. Not acceptable. Violence should be judiciously meted out, not enjoyed.

He stepped into the church, the coolness wicking sweat from his brow. The musty air brought back long-forgotten memories of being an altar boy—before the lure of the *famiglia* had changed his path.

His footsteps echoed in the cavernous space, the hitch in his left hip making for a slightly longer reverberation with every other step. An old woman lit a candle at a side altar. The cathedral ceilings, soft luminescence, and intricate tapestries soothed him. Stained-glass windows depicting the saints offered a promise of solace. The space was the perfect intersection of history, religion, and culture—all crucial pillars in his life.

"Wait here," he told Luciano.

His nephew slipped into the last pew and knelt in prayer. Prospero shrugged. At least his sister had taught the kid the importance of faith.

He strode down the aisle toward the front. The plane dominated every thought. *Did they have it?* Time was of the essence. He rubbed his five o'clock shadow and joined the three-person line waiting for the confessional. Plenty of sinning going on in this corner of Sicily, if the perpetual backlog at St. Ignacio's was any indication.

A withered woman wearing a head scarf exited the booth. Prospero nodded a greeting—she was a friend's great-aunt. He paused to let the octogenarian next in line enter the confessional, but the man tipped his hat to Prospero and stepped aside. Two elderly ladies behind the old man gave gentle waves, encouraging him to enter first.

Respect. Sadly lacking in today's youth but robust among his hometown's elders.

"*Grazie.*" He stepped up to the booth. The green light was on, indicating that the priest was ready for the next parishioner. He pulled aside the drape, moved inside, and gently lowered himself onto the kneeler.

Positioning most of his weight on his right knee, he traced the cross that was mounted on the lattice separating him from the priest. The Act of Contrition was posted off to one side.

"*Saluti, sacerdote,*" Prospero said. "*Sono io.*"

A sharp intake of breath told him that Father Anthony realized it wasn't the usual henchman making contact via the confessional. No, the *capo* was here today.

"An honor, sir," the priest whispered. "Thank you for coming."

The catch in Father Anthony's voice showed Prospero that the priest was nervous. *Good.*

Since he was already here, he might as well get a few things off his chest. "Forgive me, Father, for I have sinned. It has been three weeks since my last confession. I accuse myself of the following sins. I have committed adultery seven times since my last confession." His remorse was genuine. But given that his wife, Violetta, had less than zero interest in sex these days, what was a man like him to do? He still had an appetite, even if she had excused herself from the dining table long ago. Besides, he never got emotionally involved with his paramours—he loved his wife too much for that.

"I had to teach one of my men a lesson for stealing." The young man in question was currently in the hospital, but he'd live, and that was better than he deserved. "I'm sorry for these sins and for the sins of my whole life, especially the mortal sin of killing others." He wasn't all that remorseful about certain hits, but discretion was necessary in church.

Father Anthony's throaty voice wafted through the lattice. "Remember Isaiah 1:18: 'Come now, let us settle the matter, says the Lord. Though your sins are like scarlet, they shall be as white as snow; though they are as red as crimson, they shall be like wool.'" A long pause. "You must absolve yourself of these sins."

Red as crimson, that's for sure. He stared at his hands, almost expecting to see blood on them. He shook off the image. "Yes, Father." He recited the Act of Contrition. "Oh, my God, I am heartily sorry for having offended You . . ." He hoped *Dio* was in a forgiving mood today, because he'd need every advantage for his plans to succeed.

Prospero finished the prayer.

"Anything else, my son?" Father Anthony asked.

He hadn't made the trip just to unload his conscience. "Three million euros for your charity."

Father Anthony cleared his throat. "But the last donation was only a week ago."

"Expediency has proven expensive." His words were tight, clipped. Laundered money was critical to the plan.

"Of course. A delivery will arrive soon."

"Think of the future, Father, how you're protecting your flock." *And consider your own health.*

"It would be difficult to ponder our future if this mission fails."

"Yes, Father." But Prospero lived by the same credo as Marcus Aurelius: *Each of us only lives now, this brief instant. The rest has been lived already, or is impossible to see.* Prospero shifted weight off his bad hip. "There is one more thing, a complication." He relished a challenge, but this new development gave even him pause. Still, he couldn't resist taking a little delight in toying with the high-strung priest.

"What is it?" Trepidation lent a quaver to Father Anthony's voice. The holy man didn't want to get more involved than he already was; laundering money through the Vatican bank was already jeopardizing his immortal soul, not to mention threatening his mortal self with substantial jail time—or worse—if he were ever caught.

"*Liberata*—she's on the plane." Prospero felt the temperature in the booth plummet.

"The kidnap negotiator?"

"*Sì.*"

A long hesitation. "We should pray."

No kidding.

Chapter 3

Thea's shoulders and arms were beginning to tire from perform-
ing CPR on the unresponsive passenger. Still no pulse. She felt
slightly dizzy from her efforts, and the copilot's words did nothing to settle her thoughts.

What the hell is happening in the cockpit?

Bernard returned from conferring with his fellow flight attendant and placed a hand on her shoulder. "Here, let me take over."

She finished the cycle and moved aside, allowing him to continue
the CPR. His colleague, Madeira, moved among the passengers, reassuring them and asking them to remain seated as they craned their
necks in an effort to figure out what was going on at the front of
the plane. They'd been working on the man for at least ten minutes.
Even the AED hadn't kick-started his heart. It wasn't looking good.

She stood and extended a hand to the copilot. "Thea Paris. I'm a
security professional. Can we speak up front?"

"William Laverdeen. Absolutely."

She looked back at the boys, Jabari wrapping his larger hand
around his brother's. It made her miss Nikos. She strode up the
aisle, aware of the passengers' gazes glued to her back. Since the

older man had collapsed, an intense silence had settled across the plane, everyone absorbed by the emergency. Only the Asian woman in black seemed unfazed by the chaos, casually flipping through a fashion magazine. The woman looked up briefly as Thea passed, then went back to reading.

Thea hurried to the front of the plane. At least the turbulence seemed to have settled down.

She met Laverdeen outside the cockpit door. His face showed irritation and a pinch of panic.

"The pilot locked you out?"

"I've tried the interphone, banged on the door, but Captain Rivers hasn't responded."

"You entered the emergency code?" she asked.

"Let me try again." He punched a code into the touch pad. If it worked, it would send an alarm to the cockpit warning that someone would be cleared to enter in thirty seconds.

The light turned yellow, then back to red. "Dammit. Rivers toggled the lock mode again. We won't be able to try again for at least five minutes."

"And the lock mode could last for as long as twenty, correct?"

"Actually, he can keep switching on the lock mode, keeping us out indefinitely."

This safety feature prevented hijackers from storming the cockpit. But what protected passengers from an unstable captain? Thea's thoughts immediately went to Germanwings Flight 9525, on which copilot Andreas Lubitz locked the captain out and crashed the commercial airliner straight into the French Alps, taking all 150 souls aboard with him into oblivion. She forced the thought out of her mind.

They needed to get inside. But after 9/11, cockpit doors had been reinforced with a solid steel bar that ran horizontally across the door into a strike plate on either side. These upgraded doors were supposed to be bulletproof, too—even able to withstand the force of a grenade. The cockpit did have a trapdoor, but it could only be opened from inside.

She checked her cell to see if the in-flight Wi-Fi was still working. Nope. Rivers had shut it down. "How was the captain's mood?"

"Normal. Guy's kind of an asshole." Laverdeen punched the code on the keypad again. The red light flashed. Locked. "I urgently needed the toilet. Sounds crazy, I know, but I think he slipped something into my coffee."

Maybe not so crazy. She picked up the interphone to test it herself, on the off chance that Laverdeen wasn't telling the truth. The two pilots might have had words, or they could be embroiled in some personal drama. The phone rang and rang. No answer.

Laverdeen banged on the cockpit door again, hard. Several passengers craned their necks, trying to see what was going on. After all, pilots were supposed to be *inside* the cockpit. The Asian woman still casually flipped through her magazine.

Laverdeen pounded hard again.

Suddenly the world tilted upward, the plane's nose pitching skyward sharply, engines spooling to an angry whine. Thea crashed backward into the first row of seats. Bracing herself on a seat back, she tried to stabilize her footing.

Too late. The plane did a snap roll, the right wing pivoting toward the sky, the left one toward the ground. It felt like a ninety-degree bank, though Thea knew that was impossible— a bank that steep would exert enough g-force on the plane to start tearing it apart in midair.

A steel coffeepot flew through the forward galley and crashed into the lavatory door. Screams reverberated throughout the cabin. Thea groped at the overhead compartment, her fingers connecting with the latch. She clung to it, but as it took her weight, the latch popped open. She flopped backward, then kipped herself forward, releasing the bin door and grabbing the inside lip with both hands. With the increased g-forces, her forearms ached from the effort and her body felt much heavier than normal, swinging back and forth like that of a rock climber hanging from a dangerous precipice.

The lights flickered—off, on, off, on—the world reduced to snapshots. Laverdeen crashed against an emergency exit. Blood oozed from a gash on his head. He clung to the galley's ledge, mouth twisted in agony. She looked back for a glimpse of the boys, but to no avail—the angle wasn't right.

Movement caught her eye. The heart attack victim's body smashed against the cabin's overhead compartment, then hovered in midair, limbs loose and flailing like those of a scarecrow in a high wind. Seconds later, the corpse dropped into the lap of the man wearing the fedora. He thrust the body into the aisle, disentangling himself in a panic.

The plane continued flying on its side. With her entire body weight dangling by her fingertips, Thea wasn't sure how much longer she could hold on. She stole a quick glance at a nearby chair's TV screen: still at 37,000 feet. She peered through the windows directly below, then wished she hadn't. The earth stared back at her. She felt disoriented, nauseated.

Before she could adjust her grip, the pilot rolled right, then yanked the nose skyward again. Both engines howled. A beverage cart bounced off the bulkhead and smashed painfully into her legs. Her left hand slipped off the lip of the overhead bin.

Without warning, the captain snap-rolled the aircraft 180 degrees to the right, jabbing the left wing skyward. The move threw frightened, screeching passengers against their seatmates. Everything that had been pointed up was now down, and carry-on bags, jackets, and other debris began flying around the cabin. Her grip failed. She crashed into the front-row seats, an armrest sucker punching her in the solar plexus. All the air evacuated her lungs. She clung to the armrest, praying for the aerobatics to stop as she gasped for oxygen.

Suddenly, the plane rolled back to wings-level. She inhaled a few shallow breaths, recovering her equilibrium. Seconds felt like hours as she waited for the next move from the pilot. But the plane remained level, stable. She steadied herself on the aisle seat. Laverdeen staggered toward her, a towel from the galley pressed against his bloody temple.

"You okay?" she asked.

"Just a little dizzy."

"We need to get into that cockpit and find out what the hell is going on with the pilot. I'll be right back."

She headed down the aisle, grateful the boys were in their seats, unharmed. Bernard and Madeira were strapping the heart-attack victim's battered body into an empty rear seat. It was too late to save him, but maybe the rest of them could find a way out of this insanity.

Ayan and Jabari huddled together, arms wrapped around each other. So much for their first flight being uneventful. She rummaged in her SINK for her satphone.

"Some ride, huh?" She tried to smile.

"The airplane went like this . . ." Jabari held out a hand and tilted it so that his thumb and pinky were north and south.

"You looked like a monkey hanging from a tree." Ayan's eyes were saucers, big and round.

She smiled as she looked them over. Thankfully, not a mark on them. "I'm proud of you both for being so brave." She strode toward the flight deck.

The man with the wire-rimmed glasses and bow tie grabbed her arm. "What's going on up there? Have we been hijacked?"

"We're handling the situation. Stay belted in."

Rejoining Laverdeen, she glanced at her watch, calculating their approximate location. The trip from Nairobi to London was over four thousand miles. "We're over the Sudan, correct?"

The copilot nodded, wincing. She hoped he didn't have a concussion. If they could get back inside the flight deck, he'd have to fly the plane.

She dialed the familiar number on her satphone. It rang several times, then bumped to voice mail. Dammit. "Rif, bit of a situation on board. Possible 7500," she said, using the code for hijacks. "We're over the Sudan right now. Call me." She hung up, wishing Rif was there with her—he could fly just about any aircraft in the world.

Air traffic control would be in Khartoum. Dialing the operator, she asked to be patched through to the closest control tower. Within thirty seconds, a man with a British accent answered.

"This is Thea Paris from Quantum International Security calling from Flight 855 on a BBJ 737." The TV screen on the nearest seat provided the flight details, which she relayed to the operator. "I'm with copilot Laverdeen, who has been locked out of the cockpit. Captain Rivers isn't responding. Could be a 7500. Any chance you could patch us in to Guard?" Usually most planes had Guard, the emergency frequency, set as their second channel option.

"Give me a moment."

While air traffic control located them on their system, she placed her hand over the phone. "What else do you know about Rivers?"

Laverdeen shrugged. "Divorced, fanatical soccer fan, drinks tons of coffee—he's not much of a conversationalist."

"Kids?"

"Not sure."

"Political leanings?"

"Sorry, I don't know him that well. We sit together for hours, but we don't say a whole hell of a lot."

"We know he has a temper," Thea said.

Air traffic control came back on the line. "Patching you in now. I'll alert the authorities about the possible 7500."

Because of their location, she wasn't optimistic they'd get much assistance. But that was probably part of the hijacker's strategy. She wasn't even sure the Sudanese had an emergency action plan for skyjackings.

A series of clicks sounded. "Ms. Paris, you have been patched in to Guard on Flight 855."

"Captain Rivers, this is Thea Paris, one of your passengers. Could you let me know you're okay?"

Silence.

"We have a medical emergency back here. One of the passengers is having a heart attack." The pilot didn't need to know the man had already died. Maybe she could appeal to his humanitarian side. "We need to land at the closest airport for medical intervention."

She waited. No response.

Time for a more direct approach. She covered the phone with her hand and thrust it toward the copilot. "Keep trying, but stay calm. We don't need another aerobatics display."

She passed Laverdeen the satphone and headed for the rear of the plane, waving to the boys as she walked past.

Reaching the rear galley, she interrupted Madeira as she was cleaning up the mess caused by the pilot's maneuvers. "You have an IV bag and a fire extinguisher?" Thea's ears popped. They were descending.

"Yes, right here." Madeira reached into the cabinet. "What's Captain Rivers up to?" Her mask of professionalism was beginning to crack.

"I'm trying to find out."

"Let me know what I can do to help." She passed Thea the IV bag and a red fire extinguisher.

"Keep the crew's oxygen close at hand. He's descending—tough to predict what he'll do next."

"I hope you know what you're doing."

"You have any gloves?"

"Only oven mitts," Madeira said.

"Perfect."

She strode up the aisle, Madeira on her heels. Opening the overhead compartment above her seat, she grabbed her SINK bag again and headed for the front. Laverdeen leaned against the bulkhead, still on the phone with Rivers. "Let's talk Premier League Championships, then . . ." His voice was calm, level. Impressive, given the circumstances. At her questioning look, he shook his head.

The nearest screen's flight data reported they were at 24,000 feet. Why was Rivers descending? Was he planning to land somewhere?

She leaned back and whispered to Madeira. "See if you can engage the captain in conversation. So far we've been given the silent treatment. Just keep it low key, no accusations, and take the phone to the rear."

She shrugged. "I'll give it a try."

Laverdeen handed the satphone to Madeira. The flight attendant left the galley area.

"We need to get inside now," she told Laverdeen. Opening her SINK, she retrieved the detonator she kept hidden inside one of her glass ampules of insulin and the cylindrical plastic booster hidden underneath some tampons. Her fingers wrapped around the shock tubing, which looked like a set of brightly colored earphones she kept in an Apple case. The three-layer hollow plastic tube had an inner layer of a reactive explosive compound that could deliver a firing impulse to the detonator.

The copilot studied the items she'd collected. "What are you doing?"

"Creating an alternative form of ingress." The cockpit door was reinforced, but the bathroom wall connected to the cockpit was not.

"You could blow a hole in the fuselage." Laverdeen's voice was tight.

"Or knock Rivers unconscious. But we're out of options. Just get ready to rush in and grab the controls."

She duct-taped the booster and detonator to the wall connecting the lavatory to the cockpit, then placed the IV bag over it. Water was an excellent dampener for explosions, so the IV bag would protect the passengers and direct the concussive force into the cockpit. To protect the outer wall of the plane, she propped up two carry-on bags near the toilet.

Satisfied, she glanced up at Laverdeen.

He still looked panicked. "One more try on the phone?" he suggested.

Her ears popped again. "We need to do this now." Connecting the shock tube to the detonator, she lengthened the cord, attached the trigger to the shock tubing, and positioned herself behind the sturdy bulkhead. The fire extinguisher sat beside her. She hoped she wouldn't need it.

She glanced back to see most of the passengers staring at them. The man wearing seersucker pants and a panama hat sat in the third-row aisle seat, too close for his safety.

"I need you to move back a few rows, sir."

He looked at her, indignant. "I paid a lot of money for this ticket; I should be able to sit where I want."

"Okay, then consider the upcoming fireworks part of the pampering."

The man unstrapped his seat belt and hurried to the rear.

She turned to Laverdeen. "Head for the back. We can't risk you getting hurt."

"You sure this will work?"

"If you have a better idea . . ."

"I'll be in the other washroom." Laverdeen gave her a half smile and strode down the aisle.

The plane descended at a brisk pace. They had reached 15,000 feet.

Thea protected herself behind the bulkhead and took a sharp breath. She pressed the trigger and covered her ears.

Microseconds ticked by in slow motion.

A loud blast erupted from the cockpit area. The concussive force crashed over her on its way down the length of the cabin. Screams filled the air. Thea shook off the aftereffects of the explosion and headed toward the cockpit, Laverdeen rushing up the aisle behind her. Pieces of the cockpit wall littered the floor. Shrapnel had embedded itself in the fiberglass bulkhead. Dust sifted through the air.

The makeshift bomb had done its job, and the fuselage was still intact.

Oven mitts on to protect her hands, she pushed through what was left of the bathroom door. Through the ragged hole in the wall, she had a view into the cockpit. Captain Rivers was conscious and in full control of the descending plane. A small piece of debris was lodged in his right shoulder, and the wound was bleeding, but he seemed more or less okay otherwise. One hand manipulated the controls as he gingerly probed the shrapnel in his shoulder with the other.

The first and only instance of a hijacking being foiled while the plane was in flight happened in 1996, when officers of an Austrian special-ops unit known as EKO Cobra saved a prisoner transport bound for Lagos from being diverted by a knife-wielding passenger.

With a little luck, Thea thought, maybe this will be the second ever.

Chapter 4

Innsbruck, Austria

Johann Dietrich's gangly legs pumped up and down like pistons, knees shooting up toward his ears and falling back down again, skis bouncing off the moguls. The sunlight danced on the snow with almost blinding intensity. Fresh powder blew by his goggles in a mist of white, and the wind screeched in his ears like a train whistle. Breath shallow and sharp, he bulleted down the mountain face, his focus on the mounds of snow, on hitting the sweet spots again and again.

Nothing invigorated him more than taking the zipper line down the ominous peak. The exhilaration helped him forget about his Marfan syndrome and its impact on his life—mild scoliosis, a sunken chest, poor eyesight, and a frame that was so tall and thin that he attracted attention everywhere he went. Today, on his birthday, he wanted to feel normal, to put all that aside. And he couldn't imagine a better way to celebrate than skiing, which he had always loved—except for the fact that all his classmates were also on the slopes.

He tucked his poles into his sides and flew down the mountain. *Sensationell.* All worries about his physical and social awkwardness vacated his mind. The double black diamond run dominated every thought—until he pulled up in a spray of snow at the base of the mountain, right in front of some of his schoolmates.

"Look, guys, it's Slender Man," David Taddington said, a smirk on his fine-boned face. "Watch out, kids, you're in danger of being taken."

His classmates laughed. David, the son of an American pharmaceutical tycoon, took great delight in persecuting him at every opportunity. Johann studied hard, got good grades, and tried to remain invisible.

Easier said than done at six feet, five inches and 160 pounds.

Vater had sent him to the Hapsburg yellow building on Moosstraße called the American International School, formally Salzburg International Preparatory School. Although Austrian by birth, his father was a diehard Americanophile and felt that his only son mingling with wealthy children from the land of burgers and fries would lead to good connections.

Johann hadn't made a friend yet.

Without saying a word, he stabbed his poles into the ground and skied toward the chairlift, dusting off the snow and the smirks of David and his friends. Normally he would have stood up for himself somehow—*Vater* would have insisted—but, given recent events, he just didn't have any fight in him.

It'd been an emotional ten days for all Austrians following the country's deadliest-ever terrorist attack at Schönbrunn Palace, a UNESCO World Heritage Site. Five suicide bombers armed with automatic weapons had stormed the castle and detonated their IEDs within its walls, destroying much of the structure and leaving 842 dead, including themselves and one of his father's closest employees. They'd attended the man's funeral a few days ago, witnessing the crushing impact on his widow and two sons. An intense manhunt was under way for a sixth

attacker, who'd disappeared using the famed maze and labyrinth on the property.

It made Johann sad, all this death and hatred. And it worried
him that there were moments when he wished he'd been one of
the victims.

He queued up for the high-speed quad lift and patiently
waited his turn for another chance to escape from school trip
hell. The brave part of him wished he'd had the guts to challenge
David to a race down the mountain.

He was pushing himself forward in the lift line when the
slim girl standing in front of him, bundled from head to toe in a
white down snowsuit that made her look like the Michelin Man,
stumbled, tripping on her skis. Definitely a newbie. She scrambled to reach the red line for the chairlift, almost toppling over.
Two other skiers held back, so the operator waved Johann forward with a gruff, "*Beeile dich, sonst verpaßt du es.*"

He skied forward and helped the girl before the lift chair
swung around behind them. She fell backward and plopped
down. Hopping onto the chair, he lowered the bar over both of
them. A quick glance at his companion revealed a blue hijab
tucked neatly underneath the hood of her white suit.

Fatima Abboud, from his math class. He hadn't recognized her
at first. Fatima was from the United Arab Emirates, her huge
chocolate-colored eyes surrounded by long, dark eyelashes.
Since math came easily to him, he had plenty of time in class to
stare at her while the teacher droned on about precalculus.

But he'd never spoken to her before.

She smiled. "You're Johann, right?"

He nodded, not trusting himself to talk.

"You sure can ski. Any tips? Where I come from, there isn't a
lot of snow."

"Thanks. I've been on the slopes since I was four."

"You make it look easy. I get going too fast and fall."

"Just snowplow to slow down, like this." He pointed the tips of
his skis inward, feeling a little more comfortable now.

"The chairlift terrifies me. I couldn't sleep last night, thinking about ski day."

You weren't the only one. "It'll be okay. I'll help you." The words were out of his mouth before he could stop them. Her openness about her fears surprised him. *Vater* always told him never to show weakness of any kind. It wasn't tolerated in the Dietrich family.

"That'd be nice. Maybe one more time down the mountain. I need to find a quiet place to say my afternoon prayers."

"To Allah?"

She smiled broadly. "You're familiar with Islam?"

"A little." His skin reddened. He respected *Vater* but did not share his views on Islam; it was something he couldn't discuss openly at home.

The chair rattled as it neared the top of the mountain. She jumped a little. He lifted up the bar and offered his arm. "Don't worry, just hold on to me."

She turned to him and smiled, accepting his help.

It made him feel strange, in a good way.

Not such a bad birthday, after all.

Chapter 5

Thea ducked through the hole blasted into the cockpit, Laverdeen on her heels. The ground loomed just five hundred feet below. Through the windscreen, a bumpy dirt road was rushing up at them.

Rivers gave them a quick glance. "Get out of here. I'm landing this plane." He was yelling, deafened by the explosion in the small space.

"Take over," she shouted at Laverdeen.

A triangular piece of debris had lodged in Captain Rivers's shoulder, but he still held the plane steady. Blood dripped down his arm.

Laverdeen belted himself in, scanned the flight deck, and adjusted a few controls.

The plane had leveled off, confirming that Rivers had truly planned on landing rather than crashing. Still, Thea wasn't taking any chances. "Laverdeen, make sure he doesn't pull any more stunts."

"I need to land at these coordinates. They'll kill my daughters if I don't." Rivers's voice shook.

"Wait, someone has your kids?" Thea demanded, belting herself into the jump seat.

The pilot gave her a glance, then turned back to the windscreen and shook his head. "Take that damn thing out of my shoulder."

"Sorry, it needs to stay in until we land. Don't want you bleeding out." Ironically, the embedded shrapnel was sometimes the only thing preventing a massive hemorrhage from a wound.

The earth surged up at them, the 737's wheels touching down, one at a time, then both at once, on the uneven ground. Laverdeen lifted the thrust-reverser handles and yanked them aft, standing on the brakes. The aircraft bounced and swerved, engines howling in full reverse thrust.

A smooth enough landing, given the circumstances. Seconds later, they slowed to a crawl, making their way down the dirt runway.

"Tell me what's going on," Thea demanded.

The captain reached into his shirt pocket and shoved his cell phone at her. A picture of two young girls showed on the screen, their mouths covered with red bandanas, eyes wide.

Her pulse accelerated. They hadn't given the pilot much choice.

"Why the hell didn't you tell me?" Laverdeen's face flushed.

"Because you would have tried to intervene."

Thea scanned the immediate area. There was a large hangar ahead, the broad doors open, men with AK-47s standing nearby.

She turned to Rivers. "Where are we?"

The captain wiped his face with the back of one hand. "In the middle of the Libyan Desert."

That made sense—in the political vacuum left by the civil war and the killing of Muammar Gaddafi in 2011, Libya had once again become a hotbed of intertribal warfare and one of the likeliest places on the planet to be kidnapped. "Tell me about the people who approached you."

"The plane needs to go into that hangar. That's what they told me to do."

Thea turned to Laverdeen. "Leave it out here in the open. Can't take off, or they'll blow out the tires, but we won't make it easy on them. Fire up the APU. We need to repressurize the plane."

She focused on Rivers while Laverdeen powered down the main engines and started up the auxiliary power unit, or APU, an extra engine used purely for powering the aircraft's pneumatic, electric, and hydraulic systems. "What did these people tell you?"

"They told me to spike Laverdeen's coffee with a diuretic." Rivers held up a vial with white powder inside. "Then lock him out of the cockpit and fly directly here, contacting no one."

"How many of them were there? What nationality were they?"

"Two guys, maybe three. No accents. They threw a hood over my head in the airport parking lot and pulled me into the back of a van. Told me that if I didn't follow their instructions exactly, they would kill my daughters."

That explained why Captain Rivers had shut them out so completely, but not much else. Thea studied the plane's GPS coordinates and gazed out at the dry, bleak desert horizon. Libya. She grabbed the pilot's rectangular canvas pubs bag and started unfolding the sky charts from inside it to cover up the windscreen and block the view from outside. She tried her satphone again, but it had been jammed.

"Did they say what they wanted?"

He shook his head. "I'm supposed to pull into the hangar, then open the plane's doors." Lines of worry were etched deeply into Rivers's forehead. He moved forward in the seat, as if he were about to stand. Thea grabbed a headset cord, leaned over, and in a flash wound it around his seat and across his upper body.

"What the hell?" Rivers squirmed in the chair as she tied off the cord, ensuring he couldn't escape, then bound his hands behind him with duct tape from her SINK.

"Sorry, you're the one they have leverage on."

"But my kids . . ."

"They have nothing to gain from harming the children now." Noticing the blood that still oozed from his wound, Thea grabbed a couple of Tylenols, popped them into Rivers's mouth, and helped him sip some water. "These will dull the pain until we can get the shrapnel out. Tell me everything you can remember."

He slumped in the chair. "They kept repeating what I told you. It sounded scripted. Hell, they had my girls. I wasn't about to provoke them."

Thea paused for a moment, then turned to Laverdeen. "You have a Magic Marker?"

"In there." The copilot pointed to a cubbyhole.

Her ears popped from the APU repressurizing the plane. She found a black Sharpie, grabbed one of the large maps, unfolded it, and wrote in large letters:

AIRPLANE PRESSURIZED. DO NOT TRY TO ACCESS THE DOORS OR SHOOT. CONTACT ON VHF 121.24.

Thea repeated the message in Arabic, writing from right to left. They were in Libya, after all, and she didn't want any communication breakdowns.

She placed the map on the windscreen with the writing facing outward. "Block off the rest of those windows with these maps, and keep the plane's air conditioning on. If they contact you on the radio, come get me," she told Laverdeen.

Returning to the cabin, she found passengers staring out the windows. There were bags, blankets, and pillows littering the floor. She flicked the polarization switch to darken the windows and grabbed the interphone.

The passengers turned to face her. "I'm sure you're all concerned about the unexpected and rough landing." *An understatement, for sure.* "Could everyone join me up front? Watch your step."

For now, the plane was secure. The hijackers wouldn't risk hurting whomever or whatever they were after by blowing open the doors without trying to talk them down first—at least, she hoped not.

As the passengers scurried to collect their strewn luggage, she made her way to the boys. They looked shell-shocked, but their faces lit up when they saw her. Poor Ayan had thrown up all over his shirt and looked green. She grabbed a napkin, wiped his face, and lifted him into her arms. "It'll be okay, buddy. How are you feeling?"

"My belly aches."

"That was quite a ride for your first airplane trip."

He looked down at his shirt and shrugged.

"Don't worry, I've been sick on many flights. Happens to everyone." She wanted to strangle whoever was behind the hijacking for putting the boys through this hell.

She slung Ayan's knapsack over her right shoulder, then navigated the remaining debris to take the little guy to the lavatory. At the rear of the plane, she set him down so she could find the clean shirt she had stored in his knapsack. "Give me a touchdown signal, so we can get this shirt off." She had introduced the boys to American football, and they loved watching the game.

Ayan's sticklike arms rose straight into the air, and he wriggled as she helped him remove the soiled shirt. "Let's get you washed up." The lock mechanism on the lavatory door was set on VACANT. She slid the knob aside and pushed the door open.

But the lavatory wasn't empty. The guy dressed in Versace was in there, a Glock in his right hand. Their eyes locked across the threshold. He raised the gun.

"Run, Ayan." She slammed the front of the muzzle with her right palm, forcing the slide back.

Versace's right finger pressed the trigger, but nothing happened. She'd knocked the slide back half an inch, far enough to make the weapon useless. With her left hand, she encircled his wrist and rotated it, forcing him against the back wall.

He dropped the gun to avoid a broken wrist.

Thea shoved her way into the lavatory, the door closing behind her. The small space was oppressive, airless, and now very crowded. She brought her right forearm up to crush his throat. His breath felt hot against her cheek.

Neither of them had room to maneuver.

His left hand slammed into the side of her ribs, but he didn't have enough space to wind up for the blow, so the pain was tolerable. She lifted her knee, then crunched her boot down on his dress shoe. A snapping sound. A grunt. Versace snaked his left arm around her neck, turning her around. He wasn't a big man, but he was whipcord strong. Her head was now pressed against the side of the mirror. She let go of his right hand and tried to free herself but couldn't. He tightened his hold.

She elbowed him in the gut. Hard. His grip faltered, and she was able to twist away. Turning her head, she butted him in the nose. Blood spurted onto his shirt.

Slipping her right hand beneath his left arm and grabbing his neck, she pressed her thumb hard against his carotid artery, cutting off the blood supply to his brain. He squirmed, trying to get a purchase on her hand, but time worked against him.

Seconds later, he slumped onto her.

The door opened, the sudden light causing her to blink. She craned her neck.

Ayan stood outside, a big umbrella in his hands, eyes wild. He whacked Versace hard on the back. He lifted the umbrella again, then smacked Versace again.

"It's okay, you can stop, Ayan."

The boy made as if to hit the man again.

"Stop, buddy. We're good, we're good."

Thea shoved Versace out of the lavatory. He slumped in a heap, half inside, half outside the door. Thank goodness he wasn't a big guy, or she could have been in serious trouble. She stepped on him as she exited the bathroom, securing his Glock in the back of her pants.

"Where'd you find that?" She indicated the umbrella.

"There." Ayan pointed to the floor behind him.

"Thanks for your help." Fearless and battle ready. She'd hoped that part of his life was over.

Footsteps sounded. Bernard must have heard the commotion.

"Help me tie this guy up, would you?" she asked him.

"What the hell happened here?" The flight attendant's eyebrows arched.

"I'm guessing he's an inside man."

Bernard gave her a look, then reached into one of the cabinets and retrieved two zip ties from the security kit. "Here you go. What now?"

"Let's belt him into a seat."

Bernard grabbed the guy's upper body while she secured his legs. They strapped him into a seat in the last row, belt snug, zip ties on his wrists and ankles. His head lolled to one side.

She removed the umbrella from Ayan's clenched fingers and handed it to Bernard. "Can you give this back to its rightful owner?"

Reaching down, she scooped Ayan into her arms and carried him up front, her heart overcome with affection for this little boy. She snatched a couple of blankets along the way and wrapped one around Ayan. Both boys were in shock, but as much as she wanted to reassure them, she had to focus on finding a way out of this mess.

"Please take care of your brother, okay?" she asked Jabari, giving him the other blanket.

The older boy draped both arms around Ayan.

Several other passengers had moved to the first few rows. Only two people were left in the rear of the plane—the unconscious man and the dead man. As she walked to the front to address the passengers, they all started talking at once.

"What the hell's going on?" the Texan with the impressive mustache grumbled. "Where are we? I saw men with guns out there."

"My phone won't work. Did you call for help?" the man in the seersucker suit asked, clearly agitated.

"Please, one question at a time, and I'll do my best to help. I'm Thea Paris. I work for a company called Quantum International Security handling risk management and kidnap negotiations."

"My name's Mike Dillman. Is this a hijacking?" The Texan stroked his mustache.

"Good question. The pilot was forced by unknown persons to land at these GPS coordinates in the Libyan Desert, but we know little beyond that. Does anyone here have a security background?"

Silence greeted her.

She was on her own.

Chapter 6

Johann adjusted his knapsack as he hurried home, pleased about how his birthday was turning out. He'd sat beside Fatima on the bus coming home from their ski day in Innsbruck. She'd entertained him with stories about her crazy sisters and what life was like in the United Arab Emirates—fascinating tales that had shown him an alternative universe, a world away from his European lifestyle.

When he'd told her it was his birthday, she'd penciled a quick sketch of him on skis as a gift. A talented artist, Fatima had somehow captured that feeling of freedom he experienced on the slopes in just a few strokes of her pencil. In return, he'd shared his Toblerone bar with her. Used to people making fun of him for looking like a string bean, he was relieved to just feel normal with someone.

As he walked at a brisk pace down the lane to his home, anticipation sparked up and down his body at the thought of asking her to the upcoming school dance. Just one major stumbling block: Fatima was Muslim. His father would never approve.

Well, Father didn't have to know everything about his life.

A little spring quickened his step. Maybe *Vater* would take the evening off work and spend it celebrating his only child's birthday. Father was a successful weapons manufacturer with clients around the world, so he was always on the phone or on his laptop. Johann knew he shouldn't get his hopes up, even if it was his birthday. *Vater* had changed dramatically over the five years since Johann's mother died in a car accident: the man who'd once taken him to countless sporting events, musicals, and museums had lately surrounded himself with cronies, spending less and less time with his son.

Johann knew his father loved him, and it wasn't as if they didn't spend any time together. Beginning nearly every morning at 06:00, they trained together in a challenging routine of physical fitness and firearms training. It was grueling, especially given his illness, but Johann treasured the routine just the same. It was the one time of day when all the electronic devices were shut off and it was just father and son, working toward a common goal.

Once, late at night, Johann had found his father sobbing at the bedroom shrine he'd created for his beloved wife. His grief was genuine, but over time it had morphed into anti-Islamic xenophobia. The man who'd been driving the car that killed *Mutti* was from Dubai, and ever since then *Vater*'s views of foreigners had hardened into something ugly that Johann couldn't understand.

Turning the corner, Johann studied the fortress he called home. An Austrian castle, the thirty-thousand-square-foot *schloss* had been in their family for seven generations. Flags featuring the Dietrich coat of arms flew proudly on each of the turrets. The ancient walls were covered in moss, like an old man's scraggly beard.

As he stared at the array of vehicles in the large driveway, Johann's enthusiasm drained away: Father had his "associates" over again, including his best friend, Leopold Mueller, a supposedly brilliant biochemist who gave Johann the creeps. Uncle Karl had told Johann that Leopold had been working on groundbreaking gene therapy techniques when the university that employed him discovered that key portions of his work had been plagiarized. He had been thrown out of academia and gone to work for a Dutch biopharmaceutical company with labs in Europe, India, and Africa.

Vater and his friends had probably barricaded themselves in the basement as usual to talk business. Johann wondered if his father even remembered it was his birthday. He missed the man who used to inhabit his father's body.

Johann slipped his key into the side door, knowing a quiet dinner alone with *Vater* wasn't likely. He'd wanted to ask his father's advice about asking a girl out, but how could he do it without revealing who she was—or what she was? He felt a familiar sinking sensation in his stomach. Why did religion or culture matter so much? Wasn't it more important what kind of person Fatima was?

He hung his knapsack on the antique coatrack and headed for the kitchen, praying that Chef Rudy might have made *Salzburger Nockerl*, his favorite dessert. The mounds of airy soufflé represented the surrounding mountains, and Rudy usually smothered the peaks in thick raspberry sauce. *Delicious.* Johann's stomach growled. As he hurried to the rear of the house, familiar footsteps echoed on the marble floors.

He came face-to-face with his father, Gernot Dietrich, all six-foot-six of him. Unlike Johann, his father was thickly muscled with broad shoulders, an intimidating figure with deep-set blue eyes that radiated intelligence. "Ah, you're home. Happy birthday, son."

He'd remembered.

"Join me downstairs. I have a surprise for you."

All the cars outside—Johann prayed it wasn't some stupid birthday party. Who could possibly be there but his father's friends? It wasn't as if he had many of his own.

Vater grabbed his arm, his face animated. "This is more than just your birthday—you're about to become part of something bigger than all of this." He waved his hands to indicate their surroundings.

"What—"

"You'll see soon enough. Come."

Dazed, Johann followed his father down the spiral staircase. Something bigger? What was his father talking about?

Johann hoped that Uncle Karl would be there. Karl Wagner wasn't an actual relative, more a longtime friend of his father's, a kind man who had taken a genuine interest in Johann. They had been playing chess together nearly every week, and Johann had started to win more matches lately.

The cavernous basement held an impressive wine cellar along with his father's firearms collection. The Dietrich family had been in weapons manufacturing for generations. Johann had been going to the firing range since he was seven and was comfortable shooting everything from a Walther PPK to a .50 caliber machine gun.

The light dimmed as Johann entered the antechamber. Built like a bunker, the cellar had thick concrete walls and old-fashioned oil lamps. Twelve men were gathered around the grand mahogany table in the wine cellar, clasping metal beer steins or pewter goblets of wine. The cellar, with its heavy wrought-iron chandeliers and dark wood paneling, transported one back in time. It was also a little chilly, and a tiny shiver darted down Johann's spine.

"We all wanted to wish you a happy birthday." His father handed him a goblet of wine.

Johann looked around at the men's expectant faces and forced a smile. He would have preferred beer over wine, but he didn't dare interrupt his father.

Father lifted his beer stein. "*Prost*. To manhood." The men raised their drinks and repeated the toast.

"Where's Uncle Karl?" The one person he actually wanted at his party wasn't there.

His father sipped his beer. "Karl had to leave town—something about a family illness. Not sure if he'll be back tonight."

Weird. Johann thought his uncle would have mentioned something like that. He'd send him a text, find out what was up. For now, though, he was stuck with *Vater*'s crew.

A small package with a black bow sat on the edge of the table. A gift?

"We should have brought him a woman. That's probably what he really wants," Leopold said. Raucous laughter filled the room. Johann tried not to cringe.

"Sit down, son." His father pulled out an empty chair.

Johann collapsed onto the wooden seat, his long fingers gripping the carved arms. He wished he could go to his room and text Fatima. Instead, all eyes were focused on him.

"You're seventeen, and it's time to fully understand your responsibilities. When your great-grandfather, Otto Dietrich, returned from the Second World War, he understood that the communists posed a threat to our country—and the world."

"Hear, hear, raise a glass to the Dietrich family for their foresight. *Prost*." Leopold lifted his goblet. A faint wine stain lingered in his blond beard.

"Your great-grandfather was instrumental in founding a secret organization formed to guard against communism." Father straightened his shoulders. "Otto supplied the arms. The *Kommunisten* were everywhere, and we had to protect ourselves from an invasion."

"The CIA and British Secret Service helped train them." Falco Kerner, a wealthy industrialist, rarely spoke, but when he did, he commanded attention with his rumbling baritone. "They were hidden throughout Europe."

Johann tried to take it all in. What were they talking about? Secret armies and weapons . . . weren't the communists ancient history?

Father placed a firm hand on his shoulder. "Even top officials in the Austrian government had no idea this group existed, but your great-grandfather considered participation his patriotic duty. And he built strong partnerships with other European nations and the United States by offering discounted munitions. The relationship resulted in profitable American contracts." He smiled. "It is what enables us to live like this."

Johann shifted in his seat, dying to get this over with. Some birthday celebration.

"Even the few who know about the existence of organizations like ours believe they became defunct years ago. But we've become stronger than ever. And we'd like you to join us."

Several men pounded their fists on the table and raised their steins and goblets in another cheer. "*Jawohl.*"

Johann tried to process this information. His father was part of a secret society, and now he was being inducted into it? And no one had asked him if he was actually interested.

Father passed him the small box. Johann drew a deep breath and untied the black bow, steadying his hands. He sensed that this moment was important to his father, and he didn't want to disappoint him.

Inside, a gold medallion hung on a simple chain. It seemed familiar, tugging on a memory he couldn't quite access. He touched the pendant, then turned it over. On one side was the imprint of the Hapsburg crest, on the other side the word *Freiheitswächter* was engraved on the medallion. *Freedom Guardians*.

Father secured the medallion around Johann's neck. "I still remember the exact moment when my father gave me mine. We wear them on every mission."

Missions?

There were solemn nods around the table. It felt odd, almost absurd, to be talking about secret armies and "missions," but if that's what it took to get closer to his father again, he'd try to understand exactly what being a *Freiheitswächter* meant.

"Will you join us?"

"I'd . . . be honored." What else could he say?

"I couldn't be prouder," *Vater* said.

Johann's skin pinkened, and his chest tightened. His father had never uttered those words before.

"You'll need to swear an oath tonight. Normally your induction would be a gradual process, but at this moment we are teetering on the brink of history." Father's tone shifted. "I have something very important to show you. Follow me."

Instead of heading up the stairs, his father strode to the ornate wooden mantelpiece and beckoned Johann closer. *Vater* pressed a series of previously hidden buttons. Johann felt utterly disoriented now, unable to resist the course of events.

The wall of shelves showcasing many of his father's prized hunting trophies opened onto a tunnel that Johann had never known existed.

"Come," Father said, a strange light in his fierce eyes.

Fingers of panic crawled up Johann's throat, as if the dark tunnel led to a place from which he would never return.

Chapter 7

Rif Asker paced the situation room at Quantum International Security headquarters in London. He'd just finished a lengthy call with their top Latin American response consultant. Paco Martinez had negotiated the release of three female hostages who had been held captive in Argentina for 254 days. A strategic thinker gifted with more patience than Rif could ever muster, Paco had sounded simultaneously excited and exhausted as he shared the details of the ransom and exchange.

Debriefings like this were critical. There was always a lesson to be learned, and sharing these experiences allowed every member of the team to improve. When it was impossible for the whole team to be together in person, as it often was, debriefings would take place with a senior member of the team, such as Rif or Thea. And what a case it had been; the situation had gone on so long that continuing negotiations had been balancing on the razor's edge of an attempted extraction. Had it come down to an exfiltration, Rif—director of operations at Quantum—would have stepped in. Rescues were attempted fewer than 10 percent of the time, because the risk of the hostages being injured or killed during exfil was high. Only when absolutely all efforts at negotiation had been exhausted and the hostages' lives were in peril, Rif would lead a team of operatives into the field for an extraction. But by using his familiarity with the relationships between the local police and cartel operatives, who had a mutual interest in keeping the peace in the region, Paco had been able to put pressure on the kidnappers to accept the final ransom offer.

In exchange for the assistance of the corrupt cops and traffickers in bringing the kidnappers to the table, Paco had offered to keep the Policía Federal Argentina in the dark about certain smuggling operations going across the Altiplano and into southern Bolivia. Thanks to Paco's savvy and tenacity, not to mention Quantum's state-of-the-art satellite and drone reconnaissance, three more hostages were on their way home without a shot fired.

It was a good ending, and Rif should have been pleased, but unease elbowed his gut. Something was wrong. His cell buzzed again in his pocket, reminding him that he had a message. He'd felt the phone vibrate twenty minutes ago when he was on the other line.

He pressed the button to start the message. His spirits rose for a second at the sound of Thea's voice, then nosedived. *Possible 7500.* As a seasoned pilot, he knew the code well: *skyjack.* The room suddenly felt cold.

He pressed the end button and called her satphone. No answer. Her cell. Nothing.

Rif thought back to his last conversation with Thea. It had been several hours ago, when Thea, Jabari, and Ayan had missed their connection in Nairobi. He'd phoned the owner of Transatlantic Airlines, a client of theirs, and secured seats for them on a Boeing Business Jet headed for London.

But where were they now?

The whooshing sound of the situation room door opening demanded his attention. Hakan Asker, the owner of Quantum—and Rif's father—strode in. "How did it go with Paco?"

"He talked his way into the kidnappers' hearts, the suave bastard—the hostages are on their way home. But listen: Thea's plane might have been hijacked. I can't reach her."

"What do you know?"

Rif glanced at his watch. "She left me a message twenty-one minutes ago saying it was a possible 7500."

"You have her flight number? I'll call the authorities."

Rif admired the way his father got straight down to business during a crisis. Unflappable, laser focused.

"Transatlantic 855, a business charter." The fact that it was a BBJ meant fewer passengers than on a commercial flight, so finding out the reasons behind the skyjacking might be a little easier.

Father and son worked the phones for half an hour. If you knew whom to call, you could procure information quickly. Given there were more than eighty abductions a day worldwide, Quantum always had a finger on the pulse of the global security feed and had contacts in most countries.

Hakan clicked off his mobile and placed his left hand on the desk, his face drawn. "The Sudanese authorities lost contact with Flight 855 at 04:00, and the transponder isn't transmitting. One of the air traffic controllers actually spoke to Thea. The captain had locked the copilot out of the flight deck and was unresponsive."

Unresponsive. A pilot suicide? But why would the captain turn off the transponder if he only wanted to crash? Transponders were a secondary way to display an aircraft's position on an air traffic controller's radar screen, transmitting the location of the plane as well as details about the altitude, speed, and type of aircraft.

"What about ACARS?" Rif asked. The Aircraft Communications, Addressing and Reporting System was the unseen backbone of a plane's communication with the ground, sending electronic messages back and forth. Often engineers on the ground would know about an engine malfunction long before the pilots suspected a thing.

"Disabled or not working."

Someone wanted to obscure the location of the plane. The lack of communication could mean the jet had crashed, but he refused to give up hope—something unusual had happened here. Thea and the Kuria boys were out there, and if they were still alive, he would find them.

"I'll call Inmarsat," Rif said, referring to the satellite telecommunications company that had tracked the path of the doomed Malaysia Airlines Flight 370 that had seemingly vanished somewhere over the South China Sea in 2014. Inmarsat had ways of locating planes even if their transponders were shut off, and Rif had worked with them before.

"I'll contact our people in Sudan," Hakan said.

Rif's phone buzzed with a text. Flight 855 had just been categorized as DETRESFA, meaning there was a real possibility of danger to the passengers and crew. The flight manifest listed several American passengers, which made him think of Gabrielle Farrah from the Hostage Recovery Fusion Cell. Thea and Rif had worked closely with the extremely capable Lebanese-American agent on Christos Paris's kidnapping. A former CIA operative, Gabrielle was well connected on both sides of the pond. He searched for her name in his contacts and made the call.

Gabrielle answered with a laugh, her husky voice sounding as if she were next door instead of halfway around the world. "Rif Asker. Hmm, must be a desperate situation if you're calling a Yankee in."

He wished they could joke around, catch up, but Rif had no time to waste. "Our mutual friend is in trouble."

"Thea? What can I do to help?" Her tone immediately changed to professional and serious, ready to assist.

"She's on a BBJ that has been hijacked. Americans are on board, so you'll undoubtedly be involved. I thought sooner would be better than later. Could you keep me posted if you hear anything?"

"Of course. Text me the info. And don't worry: Thea can take care of herself."

"She has two boys from the orphanage with her . . ."

"I get it—Mama Lion will be protecting the cubs. I'll be in touch."

Rif hit the end button, relieved the HRFC agent would be feeding them intel. Any extra background information on the passengers would help them figure out if one of them had been targeted in the hijacking or if there was another reason that particular plane had been attacked.

As Rif scanned his e-mails for updates, the door whooshed open again, and Aegis, the Paris family dog, ran straight for Rif, wildly wagging his tail. Rif loved the ridgeback as if it was his own. He reached down and gave him a good head scratch. Thea's father, Christos, followed, his gait far slower; he'd lost part of a leg in Zimbabwe and been lucky he hadn't lost his life as well.

Christos was Hakan's longtime friend, Rif's godfather, and one of the most prominent oilmen in the world. "I'm off to pick up Thea and the boys at the airport. Thought I'd drop in on the way."

The brief flash of happiness Rif had experienced evaporated.

Rif looked at Hakan, his father's expression mirroring the same dread.

"What's with the long faces? I was hoping we could all go out to dinner, welcome Ayan and Jabari to jolly ole London. I bought jackets and gloves for the boys—they aren't used to this frigid weather." Christos brushed a light dusting of snow off his sleeves.

Rif swallowed hard. "We need to talk."

Chapter 8

Johann followed his father and Leopold through the dimly lit tunnel, the cool cellar air dank and musty. The soft patter of his rubber soles echoed in the corridor. It was a surreal experience to be traveling this secret passageway in his own home, with Father and the rest of the *Freiheitswächter*, most of them strangers.

Are the Freedom Guardians a neighborhood watch or something?

They arrived at a dead end and stopped, facing a stucco wall. Father lifted a panel and typed in a long series of numbers on the keypad beneath it while Johann watched. The wall shifted, creating an opening.

Bright lights blinded him. He blinked as he surveyed the room. Behind a glass wall, high-wattage bulbs illuminated what looked to be a fully kitted-out lab. Stainless steel gleamed on every surface. Yellow hazmat suits hung on one wall. Two men dressed in the bug-like costumes waved to them as they entered the secret area. Did Uncle Karl know about this part of the house? If so, why hadn't he mentioned it?

Father stood tall, his voice commanding. "As you can see, we have positive pressure suits, a segregated air supply, multiple

showers, and other safety measures in place. I've taken every pre-
caution to protect us."

Protect us from what?

"We still guard against communism, but the current threat
to our democracy and safety is another kind of blasphemy." His
father tapped on the glass and signaled to the two suited figures
inside the enclosed space, then turned back to Johann. "What
threatens world peace the most today?"

Johann's mind was paralyzed by the pace of these revelations.
Seconds ticked by with agonizing slowness. *What is the right
answer?*

"Arabs," Leopold said. "You've seen what happened in Paris,
Brussels, Orlando, Barcelona . . . and all the other endless jihads
across the globe. And last week in Vienna, right here in Austria.
These people must be stopped."

"Arabs?" The word felt awkward on Johann's lips.

"Yes. Muslim apologists say the Koran promotes peace, but
their actions tell a different story," Father said.

Several of the *Freiheitswächter* nodded. *Arabs.* One face filled his
vision: Fatima's. How could she possibly be the enemy?

"But I know some nice Arabs at school," Johann said. "And one
of them isn't even Muslim."

"World leaders are trying to fight jihad by conventional
means, but that approach will never work. Lone warriors and
small cells are the future of jihad, and they are impossible to
ferret out before they strike," *Vater* said, ignoring Johann's com-
ments. "The nations of the West are at great risk, unable to com-
pete with the slick propaganda videos and networks of operatives
who encourage self-radicalization. But we've found a solution."

Johann agreed that terrorism had to stop, but a deep-seated
trepidation took root inside him as he considered where all this
talk might be headed.

The two figures in the yellow suits left the enclosed lab. He
wondered how long this underground facility had been here.
He'd ask Uncle Karl, who must know something about it.

"Falco, it's time." Father opened the first chamber that led to the glassed-in room.

Falco placed a hand on Johann's shoulder. "I'm proud of you, boy."

Why does it feel like he's saying goodbye?

Falco removed his hand and stepped inside the antechamber, closing the door behind him.

"What's happening?" Johann asked.

"Watch." Father directed everyone to gather near the glass wall.

The two figures in hazmat suits returned, but now they weren't alone. They frog-marched a man in handcuffs and leg chains, dressed in dirty white underpants, inside. The man was sweaty and his skin was swollen and discolored in places. The yellow-clad figures secured the man's handcuffs to a pole on the right side of the spacious chamber, then left.

Something about the man's disfigured face seemed familiar. Johann tried to place it . . . *TV. The news. The manhunt.* This was the lone surviving terrorist responsible for the horrors at Schönbrunn in Vienna.

Omar Kaleb.

Chapter 9

Thea's day definitely wasn't going according to plan. Instead of meeting Papa at Heathrow and introducing Ayan and Jabari to their adoptive family, she was trapped inside a hijacked plane in the Libyan Desert, surrounded by armed men. One passenger was dead, one was unconscious, and eleven hostages were now relying on her to make the right decisions to get them out of this situation alive.

They all spent a few minutes introducing themselves. From what they shared, it seemed that the passengers were mostly businesspeople commuting from Nairobi to Europe. Lots of deals to be made in Kenya, with its rich reserves of minerals, gemstones, and other natural resources. Papa himself could have been one of these travelers, just returning from negotiating an oil-rights deal.

As the passengers spoke, Thea studied them for tells to see if Versace had been the only inside operative. It was difficult to see if they were lying or holding back information, though, because the stress of their predicament was making it hard for her to read their microexpressions.

The Asian woman, whose expression seemed oddly blasé, would have been impossible to read under any circumstances. Thea was impressed by her calm when she introduced herself.

"Ocean." Her voice was soft.

"No, honey, we're on land," the Texan named Mike Dillman said, but the joke fell flat. "What's your last name?" Dillman again—the Texan really liked to insert himself into the conversation whenever possible.

"Just Ocean," the woman repeated.

"That's not a real name," Dillman told her.

"Why not?" Nick Karlsson said. "Madonna, Cher, Sting . . . they're all real names."

Ayan was listening closely. "We lost our parents, so we have room. You can share our last name—it's Kuria." Ayan reached out and touched the woman's hand.

The first suggestion of emotion surfaced on Ocean's face as she gazed at the boy. "I lost my family, too."

Thea sensed a tumultuous story beneath the deceptively calm surface, like the depths of any ocean. She turned to address the flight attendants. "Any chance you could give everyone a snack and a drink? But conserve our supplies—we don't know how long we'll be here." Thea had noticed distressing numbers on the app reporting her continuous glucose monitoring results. Her blood sugar level had dipped, and she would need food soon to keep herself on an even keel, her mind clear.

"If anyone has sensitive information that might be helpful, please feel free to speak to me privately." She didn't want to put too fine a point on it, as the realization that there was a target on board could create conflict among the passengers. Someone had gone to a lot of trouble to hijack this plane. Which passenger did they want, and why?

"Could be my ex-wife," Dillman said. "She has loads of money and an ax to grind."

Thea gave him a faint smile. *If he didn't shut up, he might have to be stashed at the back of the plane with Versace and the dead guy.*

Matthias Houndsworth pushed his wire-rimmed glasses higher on his nose, still clinging to his messenger bag as if it was the only life preserver in a storm.

"Do you have a minute?" She grabbed a granola bar from the tray of snacks Bernard offered and waved Matthias to the rear of the cabin.

He followed her, his tight blond curls plastered against his head, giving him an impish look. "What is it?"

"Care to share what's inside that bag?"

He blushed.

"I'm sensing it's important, given you haven't let it out of your sight. Are you hiding something?"

"I've developed advanced encryption software. It's possible that terrorists would want the technology."

"What makes your product special?"

"It allows for large-scale peer-to-peer data sharing and currency exchange without any possibility of being cracked or traced short of quantum computing."

She could think of quite a few countries and organizations that would like to get their hands on something like that. "And the software is on your computer?"

"Yes."

"I appreciate your being straightforward. Let's see what happens when the hijackers make contact."

She returned to the front and grabbed her SINK again. The boys were standing nearby, chewing on brownies.

"Our new parents were going to meet us today. You don't think they'll adopt two other boys if we're not there, do you?" Jabari's expression was serious, troubled.

"Not a chance. You and Ayan are special, irreplaceable." She gave them both a hug.

Ayan lit up. "And you'll still take us to ride the London Eye?"

"You can handle hovering four hundred feet above the city?" The massive Ferris wheel would be just one of the highlights of living in London.

"Yes, yes, yes!"

"Okay, hold that thought while I head to the ladies' room." She needed to use the facilities and check her insulin pump. It promised to be a long day, and she wanted to be prepared.

Chapter 10

Johann stepped back from the glass wall in the laboratory, trying to distance himself from the handcuffed man. The thick, matted beard, the sunken eyes. Johann's mind flashed back to the photo that had been on television for the last week. No doubt. This man was the missing terrorist.

How had Omar Kaleb ended up in their basement?

His father gave him a thin smile. "I see you know who this is. Omar Kaleb and his compatriots are responsible for murdering over eight hundred Austrians at Schönbrunn."

"How did you find him?"

"One of our *Freiheitswächter* discovered him hiding in a local farmer's barn."

Leopold wiped sweat off his forehead. "We're ready, Gernot."

"Ready for what?" Johann asked.

Falco was now in the glassed-in room with Kaleb. Was Falco going to torture the man for information?

"The US Secret Service follows their American president around, picking up anything he touches or uses, like drinking cups or tissues. Do you know why?" Father asked.

More American trivia. *Vater* was obsessed.

"Because they don't want his DNA floating around. Science has progressed rapidly, and in the right hands, a bioweapon can be targeted at a specific individual. What might be a mild cold or flu to the general population could be a deadly virus for one person."

Cold fear settled in Johann's stomach as his father's words rattled around his head.

Leopold leaned against the glass wall. "The Saudi Human Genome Program is exploring why so many Arabs have genetic illnesses, including type 2 diabetes and heart disease."

Father's eyes were animated. "Scientists have been studying the genetic makeup of over twenty thousand Arabs to determine which genes and gene variants cause these disorders in that population. We hacked their database."

Though he feared the answer, Johann asked, "But why?"

His father leaned closer. "To protect our nation, our people—that is what we're trying to do."

The two hazmat-suited figures left the chamber, a soft swoosh sounding as the air lock clicked in behind them. Falco perched on a small stool near the terrorist, the Austrian man's face impassive.

Movement caught Johann's attention. Kaleb struggled against his handcuffs and leg chains. He spat at the observers, streaks of saliva dripping down the glass wall.

"Why does he look so sick?" Johann's voice wavered.

"Approximately twenty-four hours ago, this man was exposed to a form of pneumonic plague, enhanced with an accelerant." Leopold's face was a study in concentration as he spoke, his eyes fixed on the tableaux before them. "Normally it would take three days to die, but this strain multiplies rapidly and favors the major organs."

History lessons about the Middle Ages—horror stories, really—buzzed in his mind.

"*Vater*, don't let Falco die." His voice squeaked. "Why is he even in there?"

"He made the choice to be in there," Gernot said. "To prove that non-Arabs will not be affected by the cleansing power of this plague."

"Shouldn't you just bring the terrorist to the authorities, have him questioned by the police?"

Sweat trickled down Kaleb's arms and chest and he began to spasm. His head hung down, his hair flopping in front of his face, jerking in time with his body.

"It is too late for that," Gernot said. "Besides, we have all the answers we need. This is the only way we can protect ourselves."

"But—"

His words were drowned out by the terrorist's scream. "*Allahu Akbar!*"

Kaleb's torso had turned bright red, seeping blood, the rivulets sliding down his sweaty body in a twisted maze. His spindly arms and legs flailed against the chains, his head whipping from side to side. Johann ached to look away but couldn't.

"*In'a'al mayteen ehlak!*"

With a horrible gagging noise, projectile vomit erupted from his mouth, splashing against the partition, landing in a bloody puddle on the floor. Johann drew back instinctively, even though the glass protected him.

He thought of all those innocent people, including children, who had been murdered at Schönbrunn. The darkest recesses of his soul tried to tell him that justice was being served, but his saner side rejected the thought immediately. This was inhumane, grotesque.

Gushes of brownish liquid ran down the terrorist's thighs. Kaleb's body shook, his teeth chattering, as if the temperature had dropped twenty degrees inside the chamber.

Johann felt sick at the condition of the man inside.

"*Allahu Akbar.*" Kaleb's voice faded. After one final convulsion, his body slumped forward, and he spoke no more.

Johann gathered the courage to look at Falco, who sat comfortably on the stool, looking like he did every day, a smile on his lean face suggesting utter confidence that he would be safe, despite the horror that had just transpired inches away. Johann's legs felt rubbery with relief—and revulsion at the spectacle he had just witnessed.

"Falco, you will be under medical observation for two days. But strictly as a formality." Leopold clapped his hands. "I have no doubt our operation will be a success."

The men cheered.

Johann looked back and forth between Kaleb and Falco, understanding washing over him. Both men had been exposed to the plague. But only one of them would die.

Father turned to him. "A disease can be a precise bioweapon. Centuries ago in Nepal, the Tharu people used the Terai forestland, which was infected with malaria, as a natural barrier against invaders from the Ganges Plain. The Tharu had a genetic resistance to malaria; the invaders didn't. Thanks to Leopold's brilliant work pinpointing vulnerabilities in their genome, we've created a pathogen genetically designed to affect only people of Arab descent."

Johann stared at Kaleb's bloodied corpse. He considered the implications. Shame suffused his body. If he and Fatima had been inside that chamber, he would live, but Fatima would die a horrific death.

Johann remembered what his father had told him two months earlier over dinner. In the five years since his mother's death, he'd believed that her car had been hit by a drunk driver who just happened to be Muslim. A terrible misfortune, the loss devastating beyond words.

Then his father had left him shell-shocked with one sentence. "Your mother's death wasn't an accident."

"What are you talking about? The other driver was charged with drunk driving; he went to jail . . ."

"She died in a car crash, but it was no accident. It was an assassination. You were too young to understand, but you're seventeen now. You need to know the truth."

Johann had tried to absorb the news. What possible motive could anyone have had to target *Mutti*? She was wonderful, kind, generous. Everyone loved her. "Why?"

His father paled slightly. "I sold weapons to Israel. I received many threats. In arms dealing, there are always dark corners. I took precautions, but I couldn't make prisoners of your mother and you."

"*Mutti* died because of your business dealings?"

"No," Vater said fiercely. "She died because jihadis have no regard for human life. They'll kill your loved ones without blinking; they'll even kill themselves to attack their enemies. Life doesn't matter to these people." His father pounded the table, more agitated than Johann had ever seen him.

Johann didn't know what to say. He nodded at the right moments as *Vater* continued his diatribe against Arabs. Still, another voice inside his head began to make itself heard that evening, one that whispered that his father was the person truly responsible for *Mutti's* death. It was Father who had brought his dirty world home.

Chapter 11

Thea hurried down the aisle toward the flight deck, drawn there by an unfamiliar voice on the cockpit's radio. She'd asked Laverdeen to keep sending a distress signal via Guard, hoping another plane might hear them. It was their only opportunity for communication with the outside world, other than the hijackers surrounding the plane. There had been nothing but silence—until now.

Disappointment sank in when she realized it was the hijackers making contact, not a rescue team. Rivers was still tied up in the left seat. He glared at her as she slapped a strip of duct tape from her SINK bag across his mouth.

"All yours." Laverdeen handed her the radio.

"Open the doors." The voice crackling over the radio in English had a distinct Libyan accent. She was tempted to answer the man in Arabic but wanted to keep her fluency on the downlow for now. He might be sloppy, talk to his compatriots while the radio was on and reveal their plans.

"Who is this?" she asked.

"Open the doors, or the captain's daughters will die."

Rivers's eyes bulged, and he squirmed in his seat.

"Conversation is a lot easier when you know who you're speaking to."

Silence.

She waited.

"Call me Bassam."

His name meant "the one who smiles." *Just not today.*

"I'm Thea Paris."

"Open the doors."

"Bassam, why have we been detained?"

"Let me speak to the captain."

"He's no longer in charge. You can talk to me instead."

Rivers struggled against the restraints, but his efforts were in vain. She empathized, but only so much. The bastard could have killed them all, and relieving him of duty had actually helped his situation, although she didn't expect him to see it that way. Bassam had nothing to gain by hurting his kids now. But that didn't guarantee their safety.

"Last chance. We have an RPG aimed at the plane."

She peeled back an inch of the paper covering the cockpit window. Sure enough, one of the men held a rocket-propelled grenade launcher, the setting sun showcasing his silhouette. The man next to him held a walkie-talkie. *Bassam.* Tall, lean, with a *shemagh* wrapped around his head. Aviator sunglasses masked his expression.

"Now," Bassam said.

"Sorry, I'd need certain assurances first," she said.

Laverdeen raised one eyebrow.

"You have fifteen seconds to open the door."

Thea glanced at her watch. The seconds ticked by slowly, like the clunking of a grandfather clock.

"You want me to depressurize?" Laverdeen asked.

Rivers kicked and twisted in his seat.

"They sound serious." The copilot's Adam's apple bobbed up and down.

Three.
Two.
One.

Rivers squeezed his eyes shut.

She edged the paper back from the window again and glanced outside. The man with the RPG stood waiting for a command, Bassam rigid beside him.

She pressed the radio button. "Okay, Bassam, let's talk."

Chapter 12

Prospero poured four fingers of Glendronach 18 for his guest and a Rusty Nail for himself from the fully stocked bar in his study. He hoped the cocktail would anesthetize the uneasiness seeping through his body and soften his disdain for Enzo Spruilli. He hadn't liked the man's father either.

He turned to face Enzo, a long-suffering, cadaverous CIA agent. The two of them went way back—in fact, their fathers had worked together many years ago, before Enzo's dad had disappeared.

"The plan is operational." Enzo sipped at his scotch like a hummingbird dipping its tiny beak into a tepid birdbath.

"You have everything covered from your end?" Prospero had suggested the original plan to Enzo, knowing the spy was desperate to make his mark in the agency.

Both Italian, both operating in the shadows—but on opposite sides of the law—they'd found common ground as participants in Operation Gladio and since then had opened lines of communication that had been profitable financially and on the intel front. Prospero found it ironic that he was the mobster in this equation yet almost certainly had a stronger moral code than his partner in crime.

Still, the risk was his alone in this hijacking. If he was successful, he'd be doing the world a service while making a favorable deal with the CIA, one that enhanced his wealth and protected him from prosecution. If his plan blew up . . . well, he didn't want to go there now. No matter what, Gernot Dietrich had to be stopped. The *pazzo austriaco* thought he was the next Hitler, this time hoping to eradicate Arabs instead of Jews.

After the Second World War, clandestine stay-behind armies had been seeded all over Europe to protect against an imagined Soviet invasion. An expansion of Churchill's black-ops Special Operations Executive, these paramilitary organizations were secretly funded and meant to operate in the shadows, overseen by NATO and supported by the CIA and MI6 as a bulwark against the spread of communism during the Cold War.

By the 1980s, most of the groups had mutated into quasi-terrorist paramilitaries or faded into obscurity, their memberships dissolved and their secret arms caches dismantled. In 1990, the Italian branch, Gladio, had been the first to be exposed to the world, but even after coming under the spotlight, it had never gone away completely. Prospero and Enzo had both worked for Gladio, carrying out anti-leftist operations, presumably under CIA control but more often than not working for their own benefit.

The Austrian branch, the OWSGV, had gone through a number of transformations over the years, but it had survived, sheltered in the 1990s and 2000s by successive US presidents. Now, under Dietrich's leadership, they were *completamente pazzo*— bat-shit crazy.

"You have the plane—and the target is on board?" Enzo tapped his little finger on the crystal glass.

"*Sì*, the BBJ is under our control." No need to expand on the complicating circumstances. Thea Paris would eventually have to capitulate and let his men on board.

"*Bene, bene.* By the way, I suspect Rudolph Krimm is feeding the Austrians information."

Krimm was a former CIA agent Enzo used to work with. The guy was on a crusade against the Middle East, so it was no surprise to hear he was giving those murderous neo-Nazis intelligence. "You think Krimm might be supporting Dietrich's plan?"

"Hard to say."

What was it with Spruilli—had he lost his nerve? He wasn't usually this ambivalent. Or maybe he knew something he wasn't sharing? "I'll handle the situation in Libya, make sure the target is secure."

"And the truck?" Enzo paced, his fine-boned frame gliding across the hardwood floor.

"Still searching for it." That damned truck full of Syrian refugees had to be stopped.

"Any news from your informant in Austria?"

"Unfortunately, he's gone silent." Prospero was more worried than he let on; the mole was a lifelong friend whom Prospero's father had installed inside Dietrich's operation.

"I hope he hasn't been exposed."

"He knows what he's doing."

"Have you tried reaching him through the dead drop?" Enzo asked.

"Of course." Prospero felt a twinge of annoyance at being micromanaged. "Anything else?"

"Just that my contacts in Salzburg are reporting unusual levels of activity at Dietrich's property."

Prospero swore under his breath, staring at the drink in his hand. It suddenly didn't hold the same interest it had five minutes ago. With all this activity in Austria, finding that truck before Dietrich made his move was critical. But more than one million refugees from the Middle East and Africa had streamed into Europe this year alone. Locating a single truck filled with asylum-seekers was proving to be more difficult than Prospero would ever admit.

"We need more information, and fast," Spruilli said.

Prospero thunked down the undrunk portion of his Rusty Nail on the mahogany desk. "Then I'd better get going. Work your contacts. Keep looking. Let's pray we're not too late."

Chapter 13

Johann rubbed his eyes, fighting to stay awake in math class. The teacher's voice droned in the distance. After the horrifying spectacle that had kept him up half the night, he felt as if he were floating outside his body, reality having slipped its bonds.

He'd texted Uncle Karl again, hoping they could at least speak on the phone. He wanted to make sense of last night's events with someone he trusted. But no answer. His stomach twisted—Karl had given him a birthday present every year. Not even texting to wish him a happy birthday was disappointing; actually, it was unsettling, which was worse.

His nemesis, David Taddington, sat at the back of the class, surrounded by his flock of bootlickers. Johann yawned, maybe a little too loudly. David shot him a condescending glance. Despite his better instincts, Johann remembered the *Freiheitswächter* medallion nestled in his pocket, and it gave him strength. If the American boy only knew about what had happened at his house last night, he wouldn't dismiss Johann so readily.

Fatima smiled, and he smiled back. But a sudden, vivid, mental image of her gentle beauty marred by the gruesome effects of weaponized plague nauseated him, and his smile faded. Given her DNA, she would die just as horribly as Omar Kaleb had. The medallion now felt like a terrible burden.

The bell rang, jolting him out of his thoughts. He gathered his papers and books, shoving them into his knapsack. Hanging back, he let the popular kids leave the classroom first. Fatima was still typing notes into her laptop.

She closed the device and saw him standing there. Her eyes sparkled with warmth. "Free period?" Johann already knew that he and Fatima shared the same empty slot in their schedules.

"Let's go out back." The lingering mental image of the deadly gas hovering in the underground chamber tightened his chest. He craved the outdoors, fresh air, to clear his mind.

They headed out the rear door into the spacious yard, bypassing a storage shed to be greeted by a spectacular view of the surrounding mountains. The air was crisp, invigorating. A soft breeze brought a whiff of lavender. He longed to feel the same connection with Fatima they'd experienced yesterday on the bus ride home from skiing. Did she feel it too?

"You look tired. Up late celebrating your birthday?" she gently chided him.

"I've been thinking a lot about Schönbrunn." Of course he couldn't breathe a word about last night, but he had to work through some of his tumultuous feelings. He felt safe sharing his thoughts with Fatima, even though he barely knew her.

"I'm so sad. My whole family is. We prayed for the victims, their families—and the men who committed the horror."

Surprise rippled in Johann's mind. At first, he feared she might be sympathetic to the terrorists' efforts, but, looking at her kind face, he knew that couldn't be true. She was just a compassionate person.

"The attacker who got away—what do you think his punishment should be when he's caught?" he asked.

"His fate is in Allah's hands, not mine."

"Don't you think he deserves death?"

She hesitated, glancing at the ground. "I hate what those men did, what they stole from innocent people, children."

"And if you could do something to stop the next attack, how far would you go?"

She stared into his eyes, perhaps sensing a hidden conversation below the surface. "I'd give my own life, if I had to."

He could feel her conviction. She was much braver than he was. "How do you feel about secrets?"

"I have no idea what you're talking about," she said.

He looked at her blankly.

She smiled. "That's what I would say if someone asked me to divulge one."

"Oh, I see." He forced a laugh, his hand touching the medallion hidden in his pocket. Could he share this secret with her? He'd sworn an oath to Father and the other men, but this knowledge felt too monumental to carry alone.

Fatima's head snapped up, and she looked past his shoulder. He turned and followed her gaze. David and his group were headed in their direction, muttering among themselves like a swarm of angry bees.

Johann stepped in front of Fatima. "Don't worry, I've got this." But he did worry. The air buzzed with negative energy.

The group stopped a few feet away. David's chin jutted forward, his gaze focused on Fatima. "Liam says he walked by your house last night and saw a stranger going in. Is your family harboring the terrorist from Schönbrunn?"

Fatima drew back, as if physically assaulted. "My cousin Abdul is visiting from the UAE."

David looked down at her. "You didn't answer my question."

Johann straightened his shoulders. "Leave her alone—she had nothing to do with the attack."

"How do you know? You bunking up with her during prayer time instead of sleeping at the family crypt?"

His friends laughed. Fatima's face whitened. Anger pulsed at Johann's core. "Leave now."

"I need to find out what's going on at this towelhead's house."
David shot his hand toward Fatima, reaching for her hijab.

Johann's instincts, honed during countless 6:00 a.m. training
sessions, kicked in. He stepped forward, blocked David's reach
with his left arm, and slammed his right hand upward into the
bully's nose. Blood spurted into the air in a pink mist. Moving
quickly, he kicked David's feet from underneath him, toppling
him onto his backside.

The group went quiet.

Tension crackled in the air.

David covered his face with his hands, making small animal
noises. He glanced around, disoriented.

Johann grabbed Fatima's hand and pulled her toward the
school entrance.

"You're going to pay for this!" David shouted, staggering to
his feet.

"We all pay for our sins," Johann murmured under his breath.

Something had snapped inside him. He'd never hit anyone
before, but he was tired of being afraid. And now he was a *Freiheitswächter*. No one was going to bully him or his friends ever
again.

Chapter 14

Rif slammed down the landline's receiver. "She's alive!" Hakan and Christos gave him questioning looks. "I spoke to a pilot who received a call from the plane Thea is on. They landed on an old deserted runway in the Libyan Desert."

"And the boys?" Christos asked.

"Sorry, Christos, no idea. The communication was one way and didn't cover the passengers."

"That's one of the harshest parts of the Sahara. Why land there?" Christos paced the room.

"Because it's remote. An ideal place to take a hijacked plane," Rif said.

"What else did the pilot say?" Hakan asked.

"Thea's mayday gave their GPS coordinates. She also reported armed men surrounding them, but she'd repressurized the plane, so they couldn't open the doors. She's probably in a stand-off with the hijackers."

"Any way to reach her?" Christos asked.

"She would have contacted us if she could. The satphones have been jammed, and there'd be no cell service there."

"Never good to be in the middle of nowhere," Hakan said.

That's for sure. Rif recollected the sad story of the World War II B-24 bomber, *Lady Be Good*, out on its first combat mission, the wreck of which was discovered two hundred kilometers north of Kufra after it had been missing for fifteen years. When *Lady Be Good* overshot its air base in a sandstorm and ran out of fuel, the crew had bailed out, possibly believing they were over the sea. But they landed in the desert more than 600 kilometers inland and started trudging for safety across the arid sand, slowly dying from dehydration in a place so forbidding, even the Bedouins refused to go there.

Rif shook off the dark thoughts. From the sound of it, dehydration was the least of Thea's concerns.

"Any assets in the area?" Hakan asked.

"No one who can get there sooner than we can." It'd take them four hours flying time to reach the GPS coordinates. Rif typed into his phone. "The rapid response team will meet me at the airport. Wheels up within the hour." Several members of their ops teams were always on call for emergencies.

"You going to para in?"

"We'll land nearby and come in dark."

"I'll work the situation from this end, see if I can rattle any political chains, get support from the local Tuareg or Tebu tribes."

"If you reach Thea, tell her to keep stalling," Rif said.

"Be safe, son." Hakan squeezed his shoulder.

"Bring Thea and the boys home." Christos's mouth was a tight line.

Rif shook his godfather's hand. He understood a little of the torment the oilman was going through. Christos had made some horrific decisions when it came to his children, decisions that had cost him his son's life and his daughter's trust.

"I'll contact you when I know more."

Chapter 15

Johann and Fatima sat at a corner table in St. Peter Stiftskeller, the oldest restaurant in Europe, dating back to Charlemagne's time. The Dietrich family had been coming to the Salzburg landmark for generations, and Johann used *Vater*'s account whenever he dined there.

He'd wanted to escape school, David, and reality for a short time, and this was the place to do it, the familiar cathedral ceilings and dark wood surroundings providing comfort. Johann and Fatima dug into the crispy *Wiener schnitzel* and the tender beef of the *Tafelspitz* along with a host of other delicacies. He hadn't realized how hungry he was, but he'd missed dinner last night and hadn't bothered with breakfast. The maître d' treated him with respect, thanks to his father's patronage, and that made him feel good. Truth be told, he wanted to impress Fatima, and there was no better display of old-world Austria than this restaurant.

"I'm so full, I might explode." Fatima laughed, the soft sound most welcome after everything he'd been through during the last twenty-four hours.

"Finish your *Wiener schnitzel* or you get no *Salzburger Nockerl*." He'd pre-ordered dessert. If only he could freeze this moment, linger in it forever.

Fatima sparkled with enthusiasm. "Salzburg is so beautiful. I hope my family can stay here forever," she said.

"How long is your father's contract for?" he asked. She'd told him her family had come to Austria because of her father's work in plastics.

"We're going home in two months—unless the contract is extended."

She can't leave. The words came unbidden to his mind. He wondered if somehow Father could help but then realized it was hopeless. He pushed those thoughts aside and tried to enjoy the moment.

"You've heard all about my family. Tell me about yours," Fatima said.

"We lost my mother in a car accident five years ago." Johann didn't share the details.

She reached out and touched his hand. "I'm so sorry."

He never wanted her to let go. "I miss her every day, but for my father it's worse. He was never exactly a doting parent or the kind of man you'd open up to, but ever since the accident he's become . . . unreachable." Johann felt a little guilty describing his father that way, but it was true, even if it did seem like a betrayal to be confiding it to a relative stranger.

"My father, too. Although he does ask my mother's advice when he thinks no one is listening." She smiled and removed her hand, picking up her water glass.

"Women are the smart ones." He smiled back. "I miss my *mutti*. My father is obsessed with perfection, and . . . the illness I have, Marfan syndrome, it came from his side of the family."

She nodded in understanding. "So he feels responsible."

"I'm a constant reminder that his genes are *not* perfect."

"But he should be so proud of you—any father would be. You're smart, funny, kind, and a great skier, much better than I could ever hope to be." She laughed.

He laughed too, just happy to be in her company.

Her gaze became serious again. "Will you be expelled for hitting David?"

He snorted and shook his head. "Father donates so much money to the school that I could get away with pretty much anything." He pictured Omar Kaleb's bloody body and cringed.

"You okay?" Fatima asked, her dark eyes compassionate.

"I may have eaten too much. But don't worry, I always save room for dessert."

As if on cue, the head waiter pushed a gold-framed trolley in their direction, the peaked soufflé riding on top.

After they had been served, Johann leaned back in his seat. He wanted to witness Fatima's delight as she sampled the dessert for the first time.

She scooped up the first spoonful, then another and another. "Incredible. It's so light, like fluffy clouds in your mouth."

"Exactly."

"I'm going to be the size of a house if I learn that recipe."

"Nonsense—you're absolutely perfect, and you'll always be perfect," he blurted.

She blushed and smiled at him. He wanted to reach out, touch her, but the sight of his father entering the restaurant with an associate shattered the moment. Johann was sure *Vater* had mentioned having some business in Lausanne today. He swallowed, but the lump in his throat wouldn't budge. It was a large restaurant. Could they escape without his father seeing them?

But no, the headwaiter had already gestured in their direction, happily pointing them out. His father seemed even taller than his six feet and six inches as he approached the table. Father's face might look impassive to outsiders, but Johann could see the storm brewing in his deep-set eyes.

"*Guten Tag.* I didn't realize today was a school holiday." *Vater* let the words hang in the air. He was at his scariest at moments like this.

"Well, um, it's not, really. I got into a bit of a tussle at school. Thought it would be good to make myself scarce for a bit. This is my friend, Fatima Abboud."

Father's icy stare assessed her, his gaze taking in her hijab and her otherwise conventional clothes.

Fatima straightened in her seat, surprisingly comfortable in the face of Father's intense scrutiny. "Very nice to meet you, Herr Dietrich. Johann is such a gentleman, he didn't mention that the tussle happened because he was protecting me from some bullying students. You should be very proud of your son."

"Sometimes he takes things a little too far."

"It truly wasn't his fault. This American boy, David Taddington, was quite aggressive."

Uh-oh. She had just broken the cardinal rule: never criticize the great United States of America, those blessed consumers of the firearms that helped pay for this very meal. He braced himself for a tirade.

"Johann, may I speak to you privately for a moment?"

Even worse. The more controlled the manner, the angrier Father was.

"Please excuse me for a minute," he said to Fatima.

"Absolutely, but don't expect there to be any dessert left if you take too long." Fatima laughed.

He inched out of his seat and followed his father to the lobby.

"Sorry I skipped out of school—" he began hopefully.

"She's a pretty girl," *Vater* said coldly, "but remember the tale of the Trojan horse." He paused and glowered. "After you finish your lunch, I'm sure I won't see you two together again. Ever." The absolute frigidity in his voice chilled Johann to the core.

Father strode toward his table in a back corner of the restaurant, a spot that offered privacy for his arms deals—and perhaps the *Freiheitswächter* plans. *Killing Arabs.* Johann stumbled to the men's room, losing his lunch in the first stall.

Chapter 16

Although Thea had reached out to Bassam several times after the RPG bluff had failed, she hadn't heard a peep from the hijackers. Time slowed. With every hour that passed, the APU slowly chewed through their fuel reserves. Running the third engine was keeping them cool in the unrelenting Libyan heat and pressurizing the plane, protecting them from intrusion, but the harsh reality was that they could only hold out until the fuel was gone.

She had Laverdeen checking regularly for any movement or change outside, but the guards remained in their positions, alert but not aggressive. She sensed that Bassam wasn't the top dog and they were waiting for someone to arrive before making a move. That was the most likely explanation for the lack of contact.

She'd asked three of the passengers, including Mike Dillman—who'd been surprisingly helpful—to search the plane for anything that could be useful. Weapons, food, first-aid supplies, cash, phones, flashlights, blankets. She'd tried her cell and satphone several times, but communication was at a standstill other than over the frequency being used by the hijackers.

Versace was still out cold, strapped into his seat. She took a closer look at his suit. Pure cashmere with the finest tailoring, the jacket alone must have cost him more than three grand. She rifled through his things and found an Italian passport in the name of Ciaro Borolo. Born in Sicily. Thirty-seven years old, with a photo that didn't do him any favors.

She discovered a folded sheet of paper in his upper left pocket. The flight manifest. But no marks or indication of which passenger was of interest. Of course it couldn't be that easy. He carried a pack of cigarettes, a wad of cash, and three credit cards in his name. Nothing else.

No answers from him, then, at least not until he woke up. She slipped his passport into her pants pocket and strode up the aisle. All the passengers had gathered in the first few rows. A couple of people were dozing, Matthias was working on his computer, and Karlsson was nervously flipping pages of the latest Lee Child novel. Too bad Reacher wasn't there to help.

Or Rif.

By now, Rif, Hakan, and Papa would know that her plane was missing. They'd be working on tracking her flight path, but the transponders had been switched off early by Captain Rivers, so discovering the location of the plane would be close to impossible. There had been radio contact with Khartoum, but that was well before they landed. Maybe the Quantum team could tap into the military assets, use skin paint, a type of radar, to find them.

"Thea, how long do we have to wait?" Jabari yawned. Ayan had gone back to watching *The Lion King* on the small television screen.

She held his hand. "I'm not sure." She had never lied to the boys and wasn't about to start now. "It could be a long night. Why don't you and Ayan curl up with some blankets and get some sleep?"

"Okay. I want to go to London."

"Me too. Hopefully, soon."

The last time she'd peered out the cockpit window, the sun had collided with the horizon, signaling an end to this tumultuous day. Desert darkness surrounded the plane, the men with AK-47s setting up a few spotlights to keep an eye on them.

The man on the aisle seat in the first row spoke up. "Can we talk?"

She remembered the fedora he'd worn. "Sure. Hammond, right? What's on your mind?"

"I'm the chief administrator of the Herringford Trust, which has billions of dollars of equities and financial instruments at its disposal. I usually travel with a bodyguard, but mine became ill at the last minute, and I couldn't wait for another one because I'm due to speak at the World Bank Conference."

"Have you had any recent threats?"

"Usually several a day. Hence the round-the-clock security."

And here she thought *her* profession was dicey. Why was he telling her this now?

Before she could press Hammond any further, raised voices and doors slamming outside on the tarmac grabbed her attention. On this deserted landing strip, it wasn't just some passerby. She'd better head to the flight deck, see who had arrived.

"We'll talk more later."

Chapter 17

Johann slumped on a couch in a corner of the cellar, trying to maintain a low profile among the gathered *Freiheitswächter*. After being caught with Fatima at the restaurant, he'd walked her home, taking the long route to eke out every minute he could with her. An overwhelming sadness filled him. He'd finally found someone he could talk to, and now he'd been discovered and ordered to have no further contact with this magical girl.

He missed *Mutti* so much. She would have understood his feelings, his need for love and acceptance. And what would she have made of the *Freiheitswächter*?

As he looked around the room at the hard men his father had gathered around himself, he wished he could be playing on his Xbox, texting Fatima, even doing homework. Anything would be better than being here. Why did he have to care so much about *Vater*'s opinion?

Father held a laser pointer over a world map, the red dot dashing around Europe as he pointed to different refugee camps. "We'll target these locations, among others."

Johann had recently watched a documentary about the camps and how abysmal the conditions were. The reporter had said that the Idomeni camp in Greece mirrored the Second World War horrors of Dachau. Those poor people were suffering enough hardship; was it really necessary to attack them with a bioweapon? He'd also done some research since last night—the weaponized plague could infect hundreds of thousands, maybe even millions.

His father continued the presentation, the other men leaning forward, fixated on every word. If Father hadn't been talking about death and destruction, Johann would have been proud of his commanding presence. But here they were planning on slaughtering thousands of people. Innocents. People who simply had the bad luck to be born with a certain genotype.

"The pathogen will be infused via the camp showers and will be undetectable until the incubation period is over. In three days, the spread of the disease will be unstoppable."

A buzzing sound overwhelmed him, the world tilting at a strange angle. He placed his hands on his ears, trying to block out the noise that no one else seemed to notice. It slowly faded away. Johann wondered if this was another weird symptom of his Marfan syndrome. But maybe it was just shock at the obvious parallel to the Holocaust. *Showers*? His father was talking about genocide so casually, as if he was ordering groceries from the local supermarket.

"When the first symptoms appear, the initial deaths will be blamed on the unhygienic conditions, allowing the plague to spread. Surviving Arabs across Europe, not just the ones in refugee camps, will start a mass exodus. We'll reclaim our land."

"What if the men are caught installing the aerosols?" a bearded man asked.

"This is war, gentleman. Soldiers take risks."

Johann's hands shook. Should he go to the local police, share his father's plan, somehow stop him? But who would believe him? Father held such influence in Salzburg; he was a pillar of the community, untouchable.

And what would happen if they did believe him and his father went to jail? Johann couldn't bear the thought of losing his only remaining family.

Chapter 18

Thea peeked out the cockpit window. Thirty minutes had passed since two Land Cruisers had arrived on the strip. She'd snuck glimpses outside, but it was difficult to get a clear view of anything with the darkening skies. A few floodlights peppered the area, confirming that armed men still surrounded the plane. Her guess: the boss had arrived, and Bassam and his men were being reprimanded for failing to control the situation.

"I'm checking on the passengers. Keep an eye out for any changes," she told Laverdeen.

Dark smudges shadowed the copilot's gray eyes. Captain Rivers was asleep, still tied to his seat. "You think anyone heard us on Guard?"

"One can hope." But it was doubtful. Over a million square kilometers of sand surrounded them in the Libyan Desert, and the bone-dry wasteland wasn't exactly a popular flight destination. Some areas in this part of the world hadn't seen rain in more than a decade.

"The APU can keep the plane pressurized for up to seventy-two hours, but it depends on how much jet fuel there is. After that . . ."

"Every minute we hold them off buys the authorities and my team time to find us." Thea tucked her hair behind her ears.

"You're surprisingly calm."

She smiled. "We both know panic only brings disaster."

"Yeah, well, it's lucky for us that you work as a hostage negotiator," Laverdeen said.

"Maybe, but I'm not usually held captive at the same time I'm trying to negotiate a release." She scanned the instruments for the millionth time, just for something to do.

"I woke up this morning thinking it'd be another run-of-the-mill flight, and I actually said to myself, 'I hope something exciting happens today.'"

"Be careful what you wish for."

He gave her a wry grin. "I'm glad you're here."

"I'm not." She smiled and headed into the cabin.

Ayan and Jabari sat on either side of Ocean. Somehow they'd talked her into playing Go Fish, and Thea could be wrong, but it looked as if the mysterious woman might be enjoying herself. She was grateful the kids were distracted.

Karlsson beckoned to her from his seat. She strode over to him.

"Come to the back," he whispered.

She followed, wondering, *What now*?

"Can I trust you?"

Not a good start. "That's for you to decide." Trying to sway others mostly worked against you. People liked to think they made their own decisions, but universally they wanted to share whatever was on their minds.

"I'm former MI6." His face twitched.

Yet he hadn't spoken up when she'd asked if anyone had security experience. "Specializing in?" She studied his features—quite average, allowing him to blend in, like most spooks.

"Counterterrorism. I've been retired for six years, but I still have secrets locked in here." He pointed to his temple.

"Any in particular that might be worth all this?" She waved a hand.

"I'd be better equipped to reply to that question if I knew who we are dealing with. I have many, many enemies."

"Fair enough." The paranoia was obvious—but was he also nuts?

Laverdeen's voice carried down the aisle. "Thea, someone's asking for you on the radio."

She turned to Karlsson. "I've got to take this. But why don't we talk more about any African or Middle Eastern operations you may have been a part of when I'm done."

Chapter 19

In the middle of the night, Johann snuck downstairs to the cellar wearing pajamas, his bare feet cold on the stone slabs, his vision blurry. Yet another reminder of his illness, which occasionally affected the connective tissue in his eyes. *Why can't I just be normal?* He stopped for a moment and blinked a few times to get his eyes to cooperate, not wanting to trip in the gloom.

His father was out late at a meeting, and the butler, housekeeper, and chef had left for the evening. He was all alone in the castle that had once been a sanctuary and now was a house of horrors, full of dreadful secrets.

His cell buzzed in his hand.

You still awake?

Fatima. He'd have to find a way to distance himself from her, if not for his sake, then for hers. But he couldn't deny the happiness he felt when her name popped up on the screen. What was she doing up so late?

Yes.

Can we meet tomorrow morning? I think someone is watching my house.

He should tell her no, but he couldn't. He felt responsible: his poor judgment in taking her to his father's favorite restaurant might easily have resulted in this surveillance. Given what he'd learned over the past few days, nothing would surprise him. If he wanted to meet her, and he did, he'd have to be careful. School was the only safe place. Father would never remove him from the great American educational establishment, no matter who his classmates were.

7 a.m. By the shed behind the school. Now get some rest.

She sent a heart emoji. He smiled broadly and couldn't resist sending one back.

He really needed to talk to someone he could trust about this whole mess. Where was Uncle Karl? He sent him another text, asking him to call ASAP.

The basement was eerily quiet. He slipped the phone back into his pajamas pocket and approached the wall that Father had opened last night. He had no idea when *Vater* would return, so he had to work quickly. The lever was hidden behind an old book, and he had no problem remembering the code his father had typed in. Fingers shaky, he pressed the keys in sequence.

Nothing happened.

Had Father changed the security code?

He punched them in again.

A creak, and the wall shifted.

After a quick look around, he entered the dim tunnel, hurrying toward the secret area below the greenhouse. The lab. His hands felt clammy, cold. The image of Omar Kaleb's blood-covered corpse flashed in his mind. Would the terrorist's body still be there? He planned on taking photos if it was.

Unsure what he could do to prevent the planned attack on the refugee camp, he figured collecting tangible evidence would be a solid first step. But fear mixed with love for his father made him hesitate. He'd never defied Father before, not in any real way, and now he was on the brink of a massive betrayal. He shuddered to think what would happen if he were caught.

He hurried along the dark tunnel until he finally reached the wall masking the lab. Once again, he keyed in the code and held his breath.

The door shifted open. He stepped inside, turned the lights on, and braced himself for the horrors inside. But the lab was empty. The same yellow suits hung on the walls, the stainless-steel surfaces gleamed, and the glass partition that had been sprayed with Kaleb's vomit and blood was spotless. He stood in the middle of the room, searching for any sign of what had happened last night.

No trace of the Arab man, no trace of his murder.

Johann shook his head, blinked, and looked again.

Nothing.

He almost wondered if he'd imagined the whole horrific incident.

But that was wishful thinking.

He edged toward the locked area through which Falco had entered the hot zone. His palm pressed the large red button. A whooshing sound emerged as the vacuum unsealed. The door opened. Johann stepped inside, searching the floor for spots of blood, anything. But the lab was pristine, sterile. Someone must have spent the entire day cleaning.

Two doors loomed at the other end of the chamber. He glanced at his watch and hurried forward to explore. The first room was an office. Three computers perched on a white melamine table. He searched for papers, information, anything that might offer proof of what his father had planned. But the table's surface was clean, uncluttered.

He sat down in front of the first computer and switched it on. Father might monitor their use, but given their remote location, maybe he hadn't bothered to install spyware the way he had in the laptop Johann used for school. But Johann was much better versed in computers than his father, so he'd been able to block the reporting function on his laptop, allowing him to surf the net as he pleased without being monitored. A secret rebellion that gave him mild satisfaction.

He found a map with all the refugee camps marked on it, including the population of each site. The ones with lower populations had an X marked across them. Father probably felt there were too few people to contaminate. Disgust filled him.

Next, he discovered a live sonar map. *Weird.* One of the blinking lights was right on top of their home. He scanned some of the other files on the computer. Most of the documents looked like lab tests and other scientific stuff. Nothing helpful. For now, he'd leave the computers alone, see what was in the next room. He headed for the door—a heavy steel one—and opened it. A blast of cold air. He stepped inside, goose bumps rippling down his arms. He switched on the lights.

Medical instruments rested on a stainless-steel cart. An odd-looking saw perched on the farthest counter. Two gurneys sat in opposite corners. One was empty; the other held a black canvas body bag.

His pulse quickened.

The terrorist. Johann stepped forward, his breath short, raspy. Stopped.

Could he possibly become infected by the plague that had killed Kaleb? No, Falco had been in the same room and hadn't been affected, even days after exposure. The disease only infected people of Arab descent. Still, it was a plague. *Could he transfer the plague to Fatima?* His gaze was frozen on the black body bag. *No, if the body were still infectious, they would have disposed of it.* He had to take a photo of Omar Kaleb, proof that he wasn't imagining all this if he decided to report it.

His right hand touched the zipper. He hesitated for a minute, inhaled deeply, and held it, bracing himself for the horror of the terrorist's disfigured face and body. He unzipped the body bag, peeling back the black material, unveiling the corpse.

But it wasn't Kaleb.

The dead man was Uncle Karl.

Chapter 20

Prospero's Gulfstream had arrived in Libya, touching down on a hard-packed desert runway without incident. They'd had to land on a nearby strip because the BBJ with the target aboard hadn't followed orders to park in the hangar and was blocking the single runway. Thea's doing, no doubt. After inhaling a shit-load of desert dust riding in an open-air Land Cruiser, Prospero and Luciano had finally reached the tarmac.

Prospero had first hired Bassam Fakroun, who led a group of Tebu mercenaries battle-hardened by the civil war, two years ago. Like many former soldiers who had fought on the side of the National Transitional Council, Bassam and his men had been through hell during the hunt for a Muammar Gaddafi, only to be cast aside by NATO once the Colonel had been found and killed. Having turned to kidnapping, smuggling, extortion, and other violent means of survival, Bassam's team had been perfect for the job: A former colleague had been struggling to correctly calculate the earnings he owed Prospero, and sadly met with an unfortunate accident on a business journey to Tripoli. Back in Italy it was considered yet another bad-luck story about traveling in northern Africa, especially to Libya, now that Gaddafi was gone. *Those crazy desert Arabs, blowing themselves up—you know how dangerous it is over there.* But it hadn't been luck at all.

Prospero shook his head at the sight: A brand-new 737 parked on the cracked asphalt of an abandoned facility falling into ruin. Before the overthrow of Gaddafi, these airstrips had been bustling, used by international oil companies to reach their remote oil fields. But that had all ended in the chaos that followed the revolution. Now these regions were ruled by the likes of Bassam and his armed men, who currently surrounded the business jet.

"This Thea Paris—she refuses to let us board." Bassam's Italian was very good, a reminder of Libya's colonial ties to the European nation. In the torchlight, Prospero could see sweat coating the mercenary's face. He radiated tension, and for good reason. He'd been given an assignment, a relatively simple one, and failed.

Luciano pushed his hand against Bassam's chest, forcing the man backward. "You let a woman best you?"

"Let him be, Luciano. You're only showing your ignorance. This particular woman is a worthy adversary." He turned to Bassam. "Has the mechanic arrived?"

"All set," Bassam said.

"Let me speak to Ms. Paris first."

"She shaded the windows, blocked the cockpit from our view, and repressurized the plane." Bassam wiped sweat from his forehead.

Smart. Prospero wondered who the real hostage was here, Thea and the passengers or Bassam and his men. "Nonetheless, I will talk to her. Ms. Paris and I have history," he said.

"Yeah, but that didn't end so well." Luciano stared at his uncle, challenging him.

"It ended exactly the way I wanted it to." Prospero kept his voice calm.

"*Che cosa? Non è quello che ho—*"

"Later." Prospero would have to find a quiet moment to talk to Luciano about his manners. "For now, we need to get inside that plane before *Liberata*'s allies arrive."

Chapter 21

Johann stared at Uncle Karl's body, willing him back to life. This man had given him so much time and attention, becoming almost a second father. A warm, kind, encouraging one. And now he was gone. Johann could feel his soul cracking in two.

Shivers rippled down his body, the cold air sneaking into his pajama top. A sound startled him. Was someone coming into the lab? He zipped the body bag back up and slipped through the door, his bare feet quiet on the stone floor.

Making his way past the lab, he saw that a soft light glowed on the stainless-steel counters. He stopped and listened. On edge, he wondered if he had imagined the sound. He pressed his nose against the glass and scanned the chamber, noticing a small refrigerator tucked inside a cubbyhole. He suspected the plague was stored in there; he'd read online about the procedures needed to keep bacteria viable.

He shuddered. If Father released the plague in Salzburg, Fatima and her family along with thousands of others would die. Horribly. And what had they ever done to deserve such a fate? He understood wanting to stop terrorists, but bacteria couldn't tell if people were good or evil. Disease killed indiscriminately.

He felt a sudden need to get the hell out of there.

Footsteps. Scuffling. His ears buzzed. Was Father coming? He glanced around. No place to hide.

Johann came face-to-face with the man who made his skin crawl: Leopold, who had created the nightmare plague.

The scientist peered at him from behind his glasses. "What are you doing down here?"

Johann straightened to his full height. "I could ask you the same. This is my house."

The scientist stepped closer, the stench of bleach wafting off his hands. "Gernot knows I work best at night. I don't imagine you have permission to be here."

"I'm a *Freiheitswächter* now. I want to help."

"This is no game, young man. We're at war."

"Then you need soldiers."

Leopold studied him closely. "I told your father that you were too young to join, but he insisted."

"Omar Kaleb murdered hundreds of innocent people. The terrorist deserved to die." Johann didn't have to fake his feelings about the attack on Salzburg, though capital punishment was something he considered wrong, and last night's spectacle had showcased perhaps its most horrific form.

Leopold looked skeptical, so Johann plowed on. "We need to exterminate these people. Teach me what I need to know to be of assistance."

"Your father would never allow me to risk your life in the lab."

Johann had to turn this conversation around. "*Yersinia pestis*. I looked up the name of the bacteria."

Leopold raised his eyebrows.

"It has an untreated mortality rate of almost one hundred percent and attacks its victims through the lungs," Johann said.

"Correct."

"Ninety-eight percent of modern cases occur in Africa."

Leopold folded his arms across his barrel-like chest. "You are certainly a quick study."

"This is my cause as much as it is yours."

Leopold hesitated, then nodded, his mind made up. "The truth is, I could use a lab assistant with brains. But if your father finds out, we will tell him that you were doing clerical work, nothing more."

"Agreed. Thank you, Leopold. When do we begin?"

Chapter 22

Thea couldn't believe who was on the other end of the radio.

"*Liberata*, we meet again." The rumbling baritone, heavily accented, coming over the plane's radio brought the past rushing back, reminding her of the case that had earned her that nickname. She'd never forget him; voices imprinted themselves on her memory, and Prospero Salvatore was one of the most intriguing criminals she had ever met—ruthless but a born philosopher.

She pressed the record button on her cell as she spoke into the radio. "Don Prospero Salvatore." Laverdeen gave her a curious look. Rivers was awake now, mouth still duct-taped, his angry stare focused on her.

"Ah, so you remember." He was clearly flattered.

"What an unusual way to reconnect. Given we're old friends, let's dispense with the formalities and get down to business. Why are we here, Prospero?"

"You need more food?" he asked.

"We have all the supplies we need." *Nice try.*

"Why not join me for an espresso in the hangar? As I remember, you enjoy quality coffee," Salvatore said.

He hadn't changed one bit. "Tell your men to stand down and let us take off; then we can meet for grappa in Sicily."

"But we're both here now." He was actually managing to sound hurt.

"I'm going to have to decline your thoughtful invitation," Thea said.

"Ah, but now you're just being stubborn."

"A wise man once said, 'This is my way—where is yours?' My goal is to get this plane safely to its destination. What about you, Prospero?"

A hearty laugh. "Nietzsche! I've missed our little conversations, Thea."

"Just tell me what you're after. I'm sure we can work something out." Silence greeted her. She waited patiently. It wasn't long before his voice returned, but the tone was different now, harder.

"I saw the news a few months back. My condolences on the loss of your brother."

The words caused a pain that was still sharp, visceral, as if he had impaled her with an ice pick. She missed Nikos every day, even with her memories of him muddied by the monster he had become before his death. "Let's stick to the subject at hand."

"But that's exactly what this conversation is about—*famiglia*. You want to get back to yours; I want to get back to mine. I'm sure the other passengers feel the same way."

"But what do *you* want?"

"A private talk with you."

"We both know it's not me you're after. I was a last-minute passenger on the plane, and this kind of operation took time and planning."

"Don't undervalue yourself. Come out so we can have a proper chat."

"I can ask the pilots to leave the cockpit so we'll have privacy." He didn't need to know that one of them was bound and gagged.

"Sadly, this is not the kind of discussion you have over a radio."

"That's the best I can offer." No way was she opening those doors. Prospero Salvatore's men would rush the plane, and any bargaining advantage she had would vaporize.

"Don't you want those boys to meet their new family?"

Dammit, he knew about Ayan and Jabari. "Don't you want your man back?"

"That *bastardo*? You can keep him. He's safer with you than he would be out here." She had no doubt he was serious. Prospero could be very charming, but he hadn't survived as capo for twenty years because of his compassion for *soldati* who couldn't get the job done.

"Thea, Thea, Thea. You must realize that if you don't agree to join me soon for a *caffè*, I'm coming in."

"You can't do that. The plane is pressurized."

"I'm giving you more latitude than I would anyone else because I am so fond of you, but even my patience will run out very soon. Come out now—for everyone's sake."

"We're comfortable here."

Radio silence.

She had to stretch out the negotiations as long as she could in the hope that help would arrive, and soon. A chill ran down her back. She wouldn't put it past Prospero to kill them all if what he had gone to all this trouble for was, as she was beginning to suspect, a *something* and not a *someone* on the plane.

Chapter 23

Johann skirted the edge of the yellow building, making a bee-line for the shed behind the school. He was twenty minutes late to meet Fatima because he'd overslept; after a couple of hours in the lab with Leopold he'd tossed and turned the rest of the night, finally falling into a fitful sleep in the early morning, only to have a nightmare about men in lab coats chasing him down an endless corridor.

Uncle Karl was dead—strangled, by the looks of it. He still couldn't believe it. Johann touched his Adam's apple, remembering the thick red welt around Karl's neck. His own father might have killed him—but why? Karl had been a good man, Johann's biggest supporter, and a dear friend to his father. Had they disagreed about using the bacteria?

Johann couldn't make sense of this mad world *Vater* now inhabited. It was anathema to everything his mother had stood for; *Mutti* had taught him that everyone was equal and special. She'd be horrified by the *Freiheitswächter*. He understood how Father could detest terrorists, but how could he justify indiscriminately murdering innocent people? Wouldn't people with any Arab blood at all be at risk? That could include many Jews and other Europeans as well.

He hurried down the path leading to the shed, then turned the corner. Fatima sat cross-legged on the ground, reading her math textbook. She looked small and vulnerable, but when she looked up at him, her large brown eyes held hope—hope he was about to crush.

She scrambled to her feet. "Thank goodness. I thought you weren't coming."

"Sorry, rough night."

"Are you okay?" She touched his forearm.

He longed to hug her, to tell her everything would be fine, but he couldn't lie. "It's you I'm worried about. Someone is following you?"

"The same guy who was outside my house was at my bus stop this morning. I'm scared."

Only one possible explanation. His father making sure Johann didn't go near Fatima. He wanted to believe *Vater* would never hurt her, that he just wanted to keep them apart, but Uncle Karl's body was proof that he could no longer be so sure.

He took a deep breath. "Fatima, we can't spend time together anymore."

She drew back, as if stung, comprehension dawning. "Your father doesn't like me."

"He doesn't like . . . anyone."

"Because I'm Muslim?" Seeing the pained look on his face, she said, "Don't be afraid of hurting my feelings. My family has met people with limited views before."

Not like this. "If the man following you doesn't see us together for a couple of days, I'm sure that Father will call off the dogs. I'm sorry."

Fatima looked up at him. "Do you care about me?"

"Of course."

"Then tell your father you can see who you want."

He pictured Uncle Karl's unseeing eyes. "I'm sorry, but I can't."

"You stood up to David." Her voice trembled.

"It's better this way." He felt sick inside.

"Better for whom?" The bitterness in her voice stung. "I thought you were special, different."

The first bell rang. "We'd better go. After school, I'll wait fifteen minutes, so you can leave first."

"Maybe I'll tell my stalker what I think of him."

"Please don't. It's not safe." The words were out of his mouth before he could stop them.

"Not safe? What aren't you telling me?"

"Just ignore him and pretend everything is fine."

The second bell rang. Students were filing into the building.

"We'd better go," Johann said.

"We're not done." Her eyes sparked with indignation.

He felt numb inside, uncertain what to do. His mind was overloaded by the horrors he'd experienced. There was no road back to normal.

Chapter 24

Thea tossed the plastic covering of a chicken wrap into the galley rubbish. Keeping her blood sugar in a healthy range was a priority. She needed to stay sharp, especially given Prospero Salvatore's involvement in her current situation. Usually the Sicilian kingpin exercised his persuasive powers closer to home. What was he doing in Libya?

Mike Dillman exited the rear lavatory and joined her in the galley. "How long can we hold them off?"

"Let's hope someone heard the distress call. My company will be looking for us, and so will the airline."

"I'm guessing they want someone on the plane."

"*Could* it be you?" she asked, given the joke he'd made earlier.

"It *could* be. I'm stinking rich, and my business takes me abroad a lot, so I have a hefty K&R insurance policy." He smiled. "But I doubt it."

Thea nodded. This hijacking wasn't about money. She'd asked the passengers when they'd purchased their plane tickets, as anyone with a last-minute booking was unlikely to be the target. Prospero had tiger kidnapped Rivers's kids, and that meant he'd done his homework, had an inside track on who'd be flying today. "You said you own a mining company?"

"Yes, ma'am. Unlike most Texans, I'm not an oilman. Or a pickle maker, as my name might lead you to believe." Dillman laughed. "I have several patents, business offshoots—that kind of thing."

"Anything worth going to all this trouble for?"

"Hard to say. One man's trash is another man's treasure."

Ayan ran into the galley and tugged at Thea's shirt. "The bad man woke up."

Prospero's soldier—maybe he'd have information.

"Thanks, Ayan. Why don't you see if Ocean wants to play poker?"

"Texas stud." Ayan craned his neck to look up at the strapping Texan. "You want to play, Mr. Mustache?"

"Sure, son, why not? I have time and money to burn."

Ayan grinned. The Texan had better watch his wallet; the boys had more than a little hustle in them, and they had played a *lot* of poker in the orphanage.

Thea left them to their cards and headed toward the rear of the jet. The thug's eyes followed her as she approached. For a macho mobster, being taken down by a woman had probably done more damage to his ego than her forehead had done to his shattered nose.

She ripped the duct tape off his mouth.

"You're going to regret this," he said in English, his voice nasal.

"Yeah, yeah. Why don't we skip to the part where you tell me everything."

He sat there, silent.

"Okay . . ." She pulled out her cell and played the recording she had made of her conversation with Prospero. *"He's safer in there with you than he would be out here."*

His face blanched.

"I'd recommend cooperating with me if you want a chance to make it through this alive."

He remained silent.

"Who's the target?"

Nothing.

"You and I both know the capo doesn't take kindly to men who fail him."

Versace assessed her.

"One last time, then I tape your mouth back up. Who are they after?" she asked.

He sighed. "I don't know. I just had to make sure the plane reached these coordinates."

She studied his calculating gaze and decided he was telling the truth. He seemed to be exactly the kind of rat who would switch allegiances to save his own skin.

"Do better than that, or I'll give you back to your boss."

"Gladio," he blurted. "We are Gladio."

"What the hell is Gladio?"

The lights flickered off and on. One second she could see the man's face; the next, the plane went completely dark. The comforting drone of the APU was gone, replaced by silence. A blue glow lit the aisle, the emergency lights providing soft illumination. A hush fell over the passengers.

It was too soon for the fuel to be gone. Prospero had made his first move.

Chapter 25

Prospero glanced at his watch. The intel he'd procured on the Freedom Guardians' plans was time-sensitive. He couldn't afford to outwait Thea Paris—especially not when she could be useful. Bassam had blocked cell and satphone service, but *Liberata* had stalled for time while undoubtedly calling for help through the plane's Guard system.

He half smiled. It had been several years since he'd crossed paths with the kidnap negotiator, but he'd suspected they'd meet again. He had always preferred a *donna forte*, even though his father used to caution him that while men were simple creatures, easy to predict, women could always surprise you. Prospero couldn't agree more.

Smart, wily, and fearless, *Liberata* had manipulated one of his associates into giving up a hostage without one cent of ransom money changing hands. He could have stepped in but decided not to, the end result suiting his needs. And now, here they were again, this time direct adversaries in a dangerous game.

He picked up the radio. "In case you're interested, the outside temperature is thirty degrees." His linen shirt was soaked through, matted against his chest.

"Excellent. It's too cold in here. Had to put on a jacket." Her voice was strong, energized.

Normally he wouldn't want to play poker with her, but in this case he held the winning hand. With the APU off, the next thirty minutes would turn the plane into a Turkish bath, and by the time the sun came up, the temperature would become lethal. Long before then, passengers would be at risk of heat stroke, tempers would flare, and Thea would have a mutiny on her hands.

Raising an arm, he wiped sweat from his brow. "Airline coffee is terrible. Come out, and I'll make you a proper espresso, *ragazza*."

"Trying to reduce my caffeine intake, but thanks anyway, *ragazzo*."

He smiled. "I'm not going to ask nicely again. Tell Captain Rivers that his youngest is about to lose a finger."

On the other end, he heard sounds of someone struggling, a muffled yell. Then someone must have hit the mute button. As expected, she'd incapacitated the captain.

At least fifteen seconds of silence passed before she came back on. "Mutilating the girl won't help anyone. Imagine having to confess that sin to Father Francisco. There aren't enough Hail Marys in the universe to make up for harming a child in cold blood, Prospero."

Her memory was spectacular, zeroing in on the name of the priest who had been involved in the kidnapping all those years ago. And she'd called his bluff. Women and children were good bargaining chips, but Thea knew he would never maim or kill one. "Sooner or later, you're coming out. For every minute you make me wait, there will be a price." This time he wasn't bluffing.

"What does *Gladio* mean?" she asked.

"I have no idea what you're talking about." That *inutile bastardo* was spilling his guts. Good thing he didn't know much. Even so, Prospero didn't want to give Thea any more time to question him.

He gave an emphatic nod to the mechanic.

Chapter 26

One moment, Thea could see; the next, the plane was plunged into utter darkness. Even the blue emergency lights died this time, and nothing took their place. Prospero or one of his people must have accessed the "hellhole," where the hydraulics and other guts of the plane were located, and disabled the batteries, killing all power.

The passengers gasped. A few cried out. With all the lights gone, the fear inside the plane was palpable.

"Stay seated and remain calm." She fumbled in her pants pocket and found the 5.11 mini LED flashlight she always kept on her key chain. A quick flick of her finger, and a beam of light sliced through the darkness. She strode down the aisle to access her SINK and dug out two small LED beacons and a larger flashlight. She gave one beacon to Dillman, the other to Matthias. The soft glow of light dissipated the initial panic.

Ayan and Jabari sat quietly beside Ocean and Dillman, their playing cards resting on a fold-down tray table. When the flashlights came on, the boys did not look panicked; they looked vigilant, alert. Former child soldiers, they knew that nighttime was an ideal time to attack and that staying calm was a good strategy for staying alive.

"What's going on?" Hammond asked.

"The hijackers are trying to force us out. I'm trying to buy enough time for another plane or air traffic control to hear our distress signal and send help." She didn't want to share that she was beginning to think it unlikely that help would come in time; hope was a balm. "Time is our friend and their enemy."

"But isn't the plane depressurized now that we've lost power?" Hammond adjusted his fedora.

"Not exactly. It's in the process of depressurizing, but we're not down for the count yet. Hang tight."

"Maybe we should let them in, start negotiating face-to-face," Matthias said.

"These guys negotiate with AK-47s. We have no answer for that aboard the plane." She nodded to the boys and headed for the cockpit.

Laverdeen had ripped the duct tape off Rivers's face and was giving him a drink of water. She passed the large flashlight to the copilot. "Use this as needed."

She pointed her light at the cockpit window and tried to open the crank. It didn't budge. The plane was still pressurized. Soon enough, though, she'd be able to open the window.

"I need to take a piss," Rivers said.

"Unzip him and give him a cup," she told Laverdeen.

"This is fucking ridiculous. Let me go." Rivers was sputtering, saliva flying.

"You do remember who hijacked the plane, right?"

"Because they have my kids—I had no choice."

"We always have a choice."

Rivers became shrill. "I want privacy."

"Sorry, the cup is what you get. If you really want privacy that bad, you can piss in your pants." No way would she risk cutting Rivers loose.

"Get me out of this seat now!"

She grabbed the duct tape and slapped it across Rivers's mouth, muting his screams. Pilots were trained to remain calm at all times, but Rivers had officially lost it.

"I don't want to hold the cup," Laverdeen said.

"Just do it." She pressed the radio button. As she feared: dead. Prospero's men had disconnected the battery, so they had no lights, no radio, and—the most critical development—no ventilation.

Smart bastard.

Even though it was pitch-black outside, it was still hot out on the tarmac, just as Prospero had said. She could already feel staleness in the air. Soon enough, it would feel like a sauna inside the plane, which would be especially dangerous for any passengers with health problems, including her. People with diabetes didn't dissipate heat all that efficiently, and that could trigger a whole cascade of problems.

She calculated all the possible moves left to her and realized that none of them was very good.

Thea pulled back the map covering the cockpit windscreen and tried opening the small window again. This time the crank budged, indicating the plane had depressurized. She slid the window along the track, and hot air rushed into the cockpit. The entire plane would feel like the Sahara soon.

She spoke through the open window. "You there?"

Prospero's baritone rumbled back from somewhere in the darkness. *"Buona sera, Liberata!"*

"Put the APU back on, and I'll come out."

"No pressurization."

She hesitated, then realized she was out of options. "Agreed."

"You have three minutes."

The lights kicked back on. A blast of fresh air entered the cockpit.

"You're leaving us?" Laverdeen asked.

"No choice." She reached for the Glock tucked in her pants. "You know how to use this?"

"I've been to a shooting range a few times."

"Keep it hidden and be cautious. If there's a way to negotiate us out of this mess, I'll find it." She passed him the Glock. "Come with me."

She hurried into the cabin, the copilot on her heels.

The passengers' attention was focused on her as the lights and air came back on.

"What's happening?" Matthias asked.

"I bought us as much time as I could, but the plane is depressurized now, so we have to switch tactics. I'm going out there to meet with the hijacker. Laverdeen will keep trying the radio." She touched the copilot's shoulder. "He's the boss. Do what he says until I get back."

Ayan ran toward her, then strangled her legs in a tight hug. "Don't go."

Jabari's lips pinched together, but he remained silent.

The last thing in the world she wanted was to be separated from the boys.

She picked up Ayan and held him close. "Sorry, buddy. I have to do whatever it takes to make sure you and Jabari are safe. I'll be back soon."

Jabari's eyes misted. The boys had experienced horrible things, but they were still kids at heart. She returned Ayan to the floor, squatted, and held up her right pinky. "Promise me you'll be good."

Jabari leaned over, and both boys entwined their little fingers with hers. "We promise."

She stood and addressed the group. "Treat these two like your own."

Dillman nodded. "I'll keep an eye on them."

She trusted his promise. He'd come across as a blowhard at first, but he'd proven himself to be a solid guy, albeit with a unique sense of humor.

A quick glance at her watch told her she had less than a minute to get outside. She forced herself to turn and walk toward the cockpit. Laverdeen followed.

"Don't try to be a hero. The guy we're dealing with, he's a pro," she said.

"Got it. Be safe out there."

Rivers glared at her, but she just ignored him. As Laverdeen settled back into the copilot's chair, she checked her glucose levels, which were in the normal range. She'd be all right for a little while, and the peppermint candy she kept in her pocket for emergencies would keep her going a little longer, if necessary. She hated to leave behind all her gear, but it would just be confiscated anyway. Final preparations complete, she climbed over the controls and shimmied out the cockpit window.

Her fingers clutched the window's ledge, her legs dangling below. Fully stretched out, she released her hands, dropping fifteen feet to the ground. Her knees absorbed the impact. She rolled over her right shoulder to soften the landing.

Crouched on the ground, she brushed her hair back from her eyes. Prospero Salvatore stood nearby in a sweat-soaked black linen shirt, looking like a rich gangster on vacation. He stretched his arms wide, a big smile on his lips.

"*Liberata, bienvenuto a Jufra.*"

Chapter 27

Thea climbed to her feet, then brushed off the red dirt covering her hands. Prospero moved toward her, a few more lines in his craggy face since their last meeting but otherwise unchanged. A slick-haired younger man decked out in a three-piece suit stood beside him. Interesting wardrobe choice for this heat. Behind them, three Libyans swathed in desert gear pointed AKs at her.

"I thought we were having a friendly coffee, just the two of us, Prospero." Thea counted twenty men surrounding the plane. There could be more inside the hangar.

"Best to have a chaperone or two to make sure I behave." A quick smile. "I don't think you've met my nephew, Luciano," he said, sweeping his hand to indicate the young man in the suit.

"B-b-bout time you got off." The nephew's malevolent glare left her unsettled, as if she was one comment away from a pistol-whipping.

"Forgive me, but I need to pat you down." Prospero moved toward her.

She stood with her legs apart, fingers linked behind her head, while his hands brushed down her back, then front. Her face inches from his, she remained relaxed, a challenge in her eyes as he skirted the gap between her breasts. He was being reasonably thorough, but some outdated notion of gentlemanly behavior caused him to miss her insulin pump. Better that way.

"Okay, time for that coffee." Prospero headed toward the hangar.

The Libyan guards escorted her along the runway, tracing the route Rivers was supposed to have used to park the plane. The steady hum of the 737's APU gave her some comfort. At least the passengers would remain comfortable inside the jet until she could return.

For a middle-of-nowhere locale, the hangar was surprisingly large. That's what oil money did for you. But the building looked neglected, abandoned. Gunmetal sheets of steel soared high above her, although time and sandstorms had corroded parts of the upper loft, leaving gaping holes. A catwalk ran around the interior high above the ground, but the ladder leading up to it was little more than a twisted wreck of broken side rails and missing rungs. Inside, the temperature was sweltering, the air stale and sour. She'd prefer a cold glass of water to an espresso.

She followed Prospero into the kitchen, which had definitely seen better days. The plastic chairs had black smudges on them, and the melamine counter was chipped and stained. But an old espresso machine rested on a shelf in a corner.

With the Libyans on guard outside, the three of them sat at the card table in the middle of the room. A pack of unfiltered cigarettes and a lighter rested on the table. She was surprised to see a pot of cooking oil perched on an electric stovetop beside a plate of *sfinz*, delicious Libyan doughnuts served with honey or other sweet toppings. Fresh snacks, even in a hangar in the middle of the desert. Her stomach growled.

Prospero nodded to Luciano, and the younger man started making the espresso.

"You have cinnamon?" she asked.

The capo raised his eyebrows. "You shouldn't mess with perfection."

"Try it before judging."

He shrugged. "If we have it, add some to mine as well," he told Luciano. The espresso machine gurgled, and a heavenly scent filled the kitchen.

Prospero's voice dropped and he leaned forward. "Forgive me, Thea, but we don't have much time. The thing is, I need you to do something for me. Once you complete the task, the passengers are all yours."

"I'm not going to like this mission, am I?"

"A truck full of Syrian refugees is coming to Budapest. You and your team need to commandeer the truck—not the passengers— and then take the M5 to Serbia, switch to the A1, pass through Novi Sad and Belgrade, then on to Sofia in Bulgaria, finally to the E80 inside Turkey to the town of Edirne, where my team will take over."

She studied his face. "What, exactly, is on that truck?"

"That's not important."

Luciano plopped a plate of doughnuts and two espressos down on the table, a dash of cinnamon haphazardly sprinkled on each.

"Then what?" she asked.

"We do the exchange—the truck for the plane, minus the one passenger I want."

"And who would that be?"

"Also unimportant."

"For me to agree, the two boys need to be freed now."

"That's not going to happen," Prospero said.

"Then I'm not doing it."

He smiled, a look of regret creasing his forehead. "You're in no position to bargain."

She took a deep breath. No way was she leaving the boys behind. "Why can't your men handle this themselves?"

"Your team has special . . . capabilities." Prospero tapped his right index finger on the table.

"And you avoid putting your own men at risk." Knowing the mafioso, he'd had a plan in place long before he discovered she was on the hijacked London-bound flight. He'd have other contingency plans too, but her presence on the plane was too good an opportunity to pass up.

He managed to look a bit hurt at her accusation. "I promise my men will keep a watchful eye on you." He downed his espresso.

"And where is this truck coming from? How will we find it?"

"We're not sure how it will arrive in Budapest, but we'll tell you how to identify it when we know more." He shrugged.

"What's so important about this vehicle?"

"You know, the cinnamon's not as bad as it sounds." He put down the cup, took an envelope from an inside pocket, and slid it across the table.

"What's that?" she asked.

"Information." He stood. "Please excuse us for a moment."

Prospero headed for the kitchen door, Luciano at his heels like an obedient guard dog. She attempted to follow, but the three Libyan guards outside blocked her way, AKs raised.

"You wait here," Prospero said over his shoulder.

"I won't do this unless you release the boys," she called out over the guards.

"Their future is in your hands." He gave her a parting grin as he strode toward the exit.

The door slammed in her face. Frustration bubbling inside her, she ripped open the envelope Prospero had left behind and scanned the contents.

MY MEN WILL TAKE YOU TO BUDAPEST. GET A TEAM TOGETHER AND CALL ME AT EXACTLY 15:00 EVERY DAY. DO NOT BE LATE.

A phone number followed.

What the hell? She headed straight for the window overlooking the runway. A familiar, high-pitched whine set her teeth on edge—the blades of the BBJ's engines were starting to spin.

The Libyans must have accessed the 737 during her discussion with Prospero. She recognized two silhouettes climbing the set of mobile stairs now up against the aircraft: Prospero's muscular frame moved with a faint limp, and Luciano's wiry build was distinctive.

Dammit to hell.

She pounded on the windows, but they were made of glass reinforced with chicken wire.

The plane was leaving without her, the boys and the hijackers on board.

Chapter 28

Prospero climbed the steps of the Boeing Business Jet with Luciano, the engines already running. He wished he'd had the luxury of more time with Thea. If he were kidnapped, he'd want *Liberata* on the case. *Or maybe not; after tonight, she'd likely pay the kidnappers to finish the job.*

While he'd been talking to Thea, his Libyan associates had wheeled a flight cart to the 737, opening the door without deploying the emergency chute. Exactly as he'd planned. With Thea out of the way, the copilot had no choice but to welcome the heavily armed men on board.

Prospero stepped inside the plane and found Bassam guarding the cockpit, as instructed.

"Get ready to take off," he advised the pilots. Bassam had untied Rivers, allowing the captain to reclaim the helm.

"We can't leave without a full inspection. The cockpit has been blown open. The plane might have structural issues after what it's gone through," Laverdeen said.

"Make it work," Prospero said.

"We can fly low and slow," Rivers said. Sweat poured down the pilot's face, and he had a bloody bandage on his shoulder. The copilot had removed the shrapnel at the captain's insistence and administered first aid.

Prospero left Bassam to oversee the preparations for an immediate takeoff, including rolling away the stairs. He entered the cabin, where Luciano and two of Bassam's men pointed AK-47s at the wide-eyed passengers. After a quick survey of the plane, he found his inside man sitting near the rear, tied up like a trussed turkey. He half smiled. The man seated beside him had a bluish tinge to his face—obviously dead. Quite an eventful flight so far.

"Where's Thea?" the younger child asked.

"What's your name, young man?"

"Ayan. What's yours?"

"Prospero."

"I want Thea."

"She's doing a favor for me."

"Then we're going to help her. Come on, Jabari." Ayan grabbed his brother's hand and headed down the aisle toward him and Luciano.

"She asked me to keep you safe here." Prospero blocked the aisle so they couldn't leave. The kids were his best leverage.

"You're lying." The older one, Jabari, glared at him.

He admired the boy's bravado. "Sit down. You can join her soon enough."

"We want to see her now," Ayan said.

"Sorry, but that is not happening."

The boys assessed him with knowing eyes. *Could they dodge by him and make a run for it?* Before he could talk them out of it, Luciano pushed past him, grabbed both boys by the backs of their collars, and hauled them down the aisle. Ayan kicked Luciano; Jabari punched him. Ignoring their protests, Prospero's nephew tossed the boys like sacks of potatoes into their seats.

"B-buckle up," Luciano said.

"Enough." Prospero didn't want to discipline his nephew in front of the passengers, but what was he thinking, manhandling kids like that?

A large man with a handlebar mustache stood up and moved toward the brothers. Prospero recognized the man from his passport picture. Michael Dillman.

"Settle down, boys. Thea would want you to stay safe." The Texan gave Luciano a hard look and scooped up one kid in each of his gigantic arms. Ayan and Jabari calmed down, clearly comfortable with the man.

"Stick to the plan," Prospero said to his nephew.

Luciano glared for a second, then headed to the rear of the plane, where Prospero's man sat handcuffed. His nephew undid the man's seat belt, then hooked him by the collar and marched him to the front of the plane. The man's eyes pleaded for mercy as he passed by, dragging his expensively clad feet.

Prospero shook his head once. No sense giving him false hope.

Luciano forced the thug to the open door, raised his Glock, and fired two bullets into the back of the traitor's head. His body fell onto the runway below.

"Get rid of the dead guy, too. I don't want the plane smelling like a meat locker," Prospero instructed his nephew.

Luciano returned to the rear, wrestled the heart attack victim's body onto the floor, dragged him to the opening, and pushed him through. The team below cleared the runway.

Prospero stopped in front of a man wearing a fedora. "Come with me."

The older man blanched but unbuckled his seat belt and followed Prospero up the aisle. They entered the cockpit, where Bassam was supervising the pilots.

"Give me the Glock," Prospero told Laverdeen.

"What are you talking about?" The copilot shrugged as he said it. He wasn't a half-bad actor.

"Now."

"I don't have a weapon."

Prospero nodded to Bassam. The Libyan pointed his AK at Fedora's head. "You have three seconds."

The old man's body trembled. "No, please."

Prospero's gaze locked with Laverdeen's. The copilot needed to know he was serious. "One, two . . ."

"Wait!" Laverdeen opened a cubby and retrieved the gun, handing it over.

"Go take a seat," he told Hammond.

The man wearing the fedora rushed out of the cockpit, stumbling in his haste.

Rivers pressed several buttons on the console, which was followed by the whir of the second engine.

"Wheels up, gentlemen."

Chapter 29

Thea didn't have much time before the 737 took off. She rummaged through the hangar's kitchen, ripping open cabinets until she found items she could use to escape: a lighter and a can of aerosol cooking spray. She tipped some of the hot oil from the pot onto one of the burners, then moved the pot, the cigarette lighter, and the cooking spray onto the counter beside the door.

Thunder rumbled outside. A storm must be closing in—odd in this part of the world. A couple of seconds later she heard something else. Not weather this time: the plane's second engine had whirred to life, spurring her on.

Standing as far back as she could, she turned on the gas burner covered in oil. A soft clicking noise and *whoosh*, the oil spun into a flaming ball. A burning stench filled the kitchen. Smoke plumed from the burner.

She banged on the door. "Fire, help!"

Seconds later, two of the guards rushed in, focused on the smoldering stove. She launched the pot of oil toward them, dousing them with the scalding liquid. While the men batted frantically at the oil on their faces, she grabbed the lighter and the cooking spray. She flicked on the lighter and pressed the spray nozzle, sending a bright arc of flame leaping across the kitchen and turning the men into human infernos.

Primal screams shattered the air.

The third guard rushed in, rifle raised. She attacked him from the side, a sharp kick into his kidney, forcing him against the wall. He turned. She grabbed his AK-47 and twisted it to the right. His index finger crunched, stuck in the trigger guard. He fired off two shots, hitting one of the guards who was on fire. She jumped onto the man's back, snaking her arm around his neck in a sleeper hold. He smashed her back into the wall and tried to shake her off, but she just increased the pressure.

Seconds passed, and he finally slumped to the ground. She checked to make sure he was out cold. The guard who'd been shot was dead, and the other was groaning, curled into a ball with his face in his hands. After grabbing two of the AKs and extra magazines and grenades, she sprinted down the length of the hangar, closing and locking its huge doors.

The commotion in the kitchen and the guards' screams had masked the noise of the jet accelerating along the runway. Through one of the small windows on the hangar doors, she watched the wheels of the BBJ lift off the ground.

She slumped against the steel panel, her mind on Ayan, Jabari, and the other passengers on a potentially damaged plane, Salvatore in charge, all of them heading to points unknown.

Chapter 30

On board the C-130 above the Libyan Desert, Rif completed his final safety checks. The team was preparing for a HAHO—high altitude, high opening—insertion from thirty-five thousand feet. They'd discussed tactics during the flight: speed was key, but they also had to remain invisible and avoid injury. It was for moments like this that the Quantum team trained so tirelessly; while on a mission, even the smallest setback could balloon into disaster. And any jump was physically demanding, but on a high-altitude maneuver the ambient oxygen was low, so hypoxia was an added concern.

Nodding to his mates, Rif adjusted his night vision goggles and moved toward the opening, oxygen mask on. With unexpected scattered thunderclouds in the area, they'd had to spend precious moments searching for a clear zone for the drop. He channeled his inner Charles "Nish" Bruce, the British SAS soldier who'd been pivotal in developing the HAHO method of conflict insertion, and triple-checked his equipment.

"Five kilometers out." The pilot's voice sounded in his earpiece.

Rif wore a square-type ram-air parachute, which he found more maneuverable than a standard round or elliptical chute.

A backpack containing the weapons and supplies they'd need rested between his legs, secured by a lanyard. He signaled to his teammates: Johansson, Jean-Luc, Brown, and the two Scots, Neil and Stewart. He'd jump first, setting the course and acting as a point for the rest of the team.

"Thirty seconds."

Close to Jufra in enemy skies, they didn't want to be compromised by the sound of parachutes opening at low altitude. HAHO jumps also allowed them to cover more distance by deploying early and taking advantage of the increased canopy time.

"Five seconds."

His thoughts flashed to Thea and the boys in the hijacked 737 below. He had no idea who had control of the BBJ, but whoever it was, he wasn't expecting a warm welcome.

"Go."

Rif dove from the plane into the black abyss of the sky, the bitter embrace of the icy air slicing through his flight suit. The temperature was minus fifty degrees Fahrenheit. His polypropylene knitted undergarments, face mask, and gloves would protect his body from frostbite. Despite the bitter cold, despite the danger, night jumps were magical, darkness blanketing the earth in tranquility, the scattered lights below like twinkling stars in the sky.

Moments later, his teammates joined him, forming a stack in the air. Ten to fifteen seconds passed. When they'd reached twenty-seven thousand feet, he tugged on his ripcord, the rustle and *flump* of the parachute opening a comforting sound even as it jerked him in the harness. They'd started around fifteen miles upwind of the planned landing site and would glide in.

Glancing at the GPS on his wrist, he guided the group in the correct direction. They aimed to land in the wadi north of the airstrip, an ideal location—far enough away from the plane to avoid detection but close enough that they could reach Thea and the other passengers quickly on foot.

The team drifted toward the valley in the night breeze. Lightning zigzagged in the distance, a branching bolt lancing through the black sky. Dark, soundless—he relished this part of the jump, silent except for the wind rippling through his clothing. But it was about to get noisy once they hit the ground. He pulled on the right-hand cord on the chute, adjusting his trajectory.

He checked his GPS again. He didn't want anything going sideways on this mission. There were kids involved—and one of Quantum's own.

Rif and Thea had known each other since they were children, their fathers lifelong friends. During Christos's kidnapping, they'd made headway in their sometimes-complicated relationship. But the loss of Nikos had made Thea shut down emotionally. Understandably so. Both her brother and her father had betrayed her trust. As a result, she'd become even more dedicated to the work of bringing hostages home. It made him worry about the lengths she'd go to for the hijacked passengers below.

The rain started, and thunder sounded in the distance. Damn, just what they didn't need.

As the team aimed for the landing spot, the roar of jet engines caught his attention. He looked south to see the BBJ accelerating along the runway, wheels lifting into the air.

What the hell? They'd have to search the tarmac and surroundings to make sure Thea and the passengers were still on board.

He pressed the radio button. "The eagle has flown the coop. Track it." The pilot would relay the message to Hakan at headquarters. They'd mobilize every asset to follow the 737's flight path. Wouldn't be easy. They were in the middle of nowhere, and the plane's transponders had been turned off.

Had the hostages disembarked, or were they still on that plane?

A couple of hundred feet above the wadi, the engines of the BBJ faded into the distance, replaced by another disturbing sound: gunfire.

Guess there's at least one passenger down there.

Rif adjusted their trajectory once more, this time headed directly for the landing strip.

Chapter 31

Prospero sat in the jump seat behind the pilots, keeping a close eye on their movements as the plane flew through heavy rain that no one had counted on in this part of the world. Yet another complication in an already complicated situation. The glowing lights of the flight deck reminded him of sitting vigil in his father's hospital room late at night, studying at the feet of a dying man. Stefano had taught him that self-respect trumped public opinion. Before making any decision, Prospero would cut away all extraneous opinions and confirm to himself that he was doing the right thing, instead of trying to appease others. Life wasn't a popularity contest.

Considering the two men at the controls, Prospero was concerned about Laverdeen. He seemed the heroic type, someone who might put the safety of others before his own, as demonstrated by his concealing that gun. Prospero would rely on Captain Rivers—the pilot wanted his kids back, so he'd do what he was told.

Prospero had left Thea under guard so the 737 could take off without interruption. Now that he had the two boys and a plane full of hostages, she'd have to help him. He would radio back and tell his men to release her.

A blaring alarm erupted on the flight deck.

"What is it?" Prospero asked.

"Master warning for cabin pressure. The jet has a slow leak, I bet. We pushed the pressurization system too hard on the ground," Rivers said.

"We have to stay at ten thousand feet or the oxygen masks will drop." Laverdeen fiddled with the controls.

"We'll burn more fuel if we stay down there. How far are we going?" Rivers asked.

"The transponder and sat comms systems are still off?" Prospero didn't want any surprises.

"I neutralized them both before we landed, as instructed. But flying low means we can't go very far at all." Rivers studied the fuel gauge. "Only thirteen hundred pounds left in the tank. Even at our current altitude, our maximum range is around a hundred and forty miles."

"Head here." He passed Rivers the coordinates of where his Gulfstream was parked. After dropping Prospero and Luciano off, the pilot had flown to a more secluded airfield about one hundred and thirty miles away, in anticipation of a rendezvous.

They'd be cutting it close.

Prospero turned to Bassam, who remained at the entrance to the cockpit, rifle in hand. "Keep an eye on them while I check on the passengers."

He headed for the cabin, where Luciano had moved everyone into the first few rows.

Bernard and Madeira were giving water to the passengers, who seemed quite subdued, no doubt thanks to the execution they'd witnessed. Showing always worked better than telling when it came to these things.

Matthias pointed to his computer. "Hey, I'm not sure what you're after, but if it'll help, I can wire money for my release. All I need is Wi-Fi."

"How much to get off this nightmare ride?" Karlsson asked.

"I'll give you whatever it takes to get me and these boys off," Dillman said.

The Asian woman remained silent, her intelligent gaze assessing the situation.

"Sit down and shut up. No one is getting off this plane until I say so." Prospero rested most of his weight on his good hip.

Any hope of a quick escape evaporated from the passengers' eyes. *Hell, maybe I'm in the wrong business.* It seemed easy enough to kidnap people—and as a bonus, the hostages were offering their own ransoms. Then again, this had been an expensive operation, so they'd have to pay a lot of money to make it worthwhile.

But there was no time for distractions. He had what he needed: the target seemed fine, unaware of what lay ahead.

White light flashed through the windows. Lightning, quickly followed by thunder. *Very close.* He headed back to the cockpit.

Chapter 32

It was clear to Thea that Prospero wanted her to leave for Budapest with the guards he had left behind, but she had no intention of following anyone else's script. There still might be time to track the BBJ. If they had forced their way onto the plane, Prospero and his men wouldn't get far—the plane's seals were now compromised, and they had burned a lot of fuel during the landing and while on the tarmac. She slung the two AKs that she'd taken from the kitchen guards over her shoulder and grabbed a few extra magazines and grenades from the dead men.

Outside, Prospero's remaining men fired a few shots into the air and pounded on the hangar doors, but she had locked them from inside. It was only a matter of time before they forced their way in. Thea needed a plan. An old Cessna perched in one corner beside a pile of tires. Spare parts cluttered another corner. She searched the debris, finding a wrench and an old frayed rope. She stretched it in her hands to test its resilience. Not mountain-ready, but it would do.

She tied the wrench to one end of the rope, then tossed it over one of the hangar's transverse rafters. The wrench end dropped down near her. A quick slipknot, and in no time she had cinched the rope to the beam. She tied the rifles to the bottom of the rope so she wouldn't have to carry them as she climbed, then shimmied up, using her feet to hold her weight as she pulled her body upward with her hands. The ragged nylon cut into her fingers, but she ignored the pain.

Grabbing the rafter with both hands, she swung herself over to another, higher steel beam that extended across the width of the hangar. Grabbing the rope, she pulled up the AKs and secured them around her shoulder, then coiled the rope on top of the rafter. She crawled forward to reach the relative comfort of the six-foot catwalk running around the perimeter of the hangar.

The noise of the BBJ taking off had long since faded, leaving just the pinging sound of rain on the hangar's steel roof, the hiss of the soldiers' radios in the desert night air—and the pounding on the door below. She sprinted across the catwalk toward the window above the hangar's entrance. Kneeling, she cracked the window open and could see three of the soldiers pounding the entrance with a makeshift battering ram. It wouldn't hold for much longer.

Thea clicked one of the AKs to semiauto. She sighted down the barrel at one of the men and fired. He fell. The other two men glanced up, startled. Before they could react, she squeezed off two more shots, but the angle was bad. Just the same, the two men dropped the ram and scattered for cover.

Four down, counting the men in the kitchen, but she'd only made a dent. There had to be at least twelve more soldiers. Her only hope was to hang on to the tactical advantage provided by controlling the building. She had to be patient, keep them at bay, and pick them off one at a time as they came for her.

Thea tilted her head at the sound of pounding footsteps and voices yelling in Arabic outside the rear of the hangar.

She grabbed the AK and ran along the platform. Two men were climbing a ladder they'd leaned against the outer steel wall. She smashed the window they were trying to reach and fired off two rounds. The first man screamed and dropped to the ground. Behind him, the second one sprayed a burst of bullets her way. She ducked for cover, waited for the barrage to end, then popped her head back out and fired another two rounds. The soldier fell backward off a middle rung, landing in the mud below. She tried to push the ladder away from the hangar to deter any more intruders, but the damned thing was jammed, immovable.

Noise from the opposite direction caught her attention. She ran back to see two of the Libyan soldiers cutting a hole in the steel wall with a blowtorch. She shoved in a fresh magazine and fired several shots through the window above the door, but the angle didn't work—the men were directly below her. She flicked the switch to full auto, eased her entire arm out the window, pointed the AK downward, and squeezed the trigger. The assault rifle shook in her hand and rattled against the wall, her shoulder absorbing the full brunt of the recoil.

Enemy bullets slammed into the steel around her extended arm. She felt a sharp stab of pain. Unable to hold on, she dropped the rifle and pulled her arm back inside. Blood soaked her shirtsleeve just below the elbow. A quick look under the sleeve revealed a flesh wound. She tore off her sleeve and used it as a makeshift bandage.

A car engine cranked to life. She looked up. Four soldiers had climbed into an open-air Land Cruiser and were lining it up with the large garage doors. The tough, all-terrain vehicle had a reinforced front end protected by a massive grill. They were going to ram their way inside.

Removing two grenades from her pocket, she pulled the pins and tossed the first, then the second, toward the approaching vehicle. She sprinted down the catwalk and ducked in a corner, covering her ears with her hands.

Two explosions resounded harshly around the metal walls, followed by a third. The vehicle's gas tank. The window at the front of the hangar briefly glowed orange as the flames from the burning gasoline shot through the air, the concussive force rattling the entire structure. Screams pierced the night air. She inched her way toward the front to assess the damage. A large hole now appeared in the steel wall near the hangar doors, a corner of which was bent inward.

Shimmying forward, she climbed onto her knees and snuck a quick look outside. Several men were yelling, heading toward the gaping hole in the hangar wall below her. She aimed the remaining AK-47 through the window and fired, dropping a couple of them before they reached the hangar, scattering the rest. She reached into her pocket for another magazine. Last one. She'd have to use these thirty rounds sparingly.

Two soldiers fired a stream of bullets at her from behind the smoking wreckage of the Land Cruiser. She flattened herself against the catwalk as a hail of metal pounded into walls and blew out the remaining glass of the window. Another sound, coming from behind her. She turned. One of the men had climbed the ladder resting against the hangar and was entering through the rear window.

He hadn't spotted her yet, but it was only a matter of time. She'd have to fire from her position lying on the catwalk, waiting until he was closer. Risky, but she had no choice.

Three, two, one . . .

She raised the AK to her shoulder and lined up the sights.

Framed by the broken window, the soldier met her gaze, his eyes drawn by her sudden movement. He lifted his rifle, but before he could fire, the soldier staggered forward and face-planted onto the platform. She scanned the hangar to identify what had brought him down. Had he been hit by friendly fire?

She waited a beat to see if anyone else would come up the ladder, then peeked out the window just in time to witness two more men collapse outside the hangar. Another sprinted toward the building, but before he could take ten steps, his body spasmed in a barrage of bullets from an unseen assailant. She drew in a deep breath, trying to figure out what the hell was going on. More gunfire, then an eerie silence pervaded the night.

She waited, listening for any sound of movement.

Nothing.

"Friendlies! Is the interior clear?"

The familiar voice buoyed her spirits. *Rif.*

"All clear! Welcome to Jufra."

"Bit of a hellhole, wouldn't you say?" Rif crouched and entered through the ragged hole in the hangar wall with three Quantum soldiers, all of them in flight gear. Her team had arrived.

"I was planning my next vacation here, but the accommodations leave a little something to be desired."

"I can see that. Where'd the plane go?" Rif asked.

"AWOL. We're in for a long night," she said.

Chapter 33

Prospero brushed by Bassam and entered the cockpit, plunking down on the jump seat. Both pilots studied the radar map, the tension palpable. Lightning streaked across the sky, illuminating the clouds in blinding lavender flashes. Waves of thunder followed, rattling the 737. Rain splatted against the windscreen in heavy, fat drops. Even Prospero's nerves felt raw.

"Can we go around it?" Prospero asked.

"Not enough fuel." Rivers looked up from the gauge.

"I'd do a one-eighty and turn back. It's not worth the risk," Laverdeen said.

Sudden turbulence kicked in, jerking the plane back and forth. Prospero steadied himself, one hand gripping the jump seat. "Rivers?"

"We should try going between the two cloud banks." The captain thrust the controls forward, increasing their speed.

Laverdeen's face reddened. "Have you lost your mind?"

"Isn't faster better, so we get out of the storm quicker?" Prospero asked.

Blood soaked Rivers's right shoulder. "TPS—thunderstorm penetration speed. We need to do two-seventy to three hundred knots to keep things as smooth as possible."

"We're sucking up too much fuel. We won't have enough to make it through the storm front," Laverdeen said as the plane lurched again, buffeted by crosswinds.

Screams sounded from the cabin. The lights flickered.

"It'll be close, but we can do it." Rivers studied the instruments. "Strap yourself in."

The fuselage shuddered.

"The plane's already damaged from before. Keep this up, and rivets will pop—the tail could shear off." Laverdeen's voice held an edge.

Prospero turned to Bassam, who was having trouble maintaining his footing. "Go sit down." He secured his own seat belt.

Rat-a-tat-tat. Massive chunks of ice slammed into the windshield, one after the other, sounding like machine-gun fire. Spiderwebs of cracks erupted in the glass as the hail pounded it. Ice collided with the fuselage, sounding like an out-of-control steel band. Surely they'd be through the worst of it soon. He thought of Violetta. She'd always worried that he'd come home from work in a pine box, a bullet lodged in his heart. She'd never been concerned about his flying.

Purple and green waves of electricity zapped across the windscreen, arcing like mini lightning bolts. The neon colors bursting across the night sky were terrifying. "What the hell is that?"

"Static electricity from the penetrating moisture," Rivers yelled over the din of the hailstorm.

Fuck me! It took a lot to unsettle him, but this was a nightmare. The hail became larger, louder, overwhelming. He could barely think.

More beeping from the instrument panel. A red light flashed, and the plane shook even more violently than before. "What now?"

"We've lost the left engine," Laverdeen said.

Chapter 34

Johann sat across from his father at the kitchen table. Chef Rudy always had one night off per week, and on these days father and son would cook together. Tonight they'd made a huge pot of *spaetzle*, roast chicken, and thick gravy. They devoured the rich comfort food in large bowls, eating the chicken with their hands. The ritual was comforting, even in these disturbing circumstances. Johann wished he could wind back time, erase all knowledge of the *Freiheitswächter* and the lab downstairs, so he could truly enjoy what until now had been one of the few moments of quality time he and *Vater* spent together lately.

"How was school today?"

Father always asked about his studies, but Johann knew that tonight he was inquiring about something else. His appetite began to fade.

"I'll stay away from Fatima; just promise you won't hurt her or her family."

His father remained silent, studying him. "I'm trying to protect you. You're a man now. Men have certain . . . weaknesses."

"Love isn't a weakness."

"Love? What do you know about that? This is infatuation, at best. Anyway, love *is* a weakness if you waste it on the wrong person."

"But Fatima is warm and kind."

Father stared at him for a long moment. "Two years ago, I was in Afghanistan, selling arms to the Americans. I met a woman named Latifa at the hotel, the sister of the owner. During the weeks I was there, we spent a lot of time together."

"You loved her?"

"I've never loved anyone other than your mother. But Latifa was beautiful, smart, sophisticated. She gently pumped me for information about the weapons I was selling. I was so lonely, so grateful for her attention, I didn't notice what she was doing. Then, the day before the delivery of the merchandise was to take place, I received a call that you needed emergency surgery."

Johann remembered how ghastly ill he'd been. He'd been suffering from terrifying shortness of breath and debilitating exhaustion; when he wound up at the hospital, he was diagnosed with an aortic aneurysm, thanks to his Marfan syndrome. Uncle Karl had been the one who brought him to the emergency room.

"I came home straightaway." His father inhaled a deep breath. "You saved my life. The entire convoy delivering the weapons was decimated by IEDs on a remote stretch of highway. Your mother's death was a clear sign, but this event made me fully realize just how dangerous these people can be."

"Are you sure it was Latifa?"

"Absolutely."

"And . . ."

His mouth twisted. "I behaved like a fool in a moment of weakness."

"I'm sorry." It hurt Johann to see Father in such obvious pain.

"How do you fight people who stand in line to die for their cause? Their beliefs, their conviction—it's an organized evil unsurpassed in history. And now Islam is the fastest-growing religion in the world."

It was true that some Islamic terrorist groups had displayed a shocking disregard for human life, but it seemed that only a tiny minority of Muslims felt this way. Johann had read about countless imams, Islamic academics, and world leaders condemning violence committed in the name of Allah.

"Fatima isn't like that." He held his breath, bracing himself for his father's temper.

But Father looked more deflated than anything. "Johann, you never know where someone's loyalty lies until it's tested."

"You and *Mutti* taught me to treat everyone with respect."

"And so you should—but evil exists. Millions of refugees from Arab countries are flooding into Europe. And violence follows them, brought in with their religion. Bloodshed and terror have been inflicted on Paris, Brussels, Nice, Berlin, Barcelona, now Vienna—the list goes on. When I took my oath as a *Freiheitswächter,* I had no idea of the lengths we'd have to go to protect our country, our people, but this is just the kind of threat we were created to handle."

Johann swallowed the lump in his throat. "Was Uncle Karl a threat, too?"

Seconds ticked by. A look of understanding passed between them. Father knew that he knew. "He was a spy, leaking information about our plans to the Gladio."

"The Gladio?" He couldn't believe that Karl was anything but a loving uncle figure, a friend, someone who'd always been there for him.

"Groups like the *Freiheitswächter* were set up throughout Europe by the Americans and British after the Second World War, originally to stop the spread of communism. The Italian group is known as Gladio, but their organization is run by mobsters, greedy priests, and corrupt politicians."

Instead of arms dealers and mad scientists.

"But Uncle Karl—"

"Was a traitor and got what he deserved."

Johann played with his spoon, moving the *spaetzle* around the bowl. He'd completely lost his appetite.

Chapter 35

Prospero wondered if taking the damaged BBJ back into the air might have been the worst decision of his life. A hailstorm, minimal fuel, and now they were running on only one engine. Rivers and Laverdeen remained methodical and calm, but their white shirts were drenched in sweat. He swore with each jerky movement of the plane.

"We're only a few miles from the coordinates," Laverdeen yelled.

"Prepare for a hot landing," Rivers called to Prospero.

"What does that mean?" It didn't sound good.

"Too much speed when we hit the ground. It's going to be bumpy."

Somehow this sounded like understatement.

"Almost there. Brace yourself."

"Flaps are uneven," Laverdeen said.

"What?" Prospero asked.

"Hard to control." The altimeter spiraled as they dropped through the clouds.

"We'll need your help with the brakes. Just follow my lead," Rivers said.

Prospero murmured a few Hail Marys. Through the cracked windscreen, he could see the faint lights of the runway below. Lights that were coming at him way too fast. His hands clenched the bottom of the jump seat. It felt like they were on a spiraling roller coaster plunging into an abyss.

The wheels hit the ground hard with a jolting bump. His torso whipped forward, then back, his neck straining to keep his head upright.

"Reverses are useless. Maximum brakes. Do it!" Laverdeen pulled the brakes hard. Rivers and Prospero grabbed hold, dug their heels in, and yanked with all their strength.

Prospero's body slammed to the left, then right. His grip on the brakes tightened; his chest strained against his seat belt. The plane wavered back and forth.

A loud blast and the plane jerked to one side.

"Tire," Laverdeen said.

The screech of metal hitting ground. The plane careened down the runway, rotating until it finally jumped the tarmac and struck the rain-soaked verge. When the undercarriage met the earth, the plane lurched forward and down, slamming into the ground amid the sounds of the aircraft being torn apart from below.

Prospero felt himself blacking out, his eyeballs straining to jump out of their sockets.

Chapter 36

As a pilot, Rif had been inside countless hangars, but none of them had ever featured a scorched, truck-sized hole as an entrance. He glanced up at the rafters as Thea rappelled down the frayed rope to join him. She moved with grace and fluidity, landing smoothly and striding to where he stood.

"Sorry to crash your party." Rif assessed the bullet holes peppering the steel walls.

"Thanks for the save."

"I'm sure you had the situation well in hand." The dirt and oil smears on her face looked like a nighttime camo paint job gone wrong. He smiled, fighting the urge to hold her and tell her everything would be okay.

"Not really. Prospero Salvatore just took off with the passengers, including the boys." She looked simultaneously exhausted and fired up.

"What is he doing making a high-risk snatch in the middle of the Libyan Desert?"

"I doubt he's entering the kidnap business. He must want someone or something on that plane."

"I radioed Hakan to let him know the 737 is AWOL."

"It'll be challenging to track it with the transponder turned off," she said.

"Yeah, but Hakan will find a way. Meanwhile, Johansson and Brown are mopping up the rest of the area, making sure we didn't miss anyone."

"The bastard gave me no choice but to get off the plane. Then he stole it from under my nose." He could see that her professional pride was hurt, but there was something else, too. "I just keep thinking of Ayan and Jabari."

Of course. "Hey, those two are full of piss and vinegar—I'm sure they're going to be fine." He hoped he sounded more convincing than he felt. "And you did a great job, holding Salvatore off for as long as you did. What were his demands?"

"Madness." She reached into her pocket and held out the crumpled envelope to Rif. "He wants us to hijack a truck full of Syrian refugees trying to reach Budapest. We need to grab the truck and contact him after we have it. Then he wants us to deliver it to him somewhere in Turkey. The truck for the plane."

Rif was born in Turkey and had completed his yearlong compulsory military service for his country before heading to West Point. Based in London now, he hadn't been home in more than a year. From the sound of it, that was about to change.

"If he wants the truck, why hijack the plane?" Rif asked.

"He wants one of the passengers, but wouldn't say who. I think he's improvising with the truck, a plan he devised when he realized I was aboard. Reduce the danger to his own organization."

"Did anyone on the plane stand out to you?"

"Not really—I didn't have much time to debrief the passengers. I'm assuming Hakan has the analysts digging into their backgrounds?"

"Absolutely. Anyone stand out?"

"Hard to say. The target is likely to have booked the trip well in advance. Prospero tiger kidnapped the pilot's kids, so it took some planning. He also had a plant on the flight."

"You get anything from the inside man?"

"He said something about them being 'Gladio,' whatever that means."

"Huh, that's odd. Operation Gladio was part of a multinational cluster of sleeper militias scattered across Europe, formed to provide armed resistance against a Soviet invasion after the Second World War. I thought they had all been disbanded."

Thea laughed. "WikiRif strikes again."

"Hardly—just my obsession with military history. *Gladio* means 'sword' in Italian. NATO, MI6, the CIA, and even the Vatican were said to be involved in creating it," Rif added.

"Sounds to me like the conspiracy theorists have too much time on their hands."

"No, no, there's proof. The organization was exposed in a big court case in 1990 that ripped the lid off the story. The CIA and MI6 denied it all, of course."

"I know the Cold War was a time of international paranoia, but a modern-day secret army?" she said.

"President Truman himself signed a top-secret order in 1950 that permitted an *invasion* of Italy if the country went red. The Western nations were that worried about the commies. Hell, in the end the Italian secret service, right-wing militia, the Mafia, and the CIA were all involved."

She bit her lip. "Fear of the Red Menace made for some strange bedfellows, no doubt about it, but communism isn't the threat it used to be. Let's get the analysts working on what the hell Gladio could be up to today."

Rif turned away to call Hakan while Thea considered everything that had happened since she'd boarded the 737 with the boys. What did a hijacked plane and a truck full of Syrian refugees have to do with a Cold War paramilitary organization, and why was Prospero Salvatore involved? The mafioso was all about the bottom line, as far as she could remember; he was smart, sure, but not an ideologue. What could possibly be worth all this effort? She shook her head, trying to make the pieces fall into place.

Finished with the call, Rif reached into his pocket, pulled out a protein bar, and handed it to her. "How are you feeling?" He knew about her diabetes but tried not to make a big deal of it in case Thea felt uncomfortable; she had hidden her condition from him for most of their lives. Of course, he wanted to make sure she took care of herself, kept her blood sugar stable. She had a habit of putting others before herself.

"Thanks. I'm starving."

The roar of an incoming C-130 made further conversation impossible. The runway had been cleared so their ride could land. Next stop: Budapest.

Chapter 37

A rush of intense heat made Prospero wonder if this was what it would feel like arriving in hell. The intense g-forces created by the gyrating plane as it funneled down the runway had stretched his skin tightly across his face and made him dizzy, nauseated. Just when he felt he couldn't take any more, the plane had finally shuddered to a full stop, metal groaning against metal.

Then silence. And the heat. Prospero shook his head, pulling himself together. His pulse was steady, like an underwater heartbeat in his ears. He scanned his body for injury. Other than the pain in his hip from the seat belt digging in, he seemed to be in one piece.

Euphoria filled him. He had once again looked death in the eye and said *fuck you*.

"*Bravo*, gentlemen." He laughed. "Still, let's avoid any more 'hot landings' in the future."

Both pilots were already flicking switches and scanning the instrument panels. They paused to look at Prospero, but neither one said a word in response.

Prospero unbuckled his seat belt and stood, legs shaky from the nail-biting landing. "Why is it so hot in here? Is the plane on fire?"

Laverdeen checked the gauges again. "I don't think so. But none of the environmental systems are working, so no air or recirculation. We have to get off the aircraft."

Prospero nodded and left the cockpit, instructing the flight attendants to try opening the front door. He glanced into the cabin. Everyone had survived, but terrified faces greeted him. Perhaps this was a blessing—the dicey landing would keep the passengers obedient for a while. The sound of the door opening behind him made him smile.

Prospero's flight crew had seen the landing and wheeled over a set of stairs from a nearby hangar when the plane came to a stop. Even with the position and angle of the downed jet, which had raised the door several feet higher than normal, the crew was more or less able to align the stairs with the opening. He eased himself down the steps gingerly, the first to exit. His hip hurt like a son of a bitch, but he was glad to be alive.

Che spavento! He'd never seen hail like that before, and that purple and green electricity had been something out of a B-movie. But they'd made it, *grazie a Dio*. They had survived.

The desert heat was insufferable, and his stomach growled. He couldn't wait to enjoy a long shower and a gourmet meal inside his plane.

Bassam followed him down the stairs, where they met the ground crew. Prospero told his men to enter the plane and start shepherding the passengers onto his Gulfstream. Meanwhile, Bassam tried to reach his men in Jufra but received no answer. Whether or not Thea had managed to escape, they were likely all dead. Bassam was not happy about it, but Prospero wasn't worried. All that mattered to him was that she'd do whatever it took to save the lives of the two African boys. The loss of Bassam's crew was the cost of doing business. As Machiavelli had said, "Never was anything great achieved without danger."

The slightly dazed passengers traipsed down the stairs of the 737, carry-ons in hand. Ocean walked beside Ayan and Jabari, avoiding Prospero's gaze.

Karlsson stopped in front of him. "I need my checked bag."

"Hand luggage only." *Santo cielo*, this was a hijacking, not a connecting flight.

"But I have presents for my grandchildren."

"Your safe return is the only gift they need. Move."

Karlsson trundled off, eyes downcast, mumbling to himself.

But the exchange had given Prospero an idea. He turned to Bassam. "Have the crew bring any leftover bags from inside the plane." He'd be interested to see what *Liberata* kept in her carry-on.

Rivers and Laverdeen descended the stairs, followed by one of Bassam's men, the last of the passengers and crew to disembark.

"I did what you asked. Let my kids go." Dark, puffy bags shadowed the captain's eyes, and blood from his shoulder wound was crusted in dark clumps on his shirt. All in all, he looked like shit.

"Remain useful, and we'll see."

"What kind of monster are you?" Rivers's face purpled.

"Shut the fuck up and get on the plane."

Rivers stomped off to the Gulfstream.

Laverdeen lingered. "You don't need the stress of babysitting all these exhausted hostages. Take me, and let the others stay here. You could give them a satphone to call for help after we leave."

"How about I start eliminating hostages? That'll minimize my stress."

"Thea Paris is going to find us."

Prospero could tell from one look at Laverdeen's face that the pilot had more than a passing interest in the kidnap negotiator. "You'd better hope she doesn't."

"What's that supposed to mean?"

"Don't be a hero. It won't end well."

Chapter 38

Johann had barely been able to pay attention in class, his mind circling back to his father's monstrous plan. The sheer number of people that could be wiped out was staggering. Unlike other forms of the plague, which was spread by insect bites, pneumonic plague could be transmitted directly between humans. In just one of the refugee camps Father was targeting, hundreds of thousands of people could be infected in a very short time.

Now he was in the shed behind the school, reluctant to go home. Father had invited the *Freiheitswächter* over for a meeting tonight, and he wasn't sure he had the stomach to pretend he was in favor of genocide. Instead, he had his laptop out and was reading online about the Second World War, staring at grisly pictures of concentration camps. That was what mass extermination looked like.

He could never understand why Hitler had wanted to kill all the Jews, homosexuals, and other minorities. Johann thought of those ancestry tests that detailed the genealogical makeup of individuals. Sometimes people were surprised at the results. What might Hitler have found if *his* DNA had ever been analyzed?

A soft knock at the door.

Fatima.

"Am I interrupting?" Her eyes were tear-stained, red.

"Not at all. What's wrong?" He closed the screen of his laptop so she wouldn't see the horrific pictures.

She plunked down in one of the battered wooden chairs and wrapped her arms around her knees. "Remember my cousin, Abdul, who is staying with us?"

"Did he hurt you?" His protective instincts surfaced.

"No, no, nothing like that." She wiped away tears. "He pulled me aside last night, told me I was becoming too Westernized."

"He's religious?"

"Extremely." She bit her lip. "I'm ashamed to admit this, but he despises people who aren't of our faith. He's pushing for my father to send me back to the UAE, telling Papa that I'm of marrying age and need a husband to guide me."

"Why is it his business?"

"Women in my country have no say in these decisions. The marriage would be arranged for me. To a stranger, probably."

"That's terrible. Do you think your father would do that to you or your sisters?"

"I don't know. It's probably silly of me, but the worst part . . . would be leaving you." She leaned over and grabbed his hand.

He intertwined his fingers with hers and squeezed gently. The touch of her skin left him breathless.

"Wait, doesn't your father support you becoming a doctor? That would be a lot harder back in the UAE, right?"

"He does, but Papa also doesn't want any shame clouding the family name. Our cousin is very influential back home, and he could make trouble for my family."

His chest tightened at the thought of Fatima leaving Salzburg, only to be forced into a loveless marriage. "But why does he want to control your life like that?"

"You don't understand, Johann. Women have no rights in the UAE—I will have to do whatever my husband tells me to, think what he wants me to think. I couldn't stand being married to someone who wouldn't let me have my own views, but if I go back, that is exactly what will happen."

"Then don't go."

"If I don't, Abdul could destroy my family."

He couldn't bear the thought of her with anyone else. In that moment, he decided he could trust her. He had to trust her. "Fatima, my father also has hate in his heart. He sells weapons to murderous governments and individuals around the world, but he doesn't think twice about it. Instead, he blames the world's problems on Muslims."

"That's why he doesn't want us together, right?"

Johann nodded, embarrassed. "He lost all perspective after my mother died, killed by an Arab driver. And he's fallen in with some bad people." He couldn't bring himself to admit that his father was actually the kingpin, leading the others.

"Are you saying he's dangerous?"

He hesitated a long moment. "Yes."

"How dangerous?"

His stomach twisted. He'd never felt so disloyal to his father, but he'd never been this desperate to confide in someone. "I think his intentions are good. He wants to stop terrorism."

"But . . . ?" She waited.

"He's blinded by hatred. Instead of focusing on just the individuals who perpetrate terrorist attacks, he has lumped all Arabs together."

"What aren't you telling me?" she asked.

"I can't tell you. It'll only put you in danger."

"Now you're really scaring me."

"It's all I can think about."

"If you can't tell me, why don't you go to the authorities?" she asked.

"They would never believe me."

"Isn't there anyone you can trust?"

His mind's eye saw Uncle Karl's dead body. "I don't think so."

"Then you'll have to trust me. Whatever it is, I'll do my best to help."

He wavered, weighing the pros and cons of sharing some or all of the nightmare. Then he thought of Father, how telling Fatima would put *Vater* in jeopardy and threaten to put an end to the only family Johann had left. He'd have to deal with the problem alone.

"Just knowing you're there helps." He slid his computer into his knapsack. "Come on, we don't want to be seen together. You leave first."

She squeezed his hand again before releasing it. At the door, she turned to look at him. "I grew up in a culture that puts women down. It made me a fighter. And I know that you're a fighter too."

Johann hoped she was right. He was in for the fight of his life.

Chapter 39

Prospero stepped out of his Turkish contact's Mercedes into the sunshine cascading over the snowcapped Pontic Mountains. They had flown into Trabzon and driven to his friend Aslan Barak's villa, south of Rize in Turkey, a rural region near the Black Sea. He looked forward to enjoying a cup of the locally grown tea.

While he settled in at the main house, Luciano and Bassam herded the travel-worn passengers into an outbuilding on the property, a large shed with running water. They had followed the Mercedes along the coast in a bus chartered by Bassam in Trabzon. Here, the hostages would be fed, offered the use of a shower, and given blankets. He hoped they'd stay out of trouble until he had gotten his hands on the truck of Syrians; at that point, they would become someone else's problem. Then he could focus on dealing with the Austrian and, finally, head home to Violetta.

His breakfast had been soured by a report from Bassam's contacts in Libya. As he'd suspected, there'd been a bloodbath at the airstrip in Jufra. Thea had decided not to accept his offer of a personal escort. No contact from her yet, but she'd get in touch. If she didn't, he'd be forced to eliminate one of the passengers to show her he was serious—and *Liberata* would do anything to protect her precious hostages.

Identifying and targeting people's weaknesses was key. Everyone had them, even him. It was *how* people faced their fears that mattered. In one of his last conversations with his father, Stefano's dark eyes had filled with fire as he explained about the autonomic nervous system kicking in—the body sweating, shaking, breathing heavily when under duress.

His father explained that if you could find a way to harness the physiological symptoms instead of letting them paralyze you, fear could work to your advantage. Identify the response, embrace it, and then use the adrenaline while battling your enemy. Prospero had confirmed more than once that the process worked. Stefano had taught him many lessons, some inadvertently, and a critical one involved Enzo Spruilli's father.

Prospero was seventeen, bored at school, often whiling away the evenings with his friends. He didn't know much about the family "business," but he knew his father, Stefano, was a capo di famiglia. *For months Prospero been working on Papa to let him quit school and learn the business. This particular evening, he was at home with Stefano, who didn't want to hear any more nonsense about quitting school.*

"An education is never wasted. Be patient, son."

"Let me learn from you—there's no better teacher." Flattery often seemed to soften his father's hard edges, so he worked it, but cautiously—Stefano could smell bullshit from a hundred meters.

"You really want this to be your life? Once you're in, there's no going back. I worked hard so you would have choices. You could become a doctor, a lawyer—"

A knock sounded at the door. "Come in."

His father's protégé, Karl Wagner, entered with Marco Spruilli, a round-faced, doughy man with sandy hair. Prospero was surprised to see Marco; rumor had it he had suddenly left the country, taking his fat wife and sniveling son, Enzo, with him. No one knew where they had gone, but it had been at least six months since Prospero had seen Enzo at school.

"You have a minute?" Karl asked.

"Sit." Stefano waved them into the leather chairs in front of his carved desk.

Karl looked a little uncomfortable. "Maybe Prospero could bring us some coffee?"

His father stared at Prospero for a long moment, then turned back to Karl.

"No," Stefano said, "he can stay."

"The matter is a delicate one." Karl smiled at Prospero. They were good friends—Karl was only four years older—but of course they never talked about the business. Instead, they discussed books, philosophy, horses. Karl never spoke out of turn, which made him a shining star in Stefano's books.

"Go ahead."

"Marco was blown." Karl didn't mince words.

Blown?

Spruilli stared at the floor, his face reddening.

"Dietrich's son, Gernot, became suspicious and started following him—he'll never be able to infiltrate the Freedom Guardians now."

Infiltration? Freedom Guardians? Prospero wanted to ask a million questions, but he forced himself to remain silent.

Stefano placed his hands on the desk and looked thoughtfully at Marco. "These things happen. Though with your fair complexion, I thought you'd blend in well."

"Perhaps Marco is better suited to other jobs?" Karl, who had a compassionate side, was acting as a buffer for Marco, but Prospero was surprised his father was taking this failure so well. He'd seen his temper flare over much less.

"Marco, you're good with numbers. How about you move back and work the ledgers?" Stefano grabbed a cigar from the humidor, lit it, and sucked in a lungful of smoke.

"I'd like that." Spruilli's eyes were still downcast.

"Bring your family home. And ask your wife to make me some of that cannellini."

Spruilli stood, knowing he was being dismissed, probably wanting to get out before the capo changed his mind. "Of course."

After the man had slunk out, Prospero's father leaned forward in his chair, gaze focused on Karl. "I know it's a lot to ask, but I need you to move to Salzburg—permanently."

Prospero guessed that whatever they were, the Freedom Guardians were in Austria. A sustained silence followed the request.

"Of course," Karl said, finally.

And that day Prospero lost his best friend.

"You understand about Spruilli?" Stefano asked.

"I do." Karl didn't look pleased, but he was a loyal soldier.

"The Gladio thank you."

At the time, Prospero had had no idea what his father was talking about, but he was inducted into the Gladio the following year. They struck a deal: Prospero could learn the business as long as he continued his studies. But he sensed that his father was disappointed in him for choosing "the life," given that he could have pursued any career he chose.

Marco's son, Enzo, returned to school shortly after that meeting, but one night two months later, his father walked out on the family, leaving some bullshit note about falling in love with another woman. And just like that, Marco Spruilli was gone forever.

That day in his father's office had been a pivotal moment in Prospero's life.

Three men sat in three chairs while their fates were written: Marco had failed and would pay the price; Karl would forfeit his friends and family to infiltrate the enemy; and Stefano strengthened his grip on his empire.

Prospero knew which chair he wanted to be in when he became a man.

A knock on the front door interrupted his thoughts. Aslan stood at the threshold, his lean face a welcome sight.

"You don't need to knock on your own door, my friend," Prospero said.

"It has been too long," Aslan said as the two men embraced. "I'm sorry we meet in such complicated circumstances, but I'm always pleased to help a brother. No one will bother you here."

This was an ideal location to house the hostages. The villa was situated on a hundred acres of private land—perfect if you wanted to avoid any questions about the sudden appearance of a group of strangers. And its position on the crest of a steep mountain ridge allowed for early detection of any visitors.

"Your hospitality's appreciated. Come visit us in Italy soon." Their fathers had both been in Operation Gladio, and now both sons took great pride in upholding the cause.

"I'll bring the whole family."

Prospero's face darkened. "Speaking of family, we lost our source inside the Freedom Guardians. Karl must be dead. He made a personal sacrifice to embed himself with the enemy all these years."

"He knew the risks, Prospero. You mustn't be sad—we'll take good care of his sister."

"What I'd like to know is how he was suddenly discovered after so many years. He was an exceptionally cautious man." Prospero inhaled a deep breath.

Before Aslan could answer, Luciano strode into the room, and the conversation shifted to the upkeep of the passengers. A housemaid served tea and Turkish shortbreads as the men spoke. The young woman wore a loose shift and apron, but Luciano's greedy eyes followed her every movement. Prospero glared at his nephew until he caught his attention. Their gazes connected long enough for Luciano to understand: none of that while they were on a job, and never while in the home of a friend and ally. Only a faint tinge of pink in his nephew's cheeks belied his resentment.

"You set up the hidden cameras?" Prospero sipped the tea. It was as good as he remembered.

"Absolutely. They have n-no idea we'll be watching." Luciano opened a laptop and activated the live feed. Bassam's men would keep a close eye on the outbuilding and patrol the perimeter of the property, but nothing worked better than having eyes and ears on the hostages themselves. The stakes were too high to leave anything to chance.

The screen came to life, offering a view of the outbuilding's interior. Reality TV at its finest. The passengers were taking turns showering in the single bathroom, squirming with discomfort at the chilly water.

Most of the hostages were gathered around two weathered picnic tables, where the blankets and pillows were piled. The concrete floor offered little comfort, but Bassam's men would bring in hay from the barn to create makeshift beds. One of the servants would deliver bread and cheese to the guards and hostages at regular intervals.

Prospero stared at the screen, eager to see more. He watched Ocean help the boys dress after their shower, talking quietly to them, as if she were their mother. Michael Dillman coordinated the distribution of blankets and pillows, smiling and trying to cheer everyone up. Prospero couldn't understand anyone wanting to sport a handlebar mustache—way too much work. But maybe that's the way things were done in Texas. He'd never been.

The passenger named Matthias slipped a cell phone out of his bag. "I always carry a backup in case my batteries die."

"Any service?" Karlsson asked, his hands trembling.

"Nothing. And no Wi-Fi, either."

Actually, there was Wi-Fi, but it was password protected. Prospero would have Bassam conduct a search of all the passengers' belongings shortly, see if there was any contraband. He was still mulling over what he'd discovered inside Thea's large carry-on. Lots of medical supplies, mainly.

"Let's call for help," Karlsson said.

"Talk sense, man. We've got no service, and we don't even know where we are," Dillman said.

Jabari Kuria rubbed his eyes. "Thea will come for us."

"I'm sure she'll try to negotiate our release, but these men are hardened criminals. The boss looks like a mobster," Matthias said.

And here I thought I blended in as a businessman.

Ayan joined his brother. "She's going to kick those guys' asses. You wait and see."

"Watch your language, young man," Karlsson said, his tone imperious.

Jabari crossed his arms on his chest. "Don't boss my brother around. Thea will make those *motherfuckers* pay."

Prospero smiled. *Liberata* had definitely won the hearts and mouths of these two kids.

"Calm down, everyone," Dillman said. "Let's figure out where we'll all sleep. We need to establish routines. And be careful around Luciano. He has a crazy l-l-look in his eyes."

Several of the hostages laughed. Prospero glanced at Luciano, his nephew's jaw rippling with tension. Michael Dillman had just made a dangerous enemy.

Chapter 40

Johann shifted in his chair, bored, the math teacher's monotone a soft background buzz. Even if the lecture had been more compelling, he didn't think it would be possible to concentrate on school today.

Fatima sat near the front, always the keen student. Every time she turned her head, he stared at her soft, clear skin and her full lips. Omar Kaleb's horrific death, Uncle Karl's brutal murder, his father's vengeance—Johann needed an oasis, a safe place, and Fatima offered that escape.

At the same time, he worried about putting her at risk.

The bell rang. His free period, at last. He packed up his books quickly, avoiding eye contact with Fatima. Leaving the classroom, he hurried downstairs, passing the library where Fatima often lingered, and headed to the basement and another favorite hideaway, a mostly unused storage room with dingy lighting and a couple of battered desks.

He rubbed his temples, then sank his head into his hands. The information Leopold had shared with him, coupled with his own research, left him cold inside. What should he do? He could report the situation to the police, but Father often invited high-ranking police officers to his parties. For all Johann knew, the police were also *Freiheitswächter*. And did he really want his father to go to jail? Johann still loved him, and what would happen to him if Father was gone? He had no one else now that Uncle Karl was dead.

His eyes burned, and his body ached. Between the lack of sleep and the stress, he worried he wasn't thinking clearly.

A soft knock made him leap to his feet. "What?"

The door opened. Fatima stepped over the threshold. "Can we talk?"

He wanted to tell her to leave, to save herself, but longing made his resolve weaken. "No one can see us together."

She looked around the windowless room and laughed. "I think we're safe here."

A soft pink hijab covered her hair. He wanted to unwrap it, unveil what lay beneath. "Is that man still following you?"

"Yes. I did what you said—pretended he wasn't there."

"In another few days he'll give up."

"What would happen if he caught us together?"

He frowned. "Let's not find out."

"I thought Austria would be different, offering freedom, and here we are, sneaking around."

"My father . . . It's hard to explain."

"Life in my country is pretty restrictive, but at least everyone knows where they stand. I thought life in Europe would be different, freer, and—I don't know—safer."

"I know. I'm sorry. You should be nurtured, encouraged, not followed around like a common criminal."

She gave him a sad smile. "I know you know. That's why I shared my dream of being a surgeon with you."

"You'll be a great surgeon. I'd let you operate on me." He felt foolish as soon as he'd said it, but her smile told him she liked his response.

"Let's hope you never need that kind of help. It doesn't make sense to me that your father, a European, is going to stop you from doing what you want because of a stereotype, because of ignorance." She stepped closer. "I won't accept that, Johann."

Her words hung in the air, a challenge. They were only a foot apart. He felt his Adam's apple bob up and down. He stared at her beautiful face, hesitating. She didn't move away. He leaned down, then brushed his lips against hers. He tried to maintain contact without becoming a fumbling fool, caressing her soft cheek with his thumb. Finally, he lost himself in the kiss.

Even though he didn't want it to end, he forced himself to pull away. What they were doing was dangerous.

"That was nice." She smiled.

Better than nice. "Yes, but we shouldn't do it again."

"I thought we were past that now."

"My father . . ."

"I'm sure in time he'll come around. Maybe if he gets to know me."

"I don't know. With the recent bouts of terrorism, he's very guarded about foreigners. He's lost all perspective." Johann took a deep breath. "You'll be in danger if he finds out we're still seeing each other."

"Then we'll be careful. I'm not losing the one person in this school who makes me feel special, just because of someone else's ignorance."

He squeezed both her hands. "I don't want to lose you either." But he knew he was putting Fatima in danger, and that knowledge sickened him.

Chapter 41

Thea sat on a couch in her room at the Corinthia Hotel Budapest, studying for the thousandth time the note Prospero had given her in the hangar's kitchen. The deadline to call was fast approaching, but she would wait until the last minute. Prospero was used to people asking how high when he told them to jump. To maintain his respect, she had to not acquiesce to his every demand—yet still allow him to feel he had control. It was a fine line to walk.

Why the hell does Prospero want that truck?

A knock on the door interrupted her thoughts. After a quick look through the peephole, she undid the locks. An eighty-four-pound bundle of muscle and joy bounded straight for her, almost knocking her over with the enthusiasm of a child.

"Aegis!"

She stroked his wheaten hair, the Rhodesian ridgeback leaning his full weight against her legs. He whined, wagging his tail as if he was trying to shake it free from his body. She hadn't seen him in two weeks, and he clearly wanted to make up for lost time. He lived full-time with her father, but Thea thought of him as her dog.

Unlike Aegis, Papa hesitated at the threshold, his dark eyes glistening. *Tears. Unusual for him.*

"I'm relieved you're okay." He finally stepped forward, still awkward on his prosthetic leg, and reached for her with open arms.

She returned his hug, her emotions jumbled. She loved her father. He'd been a pillar in Thea's life since she was five, when her mother had died. When he'd been kidnapped last year, she'd moved heaven and earth to bring him back home, but the incident had unearthed a host of ugly secrets that Papa had been hiding. In the aftermath, her brother, Nikos, was gone, his body carried off by the Zambezi River, and her father had lost a leg. And now Thea wasn't sure if she could ever really trust Papa again.

She invited him inside. "Espresso?"

"Do you need to ask?" he asked.

She half smiled. They shared a passion for coffee, the elixir that brought light to even the darkest hour.

Packing espresso grounds into the filter, she soon had the heady scent of brewing java filling the air. A dash of cinnamon, and the espresso was ready.

"Please, sit." She invited him into the suite's living room, placing their espressos on the antique mirrored table. Aegis plopped down on top of her feet. She stroked his head.

"Any news on the boys?" Christos had befriended Ayan and Jabari during one of his trips to Kanzi, and he had funded the adoption program. The boys' new family, the Wavertons, were acquaintances of his.

Thea shook her head. "I'll be calling Prospero Salvatore soon for instructions about this truck he wants us to hijack."

Papa tilted his head. "What's so special about it?"

"That's the sixty-four-million-euro question. The analysts at Quantum are working every angle, but nobody has a clue."

"Well, if you need any support, financial or otherwise, I'm here for you." Papa sipped his espresso.

"We should have it covered, but thanks for the offer."

"I mean it. Anything I can do to get Ayan and Jabari back safely."

"We're on it. Don't worry."

Christos stared into his espresso cup. "Not much fun being a hostage."

Papa would know. "I can't help feeling I let everyone down."

"From what I heard, you held off Prospero's men as long as you could."

She thought of the fight in the hangar, all the people she'd killed. *So much loss of life. More blood on the Italian's hands.* "Prospero always had the advantage."

Papa was quiet for a long moment, his intelligent eyes assessing her. "Once you get the boys safely home, why not leave all this behind, come work with me at Paris Industries?"

There had been a time when she might have considered joining the family business. But knowing the secrets and lies her father had kept and told, and the lives it had cost, she could never work with him. His expression was so hopeful, and she didn't want to hurt him, but she couldn't give him false hope either.

"Listen, Papa, I know you're profoundly sorry about Nikos. I miss him every day, despite what he had become by the end. And I know you worry about me—"

"If I could turn back time, I'd do things differently." Papa's gaze was somber.

Easy for him to say now. She hated that bitterness resurfaced whenever she and her father discussed Nikos, but she couldn't help it. "But what happened to Nikos, how it changed him—that's why I work hard to bring hostages home. To stop what happened to our family from happening to others."

"But you're in constant danger."

"I'm careful. And I have a good team."

"You're my only child now."

"Emotional blackmail won't work on a trained kidnap negotiator."

He smiled and shook his head. "Sorry. I wasn't trying to manipulate you."

"I'm not sure you can help yourself." She softened a little. Papa loved her in his own, imperfect way. He'd made grave mistakes, but then, so had she. They had a long road ahead if they wanted to heal their relationship. She had to learn to forgive, and he had to figure out a way to stop trying to control her. She wasn't sure it was possible—Christos's stubborn streak had helped him reach great success, but it hadn't made him the best parent—but they had to try.

"I respect what you do. I just worry," Papa said.

"Well, it's the boys we should both be concerned about now. Did you speak to the Wavertons? Do they know what's going on?"

"Yes, and they are very worried and upset. But they wanted me to tell you they believe in you."

A sharp knock came on the door. Aegis barked. Thea walked to the peephole, Aegis tailgating her across the room.

Rif. She let him in, his hair still wet from a shower. Tall and broad shouldered, he looked good dressed in black. Aegis pushed past her legs to get to Rif—the dog adored Christos's godson.

"Sorry, I didn't realize I was interrupting." Rif hesitated at the door, scratching the big dog behind the ears.

"Not at all, not at all." Christos and Rif had always been close, but it irked Thea a little that her father was suddenly acting as if this was his room, not hers.

Rif gave Christos a grin and turned to Thea. "We've mapped out a plan. I'd like you to take a look."

Maybe they could find a way to bring everyone back home. *Well, not everyone.* Looking across the room at her father, Thea could feel Nikos's ghost beside her. She remembered the day she'd first met Ayan and Jabari. Two years ago, she'd arrived in Kanzi in the middle of the night, heading straight to the orphanage after thwarting a piracy attempt in Somalia.

Bone tired, she'd expected everyone to be asleep for the night. But a lone light acted as a beacon, tempting her to wander down the corridor. Nikos sat in an armchair beside a single bed, a young

African boy asleep in his arms. Tucked under the covers, a slightly older boy mumbled incoherently, sweat glistening on his forehead.

Her brother looked up as she entered. Shifting the child in his arms, Nikos reached over to the basin on the night table, squeezing water out of a cloth. With his free hand, he wiped the older boy's forehead, removing the perspiration. The boy writhed and moaned.

"Fever." Nikos's voice was barely a whisper.

"Here, let me help." She opened her arms, and her brother passed her the sleeping boy. The child nestled against her shoulder.

Nikos refreshed the cloth, using it to cool the older boy's upper torso and forehead. "It spiked a few hours ago. The doc says if he makes it through the night, he should recover."

The sick boy couldn't be more than ten—he'd hardly experienced what life had to offer. He had to recover.

She pulled up a chair and joined her brother, and they kept a vigil for the boy, talking softly about their childhood in Kanzi, the orphanage, their father.

Thea wished Papa could witness this side of Nikos, but the two men clashed whenever they met—and no détente could ever be reached. Nikos's kidnapping had revealed fault lines in the bedrock of their family, and it seemed that Nikos was on solid ground only in the company of the kids at the orphanage.

Hours later, dawn brought the beauty of Kanzi to life. A massive acacia tree dominated the yard, casting shadows on the windows. The young boy sleeping in her arms stirred, opening one eye, then the other. He reached up and traced the S-shaped scar on Thea's cheek. He shifted, then lifted his left arm, revealing two jagged scars. She smiled.

His gaze swept around the room, taking in Nikos sitting beside the bed.

"Who are you?"

"I'm Nikos's sister, Thea."

"He told me all about you."

"Don't believe everything you hear." She smiled.

"I'm Ayan, and that's my brother, Jabari. What happened to you here?" He pointed to the scar on her face.

"Just a battle wound—I can see you have a few of your own." She'd long forgiven her brother for the incident that had caused the mark.

Movement in the bed drew their attention. Jabari stretched, yawning. His forehead was dry, his eyes clear. The fever had broken.

"I'm hungry. What's for breakfast?" Jabari asked. "And who is that pretty woman?"

They all laughed. Thea didn't know it then, but it was the last joyful moment she and Nikos would ever share.

Chapter 42

Rif sat beside Thea in the conference room they'd converted into a temporary operational center. The Quantum team had gathered around a mahogany table, drinking coffee, eating *kifli* and delicious little cheese puffs called *pogácsa* from the pastry shop down the block. Their sole focus since the team had checked in was finding that truck, and all the operatives had been working nonstop, discussing the vehicle's potential routes and tactics for a takedown in the middle of a busy city.

A large screen showed a detailed map of the main arteries of Budapest, bright red lines highlighting the toll routes. Both a city and a county, the capital of Hungary held a third of the country's population. Needless to say, thousands of vehicles peppered the roads. The one saving grace was the time of year: with a holiday weekend coming up, many people were already out of town, visiting their families in the suburbs or traveling, so there'd be fewer pedestrians and less traffic to worry about.

Prospero had said the truck would be coming from the east, but they couldn't trust his information. Every route into the city had to be covered. Looking at the map, Rif understood why the wily mafioso had wanted a tactical team to handle the extraction. The Quantum team had the communications, intel, and the skills necessary to locate and secure the target in this environment. Why send your own men into a situation where they might botch the job?

Rif started the party. "The colored dots represent members of our team. We have all the main routes covered, assuming the truck will have to use a major artery due to its size."

"Who's got eyes in the sky?" Thea asked, getting straight to the heart of the plan, as usual. Leaving aside her combat skills, it was Thea's ability to keep the big picture in mind even when discussing logistics that inspired such confidence in the team.

"I'll be in the bird," Rif said. "The truck will be easier to spot from above. Once I locate the target, the team on the ground will converge on its location."

"Do we know what's so special about this vehicle yet?" Brown asked.

"It's full of Prospero's mama's homemade spaghetti sauce," Johansson said.

"Thanks, asshole." Brown whipped a cheese pastry at his teammate.

Rif didn't blink; the back and forth was all part of their team's dynamic, a way of letting off steam and creating a cohesive unit. "We've secured several warehouses. Once we have the truck, we head for the closest location, dismantle the vehicle, and figure out exactly why it's so important to Salvatore."

Thea spoke without looking away from the map. "Brown, track down any calls Prospero has made from the phone number he gave me. Maybe it'll give us a lead to where he's holding the hostages."

"On it." Brown grabbed his laptop and booted it up.

"Any other questions?" Thea asked.

"We have time to catch a few winks?" A cigarette hung from the corner of Neil's mouth.

"You bet. Rest up, and stand by for my signal." Rif turned off the screen, ending the meeting.

Everyone but Thea and Rif rolled out of the room buzzing like tuning forks. It was always like this before a mission, adrenaline flowing, everyone slightly on edge. Practically the entire team had flown in as soon as they heard about Thea's skyjacking, even the members who were scheduled for time off. When someone at Quantum needed help, it was all hands on deck.

"How was your visit with Christos?" Rif had sensed the tension in her room. Not one to push, he also wanted her to know she had his support.

She plunked back down in one of the leather chairs. "Confusing. Hard."

"Yeah, well, Christos made some strange decisions." It was the understatement of the century; those decisions had put the entire Quantum team in danger.

"I love Papa, but he set off a chain of horrific events. Many people paid the price, a few with their lives—and he was lucky to lose only a limb. And Nikos . . ." Her voice broke, and she sucked in a long breath before going on. "At times, my resentment is overwhelming. I can also see the guilt eating up my father, and I know he needs my forgiveness and support, but I don't know if I ever can, not fully. Then again, he's the only father I have."

"You have every right to be angry. Anyway, we both know that my godfather is an acquired taste." He tried a smile to soften the moment. "Now it's just a question of finding a way to heal."

"Work helps. Since Papa left rehab, I've been traveling constantly, so our paths have hardly crossed."

"I'm sure Christos realizes you're avoiding him—and understands why." Rif ran a hand through his hair and smiled. "You know, he was in the Quantum offices when he heard your plane had been hijacked. He was devastated."

Thea shrugged. "I know he loves me, Rif. It's just hard to forgive a lifetime of lies."

"Maybe he learned his lesson. I know you lost your brother, but don't forget—he lost his son."

A long silence stretched between them before Thea looked up into his face, searching. "Why didn't you tell me about Nikos's past?"

"It wasn't my place." He felt guilty that he'd known more about Nikos's kidnapping than he'd let on, but the situation had been complicated—not least because he had pretty ambivalent feelings toward her brother.

"I'm sorry, Rif. Look, I don't want you to think I'm making you choose sides between me and Papa . . ."

"Not at all." He didn't think he should say it out loud, but he'd always choose Thea, over anyone else.

Brown rapped on the door.

Thea sat up straight. "No need to knock. Find something?"

The tech guru held his laptop in his hands, fidgeting with it and looking down.

"What?"

"Maybe I should talk to you privately . . ."

"Whatever it is, Rif can hear it."

"Prospero's calls. Most of it is just standard stuff, but two stand out. The first is a call to the same banker—Falcon Private Bank—that one of the passengers uses for his software business. Matthias Houndsworth."

"Could be a coincidence but definitely worth checking out. Great job. And the second?" she asked.

"Well, umm . . ."

"Just spit it out." Thea wondered what was spooking Brown.

"Prospero phoned Christos's cell yesterday. The call lasted ten minutes."

Rif watched Thea's mouth fall open. *So much for healing.*

Chapter 43

Prospero's mind wouldn't stop whirring. His cell phone was a beacon of annoyance on the bedside table. He'd left the ringer on in case Thea texted or called. Twenty minutes left to his deadline, yet still no word from her. She certainly had bravado.

He propped up a couple of pillows, grabbed his computer, and tuned in to the outbuilding's live feed. It reminded him of one of those ridiculous British reality shows his wife watched. *Violetta*. He wondered if she missed him or if she preferred it when he was away. Twenty-three years of marriage had dampened their passion but not their love; she provided a normal life at home, where he could just be himself, a middle-aged man with a bad hip. He couldn't imagine life without her, but he knew it couldn't be easy, living with him.

The screen flickered on, allowing him to see what the hostages were doing. Even though it was early morning, most of the passengers gathered near the door, drinking the bottled water he'd provided. He glanced at his watch. Fifteen minutes left. There were so many moving parts to this plan—should he have involved Thea? *Too late for that.* Anyway, *Liberata* was a pro. She'd call.

His gaze drifted over a group hovering close to a window, a few of them peering outside. They could look all they want, but if they tried to escape, Bassam's men would sort them out.

Mike Dillman put a burly arm around Ayan. "Hope the floor wasn't too hard on you, buddy."

The young boy shrugged. "Nah, we're used to sleeping on the ground, taking turns on night watch."

"Looking for animals?" The Texan's eyebrows arched.

"Enemies. Sometimes they would try to raid our camp, but then me, Jabari, or another boy on watch would go *bang-bang*, and they'd be dead."

"You shot people?" Dillman's voice deepened.

"Lots of war in Kanzi. Boko Haram killed our mom and dad, taught us to shoot, made us fighters." Ayan yawned. "But now we're going to our new home in London."

"Children shouldn't have to fight."

Prospero agreed with him there. Only adults should wage war.

"If we get their guns," Ayan said, motioning to the guards outside, "then we can escape."

"Promise me you won't try anything. For now, we wait. Remember, Thea is coming."

Ayan smiled, his two missing front teeth making him look even younger than he was. "I love Thea."

Dillman smiled. "She loves you too. Let's hang tight and see what happens, okay?"

Ayan frowned. "These men are bad."

"Yes, but right now we have to do what they say."

Prospero wondered if the man had children, grandchildren. He and Violetta had never been blessed. Probably better that way, given his profession. Still, he wondered what he'd be like as a father. When Stefano had died, he'd felt adrift, a piece of him gone forever.

Jabari sat in a corner of the room, Ocean close beside him. They were deep in conversation, but he couldn't make out any words because the other passengers' voices drowned them out.

Matthias, Karlsson, and two businessmen rifled through the cupboards in the outbuilding, searching them. They'd find nothing of consequence. A few kicked at the doggy door Luciano had nailed shut. His nephew had done a thorough vetting of the shed before locking the hostages inside. They could look all they wanted. It'd give them something to do.

A ping from his cell caught his attention.

Finally.

Chapter 44

One look at the group of cars parked outside his family's castle, and Johann wanted to slink in the back door and up to his room for a quiet evening alone. But as luck would have it, Father was in the kitchen giving Chef directions.

"You're late. Everything okay?" A further question, unasked, lingered in his father's eyes.

"I needed to talk to my English teacher about entering a creative writing contest." Since when did lies roll off his tongue so easily?

"Fiction? The Dietrichs are making a concrete difference in the world, not losing ourselves in fantasy."

They left the kitchen together, his father headed for the rear stairs. Johann could think of nothing but Omar Kaleb's death, Uncle Karl's murder, and the plan to eradicate people of Arab descent. If he put all that in a story, he'd be asking a lot from his readers, but these were now the facts of his life.

"Is there a *Freiheitswächter* meeting tonight?" Johann asked, just to make conversation, and then instantly regretted it.

"A special guest is joining us from America."

The promised land. Father wanted Johann to return home to run the family business after completing his studies. But that wasn't Johann's plan for himself—he wanted to work in environmental engineering, where he could use his math and computer skills to build bridges and water-treatment plants in developing countries. That's where he could make a difference.

"Come downstairs and meet him," Father said.

"I have too much homework." Johann started up the stairs.

"This is more important."

Turning around, Johann traipsed back down the steps, dropping his backpack on the hall table and following *Vater* to the basement. No point arguing with Father when he had that look in his eyes.

The crowd of Watchers welcomed Father with adulation. Father worked the room, scanning the crowd, his charisma drawing people to him. Johann skulked to the shadowy area at the back of the room and collapsed onto the leather couch, guilt and disgust washing over him.

The cellar used to be a comforting cave where he watched football on the big screen. He was a Red Bull Salzburg supporter, enjoying their aggressive, flashy style. He wished he could emulate their bravado, but he'd never been much good at team sports, and his build was not good for football. He was better suited to skiing and other solo athletic activities.

Johann wanted to disappear as the group grew, crowding into the antique-filled basement. *Old World Austria meets New World Order.* Clusters of *Freiheitswächter* gathered around the fireplace. Whispers of a three-letter US-based organization peppered the air. Former or current, he didn't know, but Father's guest had to be a spy. And, given the secretive nature of the work, he figured he'd never know for sure. What did it matter, really? The bottom line was that someone with connections to the CIA was helping with the plan. Had the whole world gone insane?

Johann studied the stranger when he arrived. He was of average height and weight, with brown hair and eyes, dressed in brown slacks and a white dress shirt. Johann had expected someone more remarkable, but maybe that was the whole point. Forgettable, this man could easily blend into a crowd.

Father guided the stranger to a back corner of the room, not seeming to notice that Johann was within earshot where he had burrowed into the couch.

"Krimm, the plane has gone missing. From the security chatter, it sounds like it was skyjacked. Gladio?" Father asked.

"Perhaps. The question is, can we get her back in time?"

"Doubtful, but my contacts have their ear to the ground. A kidnap specialist with Quantum International named Thea Paris was on board the flight, but she escaped. Quantum will be negotiating for the release of the passengers."

"Find those passengers before the negotiator does. It's too late to recruit another scientist." Krimm's tone was peremptory, curt; he spoke to Johann's father in a way Johann had never heard before.

"True, but even without her participation now, we can move ahead with phase one using the quantity we have," Father said. "But we will eventually need her expertise in mass-production before we can launch the phase-two attack. We will get her back."

"Good," Krimm said. "What about the mole?"

"Dealt with."

Johann shivered. *Uncle Karl.*

"Only a few of us are aware of the overarching plan, and I am sure the Gladio don't know about the bioweapon." His father's voice was clipped, intense, as he tried to reassure Krimm.

"Then we implement phase one immediately."

"The messengers will pick up the canisters tomorrow."

So soon? Johann felt dread wash over him.

"Four refugee camps to start, yes?" Krimm asked.

"Yes, then we'll expand from there. France, Germany, Greece... we'll focus on the areas with the largest Arab populations."

"You've done well, Gernot—all of you."

"Thank you. All of us know how important this fight is for our future. Now, let me find Johann, my son, so you can meet him. He recently joined the cause."

Johann wished the floor could open up and swallow him whole. The last thing in the world he wanted was to be a poster boy for the *Freiheitswächter*.

Chapter 45

Thea and Rif strode down the long plaza toward the entrance of St. Stephen's Basilica, a magnificent neoclassical church built to honor the first king of Hungary. It had been rebuilt several times over the years, once because the original dome had collapsed before construction was even completed, taking the rest of the building with it, and again after aerial bombing during World War II had damaged it. And it looked amazing these days.

She'd had a brief text exchange with Prospero, and now she was meeting his representative in the basilica, a public space that, due to the ever-present crowds within, offered excellent cover for a meeting like this. Meanwhile, her other teammates were scattered throughout the city, procuring the vehicles and equipment they'd need for the mission.

"You call your father?" Rif asked.

"That I did." She was still reeling from the revelation that Papa and the mafioso were in touch. "He claimed Prospero was making threats about the boys unless I came up with that damned truck."

"You believe him?"

"Not really. Would you, after everything he's done?"

As they climbed the steps to the church's soaring entrance, she noticed Christ's words in giant gold letters above the arch: *Ego sum via veritas et vita*: I am the way, the truth, and the life. *Papa could have as easily taken that as his motto, the way he goes around changing the facts to suit himself.*

Rif broke into her thoughts. "What possible reason could he have to work with Prospero?"

"I know, it doesn't make sense. But something is off." She stopped mid-stride, struck by a sudden thought. "Hey, do me a favor and ask Brown if he can check Prospero's phone records from during the *Liberata* negotiation."

Rif raised an eyebrow, sounding doubtful. "I'll ask, but that's time travel you're talking about. You think Christos and Prospero might have been in touch back then?"

"Maybe. Let's hope I'm wrong."

They took the next few steps in silence; then Rif spoke up. "Speaking of fathers, Hakan sent an update. No more news on the jet passengers or the truck, but get this: apparently, the motto for the Gladio is *Silendo libertatem servo*, 'In silence we serve freedom,'" Rif said.

"I'd love to hear Prospero explain how hijacking serves freedom," Thea muttered. "Did Hakan have any luck locating the 737?" she asked.

"Nothing yet. Because of the damage to the plane, they'd have had to fly below ten thousand feet, making it difficult to locate them on the radar," Rif said. "Anyway, they couldn't have gone far. Hakan will find it."

The iconic church towered above the square, history seeping from every stone. "Twelve minutes before the meet." Perhaps she would have time to say a quick prayer for Ayan, Jabari, and the other passengers.

"I'll have eyes on you the entire time." Rif inserted his earbud. Thea's was already lodged in her ear.

"We're live?" he asked.

"Reading you, loud and clear."

"Code word *yellow* if you need me," Rif said.

Thea had been to St. Stephen's Basilica once before, when she'd squeezed in a day of sightseeing on her way back to London from a mission in Syria. Two years ago, she'd led an insertion team that rescued a Dutch aid worker taken hostage by al-Nusra jihadists in the northwestern part of the country. The beautiful church had seemed like a refuge after what had been a difficult extraction, but now it felt menacing. *Context is everything.*

Rif hung back outside so she could enter first. Dark and cool, the enormous building could hold more than 8,500 people, making countersurveillance a challenge.

Precious stones as well as burgundy, black, and white marble adorned the grand interior, all set off against the gleaming gold leaf of the vaulted, painted ceiling and ubiquitous trim. The world-renowned statue of St. Stephen at the main altar, the magnificent stained-glass windows, and the massive carved wooden pews were awe inspiring, but she ignored the beauty around her and scanned the crowd for anyone who stood out or was trying to blend in. *Someone like me.*

No one so far.

She slipped a bill into the donation box and paused to light a candle for her brother, remembering their last moments together in Zimbabwe—his rage, his pain. *Rest in peace, Nikos. I miss you.*

She worked her way around the pews, looking for anything out of the ordinary. She passed the small chapel to the left of the main altar that held the "Holy Dexter," King Stephen's mummified right hand, revered for its "incorruptibility." *I doubt that, but he was king more than a millennium ago, so who can argue with the guy's rep now?*

Out of the corner of her eye, she caught sight of Rif entering the basilica, moving toward the left aisle, which gave him clear sight lines to most of the church. He strolled casually, eyes in constant motion.

A few people prayed in the pews, but most of the crowd cruised the aisles of the church, eager to check off the box on their itinerary before moving on to the next attraction.

She threaded through the throng, narrowly avoiding being impaled by tour guides' flags and selfie sticks. Slipping into the last pew, she sat close to the aisle for quick egress. With a mirror app on her phone, she pretended to text while monitoring her surroundings.

Seconds later, a large red-haired woman wearing a flower-print dress plopped down beside her, a strong British accent revealing her home country. "Lovely top, dear."

"Thanks, it's Anne Fontaine."

"Just fabulous. If my husband drags me to one more heritage site, I will go mad. I'd rather be back at the hotel drinking Pimm's and reading Jilly Cooper before we head to dinner."

Two minutes until the meet. She had to get rid of this woman. "You're not going to the event, then?" Thea improvised.

"What event?" The woman leaned closer, her face glowing with exertion.

"At the Bestsellers Bookstore, around the corner. I heard Martina Cole is doing a book signing or something there . . ." Thea glanced at her watch. "Right about now."

"*The* Martina Cole?" She pushed herself off the bench. "I've always wanted to meet her—fancy her being here in Hungary. Thank you so much." She headed off, no doubt in search of her husband, who would have to bear the brunt of her disappointment when she found out the author wasn't actually there. But at least she'd be in a bookstore and away from the historical sites.

She scanned her surroundings, spotting Rif on the other side of the basilica. He might have been trying to hold back a smile, having overheard every word.

Several large groups entered St. Stephen's, collapsing umbrellas and shaking out their coats. Must have started raining, so the tourists were seeking sanctuary.

A man with scraggly facial hair, a leather jacket, and an olive-colored messenger bag slid into the pew beside her. "*Liberata?*"

He was dry, so he must have been inside for a while—she had to admit the approach was good. She reached into her pocket and pressed a button on her cell to pair her phone with his. "What should I call you?"

He ignored the question. "The truck entering Budapest will have this Greek license plate; the refugees are hidden inside, behind cargo. Bring the vehicle to these GPS coordinates in Turkey." He passed her a sheet of paper.

"I need more details. Hundreds of trucks come into the city every hour."

He reached into his messenger bag, then handed her a grainy photo of a large GMC truck at least twenty years old. "This is it."

"What's so special about this vehicle?"

"Just do the job."

"First I need confirmation the plane's passengers are safe, especially the Kuria boys."

He showed her a live feed of the prisoners on his phone screen. The buzz of the crowds faded, her full attention on the video unfolding on the screen. Ayan, Jabari, and the other passengers were inside what looked like a large shed or garage. The boys were playing cards on the floor. She breathed a sigh of relief. They looked healthy, unharmed, unafraid. No windows in the frame, so she couldn't see outside. She studied the items in the room, searching for clues to their location.

"I want access to the feed."

"Deliver the truck, and you'll get the passengers back."

"No harm in letting me keep an eye on them."

He reached into his jacket, pulled out a second cell phone, and pushed a button. Seconds later, two of Bassam's guards appeared in the video. They aimed AK-47s at the boys, who were thankfully so involved in their game that they were oblivious.

"Tell them to back off." Thea clenched her fists.

"Find that truck." The man stood and merged into the crowds, heading deeper into the church.

"Stay on him," Thea told Rif. It would help if they could follow the man back to where he worked or lived.

Rif's height allowed him to see over the crowd. "Got him."

She headed in his direction. "You still have him?"

"He's close to the right tower."

"Coming to meet you," she said.

"Way too crowded."

"That's why he chose this location."

"Dammit."

"What?" She quickened her step, dodging tour groups speaking different languages.

"He disappeared. Turned the corner and vanished."

"No sign of him?" she asked.

Seconds passed.

"Nothing. He's gone."

She caught up to Rif, searching the area. Not a trace. They looked for any hidden doors but couldn't find any without conducting a more thorough, and attention-getting, search.

"At least the boys are safe," Rif said.

"For now."

Chapter 46

Prospero paced the Turkish carpet in Aslan's living room, talking to his contact in Budapest on a burner cell. He'd prefer to be personally supervising the hunt for the truck, but he needed to keep an eye on his insurance.

"You were right. They tried to follow me out of the church," his man said.

"They're professionals. Be prepared."

"The live feed was effective."

"If that truck reaches the Parliament Building . . ."

"We'll have a team near the Chain Bridge, ready to block it off."

"Low-key. Remember, no authorities." If discovered, Gernot Dietrich's plan would create havoc across Europe. If the police got their hands on the truck, there was no telling what would happen. "We don't want widespread panic."

"My men are keeping an eye on *Liberata*'s movements. I'll report in later."

Loud voices distracted him. At first he thought it was on the other end of the line in Budapest, but he realized quickly that the live feed was still running on a nearby computer. Something was going on in the outbuilding.

"Don't disappoint me." He ended the call and moved to the computer.

Luciano had Ayan Kuria in a headlock.

"Let him go!" Mike Dillman was a few feet away, yelling at Prospero's nephew.

"He's just a kid," Laverdeen said.

"He b-bit me." Luciano was enraged.

"What do you expect? You keep poking him with that stupid stick." Dillman gestured toward the baton in Luciano's hand.

Jabari grabbed Luciano's right arm, trying to pry his brother loose. Luciano punched him with his free hand. The other hostages circled around the fight for a better view.

Uffa! Che idiota!

Prospero rushed down the hall and out the back door. His hip ached down to the marrow. They were in for some weather—snow, perhaps, given the temperature. He hurried down the cobblestone pathway to the outbuilding, hoping he wasn't too late to prevent bloodshed.

The icy mountain air made the hairs on the back of his neck prickle. Bassam and his guards were already inside, but they seemed unsure about what they should do, given that Luciano was taking on two children. The other hostages were closing in, ignoring the threat of the rifles.

"Stop it now." Prospero's voice cut through the chaos.

Silence descended on the outbuilding.

"Get out." Staring at Luciano, Prospero gestured with one thumb toward the door.

"The k-k-id had it c-c-coming." His nephew's mouth contorted with the effort of getting the words out.

Ayan had a dazed look on his face, his chest heaving with desperate gasps.

"I'm not asking again. Leave." Prospero's back stiffened.

Luciano glared at Dillman. The Texan smirked. His nephew stormed out of the building, reaching for his pack of cigarettes.

Tension filled the air, the hostages gathered together. Prospero's patience had evaporated. "Any more disturbances like this, there will be penalties."

"Don't let that creep come in here anymore. He tortures the kids," Dillman said.

"You're not in a position to give orders." Prospero's fists clenched.

"Get him under control. He's a loose cannon," Laverdeen said.

Prospero studied the concerned faces, knowing they were right. The only person unaffected by the commotion seemed to be Ocean, though he could see a slight tightening around her eyes. Movement in a corner of the shed caught his attention. Karlsson was huddled on the floor, hugging himself and rocking back and forth.

"Ayan, Jabari, come with me."

"Wait, where are you taking them?" Dillman asked, taking a step forward.

"None of your damn business."

Bassam raised his AK-47. The Texan backed off.

The kids followed him outside, skirting the area where Luciano stood, his back to them, blowing smoke rings into the frosty air.

Prospero headed for the house, using the rear door near the kitchen to enter. Inside was one of the domestics, a young girl, baking desserts. He grabbed a plate, tossed a few cookies onto it, and perched himself on a chair at the marble counter. "Sit," he told the boys.

The boys scrambled onto stools, hungry gazes glued to the snacks.

"Go ahead."

They each grabbed a cookie, downing it quickly in big bites.

"Have as many as you like."

He didn't have to ask twice. The boys were quite thin, wiry. He remembered how much he ate at their age.

The young cook opened the fridge and brought out a carton of milk. She poured two glasses without saying a word, placing them in front of the boys. Then she started making sandwiches. He let her go ahead. Maybe he'd have one himself.

"You two need to stop irritating Luciano."

"He's a bad man," Ayan said between bites.

Prospero was inclined to agree. "But he's your boss while you're here. Do what he says, and things will be better for you."

"He should leave us alone, or Thea will get him," Jabari said.

"Yes, I'm sure she will. How do you know Ms. Paris, anyway?"

"From the orphanage in Kanzi," the older boy said. "Her brother, Nikos, saved us from the warlord. But then Nikos died. Just like our mama and papa."

"Mi dispiace moltissimo."

"What?" Ayan wrinkled his forehead.

"It's what Italians say when you've lost someone." He remembered the day of his father's funeral, how so many backstabbing sycophants had expressed their "deepest regrets" with those very words. Mouths moving in all the right ways but eyes revealing their true feelings.

The housemaid placed a large stack of ham and Swiss cheese sandwiches in front of the boys. They dove in, and Prospero joined them.

"These are better than in the airplane," said Jabari.

"Of course. Airline food is horrible." Prospero smiled.

"When can we go home?" Ayan asked.

"To Kanzi?"

"London. We have a new family waiting for us. The Wavertons." Ayan waved both hands in the air.

"Soon enough."

"Can we call Thea?" Jabari chugged some milk.

"She's busy doing something for me."

"Are you really going to let us go?" Ayan asked.

Man, these two were sharp. Or maybe they'd just had their fair share of broken promises.

"You'll be in London soon." At least he hoped so.

"My feet are cold. Can we have boots?" Jabari asked.

Prospero nodded to the maid. "Find them something. And jackets." The kids must be freezing out there in the shed.

"More food?" Prospero asked.

"Can we take some back for our friends?"

"No. They can eat the slop the guards do."

"Didn't your mother teach you to share?" Jabari's face wrinkled in disapproval.

"My mother taught me plenty. She was a good woman."

"I want Thea." Ayan had mayonnaise smeared across his cheek.

Prospero grabbed a napkin and wiped it off. "Then behave, and you'll see her soon enough. And stay away from Luciano."

The maid returned with several jackets and two pairs of boots. Jabari slipped on two layers, smiling in delight. Ayan chose a red down jacket that must have belonged to one of Aslan's kids. The thermal boots more or less fit. They danced around in their new duds, admiring each other. *Amazing, the things a lifetime of deprivation made you appreciate.*

"Time to go." He called one of Bassam's guards to escort the boys back to the outbuilding. "Remember, behave."

Ayan and Jabari nodded solemnly.

Returning to the kitchen, he decided to indulge in another sandwich. But the plates were empty, all the sandwiches and cookies gone.

He shook his head and smiled. *"Quei piccolo banditi!"*

Chapter 47

Prospero was growing restless. That truck had to be found, fast. Looking for a distraction, he clicked on the live feed. People fascinated him. Some proved resilient, handling stress and hardship with grace, while others cracked under hardly any pressure at all.

Karlsson's mental state had deteriorated rapidly since the hijacking: he mumbled to himself constantly now, and his hair was askew. Bernard gave him water and tried to get him to eat, but he'd become convinced the food was poisoned. Some of the other passengers complained that he had been whimpering all night long, keeping them awake. *Pazzu*, but if he had to kill a hostage, Karlsson was quickly earning a place at the head of the line.

Ocean walked to where the basket case was huddled in a corner and sat cross-legged beside him. Her mouth moved, but Prospero couldn't hear what she was saying over the other passengers.

Footsteps sounded on the hardwood floors of the living room. He turned. *Luciano.*

"Those boys are animals."

Prospero was tempted to respond that it took one to know one, but he held his tongue. "They're kids, rambunctious."

"Nah, I've seen the look in their eyes. They've killed people. They want to kill me."

"You sound more paranoid than Karlsson."

"You do know they used to be child soldiers." Luciano enunciated every word, working hard to avoid his stutter.

"And that's a tragedy we should all feel bad about. No kid should have to go through that bullshit." Prospero returned his attention to the screen.

"They're nothing but trouble."

"Thea is key to our mission, and getting those boys back is her motivation. They'll be out of your hair soon enough."

"I don't trust them."

"*Basta, niputi!* You're letting two kids get under your skin for no reason. They're bright and kind of funny."

"If they attack me again, I won't be responsible for what happens."

"Yes, you will."

Prospero's cell rang. His man in Budapest. He dismissed Luciano and pressed the talk button. *"Che fai?"*

"They've organized equipment, even rented a plane."

"How many men?"

"Hard to tell—maybe ten, tops. I was expecting more."

"Tactical teams work better in small groups." *At least I hope so.*

"We've plotted the most likely route, and we'll have people searching the city as well."

"I don't care who gets there first, but someone needs to find that truck, *pronto.*"

Chapter 48

The sun descended below the horizon as Rif and Thea strode through Budapest's Castle District. Rif caught a glimpse of their tail as they crossed the street. Both armed, the two men had been tag-teaming their every move since they'd left the basilica.

"Looks like you have two admirers—how will you choose between them?" Rif smiled at Thea, his eyebrows slightly raised.

"That's easy: the one in the black hat. Couldn't wear my Louboutins with Shorty."

"Ah, then I'll take Black Hat, to protect your virtue." Rif tried not to laugh. "Hey, how about I show you one of my favorite places in the city?"

She glanced at her watch. "If we make it quick."

Both of Rif's parents had been born in Istanbul. And since Budapest was one of the few places in the world with authentic Turkish bathhouses, some of them dating back to the sixteenth century, his family had spent many weekends and holidays in the city. On many nights they had strolled along the Danube after dinner.

"My mother took me to the labyrinth every time we visited," he said. "And we're just in time for the evening walk-through." He guided them across the street toward the entrance.

"Your parents still planning on remarrying?" she asked.

"Yup. No firm date yet, but I accepted my father's offer to be his best man." His parents had divorced years ago, when Hakan had been an active response consultant, away from the family more often than not, but they'd never stopped loving each other. Three years after the divorce, they'd started dating each other again.

"That's a wedding I'm looking forward to," she said.

"You could go as my date."

"Tempting, but I have a date—Black Hat has already picked out his tux."

"He won't be able to dance when I'm through with him."

She smiled. "Who said anything about dancing?"

It seemed that things had shifted between them lately, and Rif hoped Thea was beginning to see him in a new light. Thea was special, different from any woman he'd known—and not just because she was a skilled combatant and spoke seven languages. She was exciting to be around, with a dry sense of humor that shone through even in the most dangerous circumstances. They'd known each other since they were kids, and now they were colleagues, but it was only recently that he'd started to feel this way. He often found himself wondering if she felt it too, but he didn't know how to ask—or if it was a good idea to explore the subject at all. *Probably not.*

Rif led Thea down the steep stairs to enter the series of caves under Castle Hill. He paid the labyrinth's entry fee while studying the reflection in the ticket booth's glass. Sure enough, Black Hat and Shorty lined up several people behind them. They were doing a reasonable job of surveillance, but they needed a larger team if they wanted to remain invisible. Clearly these two didn't have intelligence or military backgrounds; now that they were closer, Rif made a point of studying their faces, remembering them. The skill had kept him alive more than once.

Tickets in hand, Rif picked up an oil lantern and entered the caves. The labyrinth offered a special evening tour featuring oil lamps as the only source of light. The dampness sent goose bumps rippling down his arms. As a kid, he'd loved anything creepy like this. Some people found the maze claustrophobic and terrifying, but he had a feeling that Thea wouldn't be grabbing his hand for comfort. *Too bad.*

A pungent mix of mold and kerosene wafted into his sinuses. Wax figures wearing dingy opera attire stood in what appeared to be jail cells as selections of Verdi operas echoed off the travertine walls. Water dripped from the ceiling, forming little puddles on the floor.

A private guide led eight Moroccans on a tour, and he and Thea tagged along, absorbing the history lesson.

The male guide spoke Spanish, so they had no trouble following along. "These caves served as a refuge and hunting ground for prehistoric man some half million years ago. Since then, they have been used as a wine cellar, a torture chamber, a jail, and a treasury."

The guide stopped in front of the *Hospital in the Rock* exhibit. "These caverns were used as a medical facility in the Second World War, and during the 1956 uprising, they served as a command center in the event of a nuclear war. The whole cave system could accommodate about ten thousand people."

Rif couldn't imagine that many individuals crouching inside these dank, dark walls. They would be like rats in a series of tunnels, all scurrying for protection.

Their stalkers closed the distance, emboldened by the dim light. Fog machines pumped out plumes that reduced visibility. Rif made a quick nod to Thea. They slowed their pace, letting the group from Morocco forge ahead. Other than their tail, no one else lingered close behind.

They closed the distance to Dracula's Chamber, the most intimidating section of the caves. Visitors were greeted by absolute blackness, given only a handrail to guide them out of the all-consuming darkness.

"Now." Rif nodded to Thea. They entered the inky room and stepped to either side, waiting for their quarry, eyes adjusting to the dark.

The dim light near the entrance allowed them to see the shadows moving toward them. Shorty and Black Hat walked briskly side by side, probably worried they'd lose their marks in the labyrinth.

Verdi's opera hit a high note. Footsteps. Movement. The men entered the Dark Room. Black Hat's taller form was closest to him. Thea would handle Shorty.

Rif shifted his weight, then rounded on Black Hat with a quick kick, taking out the man's legs. Black Hat sprawled onto the floor. Before he could regain his equilibrium, Rif forced the man's arms above his head, then patted down his torso to find his holstered weapon, tossing it aside.

Grunting sounds echoed beside him: Shorty being manhandled by Thea. He couldn't see a thing, but he'd bet on her any day. A soft curse from Thea. Shorty must have gotten a punch in.

A thud. The clatter of metal on stone. Silence.

"He's down." Thea's voice was raspy.

Black Hat squirmed underneath him, but Rif held him fast. "Who do you work for?"

"Fuck you, *baccala*."

"Let me guess. Salvatore."

Black Hat spat in his face. Rif wiped it off with the back of his hand, curled his fingers into a fist, and slammed it into the man's nose. The crunch of cartilage breaking preceded more Italian expletives.

"If you want any teeth left, start talking."

"Fuck you."

Rif kneed him hard in the balls.

A loud moan.

"Last chance."

"Vaffanculo!" the man yelled.

Rif wrapped his hands around the man's neck and tightened them. "Why does Salvatore want that truck?" Tough guys like this one were often brave—until they couldn't breathe. Black Hat wheezed, lungs desperate for air, his legs kicking in panic.

Rif loosened his hold. "Talk."

"Need to stop the Austrians." The words were barely a whisper.

"What Austrians?"

"The Freedom Guardians."

Voices sounded in the corridor. Innocent tourists would be entering the Dark Room soon. Rif punched Black Hat in the solar plexus. The man curled up into a ball, writhing.

"Let's go."

"Shorty is unconscious, and I can't see a damn thing." Thea was right beside him.

Rif grabbed her hand, enjoying the contact. He guided them out using the handrail.

As they neared the exit of the Dark Room, the voices in the distance became clearer. Sounded like college kids. Someone flicked on a cell phone light. "Hey, I think these guys fell down in the dark. I told you it's dangerous in here."

Thea, inspecting the bloodied knuckles of her left hand, already beginning to swell from the blow to the short man's jaw that had knocked him out, had to agree.

Chapter 49

The sound of scraping woke Prospero. Metal against stone. *What the hell?* He scrambled out of bed and hurried over to the window and peered outside. One of the guards was shoveling freshly fallen snow from the cobblestone path. At least a foot had fallen while he slept. Dawn had eased in gently, soft morning light flooding the mountains, the view of the freshly capped white peaks breathtaking.

After slipping on a black cable-knit sweater, he opened the live feed on his computer. In groups of four, the hostages were allowed thirty minutes outside the cabin to get a little exercise. Prospero had given the okay, knowing it would keep them calmer. Given the tension between Luciano and the boys, they all needed to let off a little steam.

Karlsson, Matthias, and the two flight attendants were returning after their time outdoors. Karlsson seemed a little more together since Ocean had talked to him, but he still appeared fragile.

Prospero called Violetta to wish her good morning, telling her the business trip in Eastern Europe was going well. After this was over, he'd take her on a holiday, perhaps to Milan. She loved the stores at Quadrilatero d'Oro, the golden rectangle of shopaholic heaven where his credit card would get quite a workout. He smiled; he could afford it, and since it made her so happy, then why not?

The snow had lifted his spirits, and it seemed to give the hostages a morale boost as well. The boys were next in line to enjoy some outdoor time. They had already put on their new coats. Dillman and Captain Rivers were the other two hostages in their group.

"This is our first snow ever," Jabari said. "What do we do with it?"

Dillman laughed. "I'll teach you how to make a snowman—and snow angels."

Rivers grinned. "Or we could have a snowball fight."

"I'm going to dive right into it." Ayan hopped around with excitement.

Prospero left his bedroom, grabbed a *caffè* from the kitchen, and hurried outside, thinking it might be fun to watch the boys enjoy their first snowfall. His hip ached even more when he stepped outside, but he didn't care; he brushed off the snow on a nearby bench and sat down to enjoy the show.

Ayan sprinted toward a large pile of fluffy snow, diving headfirst into it with a squeal of joy. Jabari lay on his back, creating snow angels under Dillman's tutelage. Jabari made one angel, then jumped up to briefly admire it before searching for a fresh spot to make another. Even Bassam and the guards watched with amusement. Seeing something new through the eyes of a child was a wonderful experience. And Ayan Kuria—the boy was like a wind-up toy that never stopped.

Dillman kneeled beside Jabari to teach him how to make a snowman. The older boy scooped up a handful of snow and sprinkled the fluffy white powder on the man's mustache. They both laughed.

Rivers packed snow between his hands. One of Bassam's men had removed the shrapnel and treated his shoulder, and he looked to be in less pain. Rivers's snowball careened toward an unsuspecting Ayan. *Smack*. Right in the face.

For a moment, Prospero worried that Ayan might be hurt or at least stunned, but laughter echoed across the mountainside as he quickly recovered. Making his own snowball, Ayan hurled it toward Rivers.

The captain ducked, the snowball sailing straight past. But Ayan was already making another. He sent the white orb flying toward Rivers, then another. Prospero smiled. Rivers had no idea what he'd started.

War.

Jabari and Dillman joined in, and soon they were launching snowballs back and forth, Ayan hiding behind a large bin before sending more missiles flying their way. The others had joined forces with Rivers, so Ayan now faced three opponents.

Not at all deterred by the odds, the little guy hurled a flurry of snowballs in the opposing team's direction. The others closed in on Ayan, so he used a short break in the assault to run for better cover. Throwing a snowball over his shoulder, Ayan ran full tilt, his little legs stumbling in the deep snow. Prospero wanted to cry out a warning, but the words stuck in his throat. Ayan slammed straight into the back of Luciano, who was looking elsewhere, smoking. His nephew collapsed onto his knees and face-planted in the snow, his cigarette flying out of his mouth. Rivers, Dillman, Jabari, and Ayan laughed.

Luciano pushed himself off the ground, wiping the snow from his face. His expression was contorted by anger. He lunged toward Ayan, but his smooth-soled loafers slipped on the snow, and he fell again. Peals of laughter followed. Even the guards snickered. But instead of joining in the moment, Luciano rushed toward Ayan.

Before Prospero could move off the bench, his nephew cuffed Ayan hard across the temple. For a brief moment, the youngster wavered, dazed by the blow. Then Ayan gathered himself and charged toward Luciano, punching him hard in the balls.

Prospero jumped to his feet, knowing he was too far away to intervene. Time slowed, offering fractured snapshots. A flash of Luciano's Glock. Ayan looking up in fear. Dillman leaned down, lunging toward Luciano, thrusting Ayan out of the way.

Bang, bang, bang.

Prospero was almost there as the Texan collapsed onto the snow.

All three bullets had caught Dillman in the face, his signature mustache obliterated. The Texan spread-eagled on top of one of Jabari's snow angels, his arms outflung in a grotesque parody. Blood spurted onto the pristine white blanket as the man's heart pumped its final beats.

Two guards raised their rifles but knew better than to shoot Luciano. Prospero ripped the Glock out of his nephew's hand. Ayan and Jabari rushed over to the fallen man as frothy red spittle oozed out of his mouth. The Texan gurgled, a soft, mewling sound, and then went silent.

The gun felt cold in Prospero's hands.

Luciano's gaze held triumph.

An eerie silence fell, and they were all suddenly aware of the wind whipping through the courtyard. Ayan and Jabari's dark eyes filled with tears. They'd bonded with Mike Dillman, become friends. Now they had to deal with losing yet another adult who had been kind to them.

And Prospero was one hostage down. He turned on his nephew and smashed the gun across the younger man's face, sending him once again into the snow.

Chapter 50

Johann parked himself in his basement hideaway at school, wrestling with indecision. His fingers tapped on the battered desk. Time was running out: if he didn't act, thousands of innocent people would die horrific deaths. He had to find a way to stop his father from releasing the plague.

The local police weren't an option because of his father's connections, but maybe he could call Interpol. Then again, *Vater* probably had protectors there too. Johann just couldn't chance it. And he wasn't sure anyone would believe this insane story. What if whoever he told called Father, asking what nonsense his son was spouting?

His stomach twisted at the thought. It wasn't fear for himself. Father never went the obvious route with retribution. Instead, *Vater* targeted his opponents' weaknesses and exploited them. And Johann's Achilles' heel was Fatima.

During *Vater*'s conversation with Krimm, Johann had overheard them talking about Thea Paris, how she had been released from the hijacked plane and was now negotiating on behalf of the hostages. Maybe she already knew about the plan, if skyjacking the plane was part of it. He'd googled her, read articles about the company she worked for, dedicated to bringing hostages home around the world. She was completely outside his father's sphere.

And she had a tactical team at her disposal.

He clicked on the Quantum International Security website. Lots of data about kidnappings, a list of the ten hot spots in the world, lists of dos and don'ts for hostages. He studied a section on travel advisories, places Quantum recommended tourists avoid. At the moment: North Korea, Syria, Afghanistan, and Iraq, among other countries. That list was about to get a lot longer if he didn't do something.

He searched the site for photos of Thea but found none for any of the employees. That made sense. Hostage negotiators would want to keep a low profile so they could travel without being recognized or kidnapped themselves. He continued digging, finding as much information as he could on the kidnap expert.

Activating the burner phone he'd purchased, he considered what taking this next step meant. Father would likely go to jail. Johann would betray the one person who had always been there for him. He closed his eyes and remembered Omar Kaleb's horrific death, Uncle Karl's body. If he let Father move forward with his plan, many more would die. *I can't let that happen.*

Before he lost his nerve, he dialed the number for Quantum. A woman answered on the first ring. "Quantum International Security."

"May I speak to Thea Paris, please?" His voice shook a little.

"Sorry, she's not available. May I take a message?"

"I really need to speak to her. It's urgent."

"Please hold a moment."

Johann inhaled a deep breath. A man came on the line.

"Hakan Asker speaking, president of Quantum. How may I help?"

"I need to speak with Thea Paris. It's about the plane she was on, the one that was hijacked."

"Do you have information on the location of the passengers?"

"No," Johann said. "When will Thea be back?"

"Feel free to speak to me. I'm her boss."

"I only want to talk to her. I know who they were targeting on the skyjacked plane."

"Give me your number. I'll have her call as soon as she can."

"Can't you just connect me with her now?"

"Tell you what, phone again in a few hours, and I'll patch you through. May I tell her who will be calling?"

"Talk to you then." He pressed the end button, his finger trembling. Once he shared this information, there was no going back. His future would be forever changed.

Footsteps sounded in the hall. A soft knock. *Fatima.*

She entered with a sad smile on her face. Her gaze assessed the two phones sitting on the desk. "That man is still following me. How long do you think this will last?"

"Please sit."

She perched on the edge of a chair, like a frightened bird. He felt protective of her, stronger somehow. Something had already changed inside him since he'd made the decision to reach out to Thea Paris. And, like a monkey releasing his grip on one branch only after grasping another, his allegiance was shifting from *Vater* to Fatima.

"We need to talk," he told her. And talk they did. Johann shared the horrors of what he had experienced in the past few days—from Omar Kaleb's death to Uncle Karl's, the plan to release the plague, and his decision to call Thea Paris. Fatima listened with rapt attention, shock and terror crossing her face.

She grabbed his arm, a fierce look in her eyes. "You made the right decision—I want to help."

"It's too dangerous."

"You can't attempt this alone," she said.

"I'm going to steal the plague tonight, then take it to Thea Paris. If you don't hear from me, call Interpol and tell them what you know."

"Let me help. I have a cousin in Istanbul named Marush who is a biologist. We'll go there."

Having a backup plan was appealing. Still, he didn't want Fatima involved. "If anything happened to you, I'd never forgive myself."

"Marush will know what to do." She tried to reassure him.

"But if the container isn't properly sealed, you could die."

"And if you fail, I'll die anyway," she said. "From what you said, Leopold is a brilliant scientist. He must have ensured that the containers are safe for transport. He wouldn't want the plague released until he was ready. We'll do this together." She squeezed his hand.

"What about your parents?"

"I'll leave them a note, tell them I've gone to visit my aunt in Vienna."

"And when you don't show up?"

"That doesn't matter. If I don't try to stop this, we'll all be dead. I'm committed to this." Her face flushed.

"And if I don't do something, then I'm complicit, a murderer. So am I," he said.

Chapter 51

Even though he wasn't a superstitious man, Prospero couldn't shake the feeling that Michael Dillman's death was a harbinger of bad things to come. Used to staying one step ahead of his enemies, he had a sinking feeling that the greater threat might be within his own organization. Losing contact with Karl Wagner, his lifelong friend and key source inside Dietrich's group, had been a devastating blow.

The left side of his face a mass of cuts, his eye swollen shut, Luciano was confined to the villa under strict orders to stay away from the hostages. Prospero needed to de-escalate the situation, bring back a semblance of equilibrium. In the meantime, he'd have to keep a close eye on the live feed for any signs of insurrection.

None of the passengers had been allowed outdoors since the incident. Bassam's men had given the hostages more blankets and a space heater to stave off the cold. Ocean and the boys huddled in one corner, playing cards. The copilot, Laverdeen, seemed to have taken over Dillman's leadership role. Karlsson was curled up in a fetal position close to the heater, staring into the distance. Dillman's death had hit him hard.

Rivers sat cross-legged between Laverdeen and Matthias, his face coated in a sheen of sweat. Prospero hoped his shoulder wound hadn't become infected, but he wasn't willing to bring a doctor onto the property to have him examined just yet.

"Now that the psycho isn't around, we have a better chance of escape. I don't think they're going to let us go," Matthias said.

"They have my kids. I'm not going anywhere until I know they're okay," Rivers said.

"I studied the landscape while we were outside. We're in the middle of nowhere, and very few of us have warm clothes. Assuming we could escape, we'd die of hypothermia before we got very far."

"So we should just wait? For what?" Matthias adjusted his glasses.

"Thea Paris will negotiate our release," Laverdeen said.

"Your schoolboy crush is clouding your mind. She ditched us in Libya without a second thought," Rivers said.

"Says the pilot who hijacked his own plane. Did you miss the part where the mobster shut down the APU and forced her to come out?" Laverdeen's voice had an edge to it.

"What if one of us could get into the main house, use the phone to call for help?" Matthias asked.

"The kids have been there once already. Maybe they could go in again," Rivers said.

"Are we really going to ask the boys to take that kind of risk?" Laverdeen exhaled loudly. "If Luciano catches them, he'll shoot them. Look what happened to Dillman."

"Rivers is right. The boys want to make it to London as much as the rest of us," Matthias said, calling Ayan and Jabari over. "Maybe they'll help."

Prospero sat back in his chair and shook his head. Maybe he should make an example out of one of the ringleaders, settle the group down. But he'd have to be cautious. He didn't want them to know he had eyes and ears on them at all times.

Ayan and Jabari walked over to the men, visibly irritated at the interruption to their card game with Ocean.

"You guys okay?" Laverdeen asked.

"I guess." Jabari looked tired.

"I know all of this is overwhelming, but we could use your help. Did you by any chance see any phones inside the house?" Rivers placed a hand on Jabari's shoulder.

"The boss has one," Ayan said.

"A cell?"

"Yes."

"What were you guys doing in there, anyway?" Rivers asked.

"Eating." Ayan shrugged.

"Maybe tomorrow you can go for another visit. Prospero seems to like you," Matthias said.

"Do you know Thea's cell number?"

"Yeah. We phoned her every Sunday from the orphanage," Jabari said.

"Could one of you distract the boss while the other tries to call?" Rivers asked.

"If they get caught, they could get seriously hurt. We can't ask them to risk it," Laverdeen said.

"I'll do it," Ayan said.

Prospero admired the kid's spunk. He wished more of his men had the fire of this young boy.

Chapter 52

Johann tried forcing down small portions of the schnitzel, scalloped potatoes, and peas Chef Rudy had prepared, but mostly he just moved food around his plate. This could be the last meal he and his father would ever share. Once Johann revealed the *Freiheitswächter* plans to the authorities, his father would likely be going to jail for the rest of his life.

"You're not feeling unwell, are you?" Father asked, sipping from his wineglass. "I could call Dr. Kaufman."

Johann's grip on his fork tightened. "No, I'm fine."

"Well, just in case, stay home from school tomorrow. I'd like you by my side when the canisters are collected." Father dug into the schnitzel with gusto.

"I have a history test tomorrow . . ."

"I'll give you a note. We will be *making* history together. Europe is about to become a much safer place."

"Aren't you concerned about retaliation?"

"They can't fight back when they're dead."

"But what about the women and children?" Surely his father wouldn't want to hurt them.

"Son, when we have time, I'll show you films of suicide bombers in places like Fallujah and Mosul. The *fickfehlers* had women and kids sprawled on the road, pretending to be injured, luring soldiers close before they blew themselves up."

"I hate the terrorists too, but what about all the good people from the Middle East?"

"No such thing. Right this very minute, millions are being brainwashed in madrasas, preparing to fight jihad. And those who claim to be 'decent' are simply waiting to step in and help take over society when the jihad has been won. This is war, plain and simple." He refilled his wineglass.

Johann looked at his father with wonder. *He is a zealot, exactly like the Islamist extremists he hates.*

"May I be excused? I have homework."

"Of course. Are you sure you're feeling okay?"

"I'll be fine." He hesitated before leaving the dining room. "I love you, *Vater*." It was true, no matter what.

His father paused. "I love you, too, Johann. You know I'm doing all of this so you—and your children—will be safe, right?" Conviction resonated in every word.

"Yes. Thank you, *Vater*. Sleep well."

Hours passed. Johann had spent the time researching and preparing and then gone to bed, tossing and turning, waiting for his father to go to sleep. Under the covers, Johann wore a dark hooded sweatshirt and jeans, and he had two backpacks sitting beside his bedroom door. The canisters Leopold had shown him should easily fit inside.

Finally, he heard movement on the stairs at 2:38 a.m. Johann could tell by the heavy, plodding footsteps that Father had consumed a lot of wine. Hopefully he'd be out cold for the rest of the night. Waiting for yet another hour to pass was painful, the seconds ticking by slowly, but he forced himself to wait before he rushed downstairs, grabbed the canisters, and headed for the *Hauptbahnhof*.

He planned to meet Fatima at 5:00 a.m. so they could catch the first train to Budapest. From there, they would change trains and head for Istanbul. It would be a long trip, more than twenty-four hours, but he and Fatima had already come up with a schedule where only one of them would sleep at a time while the other person guarded the canisters.

He tiptoed around his bedroom, hiding his regular cell phone under his mattress with the power off. On this trip he would only use the burner phone he had purchased earlier. In his wallet were enough euros to get them there and back without ever having to use a credit card.

He planned to purchase three different train tickets to throw off the pursuit. And he and Fatima would speak to each other only after the train had left the station and was well underway. When *Vater* discovered that Johann and the canisters were missing, he'd have his men scour the city looking for him, searching camera footage at train stations and airports. If he was spotted on tape, Johann wanted his father to think he was acting alone so there would be no repercussions for Fatima or her family.

With both backpacks slung over his shoulder, he slipped on his sneakers and a baseball cap and quietly opened the door to his bedroom. He waited, listening. The soft sound of his father's snoring greeted him from down the hall. A faint hint of moonlight streamed through the windows, helping him navigate the stairs. He reached the ground floor and stopped to listen again. All quiet. He headed for the cellar.

At the bottom of the cellar stairs, he switched on the burner phone's flashlight. It was pitch-black down there, and he didn't want to bump into something and make noise. He worried that Leopold might make another midnight visit to the lab. Or that there was an alarm system he didn't know about.

He punched in the security code, the shelves slowly parting. The creaking of the hidden machinery sounded like a roaring ocean to his twitchy ears. He held his breath, hoping Father was deeply asleep. Slipping inside the tunnel, he rushed to the next set of doors, entering the code again with a shaky finger.

A slight humming noise greeted him, coming from the machines that maintained the pressurization of the lab. With the whoosh of the vacuum doors, he entered the hot zone. Every instinct told him to bolt, but the memories of Omar Kaleb's dramatic death spurred him on. What Johann planned to do was personally dangerous, but the alternative—leaving the plague in his father's hands—was unthinkable.

With uncertain fingers, he opened the fridge. An icy mist drifted into his face. He opened the first backpack and slipped one canister inside. Then he placed the other canister inside the second backpack, nestled beside a change of clothes and a toothbrush. Securing the fastenings on both bags, he slipped them over his right shoulder.

After retracing his steps and closing the lab and secret entrance behind him, Johann went out the west wing of the house so he could leave through the greenhouse. He had stashed his mountain bike by the outside door so he could leave unseen by the tree-lined paths that led to the nearby woods. Gently resting the backpacks on the ground so he could check that the yard was deserted, he turned to lock the door and noticed a red light flashing on a panel by the door.

Scheisse! He had forgotten to disarm the house alarm before he entered the greenhouse. He punched in the code quickly, hoping the security company would think it was a false alarm. Scooping up the backpacks, he locked the greenhouse door, grabbed his bike, and headed for the woods.

Chapter 53

The cold night air left Johann's face numb and his breath ragged as his legs pumped hard, the only sound the whir of the tire treads against the road. He'd installed a headlight on the handlebars so he could take the bike out for night rides, but he never imagined he'd be making a journey like this one.

Arriving at the *Hauptbahnhof*, he locked the bike to one of the racks. It was an automatic impulse, as his father would punish him if it were stolen. He shook his head and almost laughed at the ridiculousness of it. Making sure his bike was properly secured was the least of his problems.

The station was quiet, only a few commuters waiting for the first train of the day. It was too early for the information center to be open, but employees were already arriving at the fast-food restaurants, preparing for another hectic day at the busy transportation hub.

Built in 1860, the station had been severely damaged during the Second World War. Father had told him it'd taken decades for city officials and residents to figure out how to redevelop it. Now a large square greeted travelers, and underground platforms had been added for local trains. Over time, capitalism had arrived in force in Salzburg, and now the station was surrounded by temples of commerce: gleaming office buildings, shopping malls, and restaurants.

A homeless man, a couple of teenage punk rockers, and a few broken-down drunks loitered around the station. Johann avoided them all and headed inside to the ticket office. His baseball cap was pulled low over his eyes and his sweatshirt hood over that; he hoped not to be recognizable on any CCTV footage. He purchased tickets for Berlin, Budapest, and Rome.

In Budapest, he would buy the ticket for Istanbul. Maybe he was being overly cautious, but he didn't think so; *Vater* was very resourceful and obsessed with his plan of extermination, so he'd stop at nothing to find the canisters once he realized they were missing.

Johann scanned the station, looking for Fatima. No sign of her. Could she have changed her mind? He wouldn't blame her, but disappointment stole into his heart. Maybe she hadn't been able to sneak out of her house. She had three sisters and shared a room with one, so that could make it complicated for her. Or maybe *Vater*'s man was still watching her?

He walked to the escalators and headed to the tracks upstairs, still searching, hopeful. The large board listing departures and arrivals showed only fifteen minutes before their train left.

A familiar figure walking toward him in the distance sent him into a cold sweat. *Falco, who'd been inside the chamber when Omar Kaleb died. Could he know that I'm here?*

Johann averted his gaze and walked steadily until he reached a nearby pillar, slipping behind it. Becoming invisible was his specialty, a skill he'd honed at school. After a few seconds, he chanced a look around the pillar. Falco was walking down the platform, far away now, obviously headed for another train. Johann let out a deep breath. *Close call.*

A light in the distance jangled his nerves. Their train. If Fatima didn't arrive in the next few minutes, he'd be making this cross-country journey alone. The train's headlight grew larger and more blinding until the front of the train passed. The red-and-white cars zoomed into the station, the screech of the brakes the loudest sound he had ever heard. The doors opened with a hydraulic hiss.

A small figure dressed in all black, including a head scarf, emerged from the shadows at the other end of the platform and scurried onto the train. He immediately recognized Fatima. *She came.*

He stepped on board, hopeful for the first time. Maybe they would stop this horrifying disaster after all. Fatima's cousin Marush sounded like someone who'd know how to dispose of the bioweapon. Or maybe Thea Paris could help. He had been too afraid to call Quantum back from inside his house. Just knowing his father was nearby made everything seem more real. He'd try Thea again from the train.

Johann adjusted the backpacks on his shoulder and found a seat. The whistle blew, and the train pulled away from the station.

Chapter 54

Prospero showered and shaved, preparing to face the day. After Mike Dillman's death, he was worried about morale among the passengers. Once the first hostage died, anxiety set in: who would be next? But it certainly hadn't robbed the two boys of any spunk. Last night, the cookie bandits had suggested a visit to the main house, but he'd declined.

Luciano was in the kitchen, surrounded by a cloud of smoke.

"Those cigarettes will kill you—if I don't first."

"Mustache Man had it coming, m-making fun of me." Luciano gulped his *caffè*.

His nephew's stutter had been a difficult cross for the young man to bear, but it was still no excuse for his violent outbursts.

"Control your temper. We need those hostages alive."

"One won't be missed," Luciano said.

Prospero leaned closer to his nephew, speaking with intensity. "Anything could have happened when that gun went off. You could have killed the boys—or our target. Don't let it happen again." He slipped on a down jacket and a knit cap.

"I didn't start the whole mess."

Everything is always someone else's fault with this one. "How did it go last night?" Luciano had been assigned the overnight shift of watching the live feed.

His nephew shrugged. "Boring. They slept."

"You stay here. I'll check on them this morning." Luciano couldn't be allowed near the boys without supervision.

More snow had fallen overnight, and the wind had picked up, creating swirling white drifts around the property. The cold prickled his skin. Bassam nodded a good morning.

"Little chillier here than in Libya," Prospero said, smiling.

"The conditions don't bother me." Bassam had a camouflage scarf wrapped around his face.

He should think not, considering the massive sum he'd given him and his men for this operation. Bassam directed the guard posted at the outbuilding to open the door. Prospero entered the building, finding the passengers gathered near the space heater. The sound of the shower running this early surprised him. It was a little chilly to get wet, especially since the water probably wasn't even hot yet.

Laverdeen strode over to him. "We're freezing our asses off in here. Can we get another heater?"

"I'll see what I can do." He couldn't blame them for complaining. After the snow, it was damn cold. Prospero scanned the shed for Ayan and Jabari. *Must be in the shower.*

"Can I talk to my kids?" Rivers asked.

"Maybe later," he said, distracted.

Matthias was leading what looked to be a yoga class, most of the participants in a lunging pose, arms pointed into the air. Smart: it was easier to stay warm if you kept moving. Unlike Karlsson, shivering in a corner, looking completely detached.

Wait a minute. He couldn't spot Ocean either. Could she be helping the boys? He strode to the bathroom door and pushed it open. Only the sound of water splashing greeted him. No sign of anyone. He yanked the shower curtain aside. The stall was empty, the water running with no one inside.

Che diavolo?

He hurried into the small rear storage room. A few area rugs littered the floor. A broken lamp rested on a wooden table. When they'd first arrived, Luciano had nailed down Aslan's doggy door, closing it off. But now it was hanging by its hinges, having been ripped back open.

He lifted the flap and studied the hole. Maybe large enough for the boys and Ocean, given her slender frame. None of the other adults would be able to squeeze through the small opening.

Returning to the main area, he pulled his Glock from its resting place at the back of his pants. Silence filled the room. Prospero strode to Rivers, wrapped his fingers around the captain's throat, and shoved him against the wall. With the barrel pressed against the man's temple, Prospero leaned close. "You have ten seconds to tell me everything. If you leave out even one detail, I will have your daughters killed immediately."

"I had nothing to do with it! I told them not to."

"Just answer the question." Prospero jammed the barrel into Rivers's skin. "When did they leave?"

"Hours ago, in the dark." The captain's eyes bulged, his breath raspy.

"What's the plan?"

"Find another house, call for help."

"There are no homes nearby." They'd chosen Aslan's house for its remote location and the rugged terrain surrounding it. "Who came up with the plan?"

"It was Ocean's idea."

I'm sure it was.

The boys, his leverage over Thea; Ocean, his target.

Gone.

Chapter 55

Anger and anxiety warred for dominance in Prospero's mind. He forced himself to think logically. Even if Ocean and the boys had escaped six hours ago, they couldn't have traveled very far on foot. And the challenging terrain and deep snow would slow them down. Actually, his greatest fear was not that they'd get away but that they'd freeze to death on the mountain before they could be found. The boys were his ticket to securing that truck—and Ocean must be kept from reuniting with the Freedom Guardians.

"Anyone else have information?" He kept the barrel buried in the flesh of Rivers's temple as he turned to face the others.

Laverdeen spoke up. "After Luciano killed Dillman, they figured the same thing would happen to them."

"They were in no danger."

"How could they know that? They were probably more terrified of that psycho than of what might happen to them in the wilderness," Laverdeen said.

"You'd better hope they don't die out there." Prospero swept his gaze over them all, then turned to Bassam. "Go search for tracks."

As Prospero tucked the Glock back into the waistband of his pants, he thought of the food Ayan and Jabari had pilfered from the house—and how they'd asked for boots and coats. *They were planning this escape from the beginning, working me the entire time.* A hot flush ran through his body. He wouldn't underestimate them again.

"They used a metal sheet they found like a toboggan." Matthias pointed out the window toward a pile of construction materials, obviously trying to curry favor with him by providing information on the escape.

Gutsy. They'd make better time sliding down the mountain instead of walking, but they'd taken a hell of a risk doing it in the dark. He might find them unconscious or dead at the foot of a tree or boulder.

He glanced at one of Bassam's men. "No food for anyone today. Only water."

Unhappy faces stared back at him, but no one said a word. Maybe they'd think twice about letting anyone else leave.

He shoved past the passengers and stormed out of the shed. A white mist blew into his face, icy blades prickling his skin. Snow still tumbled down in large fluffy flakes. His hip hurt like a son of a bitch. *Damn, I hate winter.*

Bassam sprinted toward him. "The wind and fresh snow have covered their tracks. I can't tell which way they went."

Prospero joined him in scouting the yard, searching for evidence of their departure, but the snow had obliterated any sign of the three escapees.

"You ever driven a snowmobile?" Prospero asked.

Bassam shook his head.

"Of course not," Prospero sighed. "It's easy enough. Have your men secure the doggy door in the back room and tell them to do a head count every hour." He wasn't taking any more chances. "Back in a minute."

He burst through the front door and went straight to the kitchen. Luciano was busy wolfing down bacon and eggs.

Prospero cuffed his head hard from behind, sending food and utensils flying across the counter.

"Hey—"

"*Sei uno stronzo.* I give you one job, you lazy fuck, and you can't even do it."

His nephew oozed insolence. Prospero was tempted to beat it out of him.

"W-w-what the hell is the matter with you?"

"The boys and our target escaped is what's the matter with me. And they did it while you were supposed to be monitoring the live feed."

"It w-was dark. I didn't see anyone leave."

"Shut up. I know you weren't watching."

"We'll find them."

"Damn right, we will. Get your coat and boots. We're leaving now."

"What's so special about that woman anyways?"

"Keeping her here under our guard could help prevent a nuclear holocaust. That special enough of a reason for you?"

As he stood up, his nephew shoved a piece of toast into his mouth. "W-w-wait till we find those kids."

"You won't lay one finger on the boys. Your temper is what got us into this situation."

"But—"

"Not. Another. Fucking. Word."

Prospero hurried to his room and pulled out a scarf, down gloves, and a pair of goggles. After filling a canteen with water and grabbing a few protein bars from the kitchen on his way out, he joined Bassam near two snowmobiles. Canary yellow and white, the sleek machines both had full tanks of fuel. He fired one up, the throaty engine roaring to life.

He pointed to the controls. "Just steer and ease the throttle with the grip to speed up or slow down, but always be ready with the brake. The mountain is steep, and these machines are fast."

"You want me to follow you?" Bassam asked.

"Better to split up so we can cover more ground. Head down the west side of the mountain and look for any tracks. We'll go down the east side. Stay in touch via satphone."

Bassam climbed onto the first snowmobile and eased the throttle open, making a slow circle around the outbuilding, testing out the machine. Several of the hostages had their faces pressed against the window.

Luciano rushed outside, fastening his coat. He slipped behind his uncle on the second machine. At least that way Prospero wouldn't have to look at the idiot.

Bassam parked beside him, his engine running. "Okay, I have the hang of it."

"Head that way." Prospero pointed westbound. "And watch the steep inclines."

"Got it." Bassam goosed the engine and zoomed down the mountain.

Prospero turned to Luciano. "Keep your eyes open for tracks."

With a quick nod to Bassam's men posted outside, Prospero threaded through the alley between the villa and the outbuilding.

As they headed down the cliffside, he scanned the cascade of white snow blanketing the area. Three jagged peaks stood together in the distance. The view would be spectacular under any other circumstances. His eyes watered even underneath the goggles. It was bitterly cold—he needed to find the escapees before they succumbed to hypothermia.

His satphone vibrated against his chest. Maybe Bassam had found something? He pressed the brakes and parked sideways so the snowmobile wouldn't slide down the mountain. He reached inside his jacket to grab the phone.

He glanced at the call display.

Not Bassam. *Liberata*.

Chapter 56

Prospero killed the engine and shoved Luciano off the back. He stomped through the drifts around the snowmobile to get away from his nephew, his mind working overtime. He took a deep breath and picked up. "You have the truck?"

"We're closing in on it. But I want to see the boys first."

"The live feed isn't working," Prospero said.

Luciano wandered over to a nearby group of trees to take a piss.

"Put them on the phone. I need to know they're okay," she said.

"I'm not with them right now."

"Patch me through to your men. They can connect me."

"Have you forgotten who's in charge? Do the job; then you get the kids back."

"Then let me speak to Laverdeen or Dillman."

The Texan wouldn't be talking to anyone ever again. "So you can work them for information?"

"You need to give to get."

"Send me proof you have located the truck, and you can speak to the boys." He should have them back soon.

Another call was coming in. Bassam. *Maybe he'd found Ocean and the kids.*

"Ayan and Jabari matter to me—if I can't see them or talk to them, you get nothing," Thea said.

"Don't worry, they're flying high on sugar from eating their body weight in cookies." True enough—they'd stolen the entire plate. "Get the job done, and then we'll talk about the exchange." He pressed the button to end his conversation with Thea and accepted Bassam's call. "Tell me you have them."

"I found fresh tracks. The GPS coordinates are coming via text. I'm following them." The growl of Bassam's snowmobile's engine over the phone made it difficult to hear him.

"We're coming now." Prospero glanced at the coordinates as Luciano returned to the snowmobile. "Bassam found something. Let's go."

He cranked the engine to life, the throaty yowl echoing across the mountainside. As soon as he felt Luciano get on behind him, he goosed the throttle. The whole mission would fall apart if he didn't get the three runaways back.

Chapter 57

The snowmobile blasted through fresh powder, spraying an icy trail in their wake. Bassam had found the runaways' tracks, and Prospero wanted to be there when they were recaptured. He'd let down his guard and been hoodwinked by the kids, but they'd be under lock and key from here on in. He should have known the former child soldiers wouldn't relinquish their freedom so easily. Still, he admired the boys for being so cunning—securing food, clothing, and a partner in crime to aid in their escape.

Prospero crested the peak, gunning the powerful machine. A ray of bright sunshine burst through the thick cloud cover, turning a portion of the snowy slopes into a glimmering expanse. Bassam was bulleting across the mountain below them.

Descending, Prospero focused on keeping the snowmobile upright in the fresh powder, leaning right or left as needed, Luciano following his lead. Bassam's snowmobile disappeared into the trees for a moment, then accelerated along an open stretch of mountainside.

His gaze scanned the ridge, but he didn't see any sign of life other than Bassam.

Prospero blinked, then looked again. *What the hell?* The Libyan was torpedoing toward a pile of branches, but the thick brush actually masked a massive drop off the side of the mountain. He slowed the snowmobile and reached for his phone. He dialed Bassam's number. It rang and rang, but the man didn't answer. Instead, his snowmobile jetted toward the cliff while Prospero watched, powerless to stop him.

Seconds later, Bassam must have realized he was in trouble and slammed on the brakes. His snowmobile fishtailed left, then right, but he had too much momentum. The world slowed, the events unfolding in what felt like slow motion. The machine crashed into the fallen branches and catapulted off the mountain, flipping once and throwing the screaming passenger off before both hurtled into the snow-covered trees far below.

Luciano's grip around his waist tightened like a boa constrictor. Prospero threaded through the trees, cautiously motoring down to the area where Bassam had hurtled off the mountain. As he closed the distance, realization dawned. Small boot prints—the size of Ocean's feet or the boys'—led straight to where the branches had been.

A trap. And Bassam, out of his element in these mountains, hadn't realized until it was too late.

Prospero spotted a hint of movement about three hundred feet below, something nestled deep in a patch of forest. He studied the area, then saw it again. A flash of red. Ayan's down jacket. They were closing in on the escapees.

Chapter 58

By pairing her phone with the one carried by Prospero's man in St. Stephen's, Thea had managed to capture a recording of the live feed of the prisoners. The Italian had been careful not to include any outside views, as terrain could be an indicator of locale. Still, the smallest details could tell a story if you knew what to look for.

She studied the video again and again, freezing each frame. The black arrow painted on the floor was undoubtedly there to show the direction of Mecca. Coupling that with the delicate ceramics collecting dust in a corner and the design of a small carpet, she surmised the hideaway was likely somewhere in Turkey, which made sense, since that was where they were supposed to deliver the captured truck. Of course, it was a big country.

Rif was cleaning the weapons before the mission when Thea interrupted. "Any idea which region in Turkey this could be?"

"You've got to be kidding." He shook his head. "But Hakan has the analysts searching for any links Prospero might have there—friends, businesses, property. Let's hope he gets a hit." Hakan was a genius at this sort of thing, and his impressive skills had helped them locate countless hostages over the years.

Everyone left a fingerprint on the web, even if they tried not to. She often counseled Quantum clients to avoid posting their current location and travel plans on social media. Today's kidnappers stalked potential victims online, and being told where and when they could find you made the abduction a whole lot easier.

"Ayan and Jabari are quite capable. They'll sit tight until we can find them," Rif said.

"Stop trying to cheer me up. You know they're going to cause havoc every chance they get. It's who they are."

He smiled with genuine affection. "Yeah, especially Ayan."

"Prospero is going to have his hands full, and he's not the most patient man." Deep down, Thea knew that he was unlikely to hurt the boys, but that was little comfort when she couldn't lay eyes on them. And she wondered how Laverdeen, Dillman, and the other hostages were faring.

"Did you see the medical report on the passengers?" Rif looked up from the M4 he was reassembling.

"Two require meds: Matthias takes digoxin for his heart, Karlsson takes risperidone, a second-generation antipsychotic, for schizophrenia." At least one out of ten people needed some kind of regular medication. And kidnappers often were forced to procure it—not out of compassion, but to keep the "commodity" alive and well. And medications could be traced.

"Think Prospero will take care of them?"

"One would hope—but he may not have access to the medications if he's in a remote area. And he might just not care."

Thea's phone beeped. Hakan, with more research on the passengers. "Ocean," she said to Rif after the call.

"The woman with one name."

"That's what made identifying her a challenge. But Hakan came through," she said.

"And?"

"She might be the target." Thea was lost in thought for a moment. "Her birth name was Akira Nakamura. She legally changed it two years ago."

"It's not a crime to change your name."

"Of course not," Thea said, shaking her head. "You remember when Jihadi John beheaded Haruna Yukawa and Kenji Goto?"

Thea had been in Syria working another case when that had happened. Yukawa had been a failed Japanese businessman who'd tried to reinvent himself as a private military contractor in Syria. After he'd been kidnapped by ISIS, Kenji Goto, a freelance journalist, had headed to the Middle East on a quest to free Yukawa, but he ended up being captured and then beheaded alongside the man he'd tried to find.

"How could I forget it?" Rif was loading 5.56x45mm NATO rounds into a spare magazine.

A lot of people blamed kidnapping victims for their predicaments: *she shouldn't have been volunteering in such a dangerous region; why were they hiking in such a remote place?; he knew the risks, working in Iraq.* But these people—employees of NGOs, adventurous travelers, ambitious expats, dedicated missionaries—didn't *want* to be kidnapped. They just happened to be in the wrong place at the wrong time and ran into the wrong people.

And this was exactly what had happened with Yukawa and Goto. During the ransom negotiations, many Japanese people had felt that the government owed the two men nothing—certainly not the two-hundred-million-dollar ransom. Japan had withdrawn all its diplomats from Syria by March 2012 as the civil war was escalating, and the government had issued a travel warning. If Yukawa and Goto decided to ignore the caution, the thinking went, then they were responsible for their fates. While the hostages' families were trying to mourn the brutal slayings of their loved ones, widespread censure only added to their devastation.

"There's a connection."

"Are you saying Ocean knew one or both of the men?" Rif asked.

"No, but she went through the same thing. Three years ago, her father was captured by ISIS in Syria during a peacekeeping mission."

"Orange?" The color of the infamous jumpsuits used in the snuff videos made by the terrorist group.

Thea nodded. "Humiliated, tortured, then beheaded on video. Ocean's mother couldn't face the harsh criticism from the press and social media. She took her own life."

"Leaving Ocean an orphan," Rif mused. "No wonder she bonded with the boys." He slid the full magazines and a couple of grenades into the TacVests.

"There's more," she said. "Ocean was one of the top nuclear engineers at the Sendai plant before she left Japan two years ago. Apparently she left the industry altogether and went to work for a pharmaceutical lab in Johannesburg."

"Wait, pharma? I thought she was a nuclear scientist."

"She seems to have an advanced degree in bioengineering too."

"You think that's why she's the target?"

"Maybe. The only thing I'm sure of—we don't have a full picture of what's going on. Why would a Sicilian gangster risk hijacking an international flight? What does he want with a truck full of Syrian refugees? And what is the connection, if any, to this Japanese national who happens to be a nuclear engineer?" Thea ran a hand through her hair.

"The truck we're hunting might give us answers."

"Or create more questions." The lives of the hostages, including Ayan and Jabari, rested on them answering those questions. Those boys were her last connection to Nikos—getting them back was her first priority, not only for their sake but for her own.

Thea had taken a leave of absence from Quantum after Nikos vanished in the Zambezi River, to assist in the search for his body. After four weeks of scouring the river and surrounding areas, the effort had finally been called off, her brother's body never found. The local experts gently explained that the plethora of crocodiles in the river could be the reason why.

Exhausted mentally and physically from the grueling recovery operation, her phone battery drained, she'd headed straight to Kanzi and the orphanage, a place Nikos considered home. She owed it to the boys to tell them about her brother in person, which she dreaded. Ayan and Jabari had already lost their parents and so many others.

The midday sun scorched the red dirt, the earth's minerals sparkling like tiny diamonds. Sweaty and slightly sick to her stomach, Thea arrived to find the Kuria boys lined up with the other children for vaccinations.

"Thea!" Jabari left the queue to hug her, his wiry arms squeezing her tightly.

Ayan stayed in place, a big smile on his face. "Needle day." As if that explained it all.

She went over to the little guy and gave him a big hug too.

"Last I remember, needles weren't all that much fun." Her hands trembled, her heart beating faster than usual. She attributed it to the particularly hot day.

"We get chocolate if we let them poke us."

She laughed, feeling a little light-headed. "That explains why you wouldn't get out of the line."

"I asked if I could have two needles and two chocolates, but they said no." Ayan looked slightly disappointed.

"Someone has a sweet tooth." Both brothers nodded at this. "Listen, I need to talk to you guys. Maybe after the needles we can go for a walk?"

"Is Nikos coming?" Jabari asked.

"Just us . . ." Her vision blurred slightly.

"Are you okay? You look all white." Jabari stepped closer.

The world started spinning. She flung an arm out, reaching for support that wasn't there, and crumpled to her knees.

"Thea, are you okay?" Jabari's voice sounded distant.

Her mouth moved, but no words came out.

"Orange juice," the older boy commanded Ayan.

She shook her head, trying to gather her thoughts, but her head was muddled and too damn heavy. Movement to her right had her lifting her blurred gaze. Ayan was running toward the canteen. Seconds passed, feeling like centuries.

A figure stood off in the distance, familiar somehow. She squinted. Nikos. No, she was imagining things. Nikos was dead.

A cup was thrust toward her. Ayan and Jabari helped her sip the orange juice, encouraging her to drink more. Their voices were soothing, kind.

Slowly, the world came back into focus, steadied. Her hands stopped trembling, and her mind sharpened. She was almost human again.

She reached into her pants pocket, pulled out her phone, then remembered that the batteries were drained. That's why her Dexcom alarm hadn't sounded, alerting her that her blood sugar was running low. The toll of the search coupled with her anxiety about having to tell the boys about Nikos had made her less meticulous about monitoring her diabetes.

"How did you know?" She had always kept her disease a secret, only confiding in her immediate family, Rif, Hakan, and the Quantum team. But she'd never told the boys.

"Know what?" Ayan asked.

"The juice."

"Nikos told us that if you ever acted weird to give you orange juice. He didn't say why, but he made us promise."

Her brother, so damaged, had had the forethought to protect her even in his absence. Her eyes filled.

"Thank you both. I have a medical condition, and the juice helps." The queue had moved along, Ayan losing his spot. "I owe you both some chocolate."

"It doesn't matter." Ayan gave her a hug.

She touched her head to his, hoping another sip of orange juice would help her reclaim the use of her tongue. Recovery from a low was damned slow, but she had to do this now. "I need to tell you something. Nikos . . . he's gone."

"Gone where?" Jabari asked.

"We lost him in a river. He's with the angels now."

"He's dead?" Jabari's voice sharpened. These kids had witnessed far too much loss in their short lives to be satisfied with euphemisms.

"Yes."

"No." Ayan placed his hands on his hips.

"I'm sorry, Ayan."

"No, he's not dead. I can feel it here when someone is gone." He touched the left side of his chest.

Thea had known it would be difficult news for the boys to accept—they had been so close to Nikos—but the look in Ayan's eyes left her gutted.

Chapter 59

Rif studied the detailed map of Budapest on the large screen in their makeshift war room. Thea, Johansson, Jean-Luc, Brown, Neil, and Stewart gathered around the conference table. Shortly, they'd all be diverging to their assigned locales. The city covered 203 square miles, occupying both sides of the Danube since Buda merged with Pest back in 1873. Almost three million people lived in the city. And their target was one lone vehicle.

"Remember, eight main roads lead into Budapest, four of them motorways," Rif said, pointing them out.

"The truck is coming from the east?" Stewart asked.

"Likely, but we need to cover all the routes."

"It would be ideal to locate the target before it reaches the M0, the orbital motorway around Budapest." Thea sipped from her water bottle.

"Do we know its final destination?" Johansson asked.

"According to Prospero, it's the Parliament Building. And the drivers are armed and dangerous. We must stop the truck before it gets there . . . at any cost," Thea said.

A look went around the room—a target like that suggested a bombing. And hijacking a truck with a bomb on it would not be easy.

"I'll be in the plane above the city," Rif said, breaking the silence. "And Hakan has someone working on hacking into the local traffic cams."

"A truck full of refugees. Illegal?" Stewart asked.

"Probably. Intel says they'll be hidden behind cargo." Rif tapped his fingers on the table. "But the refugees aren't the identified target, just the truck."

"Prospero will definitely have another team working on this, hedging his bets. We need to find that truck before they do, so we have leverage to bring the hostages home alive." Thea sounded calm, but the taut lines around her mouth suggested otherwise.

"The vehicles ready?" Brown asked.

"Yup. Two motorcycles, an Audi S8—you don't want to know how much that cost to rent—a borrowed garbage truck, panel vans, and an aerobatic plane. We have it covered," Thea said.

The motorcycles would allow them access to alleys and short-cuts once they found the truck. The larger vehicles would be useful for blocking streets or forcing the target off the road. All the vehicles had e-vignettes for the toll roads.

"The refugees on the truck will likely be frightened of being discovered," Brown said.

"They'll also be terrified of us—from their perspective, we could just be a gang of thugs," Johansson added.

"Neil and Stewart will take them to safety once we neutralize the driver and guards," Rif said. "They both speak Arabic and will be able to explain what's happening and hopefully reassure them enough to get them in the vans without making a fuss."

Rif's phone pinged. "Time to go." He strode to his duffel and distributed the weapons he'd brought: M4s, MP5s, Glocks, and grenades. "Remember, we can't afford to engage with local law enforcement, so stay below the radar."

"Where's the fun in that?" Brown said with a half smile as he secreted a Glock and two grenades in his vest, probably thinking about the concealed surprises he and Johansson had left at strategic points along the shore of the Danube.

"*Sacre bleu*," Jean-Luc said, speaking for the first time.

Brown burst into laughter.

The situation was far from ideal, and they were on the wrong side of the hijacking, but no one called Quantum for the easy jobs.

Chapter 60

Prospero closed the distance to the spot where Bassam had catapulted off the mountainside. Easing the throttle back, he brought the snowmobile to a full stop. Luciano jumped off the back and sprinted toward the cliff. Prospero followed, the cold wind stinging his exposed skin. He stood beside Luciano, peering over the edge. Bassam rested in the canyon far below, his neck twisted at a fatal angle, a pool of red staining the white blanket covering the rocks. The snowmobile was in pieces.

"*Sfigato*," Luciano spat.

Heavy, wet snowflakes landed on Prospero's eyelashes. He wiped them off and scanned the nearby forest where he'd first caught a glimpse of Ayan's red coat. Pointing his gun into the air, he fired one shot.

"Come out now, and no one gets hurt." His deep voice echoed around the valley. "You'll freeze to death out here."

He waited thirty seconds, a minute. Nothing. The cold air stung his eyes, making them water.

"Drive the snowmobile to the other side of the trees in case they try to escape that way. I'm going in on foot."

"Give me my gun," Luciano demanded.

"You'll be fine without it. They can't cover ground quickly in this snow." He'd confiscated Luciano's SIG Sauer after Dillman's death.

"The little one bit me."

"Get a grip." They were tough and wily, but they were still just kids. And Ocean probably weighed fifty kilos soaking wet. Prospero stomped through the snow, headed for the forest.

Luciano started the snowmobile and looped around the perimeter of the wood—the pines were bunched too closely together for the snowmobile to navigate through them. The howling engine faded to a soft background buzz as his nephew circled the woodland.

Approaching the forest, Prospero was impressed that the escapees had made it this far. That impromptu toboggan had worked well for them. His gaze scoured the trees, the Glock in his right hand. The morning light faded as the foliage thickened. In here, their footsteps were plainly visible, protected from the wind. Farther on, he spotted a few sprigs of a cherry laurel that had been broken, and cookie crumbs peppered the ground—he was on the right track. His stomach growled at the thought of real food. The *hamsi* stew and cabbage soup Aslan's cook had prepared was sitting on the stove, waiting for his return.

A sound. The soft whispering of bushes.

He had them cornered. Stepping forward, he raised the Glock, careful to move without disturbing any foliage. A swishing sound. His gaze darted to the right.

A wild goat bulleted through the forest as if it was being chased by the devil himself. *Porca miseria.*

To the right, a flash of red caught his eye. He darted forward through the trees, bending low. It had to be Ayan's jacket—that shade of crimson didn't exist in nature. He quickened his pace. Almost there. He lunged forward, hip screaming.

Then stopped dead in his tracks.

The escapees had ripped off a piece of the jacket and secured it to a branch, the wind causing it to flutter. He studied the tracks surrounding the tree. Footprints led in every direction, making it impossible to know which way they'd headed. They'd likely walked out, then stepped backward in the tracks to return to the tree, then repeated the process. *Smart little fuckers.* He'd have to follow one track, then another and another, to narrow down which way they'd actually gone.

He called Luciano's satphone.

"You have them, boss?"

"Not yet. Any tracks on that side of the forest?"

A moment's hesitation. "Hard to tell. The wind's really come up, and it's blowing snow all over the place."

"Drive around the wooded area, and look for any sign of them. Meanwhile, I'll search in here."

He ended the call and studied the footprints, deciding which set to try first.

Chapter 61

Rif sat inside a Czech Aero L-39 Albatros, wheeling down the runway, almost ready for takeoff. Because he would need speed and agility, and because he didn't know how long he'd have to be in the air, a helicopter and its small fuel supply wouldn't cut it. After they'd left the hotel, everyone dispersed to their assigned locations via motorcycle, car, panel vans, and garbage truck while he prepared to search for the target from above.

He'd been lucky to find such a fast and agile plane on short notice. The former fighter jet was painted in the Soviet air force colors—a camouflage scheme with bright yellow bands on the tip tanks and the back of the fin. The training jet had probably been purchased after the collapse of the Soviet Union, as the financially struggling country's stockpile of L-39's was offered at a fraction of their original multimillion-dollar price tags. Still cost a pretty penny to lease one for the day. *Wait until Hakan sees the expense report.*

The Albatros had a castering nosewheel. To steer the L-39 on the ground, all he had to do was squeeze a motorcycle-style brake grip on the control stick and position the rudder pedals to direct differential brake pressure to the main wheels. Reliable and sturdy, the L-39 could reach airspeeds of five hundred miles an hour. Best of all, his large frame wasn't cramped inside the roomy front cockpit of the dual-control, tandem plane. He sat in the front seat, the rear seat empty.

The metric hardware and nitrogen took a little getting used to, but he'd flown an L-39 three years ago in the Ukraine, so it didn't take long to reorient himself. He planned on maintaining a low altitude during the search for the truck—the L-39 offered nine thousand feet of cabin pressurization differential, so he wouldn't need to use the oxygen mask below eighteen thousand feet. He'd have a couple of hours of fuel as long as he kept his speed under control.

He pressed the CommRadio, contacting air traffic control to secure permission for takeoff. Selecting flaps takeoff, he slipped the speed brakes into forward, trims neutral.

Full throttle. The jet accelerated down the runway and glided into the air. He banked hard to compensate for the high speed.

The cool air allowed him to climb 4,500 feet per minute, so he reached 11,000 feet in no time at all. Re-familiarizing himself with the aerobatic plane, he did a few barrel rolls, loops, and a Cuban Eight before settling into surveillance mode. The g-forces made him feel alive, adrenalized. Nothing compared to this feeling. He smiled, remembering the scene featuring the L-39 in *Tomorrow Never Dies*. Sadly, the weapons systems on his plane were inoperable, so he wasn't quite in 007 mode.

He contacted Thea via satphone. She picked up on the first ring, earbuds already in. "Nice moves up there." Her tone was clipped, focused.

"Thought you might enjoy a little show. Once the boys and the other hostages are safely home, I'll take you for a ride."

"As if," she deadpanned. "Be careful up there."

"As long as I keep my hands off the red handles in the center, it should be fine."

"Red handles?"

"The ejection seat controls." He regretted mentioning it immediately. Given that Thea wasn't keen on flying at the best of times, she wouldn't want to even contemplate bailing from the jet in mid-flight. "I'm scanning for the truck on the westbound roads into town; then I'll search clockwise."

"The team's in place. Hakan's monitoring the cameras."

There hadn't been time to go through normal diplomatic channels, so three tech specialists from Quantum had hacked into the CCTV system monitoring the highways and were searching for GMC trucks on any and all routes into the city.

"City looks gorgeous from up here." Every time he flew, he marveled at the beauty of the earth from above. And this time was no exception, as his gaze swept over the Danube, the historical buildings, and the grassy plains below.

"It'll be plenty interesting down here. Life comes at you fast on a bike."

She was riding his favorite BMW motorcycle, the R1200GS. He'd much rather be on the ground, where he could provide more help if something went wrong, but he was the only member of the team with a pilot's license, so his job was in the air.

Johansson spent much of his free time on the track, so he sat behind the wheel of a beastly but innocuous-looking Audi S8. Once they pinpointed the truck's location, they would all converge on it—while trying to stay off law enforcement's radar.

"I'm connecting you with the team now. Stay in touch."

A buzzing, then voices, sounded in his ear.

"Try to keep out of trouble, boys. No speeding," Rif said with a smile.

Jean-Luc's heavily accented voice came through the radio. "Not much chance of that in my garbage truck."

The former Legionnaire was behind the wheel of a hulking vehicle they had "borrowed" from the city's sanitation department. If needed, it could be used to block a two-lane roadway.

"I'd like to see the rendĐrség try to stop me," Brown said, referring to the local gendarmes. He rode a high-performance Ducati 959 Panigale, with a top speed of 134 mph.

"Stewart and I are all set." The two brothers had rented two white panel vans, and their job was to transport the refugees to a local care center where they could find food and shelter.

Rif adjusted his sunglasses and settled into his seat. The mechanical flight controls of the L-39 operated smoothly, allowing him to study the ground below, his mind focused on one goal: finding that target. How many large trucks could be entering Budapest at this time on a Saturday morning?

Apparently quite a few, judging by the massive gridlock he saw as he passed over the M0 on his eastern sweep.

Chapter 62

Thea clung to the saddle of the BMW as she accelerated past an elderly driver trundling along below the speed limit. She ignored the ache from her left hand, which still throbbed from the fight in the labyrinth, and focused on the road. Headed eastbound on the M4 motorway, she cruised back into the city, hoping Hakan or Rif would spot the truck soon. The other members of the team were making similar loops through their quadrants, waiting for a positive ID on the truck.

Each vehicle had a GPS tracker, so Hakan could see them on an electronic map in the situation room in London. He would guide them toward the target once it was found.

She dropped lower on the bike, using the windscreen to shelter her body from the wind. The full leathers she wore weren't quite thick enough to warm her bones on this chilly day, but she'd still rather be racing along the highway than be up in the air with Rif. Those aerobatic maneuvers he loved so much would have her reaching for the white bag within seconds. She was much happier on solid ground or even water. The air was his domain.

Hakan's voice rumbled in her earpiece. "Might have something. Truck with a cargo back traveling westbound on the M3, approaching the M0 cloverleaf at Sikátorpuszta. Just spotted it on the toll cameras."

"I'm on it," Rif responded.

"Johansson, take the next exit and head west on the M3. You're approaching the cloverleaf now," Hakan said.

"Got it." Johansson was on the M0, heading north toward the M3 interchange.

Meanwhile, Rif dropped down for a closer look at the truck. "Found it. Driver is aggressive, weaving in and out of traffic."

"Johansson should be there soon. Hang tight, everyone," Hakan said.

She traveled along the motorway, awaiting further instruction from her boss. All team members would remain on their routes until they confirmed it was definitely the target. They had to be sure before abandoning their positions.

Minutes passed in tense succession. She focused on the road and the vehicles around her. In a city of three million people, the search for one truck was daunting. They had a far better chance of finding it than Prospero's team did, but dumb luck could always play a role. She prayed they got to it first.

As she waited for more information, she thought of Ayan and Jabari, wondering how they were coping. She planned on calling the Wavertons with a progress report tonight. With any luck, the boys would be safely back soon. The original plan had been for Ayan and Jabari to spend a night with Thea and Christos before heading to their new home in London. A flush of shame washed over her. She'd made the plan partially so the boys would be there as a buffer between her and her father. She had to find a more honest way of dealing with Christos, or they'd never be comfortable together again. But what was he hiding from her?

"Coming up behind the truck now." Johansson's voice jolted her back to the present.

"Driver's still acting like an asshole, but he's not the only one," Rif said.

"Rear axles are low. Looks to be heavily loaded." Johansson's breath sounded in her ear.

"Remain close and monitor it," Hakan said. "License plate?"

"YRE-9912."

"Not the one we're looking for, but they could have changed plates," Thea said.

"Checking it out now," Hakan said.

"The right rear bumper has a large dent, the paint scraped off. Mud splatters on the sides of the gutters." Johansson was an excellent observer, good with details. "Passing the truck now—will check out the driver."

"Just don't spook them, Jo," Thea said.

"With my gorgeous face? Not possible."

"Sorry, but you're lucky your kid looks like your wife," Rif said.

A sharp laugh from Jo.

Seconds ticked by. No update from Hakan, nothing from Johansson. Silence.

She waited.

"Piss off!" Johansson shouted.

"What's going on?" Thea was primed to accelerate and head for her teammate's position.

"The driver threw his coffee out the window right onto the S8 as I was passing him. Looks like a local, with no respect for the environment or his fellow drivers."

"Exit for 2A approaching in five hundred meters," Rif said. The truck they were after should stay on the M3, heading for the city center. If this was the target, they'd better move on it soon.

"Blinker is on. Should I follow?" Johansson asked.

Hakan's voice buzzed through. "Just ran the plate. A leather goods' company, reputable."

"He's turning off, headed northbound on 2A," Johansson said.

Away from the city center.

"Not our target." Hakan sounded frustrated. Ten minutes focused on the wrong truck. She just hoped they hadn't missed the real one. Gearing down, she slowed the motorbike to avoid some road construction, moving into the right lane. Up ahead, a flash of black fabric caught her eye.

Chapter 63

The flash of canvas Thea had spotted wasn't the truck, but a tarp covering a Boston Whaler being towed by an SUV. Another thirty minutes ticked by as they combed the roads, Rif scanning from the air, Hakan monitoring the toll cameras. Prospero seemed certain about the time frame and type of truck. They had to keep looking, but Rif couldn't stay up in the air forever without refueling.

Her earpiece buzzed. Rif. "Spotted something."

"What is it?"

"A large military truck with canvas backing close to the city center, heading up 51." All the drivers had memorized the main arteries into the city, so Thea knew more or less what he was talking about. "It must have come up the back roads from the south while I was flying over the north. Going down for a closer look."

"Coordinates?" Thea asked.

"Sending them now. Looks like it's heading in the direction of the Chain Bridge. Could be the one."

Hakan's calm voice sounded in her ear. "Jean-Luc and Thea are closest; they'll arrive first. Everyone else, converge on the coordinates at your earliest. If it's our truck, we need to seize it immediately, before it reaches the Parliament Building. If not, we'll scatter again."

She guided the BMW onto the shoulder of the road, rebalancing the bike as the tires spun on loose gravel, and sailed past the stop-start traffic clogging the M3. Revving the throttle, she barreled down the highway, her gaze scanning for police, who might not appreciate her solution to surviving the congestion.

"I'm not far either," Johansson said.

"Coming." The howl of Brown's Italian racing bike confirmed it.

"We're on our way," Stewart said.

"What cross street should I use?" Thea asked.

Hakan guided her through the city via her earbud, using live traffic maps for the most efficient route.

"The target is following the Danube, northbound," Rif said.

"Jean-Luc, position yourself on the Buda side of the river near the Chain Bridge," Hakan instructed.

"Already idling in the parking area for the funicular." That put him beside the roundabout on the east side of the bridge, right where he needed to be if the truck tried to cross over.

"There soon," Thea said.

The L-39 whizzed overhead as she closed the distance to the truck. Shifting gears, dodging between cars, Thea broke every traffic rule trying to catch up to the lumbering vehicle. A few drivers raised fists or gave her the finger. She sympathized—she was driving like a wild woman—but they had no idea how much was at stake.

"Eyes on target," she said. "It's a GMC CCKW, one of those two-and-a-half-ton trucks with a long wheelbase. Canvas back."

Johansson's voice sounded in her earpiece. "Made it to the Buda side of the Chain Bridge. Idling on the side road."

She reduced her speed, not wanting to startle the driver. Fifty meters behind the truck, she was finally able to read the plate. "It's our target."

"Thea, you're closing on the Chain Bridge. Stay with the truck," Hakan said. "One noisy distraction, courtesy of Brown and Johansson, coming up."

She opened the throttle a little, shrinking the distance to twenty meters, then ten. She needed to be directly next to the truck. She passed several boats moored on the Danube, shivering at the thought of how cold it would be on the river today.

"Jean-Luc, block the bridge from the Pest side." Hakan was the grand master, moving pieces on the chessboard, planning a surprise capture of the enemy's king. "Johansson, as soon as Thea reaches the bridge, close it off from the Buda side."

"Got it."

"Rif, keep an eye out for any police. We have a small window before company arrives, and we want to be moving out before they do." Hakan's voice was calm, measured. It felt as if he was right beside them rather than in London.

She downshifted the BMW, preparing to turn onto the bridge behind the truck. The target trundled along the road, traveling at the speed limit. As far as she could tell, the driver had no idea he was being tailed. It wasn't easy to see a motorcycle in the rearview mirror, especially given how close she was.

The rumble of an explosion echoed in her ears. In the distance, a smudge of dense black smoke rose above the Danube. She smiled. One of the caches of harmless explosives Brown and Johansson had set up at various points along the riverbank had just been detonated. Hopefully, it would keep the cops busy enough for the Quantum team to complete the mission and melt into Budapest traffic before the police arrived.

"Brown, park your bike and prepare to drive the truck to the gamma location," Hakan said.

They had rented four different warehouses across the city in anticipation of this moment, each one coded to the first four letters of the Greek alphabet. The goal was to hide the truck as quickly as possible so they could search it and talk to the refugees somewhere private. Prospero's men were undoubtedly searching for the target—they might even have eyes on it now—and the Quantum team wanted to get to it first.

Brown had been a mechanical engineer, and Johansson knew more about cars, trucks, and motorcycles than anyone else on the team. They would take it apart piece by piece if necessary to figure out what had driven Prospero to hijack a plane full of passengers for it.

The GMC activated its right blinker, waiting for traffic to move. Thea followed suit. "Now."

"On it," Jean-Luc said. The Chain Bridge wasn't very wide, he'd blocked access to the Parliament Building from the Pest side by parking the garbage truck at an awkward angle across the lanes of the bridge. He had the hood up, making it look like a breakdown.

The GMC turned. Thea followed. A quick glance in her rear-view mirror showed Johansson right behind her, stopping in his lane so no one could access the bridge from that end. Two cars honked at the S8 in their way. Johansson flicked on his emergency lights and raised his hands in mock frustration: *What can I do?*

The cars behind the S8 turned off, headed for the next bridge crossing. Meanwhile, the GMC's brake lights came on, the driver realizing a garbage truck blocked the bridge.

Thea gunned her motorbike over to the curb, slammed on the brakes, and engaged the kickstand. Hopping off, she freed the Glock from inside her leather jacket and sprinted toward the back of the truck, the weapon in both hands, pointed at the passenger-side window. Two rounds whizzed by her ear, ricocheting off the asphalt behind her.

Chapter 64

Rif descended in the L-39 for a closer look at the action unfolding on the Chain Bridge. Jean-Luc and Johansson had sandwiched the truck from either side, boxing in their quarry. Vehicle after vehicle was trying to access the bridge but giving up after determining it was blocked. Even given the helpful distraction downriver, it would be only a matter of minutes before local officials were alerted about the traffic stoppage and arrived on the scene.

He flew past the bridge, then circled back, staring down at the Danube. A few boats were parked along the Pest side; some sort of exhibition was happening later in the day.

This mission was fluid, the plan designed to adapt to events as they unfolded. He preferred a mission with strict parameters, but you played the hand you were dealt. The team always prepared backup plans, and backup plans to the backup plans, and they'd explored countless operational scenarios, but none in depth. The ideal take-down spot would have been on a quiet road outside of the city, but now they'd have to depend on their training to make up for the less-than-ideal location.

Among the scenarios they had considered—one of them featured Thea and Brown boarding the truck from their motorcycles—many had a high risk of going sideways, so in some ways the bridge was a minor blessing. Still, the blockade ratcheted up the likelihood of gunplay. Trapped, the operators would have nowhere to go, and that would make them desperate and dangerous. And the local police and/or Prospero's men could arrive at any minute, adding to the total number of combatants. His gaze combed the area below, searching for any indication of the gendarmes or other actors approaching. But the streets below looked normal enough for what had turned out to be a busy Saturday morning.

"The vans are in position on the Buda bank," Neil said. "Ready to receive."

Rif clocked the location of the white vans and noticed Thea's motorcycle parked on the bridge; she would be preparing to engage the smugglers.

"Let's do it," Hakan said.

Seconds later, heated shouting erupted over the radio. *Here we go.* As expected, the targets weren't interested in surrendering without a fight. Rif wished he could be there by Thea's side.

Chapter 65

Thea crouched at the back of the truck, protecting herself from the man on the passenger side, who had cracked his door open and taken a potshot at her with his revolver. The round had *spanged* off the roadside and smashed into the vehicles behind her and ricocheted harmlessly off the bridge, but that was dumb luck. If he kept firing, a civilian injury or death was all but inevitable.

She snuck a quick look around the corner of the truck, poised to fire, but the shooter had retreated inside the GMC, leaving the door slightly ajar. Johansson kept low and sprinted along the bridge to her left, zigzagging to be a harder target. Just as he took up his position at the other corner of the truck, the rear canvas flap opened and terrified refugees piled out of the back.

In Arabic, Thea told the refugees that everything was going to be okay, but that they had to get aboard the two vans immediately if they wanted to stay safe. Scared but not knowing what else to do, they obeyed.

Her radio crackled again and she heard Jean-Luc's voice. "Two targets in the cab. Driver is hiding below the dash, but I have a clear shot on the passenger." He was stationed inside the cab of the garbage truck, a silenced M4 propped up on the window frame of the open door.

"Take him out," she said, trusting her teammate's aim. She didn't like the idea of killing the smugglers, who were probably victims in this plot, too, but they had to take out the hostiles quickly to protect the greatest number of people.

Even muffled, the report of the M4 was loud. The glass of the truck's windshield shattered in a ragged star as the round passed through and found its target. The passenger slumped out the truck's door, pushing it open. *One down.*

"Driver still not visible," Jean-Luc said.

"We'll take it from here. Cover us." Thea glanced behind her at the Pest side of the bridge. Neil and Stewart were shepherding confused refugees into the vans. Everyone would be taken to the nearest shelter for safekeeping after the two brothers had debriefed them. Some evacuees seemed hesitant at first, but whatever her teammates were telling them was working to keep them calm and compliant.

She signaled to Johansson, and he signaled back as they worked together to cover the driver's exit routes from the cab. Refugees kept stumbling out of the rear cargo area, one after the other. She couldn't believe how many people had been sardined inside.

Thea covered the passenger side door, approaching the truck with caution, as Johansson—his back pressed against the side of the truck—inched toward the driver's side door. He was trying to "slice the pie," surprising the driver by using the blind spot to approach the window.

Johansson moved silently and quickly. In position, he raised his Glock with both hands, stepping out from the truck until he had an angle on the target. Crouched low, the driver leaned out, raising his weapon. Before the man could fire, Johansson reached over and yanked open the door. Eyes wide with surprise, the man tried to regain his balance, but he was extended too far. Johansson delivered a crushing blow to the man's larynx with his left hand. A horrible choking sound escaped the man's throat and he dropped his weapon. Johansson shoved the driver inside while scanning for other occupants, Glock raised and ready in his other hand.

Johansson opened the door and pulled out the driver one-handed while scanning for other occupants, firearm raised and ready in his other hand.

"Clear," Johansson announced.

"Cops are headed for the Buda side." Rif's deep voice sounded in her earpiece.

Brown wheeled onto the bridge on his motorcycle, the final team member to arrive at the scene. He threaded through the fleeing refugees and parked his bike off to the side.

Sirens wailed, but no cherries were visible yet. Brown helped Thea load the passenger back into the truck, then she ran back to the cargo hold as the last few refugees jumped off the truck. One of the men, wearing a black-and-white checkered *shemagh* around his neck, knocked into her shoulder in his rush to get off. Something about him caught her attention, but she didn't have time to investigate.

"Get out now," Hakan's voice urged in their earbuds.

Jean-Luc joined them, hopping into the driver's side of the GMC and shoving the two bodies out of his way. He had abandoned the garbage truck with the keys inside, so the police could move it. The entire team had worn latex gloves to avoid leaving fingerprints on any of the vehicles.

Johansson sprinted back to the S8, turned off the hazards, completed a three-point turn, and raced off in the opposite lane, allowing egress for the truck. Brown jumped onto his bike and sped off the bridge. They would shadow the target to the "delta" warehouse to ensure it arrived safely.

Thea helped a wide-eyed young mother holding her child, two of the last wave climbing off the truck. In Arabic, she said, "We're here to help. Those men will take you somewhere safe." She indicated Neil and Stewart, standing beside the panel vans.

The mother pointed at the man wearing the *shemagh*, who strode quickly past the group of refugees. "He's one of them," she whispered.

"Thank you," Thea said as the woman hurried off to the bus. "We have a live one," she said. "Going after him."

"Roger that. Police in under five, so be quick."

Thea clutched her Glock in both hands and started after the man. As the last living member of the team that had been driving the truck, he might have important information to offer. He had a solid head start, so she ran. He glanced over his shoulder and saw her chasing him. He turned, raising a pistol. She dove to the ground and rolled. He fired off a couple of rounds, then bolted.

She jumped up, frustrated she couldn't return fire because of all the civilians. The man raced off the bridge and turned left onto the road bordering the Danube, with Thea attempting to close the gap.

A few boats were parked along the river, the owners milling about. She was still a hundred feet behind when he aimed his handgun at the men and shouted at them. Seconds later, he jumped into a sleek Cigarette boat and fired up the engine. He untied the mooring ropes, gunned the throttle, and knifed through the water, heading north just as she was catching up to him.

Thea greeted the boat owners in Hungarian. She wasn't fluent, but with the gun in her hand and her chest heaving from the footrace, her intentions were pretty clear. "Need to follow him—will bring the boat back."

Looking at the gun in her hand, one of the men tossed his keys to her. She caught them as he pointed to a red-and-white Donzi.

"*Köszönöm*," she said, thanking him.

She jumped into the speedboat, pulled in the bumpers, and cranked the throaty engine. She untied the boat from the cleats and pushed her off from the dock as the men looked on in stony silence. When she had the boat in the middle of the channel, she slammed the throttle down and raced after the Cigarette. Given the cool temperature, there wasn't much traffic on the Danube, but the man ahead of her seemed to be a little twitchy at the helm, perhaps unfamiliar with driving such a powerful racer.

But as speedy as the Donzi was, *Shemagh* still had the faster boat.

Chapter 66

Rif checked the fuel and realized he was running low. Blue and white lights flashed below as cops swarmed the Chain Bridge, but the team had escaped in time.

"The eagle has landed." Jean-Luc's gravelly voice rumbled over the radio.

The GMC had arrived safely at the warehouse. Their team would tear the truck apart and figure out what had driven Prospero Salvatore to such lengths to procure it. It would be a distinct advantage to know what, exactly, they were handing over.

Meanwhile, Thea was chasing one of the men in a racing boat—and from his bird's-eye view, it looked as if she was falling behind the larger, more powerful Cigarette.

Thea's voice, buffeted by the wind, came in over the Comm-Radio. "Rif, any obstacles ahead?"

He looked north along the Danube—it must be freezing on the river. "Clear sailing, but you're losing ground."

"The throttle is wide open—this is all she's got." Her voice was choppy.

"Leave it to me. Drop back a little."

"Roger, out."

Thea decelerated, allowing the Cigarette to plunge ahead. The man in the *shemagh* would undoubtedly feel cocky, so close to escape. He'd never expect an attack from above.

Rif went into a swift dive, banking hard right, the huge non-tumbling altitude indicator spinning in reverse. He pushed his left thumb onto the speed brakes, keeping the Albatros under 250 knots as he plunged below 10,000 feet.

The Cigarette shot under the bridge at Margaret Island, churning up a huge wake. Thea's Donzi had dropped back, allowing Rif the room he needed to maneuver. He dipped down and zoomed under the bridge in pursuit, the steel rafters mere feet above the rudder. He was nail-bitingly close to the dark water, but the Albatros was nimble.

Time slowed as Rif closed in on the boat. The man driving the boat glanced up, a stunned look on his face. The concussive force of the powerful jet engine sent shock waves rippling across the water faster than the boat could travel. Seconds later, the turbulence from the L-39 slammed into the Cigarette, lifting the prow of the craft and flipping it end over end. The driver pinwheeled into the frigid water as the boat finished its tumble, the engines swamped.

Rif lifted the nose of the plane and accelerated, heading for the airport. His fuel level was now dangerously low. He needed to get this bird onto the ground.

He pressed the button to connect with Thea. "Your man's ready for pickup."

Chapter 67

Thea's mind was still blown from Rif's stunt. Watching the L-39 zoom under the bridge breathtakingly close to the water had been exhilarating. But seeing the Cigarette flip like a playing card caught in the wind, flinging the man through the air, had been something else. She opened the throttle on the Donzi, happy to have been far away when the large boat capsized.

Reaching the accident site, she slowed the Donzi, scanning the water. It didn't take long to find the man. He still had his scarf wrapped around his neck as he paddled weakly toward the shore. His eyelids flickered, and his teeth chattered nearly loudly enough for her to hear over the purr of the boat's engine. The river had to be around forty degrees, so hypothermia would set in quickly if he didn't get out of there. She killed the engine and tossed him one of the bumpers from the boat. He grabbed hold, his hands fumbling and desperate. She pulled him in, bringing him to the aft, where he could use the ladder to climb aboard.

His hands were weak, his body shivering uncontrollably, so she pretty much had to haul him onto the Donzi. It occurred to her that he might also be concussed from the force of hitting the water. She patted him down to make sure he didn't have a weapon. His handgun was probably at the bottom of the Danube. She shepherded him to the passenger seat and sat him down.

A quick search of the Donzi yielded a first-aid kit. She wrapped the reflective Mylar blanket around him to stabilize his body temperature. Soaked and stunned, he seemed harmless enough, but she'd learned long ago not to take any unnecessary risks. She grabbed a zip tie from her pants pocket and secured his wrists together in his lap.

Shemagh pointed his hands up to the sky, where the L-39 had faded into the distance. *"Majnoon." Crazy.*

Rif definitely was, but in a good way. Instead of letting the man escape in the barreling Cigarette, Rif had stopped him cold—and now they had a potential source of information. She'd take him back to the warehouse, get him into some warm, dry clothes, and then the *majnoon* pilot could interrogate him.

Thea piloted the Donzi in a half circle and headed back down the river. She used her satphone to call Rif. "I caught the fish."

His warm laughter sounded in her ear. "Been a long time since I've been able to execute a flyby like that."

"You certainly cut it close."

"It's the only way. Just landing now. Meet you at the warehouse."

"Roger that. Meanwhile, what should I tell the Cigarette's owner?" The boat *Shemagh* had stolen was a total loss.

"That you hope he's insured?"

"Ha ha." Hakan would track down the owner and make sure that everything was taken care of. If she had her way, Prospero would buy the guy a new racing boat.

She couldn't wait to get back, tell Prospero they had secured the truck, and set up the meet. Ayan, Jabari, and the other passengers could come home at last.

Chapter 68

Jean-Luc picked up Thea and her captive in a borrowed Peugeot and took them to the warehouse, where the team was tearing apart the GMC. Neil and Stewart were working under the hood, Rif sat near the right front wheel well with a ratchet set nearby, and Brown and Johansson were in the back compartment, ripping it apart. Every inch of the vehicle would be scoured before they met with Prospero.

She'd given their guest dry clothes and food before applying another zip tie to his hands and tying him down in a chair.

With luck, whatever Prospero wanted could be removed from the truck and transported in another vehicle, as every police officer in Budapest would now be on the lookout for the GMC. If not, they'd paint the truck and change the plates before driving it to Turkey for the meet.

"How are the refugees?" Thea asked, standing near the engine block and looking over the shoulders of the Scots.

"Safely ensconced with friendly locals," Neil said.

Quantum had black-book contacts across the globe they could reach out to in emergencies. In exchange for future services,

Hakan had mobilized the Hungarian contacts to see that the refugees arrived safely at processing centers across Eastern Europe. Most of them would not stay in Hungary, which was ranked among the worst countries in Europe for its treatment of asylum seekers. They would be safe for now, though the challenge of integrating into their new countries would provide them a difficult, and in some ways more arduous, journey than the one they had just taken.

She strode to Rif, who was working to remove the front left tire for an inspection of the rim and wheel well. "Would you like the honor of chatting with our new friend? He admired your aerobatics earlier."

Rif smiled, wiping his hands as he stood. "I'd be delighted to talk to him."

Thea entered the office portion of the warehouse, closed the door, and sank into a leather chair. She hadn't had much sleep, just a short nap while flying to Budapest with the team. Sleep was a treasured commodity in their business—you grabbed it when you could. But before she could try to nap, she needed food and insulin. Dealing with her illness was a pain in the ass, but there wasn't much she could do about that.

She opened the box of diabetes supplies Hakan had sent with the team. It had been three days since her last rotation, and she always adhered to a strict regimen. Couldn't have her pump malfunctioning while in the field.

Thea ripped off the sticky tape holding down the sensor, wincing as it pulled a few hairs along with it. Her skin underneath was red and irritated—no surprise, given the recent sweat-fest in Libya. The small hole in the middle of the irritation looked puffy. She smeared Neosporin on it and covered it with a Band-Aid.

Her hands worked quickly to replace the sensor and infusion sites, as she needed to keep moving the sites to avoid infection. She'd been at the drill of looking after her diabetes for years, but the technology had changed since she'd first been diagnosed at age twelve. Remove the tube, rewind the pump, fill the reservoir with insulin, prime the pump. She liked to think that her diabetes routine wasn't all that different from disassembling and reassembling a gun.

The process completed, she tossed the empty cartridge and cannula into the garbage can on the far side of the room. In two hours, her sensor would be all warmed up and ready for action.

She grabbed the new satphone Hakan had sent and dialed Prospero's number. It rang and rang. Finally, she heard a click.

"Salvatore." He sounded slightly out of breath.

"We have the truck."

"So I heard. I'll send the coordinates in Turkey."

"Not so fast. I want to speak to the boys."

"I'm out. I'll call you when I'm back."

"That excuse isn't going to fly a second time. Put them on now."

"In two hours." He ended the call before she could respond.

Her fingers clenched her cell. Why not put the boys on the phone? She had what he wanted, and vice versa. *Something is wrong.*

Chapter 69

Rif positioned a metal chair in front of the Syrian, then straddled it, staring at him. "Remember me, from the plane?" he asked in Arabic.

The man's narrow face paled. Rif could only imagine the distress caused by having a plane buzz so close, followed by being catapulted into the Danube. The man would not forget the experience for quite some time.

"Let's talk about the truck. Where did you get it?"

Rif sensed the man was weighing his options, realizing he had none. His partners had tried to shoot their way off the bridge and failed. He was the one person left who had knowledge about the vehicle. He had something to trade.

"I want to stay in Europe."

"You're in no position to negotiate. Help me, and maybe I'll help you."

A few seconds passed. "They told me if I went to prison, my family would be safe, rich."

"Who asked you to bring the truck here?"

"The man spoke with a German accent."

"Name?"

"No names, just a bank account. I did this for my family."

"The man wired you money?"

"Not me. My colleague, Mohammed Amir. Western Union."

Hakan might be able to trace the funds transfer. Rif texted the info to his father, asking him to investigate.

"Where were you supposed to take the truck?" He already knew the answer but wanted to see if the guy was playing it straight.

"The Parliament Building."

"Why?"

"Lots of police." The man shivered periodically, undoubtedly the aftereffects of his dip in the icy waters of the river.

"So you *wanted* to be caught?" It made no sense.

"We would go to prison, but our families would be given money. But we had to reach the Parliament Building, or the deal was off."

Rif's mind raced as he tried to grasp the shape of the plan. *What the hell is this all about?*

"Rif, you need to see this." Thea had emerged from the office and was standing by the truck with the rest of the team, her tone clipped.

He went to the GMC. Brown and Johansson had ripped open a false panel in the back of the truck. Two metal cylinders rested inside the rear hatch. He read the letters: USAF. But it was the familiar black and yellow emblem that left his blood cold: the symbol for nuclear material.

His gaze locked with Thea's. What had they stumbled upon?

Chapter 70

Thea dialed Gabrielle Farrah's number. The two women had forged a friendship during Christos's kidnapping. Formerly CIA, the Hostage Recovery Fusion Cell member was based in Washington, DC, but had connections around the world. And the Quantum team needed information and advice—fast. Nuclear material had been sent in a truck full of Syrian refugees, headed for the Hungarian Parliament. And someone else wanted it discovered. Why? To start a war? What was the Sicilian's involvement all about?

Gabrielle picked up. "Last I heard, you'd been skyjacked. You drop the hijackers from thirty thousand feet?" Her tone was playful, but Thea sensed tension in her voice.

"Actually, I was the one jettisoned from the plane."

"Ever think about taking a normal vacation like the rest of us?"

Thea smiled despite herself. "The skyjacker was Prospero Salvatore, a mob capo from Sicily. He wanted me to hijack a truck carrying Syrian refugees from the streets of Budapest in exchange for the return of the plane's passengers. The rendezvous is in

Turkey. We have the truck; problem is, we found two American nuclear capsules hidden inside. What are we supposed to do now?"

Silence. Thea waited.

"Give me the serial numbers. I'll look into what those capsules are, exactly, and get back to you asap."

"Thank you. It's a major quandary. I can't exactly hand over nuclear material to a mafioso, but I need to get those hostages back."

"You never do things halfway," Gabrielle said. "Any idea where the passengers are being held?"

"None. Quantum is still searching for the plane, which we assume never left Africa. But that might not get us closer to finding the passengers before we have to exchange the truck."

Gabrielle let out a long sigh, as if she'd been holding her breath. "Okay, I'll call as soon as I have something. Meanwhile, see if you can delay the hostage exchange until we know more."

"I owe you one." Thea ended the call.

Rif stood beside her. "You didn't want to share your suspicions that the passengers are being held in Turkey?"

"I trust Gabrielle completely. But you never know who might be listening. For now, I'd like to keep everything on the downlow. We don't want to spook Prospero or the other players."

"Did you talk to Ayan and Jabari?"

"No. Prospero told me to call back in two hours."

Rif frowned. "He knows we have the truck?"

"Absolutely."

Her satphone rang. Hakan.

"Rif there?"

"Yes." She put Hakan on speakerphone.

"The wire transfer to the Syrian originated in Salzburg, Austria."

"Austria. I wonder if there's a connection to the recent terrorist attack at Schönbrunn Palace. . . ."

"Keeping an open mind."

"Rif told you what we found?" she asked.

"Yes," Hakan said, searching for a silver lining. "At least it wasn't a bomb."

"But if there is fissile material in there that can be weaponized, all that's missing is a facility and a qualified engineer . . ." Rif said. "Like Ocean. I wonder if Prospero is part of this plan or trying to disrupt it."

"Whoever loaded the truck wanted the refugees caught with it. Why frame a bunch of asylum-seekers?" Thea asked, shaking her head. "We gave Gabrielle Farrah the serial numbers in the hopes she can offer more information about the canisters. Any updates on Prospero's contacts in Turkey?" She couldn't just hand over nuclear material, no matter how badly she wanted those passengers back.

"Nothing definitive, but we're working on it. Prospero has forty-three connections in the country," Hakan said. "Oh, and a very nervous young man with a German accent called, said he had information for you. We tried to get him to talk, but he refused. He said he would call again, but I haven't heard from him. He called from a burner phone, untraceable."

"Patch him through to my satphone when he does." They had a couple of rental cars ready to drive to the meet in Turkey, vehicles that hadn't been used in snatching the truck. "Can one of the local assets pick up our guest?" She glanced over at their prisoner, tied to the chair on the other side of the warehouse.

He was just a pawn in a game. Like the two smugglers. But who were the players?

Chapter 71

Following the footsteps of the three escapees, Prospero was sweating even though the snow had started to fall again. He told himself it was from the exertion of running around in the winter wonderland, but the ticking clock definitely played a part. Now that Thea had the truck, he wasn't about to let the escapees ruin his plans.

After retracing several false paths, he finally found their actual route. He grudgingly admired their tactics. Tracing the maze of footprints had wasted valuable time, but he now knew he'd find them.

He hurried to where Luciano waited for him, the snowmobile parked just south of the trees. His nephew paced in the snow, smoking one of his foul Turkish cigarettes.

"I checked the other side of the forest. No sign of them." Luciano sucked in another lungful of smoke.

"I know where they're headed. Let's go." He hopped onto the snowmobile and fired up the engine.

Luciano flicked the butt into the snow and jumped on behind him. Prospero zoomed down the slopes, following the partially filled tracks. A small village nestled in the nearby valley. Tea and kiwi farmers lived there, cut off from the world by the surrounding mountains. If Ocean and the boys made it that far, they might have been able to catch a ride out of the area. But the tracks on the outskirts of the village were fresh, barely snow-covered, so he doubted it.

Arriving at the village, Prospero parked the snowmobile at the side of the main road, near the only petrol station. Shutting down the engine, he nudged Luciano off the back. As much as he wanted to keep a close eye on his nephew, time was of the essence. They had to split up to cover more ground.

He slid Luciano's SIG out of his jacket pocket and handed it to him. "Only use this to influence. No one gets shot."

"W-what if they run away?"

"If you see them, call me. Don't do anything stupid. I need all three hostages alive and well."

Luciano shrugged.

Prospero grabbed him by his jacket and pulled him close. "Whatever you do to them, you'll get the same, you hear?"

"Yeah, I got it."

He released Luciano. "Cover the east side of town. I'll head west." He strode down the main artery of the village, memories flooding back of getting very drunk at the local watering hole with Aslan one lazy summer afternoon. The town looked different covered in snow, with hardly anyone on the streets, the residents huddled inside the stone buildings. Wrought-iron streetlights framed the quaint street. A butcher shop sat on one corner, a bakery on another.

The blizzard intensified, blasting particles of sleet into his face. His cheeks were numb after being exposed to the elements. Grateful for the goggles protecting his eyes, he crossed the road. He glanced down the alleys between the buildings where the escapees could be hiding—from him and from the storm.

Nothing.

He passed the local watering hole, wishing he had time for a grappa to warm his insides. He peered through the front windows: except for the bartender there was just one person, of indeterminate sex, head down on the bar. The poor weather had kept everyone at home. Prospero longed for the sunshine of Sicily.

Crossing an alley, he reached the local mosque, an enormous building with an impressive minaret. The hinges on the large steel door creaked as he entered. Inside, he brushed snow off his jacket. No sign of the imam or anyone else. He made his way to the front, scanning for movement.

Empty.

Frustrated, he left the relative protection of the mosque and tromped down the street. The soft glow of the streetlights guided him through the falling snow.

His phone buzzed. "You find them?"

"I ran into a guy plowing the streets," Luciano said. "He saw strangers running in your direction ten minutes ago—said he couldn't believe people were out in this weather."

"I can't believe we're out in it," Prospero said. "Get the plow driver to give you a ride, head this way, and join me. They can't have gone far." No cars on the streets, no pedestrians, so the chances of them hitching a ride or finding help were minimal—unless they'd stolen a vehicle.

"Where are you?" Luciano asked.

He scanned the nearby shop fronts. "Near the cheese store."

"On my way."

Prospero pressed the end button, slipping his phone back into his pocket. He forged ahead with renewed energy. Up ahead, movement caught his eye. He blinked, then looked again. Maybe the snow was playing tricks with the light. No, he'd definitely seen something. He quickened his pace. An old blue-and-white phone booth stood on the corner, snow building up on the weather side. Someone was inside it.

Moving slowly, Prospero kept his eyes on phone booth. Two figures, both short. A flash of red: Ayan's jacket. Had to be the boys. He scanned the nearby area, searching for Ocean. No sign of her.

Now that he was closer, it looked as if they were on the phone.

Sprinting the final twenty feet, he ignored the pain in his hip. Jabari was talking to someone.

Propero tore open the snow-covered door and lunged into the booth.

Chapter 72

Prospero raised his Glock, aiming it at the two shivering boys inside the phone booth. The gun wasn't loaded—he wasn't going to risk hurting Ayan and Jabari—but they didn't know that. Snow covered the boys' hair and clothes, little clumps of white on their eyelashes, their teeth chattering. He reached in with his left hand, ripped the receiver out of Jabari's hands, and slammed it down, ending the call.

"How's Thea?"

The look on their faces said it all. They'd spoken to the kidnap negotiator. He knew better than to ask what they'd told her. These two would just lie.

"Where's Ocean?" he asked. She couldn't be far.

Jabari shrugged.

"That's not an answer."

Trapped inside the phone booth with a gun pointed at them, the boys were still defiant. His patience was wearing thin. "I don't want to have to use this." He lifted the Glock in the air.

"She ditched us," Ayan piped up, looking anything but scared.

A prickling started at the base of Prospero's neck and crawled up his skull as realization washed over him. All this time, he'd believed he was tracking three escapees, but Ocean had been on her own, possibly for hours. His mind recoiled at the complications this might cause.

"Which way did she go?"

"It was dark. We didn't see." Jabari wrapped his arms around Ayan, trying to keep them both warm.

So it was not that long ago. A pickup truck with a large cab and a snowplow attached to the front lumbered down the street toward them. Luciano hopped out of the passenger side and joined them. The boys shrank back at the sight of his nephew.

Prospero turned to Luciano. "Ocean left the boys. We'll need a search party to find her. Let's go."

He directed Ayan and Jabari to climb into the back seat of the truck and piled in with them, letting Luciano sit up front. He didn't want any more trouble. The driver negotiated the twisty roads with the skill of a lifelong local, following Luciano's directions to the villa while the boys huddled together in the warmth of the cab.

Propero called his Turkish host. "We have the kids, but Ocean escaped."

"Any idea which direction she was headed in?" Aslan asked.

"None."

"I'll have a search team ready to go in fifteen minutes."

"Thanks. We will have to leave with the passengers immediately—the boys called *Liberata*." Aslan's men would retrieve his snowmobile, handle the hunt for Ocean, and recover Bassam's body, which was for the best, since they knew these mountains better than anyone.

"Ah, that is a pity. It's been a pleasure having you around, my friend."

He ended the call, irritated afresh that the boys had contacted Thea. Even if the boys couldn't identify the town, Thea would have traced their call. They needed to relocate immediately.

Prospero had planned this operation meticulously, nailing down every detail, but things had begun to go sideways. One passenger had been killed, and he would miss Bassam, who was very capable. Co-opting Thea and her team to hijack the truck had seemed a better option than his original plan, but now it was beginning to look like a mistake. No matter. He still had an opportunity to get his hands on what he wanted.

His cell buzzed. Thea. He ignored the call. Let her stew a little before he gave her his new demands.

Chapter 73

Thea could barely stand the tension. The boys had escaped. But they'd hung up in mid-sentence. She recorded all her calls—it was often helpful to listen to conversations repeatedly in her job, analyzing voices, inflections, discerning ambient sounds that could help identify the location. She pressed play to listen to the conversation she'd just had.

"Thea, it's Jabari. We got away! Ocean left too, but she went a different way."

"Where are you now?"

"In a phone booth."

"Look for a sign. Any names. Tell me what you see."

"It's snowing. Lots of mountains."

"Okay, that's good. Any street signs, names of businesses."

"The letters look funny. I can't read them."

"What about license plates, any cars around?"

"No, it's snowing hard. I can't see any."

"Is there a number written on the pay phone?"

A scuffling sound. *Click.*

"Jabari, are you there?"

Silence.

"Talk to me, Jabari."

The recording ended.

What had happened to the boys? She tried phoning Prospero, but he didn't answer. At least she now knew why he'd been putting her off, not letting her speak to them. *They'd escaped.* Had Prospero just caught up with Ayan and Jabari? She kept the line free in case they called back so they could trace the call from the Quantum office.

They'd narrowed the number of likely locations for Prospero's hideout from forty-five to thirteen, focusing on the man's known associates within Turkey. Reading the clues from the live video she'd seen and based on the fact that the kids had reported signs written in a non-Roman alphabet, she was sure they were right about Turkey. Of course, even if they did find the safe house, they'd have to proceed cautiously. Rescues were dicey propositions, with only one in five successful. And in this case there were children among the hostages.

Every piece of information they gathered offered potential clues to Prospero's endgame, but the thing that she wanted to know most was what the nuclear material had to do with his plan.

Her cell buzzed. Gabrielle.

"Tell me I have nothing to worry about, that it's all a hoax, and there is no nuclear material in those containers," Thea said.

"Yeah, about that . . ."

"How bad is it?"

"Bear with me while I give you a brief history lesson. On March 10, 1956, four B-47s took off from MacDill Air Force Base in Florida, each carrying two containers of uranium 235 with a four-megaton yield, designed for Mk-21 warheads. Over the Mediterranean Sea, they descended to fourteen thousand feet for an in-air refueling near Morocco. Visibility was poor."

"Oh, no."

"One plane, serial number 52-534, disappeared. The wreckage was never found. Neither were the two nuclear cores on board—"

"Until now." Thea finished Gabrielle's sentence.

"Exactly. You've discovered a Broken Arrow."

Thea inhaled a deep breath. Okay, the nuke was American, MIA since 1956. *But how does it figure into Prospero's plans?* "Any idea where it's been all this time?"

"None. Earl Johnson, the captain of one of the other B-47s on the flight, kept searching for the missing plane, because his best friend was the captain, but he never found a thing. And Earl passed away years ago."

"How does a plane just disappear?"

"Sadly, it's not that uncommon. I'm meeting with a CIA contact in a few hours whose specialty includes lost high-powered ordnance like this. I'll let you know how that goes."

"Meanwhile, what about the trade with Prospero Salvatore?"

"Put him off, buy more time," Gabrielle said.

"I'll do what I can, but you'd better move fast. I need those passengers back."

"I hear you," Gabrielle said, then paused. "Why would a mafioso want to lay his hands on fissile material? The whole mission seems expensive, high risk, and outside his area of expertise."

"Exactly," Thea agreed. "Here's a fun fact that might be important: Salvatore is part of some vestigial post–Second World War militia called Gladio, funded at least in part by your friends at the Company."

"More ancient history . . . I'll poke around, see if that fits in with what my CIA contact has to say," Gabrielle said. "Anything else?"

"That's it for now. Let me know how the conversation with your spook goes." They said goodbye, and Thea pressed the end button.

The hostage situation had seriously deteriorated. It was no longer just about a simple exchange of the truck for the plane passengers. How could she in good conscience trade weapons-grade nuclear material for the lives of the passengers? It would be wrong. And yet, she had to get the hostages back.

Depressed, Thea shared the details of the Broken Arrow with Rif.

"This complicates things," Rif said. "We may have to attempt a rescue instead—if we can zero in on their location."

"I'm hoping it doesn't come to that," Thea mused, thinking again about the risks to the hostages in any rescue.

"As for this stuff," Rif said, sweeping a hand to indicate the nuclear cores, "Ocean must be the target Prospero was after."

"Probably. She escaped with the boys, but she abandoned them, so she's likely still in play. Anyway, Hakan is doing a full workup on her."

"Maybe all Prospero wanted was to avoid the refugees being discovered with the nuclear cores," Rif said, looking thoughtful. "What if his ultimate goal isn't so sinister after all?"

"Perhaps, though he's hardly the sort of partner I'm looking for. Also, I have no doubt he has plans for selling the nuclear material."

"Well, at least it wasn't a live bomb."

"That's what makes me think the reason for the operation was an attempt to create a backlash against the refugees."

"You're probably right." Rif said. "Right now Hungary is one of the least hospitable places in Europe for refugees, especially from the Middle East. I'm surprised they were even able to cross the border with that amount of human cargo. The question is, why the hell—"

They were interrupted by Thea's cell buzzing. Hakan. "What's up?"

"The young man who called earlier. He's on the line, insistent about speaking to you. Austrian, I'd guess, now that I'm hearing him for the second time."

"Any idea what he wants?"

"Not really. He said he would only speak to you."

"Patch him through. Rif can fill you in on my conversation with Gabrielle."

"Sounds good. Talk to you later."

Waiting for the call to be routed, Thea stared at the black-and-yellow symbol on the canisters. It wasn't every day she was in the same room with enough nuclear material to start World War III.

Chapter 74

At the foot of Aslan's driveway, Prospero climbed out of the truck with the snowplow attachment and shoved a meaty stack of Turkish lira into the driver's hand. That should keep him quiet, at least long enough for them to vacate the area.

Luciano led the boys to the outbuilding where the other hostages were already gathered, shivering in the cold. Prospero had called ahead, instructing Bassam's men to prepare the passengers for immediate departure. He had no idea how much Jabari had been able to tell Thea, but he couldn't take any chances. The kidnap negotiator was not to be underestimated, so an evacuation was in order.

If Aslan's men found Ocean, they would escort her to Bosnia, where Prospero planned to take the hostages. A business acquaintance there had a house secluded enough to hide the passengers until the exchange could be set up.

Bosnia had other advantages too, including greedy officials accustomed to working closely with the parade of smugglers, traffickers, and other organized-crime syndicates operating there. The remote property owned by his colleague was right outside

Mostar, not far from Stari Most, the "old bridge." Named after the medieval keepers—*mostari*—who had guarded the bridge over the Neretva River, the Stari Most was a relic from the sixteenth century, when the land had been under Ottoman rule.

His associate Vedad Divjak owned a mining company and had made millions selling steel to automobile and soda manufacturers worldwide. Vedad also had the mayor of Mostar in his pocket, so there wouldn't be any inconvenient questions about a group of foreigners flying into town under high security.

"Are we going home now?" Karlsson asked.

"Soon. Into the van." Normally, Prospero would tell the nutcase whatever he wanted to get him moving, but his patience was wearing thin. The insanity of the Freedom Guardians and the importance of this operation, which had already grown very complicated, had left him short-tempered.

Laverdeen greeted the boys with a warm hug. "Sorry, guys. I'd really hoped you would get away."

Ayan piped up. "We called Thea. She'll come get us now, kick their asses."

Jabari pushed his brother's shoulder. "Quiet."

"How about Ocean? Did they find her?" Laverdeen asked.

"Poof! She disappeared." Ayan flung the fingers of both hands wide.

"At least someone made it out of here," Jabari said.

Prospero again found himself admiring the boys' spirit, despite all the trouble they had caused. Why did these two war orphans turn out to be so resourceful and kind, while his nephew, raised in the arms of his family, was in a state of arrested development?

Rivers approached Prospero, looking desperate. "Are my girls okay?"

"Your kids are back with their mother. They'll be fine if you do what you're told."

"Let me speak to them."

"Later. We need to leave now."

Rivers opened his mouth to answer, but Prospero silenced him. "Just do what you're told, and everyone will be fine."

The captain stepped into the van and slammed a fist into the wall. Now that he'd spent time with the hostages, Prospero was grateful he didn't kidnap for a living. Way too much trouble to deal with other people's foibles. There were many easier ways to make money.

Laverdeen paused to speak to him. "Why not let some of the passengers go, as a goodwill gesture?"

"Who the fuck do you think you are?"

"You don't need all of us, and—"

"Keep this up, and you'll be joining Dillman," Prospero said.

Laverdeen hesitated for a moment. "I don't think so. You're not like the hothead."

"You know nothing about me, but I'll tell you this much: I never let anything get in the way of what I want. Now get in." Prospero gestured toward the van.

Laverdeen stared at him for a few long seconds, then complied.

Ayan and Jabari were the last to climb into the van. He'd had the cook give them hot soup in paper cups to warm them up. They had been well on their way to becoming hypothermic.

"Time to go."

Ayan stood with his hands on his hips. "The Wavertons are waiting for us in London. Why can't we just go there? It's not fair."

"That's life—a series of injustices. I would have thought you two, of all people, would know that by now." Prospero had a sudden thought about the family adopting the boys and wondered what it would be like, having them around all the time. Entertaining, at the very least. "Get in."

He thought of his former best friend, Karl, the sacrifices he'd made for the Gladios, infiltrating the Freedom Guardians. Karl was the reason he knew about the Austrian's insane plans. And now he was gone, probably dead. So many losses.

Luciano cranked the engine on the large cube van. They'd head for the airport in Trabzon, then fly to Bosnia on Prospero's plane. Memories from the last time he'd seen Vedad sprang to mind as he thought of their destination.

Prospero's supplier in the Ukraine had lost several arms shipments due to the civil war tearing up the country, and the weapons shortage was compromising his business. So he'd reached out to Vedad. Although Vedad kept his business dealings legitimate, he knew many entrepreneurs who were a lot less . . . particular.

A few calls and a few greased palms later, Vedad invited Prospero to Bosnia for some rakija, the local fruit brandy—and a little business at his countryside home. Vedad had warned him that his contact, Mirsad, was pretty rough around the edges but also said that the man's extensive network of arms dealers in Africa, China, and Russia made up for any lack of manners.

A former mercenary turned gunrunner, Mirsad had a fetish for conflict zones. From Vedad's stories, it sounded as if the arms dealer might have a screw or two loose, in fact, but what did it matter if he could deliver what Prospero needed? He'd brought Luciano with him, wanting to show his nephew the subtler side of the business, where money changed hands between partners instead of blows between rivals.

They sat in the villa's great room, an expansive space with an entire wall of windows looking out over lush gardens. A well-stocked mahogany bar, the dark wood paneling, and several taxidermy trophies from Vedad's hunting trips contrasted with the bright outdoors.

Mirsad was late, of course, so Vedad entertained. The Bosnian, who had thick white hair and an untamable cowlick, poured the brandy with a heavy hand. As they chatted, Vedad kept leaning over with the bottle, saying, "Let me top you up."

"Where's your man?" Prospero asked finally, getting impatient. They were supposed to be having dinner together, but now Mirsad was going to miss that as well.

"Probably cutting someone's balls off in a back alley." Vedad laughed. Say what you would, the man was a happy drunk.

Prospero preferred not to imbibe while conducting deals, but with the Bosnians, it was part of the ritual. He was used to it, of course, but Luciano was edgy, smoking like a fiend. His nephew didn't like small talk; it presented too many opportunities for his stutter to manifest.

By the time Mirsad showed up, it was close to midnight. Luciano had stopped drinking, much to Vedad's disappointment, and Prospero had surreptitiously tossed his last two glasses into a nearby potted plant when his host, now thoroughly drunk, wasn't looking.

The mercenary didn't make a good first impression, with his brusque demeanor and calculating eyes. His shaved, sweaty head glowed, a shiny, stubbly orb perched atop a fireplug of a body. A large indentation on the right side of his skull drew Prospero's attention. A little hair could have masked the concave pit, but maybe that was the point. He sensed that Mirsad liked people to know he was hardheaded in every sense of the word.

Prospero endured the convoluted story of how Vedad and Mirsad had first met in Africa, when Vedad was negotiating with a South African company for iron ore mining rights for his steel company. The gunrunner had supplied the South Africans with mercenaries and weapons with which to protect their interests. Discovering they were both Bosnian, however, Vedad and Mirsad had banded together and double-crossed the South Africans, leaving them with neither the firearms nor the minerals. The tale put Prospero on his guard.

Vedad slumped on the couch and, cradling his drink, started the conversation. "My friend, the Italian here, he needs weapons."

"How many?" Mirsad grunted.

"It'll be a large deal. Crates of handguns."

"Handguns are for pussies."

Luciano twitched. Prospero shook his head once to stop his nephew from doing anything stupid. "Not all of us live in war-torn cesspools." His men couldn't exactly go around toting M60s during their weekly collections from the businesses for which they provided protection.

"You want men, maybe, who know how to use weapons made for men?"

"Just the guns, thanks." Prospero could only imagine the thugs Mirsad would provide.

They'd negotiated through the night, Vedad passing out drunk on the couch long before Prospero and Mirsad hammered out the final details. Prospero secured a better price by far than he would have gotten from the Ukrainians, but he would not become a regular customer. Something about the Bosnian felt off. In Prospero's world, men lived by a code. In Mirsad's, brutality ruled. And while Prospero had a thick enough skull, he preferred deploying the brain inside it rather than using his head as a blunt instrument.

Chapter 75

Johann had been patched through to Thea Paris, but the connection dropped before he could speak to her. Cell service on the train was frequently spotty in the countryside. Feeling alternately panicked and frustrated, he decided to try again when they reached an urban area.

He and Fatima had switched trains in Budapest, where he booked them on a two-bed sleeper on the EuroNight Ister to Bucharest. It was a long trip to Istanbul, and the journey would have to be taken in stages. It didn't help that they felt a distinct sense of urgency, considering the bioweapon sitting between them.

They curled up on the bottom of the compartment's two firm bunks, restless, neither one able to nod off. Fatima's presence made him feel determined, capable of anything, but he worried about her because of the bacteria. He couldn't imagine what he'd do if anything happened to his girlfriend. That's how he thought of her now, as his girlfriend. He'd broken away from his father's dominance, and now he felt empowered, able to make his own decisions.

He glanced at his watch. Hours ago, *Vater* would have realized that Johann had disappeared along with the sealed containers. He might be making his own decisions now, but he had sacrificed his father's goodwill—and that could prove quite dangerous for them.

"You're thinking of your father, aren't you?" Fatima had rolled over to stroke his forehead.

"He'll be looking for me." Her touch helped settle his nerves.

"We have a head start, and it was a brilliant idea to buy several different train tickets."

"That will only delay him. He'll get his hands on the CCTV footage from the *Hauptbahnhof* and know soon enough which train I took."

"But we switched lines in Budapest."

"If there's one thing *Vater* has taught me, it's that money and connections can buy you pretty much anything. When I narrowly missed making the National Ski Team, Father hired a private detective to learn everything he could about the coach. A week later, my father leaked information to the press about the coach's penchant for much younger women. Girls, really. Anyway, the coach was replaced with someone more . . . willing to have me on the team."

"You were on the National Ski Team?"

"I faked a knee injury and didn't join. It didn't seem right to accept a spot I didn't earn. But the experience taught me that my father always gets what he wants."

"Should we split up? I could take the containers to my cousin while you create a false trail."

She was so committed, so self-sacrificing, leaving her family in the dead of night to go on this dangerous journey. The thought of them separating hadn't entered his mind until now. Should they? No, they were stronger together. "Traveling as a couple provides better cover. Hopefully *Vater* thinks I'm doing this alone."

"Is that what we are—a couple?"

"Definitely." He leaned in close and kissed her lips, exploring her face with his hands, like a blind man memorizing every surface, soaking up the memory so that he would never forget the feeling.

They talked for hours, held each other close, and finally fell asleep in each other's arms on the small bunk.

Chapter 76

In the morning, Johann's mind felt sharper. He'd slept like the dead, bone-weary after the insanity of the past few days. With any luck, he'd be handing over the bioweapon to a responsible adult soon and be free of this monumental burden. He glanced at his watch. He'd call Thea Paris right after breakfast.

A subtle slowing of the train told him they'd be approaching the next station shortly. Fatima smiled at him when his stomach growled loudly.

"How about I buy us some food while you freshen up?" His hand rested on the door handle. He wanted to give her some privacy.

"Thank you, that's very thoughtful."

"More like starved and self-motivated."

Fatima searched his face. "You okay?"

Last night had been an oasis, allowing him to forget his challenges for a few hours, but her question brought him back to reality. "There's no going back now."

"Maybe this will be a wake-up call for your father."

"*Vater* never regrets his decisions," Johann said, taking his hand off the knob. "And no matter what happens, I don't regret mine. It's bad enough—the refugee camps, the conditions people suffer when they're looking for a better life. But this bacteria . . ."

Fatima smiled wide. "I adore you and your warm heart, Johann Dietrich."

He felt himself blush. "Keep talking like that, and I'll gladly bring you breakfast every day."

She laughed. "Let's start with today. Hurry up, I'm starving."

"Lock the door."

"Yes, sir."

Johann stepped into the corridor, closed the door, and headed for the buffet car. The train decelerated noticeably, the engineer announcing the next stop. He ordered four croissants with butter and jam along with two coffees. While he waited for their food, he gazed out the window at the snow-covered countryside. *Picturesque. Too bad this isn't a holiday.*

The brakes squealed, protesting, as the train ground to a stop at the station. A smattering of people waited on the platform. Teenagers, businessmen, young mothers, a few elderly folks. He scrutinized the passengers as they boarded. No one seemed unusual or out of place.

The steward was filling the two coffee cups for his order when Johann noticed the stranger enter the far end of the buffet car. Dressed in a charcoal suit and a crisp white shirt, he looked like an average businessman, his craggy face banal—but as the man twisted to let a passenger past, Johann recognized him as one of the lackeys who had been present at the *Freiheitswächter* meetings. Which meant that the man would recognize Johann too.

Johann left the coffees and croissants sitting on the counter and rushed back to their compartment before the man in the gray suit spotted him.

Chapter 77

Johann rapped his knuckles on the sleeper door in a prearranged rhythm. Fatima welcomed him inside. Fully dressed, her head scarf back on, she smiled at him. "Where's breakfast?"

"One of the *Freiheitswächter* just boarded. We need to get off."

Panic clouded her face. "Someone you know? Did he recognize you?"

"I'm sure I've seen him with my father before. And it looked like he was wearing one of these." He reached into the pocket where he kept the medallion *Vater* had given him and showed it to her.

"Nice enough, if you don't know what it stands for." Fatima shoved her belongings inside her tote bag and slipped one of the backpacks around her shoulders. "I'm ready."

Johann grabbed the second backpack. The train whistle blew. They had missed their chance to get off the train before it left the station. He cracked open the door and peered down the corridor. The man in the suit was showing the steward a photo. He couldn't hear what the man was saying, but he hoped the *Freiheitswächter* was only looking for him and not Fatima.

He passed her the backpack he had been holding. The canisters were awkward to carry but not very heavy. "The man is to our right. We need to split up. Take the canisters, and head for the back of the train. If he follows you, hide in the cargo hold. I'll be right behind you."

"I don't like this, Johann."

He cradled Fatima's face in his hands and kissed her gently. "I'd never forgive myself if something happened to you. And we need to make sure this stuff winds up in safe hands. You have Thea Paris's number, just in case?"

The train lurched forward.

"Yes."

"I'll be there soon. Hurry."

"Be careful."

"Don't worry. I'm sure *Vater* told him not to hurt me."

Fatima raised her eyebrows, a skeptical look on her face. "Are you sure? You're ruining your father's grand plan, years in the making."

Johann wondered if Fatima had a point. Look what had happened to Uncle Karl.

Chapter 78

Johann stared through the peephole after Fatima left the cabin. The train had started moving again. If the *Freiheitswächter* followed Fatima, he would pursue the man, find a way to distract him. But for ten minutes, no one passed their sleeping compartment. Still, given that the man had spoken to the steward, he couldn't stay where he was. And with the train nearing full speed, he couldn't exactly jump out the window, either.

Johann cracked open the door and looked to the right. The man in the charcoal suit was long gone, along with the steward. He glanced to the left. No one. He slipped out, staying close to the wall, conscious of the jounce and sway of the car beneath his feet.

The doors to the next carriage opened. He sucked in a deep breath. An older woman dressed in tweed stepped inside. She smiled. Johann returned her greeting, exhaling with relief. He needed to walk through at least ten cars to get to the cargo car. He was about to pull open the doors leading to the next car and step through when a flash of gray caught his eye. The *Freiheitswächter* was in the next carriage.

Dammit, how did he get past me without me seeing him? He backed away from the window.

Johann texted Fatima: *Coming as soon as I can.*

She responded immediately: *Hiding in the freight area. All clear.*

Thank goodness she'd made it. He slipped on the leather gloves and wool cap he'd stashed in his jacket pocket. He glanced around. *Now or never.* He pressed the red button that opened the door to the next car. A soft warning beep sounded. He exited quickly, silencing the alarm.

A blast of cold air buffeted him between the cars. His gloved fingers locked around the steel safety bar, gripping it tightly. The train bulleted down the tracks through the snowy countryside, his eyes watering from the frigid temperatures. And it would only get colder up top.

Taking a breath, he swung his lanky frame from the platform between the cars onto the maintenance ladder leading to the roof. He climbed the rungs slowly, all the muscles in his arms fully engaged. A strong gust of wind threatened to fling him loose, sending his right leg off its rung and in front of the window of the carriage. In a panic, he fought to get his footing back, resting for a moment once he'd secured his shoe back on the rung.

His concern now was whether anyone had seen his leg in the window. Either way, he needed to get a move on. He tackled the final two steps, then collapsed on top of the carriage, staying under the steady stream of wind as much as possible. He wormed his way forward so he had a handhold. He took a moment to catch his breath.

The hardest part was over—at least he thought so. Then he glanced up. Two electrical wires hung parallel to the carriage. He'd forgotten that this brand of train relied on electricity. Avoiding the wires meant he'd need to stay directly in the middle of the carriage.

Here goes nothing. He edged his knees forward, preparing to stand. Before he could lift himself up, a faint sound drew his attention. He glanced back over the edge of the car.

The man in the gray suit was scaling the ladder.

Scheisse. Johann climbed to his feet, stabilizing himself. The wind billowed his clothes around his body, fabric flapping wildly. He stood dead center, avoiding the wires, slowly getting the feel of the wind resistance. Finding his balance, he ran to the end of the carriage. One quick jump, and he launched himself onto the next one. At least ten carriages stretched ahead.

A quick glance behind—the *Freiheitswächter* had already climbed the ladder. Compact and muscular, the suited man looked more than capable of catching him before he reached the end of the train. Johann looked ahead, searching for the freight car, where Fatima waited.

A chill ran through his body: about a mile ahead and approaching fast, a tunnel yawned like a great hungry mouth.

Chapter 79

Johann sprinted along the train's roof, hopping from one carriage to the next as fast as he could. A quick check over his shoulder—the distance between him and his pursuer was shrinking.

The train raced toward the tunnel.

A hundred feet away.

Fifty, and closing.

Every tunnel had a different clearance, but they were all mandated to have at least nine feet. Seconds after the train entered the tunnel's abyss, Johann dove forward onto his stomach, knowing the *Freiheitswächter* wouldn't be able to see him in the dark.

The overwhelming blackness of the tunnel swallowed him whole, the sound of the blustering wind replaced by the thunderous rattle of the train in the enclosed space. Wet, dank air flooded his sinuses. Beneath him, the cold of the train's steel roof penetrated his jacket. He rolled onto his back and raised his legs, the soles of his feet facing the direction of his pursuer. Coiling his knees close to his stomach, he waited.

Footsteps pounded closer, closer. The shadow was almost upon him. Johann unleashed his legs, his feet colliding with hard muscle. *Umph.* The impact sent Johann skidding backward on the roof, but he had the benefit of a lower center of gravity and a solid base, so he didn't go far.

Surprised by Johann's kick, the *Freiheitswächter* launched up and sideways, wheeling his arms around as he tried to regain his balance, before stumbling into the pantograph wires. A massive spray of electricity lit up the tunnel, sparks cascading in a dazzling display of pyrotechnics as the man spun from the contact.

Darkness became light when the live wires connected with the man's torso, completing the circuit from train to wire. Every muscle in the stranger's body convulsed, flinging him to the edge of the car, where he struggled for a second before tumbling off, all sound lost in the roar of the tunnel.

Johann lay there, shaken. He had just killed a man.

Seconds later, the train rocketed back into daylight, leaving the tunnel behind. Hands trembling, Johann scrambled to his feet and rushed forward to reach the freight car. He'd been able to neutralize the immediate threat, but the man had surely notified his father that Johann was on the train. And was he the only *Freiheitswächter* on board?

The next station approached in the distance. He needed to find Fatima and get off the train. They'd have to find another way to Istanbul.

Chapter 80

Thea tapped the keys of her laptop, scanning her e-mails for updates. Ayan and Jabari hadn't called back. Prospero had probably caught them, and she worried that he would punish them for their escape attempt. In group captivity scenarios, when someone attempts a breakout, they are often beaten, sometimes even executed. A powerful lesson for the other hostages.

In this case, Thea was pretty sure Prospero would keep them alive—he knew that the boys were his greatest leverage. Still, he'd have to do something to reestablish control after the escape, and the easiest way to do that was through fear.

Her phone rang, jolting her out of her thoughts.

"Paris."

"I have that young man calling again." Hakan sounded spent. She doubted he'd slept more than a few hours since the hijacking.

"Okay, patch him through." She inhaled deeply and waited for Hakan to connect her with this anonymous and persistent young man. A click sounded as he was routed to her.

"Thea Paris speaking."

"What's your dog's name?"

"Who is this?" she asked.

"Please, just answer the question."

"Aegis." It wasn't a state secret.

"And your mother's name?"

"Tatiana. What's this about?" The kid had read too many spy novels.

"I wanted to be sure I was talking to the *real* Thea Paris."

"If I were any kind of serious impostor, neither of those questions would have made me break a sweat. But now it's my turn to ask a question. Who's calling?"

"My name is Johann Dietrich. I'm from Salzburg, Austria."

"How old are you, Johann?"

"Seventeen." His voice cracked.

"Hakan Asker, the man you've been talking to at Quantum, says you know something about the hijacking of the jet in Libya."

"I know that *Vater* was angry the plane had been taken."

"Your father?"

"Gernot Dietrich. He owns Dietrich Arms Manufacturing."

She'd heard of them, a successful weapons manufacturer that supplied the US Army, among many others. He had been part of Nikos's world.

"I overheard *Vater* saying the Italians must have hijacked the plane."

Interesting. "How is your father involved in this?"

"He knows a woman who was on board."

"Ocean?"

"I think so. I overheard them talking about her being important. She's a scientist of some sort."

The earnest voice, the solid information—she sensed that he was genuine. "Do you have other information about the hijacking?"

"No. That's not why I'm calling." She heard him take a long breath. "I need your help."

"I see. What kind of help, exactly?"

"Could you meet me in Istanbul? It's important."

"That's quite an ask from someone I've only just met," Thea said with a soft laugh. "Look, I'm in the midst of trying to negotiate the release of the hostages from that jet. But I could have an associate meet you, someone I trust."

"What if I told you this was about a biological weapons attack?"

The hairs on the back of her neck stood on end. "Excuse me?"

"I don't want to go into details on the phone."

"This is a secure line," Thea said, thinking fast. "If you really want my help, you're going to have to give me more."

The words came out of the boy in a rush. "My father wants to release a genetically targeted weapon inside several refugee camps throughout Europe."

Her pulse accelerated. "What kind of bioweapon?"

"Pneumonic plague, targeted specifically to people of Arab descent."

Her mind reeled. *It would spread like wildfire in the crowded conditions of the camps.* "Do you know the locations he's targeting? We can get people in place, stop the attacks."

"I have the plague in my backpack."

"What?"

"In sealed containers. I stole it from him."

"Where are you now?"

"Headed to Istanbul with my girlfriend, Fatima Abboud. She has a cousin who is a scientist."

"You can't just walk around with a biological weapon. What if it gets into the wrong hands?"

"That's why I called you. I'll give the canisters to you or Fatima's cousin, but no one else."

"When will you reach Istanbul?"

"Tomorrow morning."

"I'll be there. Give me your number. I'll call as soon as I arrive to set up a meet."

"Okay." He rattled off the digits of his burner cell.

"And send me your photo so I know what you look like." Hakan could run a full background check on Johann and his father before the meet.

"I'm hard to miss, built like a tall string bean." He paused, then plunged on awkwardly. "I have Marfan syndrome."

Thea immediately felt for the kid. "Well, you're talking to someone who's tethered to an insulin pump as we speak."

"Diabetes?"

"Type 1." It felt good not to be so guarded about her condition.

"Do you miss chocolate? I don't know if I could survive that . . ."

"I can enjoy a small piece now and then," she said, smiling. "Johann?"

"Yes?"

"Be careful."

"I will, Thea. Thank you. See you soon."

Chapter 81

Johann felt better after talking to Thea, but the feeling didn't last long. *Vater* had nearly caught them once, and the next attempt wouldn't be far off. The sight of the man in the gray suit slipping off the train car in the dim light of the tunnel still haunted him.

He and Fatima had walked more than five kilometers after leaving the train in Romania. Googling their location, he'd found a nearby truck stop. They planned to hitch a ride with a long-haul driver to conserve their funds and to make it more difficult to track them.

Johann shifted the two backpacks slung on his shoulder. The straps digging into his muscles were a constant and painful reminder of the gravity of the situation.

"You sure you're okay?" Fatima asked.

"Just thinking about our next move." He'd told Fatima about the chase along the train roof but hadn't shared details of the man's death. Johann wanted to protect her from all the horrors he'd witnessed; she had an innocence about her that he loved. He didn't want her to change, to become cynical like him. Years of being bullied had shaped his dark outlook.

"What if none of the truckers will take us?" she asked.

"We'll find one. We're paying passengers." The bulge of notes in his pocket both comforted and unsettled him. They had more than enough money, but they could easily be robbed. Switching from the rail system to the highway made them a lot less safe.

The sun had disappeared from the sky, dusk nestling in. The neon lights of the roadside café lay ahead. Several eighteen-wheelers were sandwiched together in the large parking area, and the scent of diesel fuel made his head swim. He didn't know when it had happened, but he and Fatima were holding hands as they walked across the lot.

Signs in the window featured pictures of cakes and pies. He thought of the coffee and croissants they'd never had a chance to eat on the train. His stomach growled loudly.

Fatima smiled, looking up at him. "I could also use a bite."

Johann held the door for her, looking around as he did. A variety of truckers perched at battered Formica tables. Many looked as if they had lived hard, with deep wrinkles carved into their gray faces. A guy in greasy overalls gave him and Fatima a long stare. Some of the men were downing their food in quick gulps, eager to get back on the road, while others lingered over coffee.

Two scantily dressed women lingered near the toilets, chatting with each other and occasionally eyeing the customers. In a corner a man sat reading a newspaper, and Johann caught a glimpse of a front-page story about the investigation into the attack on Schönbrunn. His mind went to the canisters inside the backpacks, which seemed heavier with every step.

There were plenty of seats open at the counter, which had the best vantage point inside the restaurant. "Let's sit over there."

He and Fatima made their way over and plopped down on the swivel stools. Within seconds, a waitress brought them two empty mugs. "What you want?" she asked in heavily accented German.

"Pancakes and coffee, please," Fatima responded.

"Make that two," he said. "And sausage on the side for me."

The waitress grabbed the coffeepot and poured two brimming cups, slopping some of the hot liquid on the counter before heading back into the kitchen. Johann used a napkin to wipe up the mess. "Not exactly like the last place I took you," he said.

"At this point, I'd eat a spare tire." She tucked an errant hair under her scarf.

"I'm sure there's plenty of those around here."

A man sitting two stools away smiled at them. He had dark skin and a wide face with lively eyes. "*Marhaba*," he said to Fatima.

She returned his greeting in Arabic, then continued speaking to him. Johann had no idea what she was saying, but he did hear the word *Istanbul,* so he figured she was asking about his destination.

The waitress dumped their plates onto the counter, slipping the bill under Johann's coffee mug. He didn't dare ask for a refill.

He and Fatima wolfed their pancakes while she spoke to the man. They were both smiling, nodding, so he figured it must be going well enough. Suddenly, Johann felt a presence and turned to see the man in the greasy overalls looming behind them.

"You desert pigs invade our country, steal our jobs, and babble in your stupid gibberish. Shut the hell up," he said in accented English.

Before Johann could step in, their new friend raised a hand in a conciliatory gesture. "I'm sorry if I offended you, sir. I was just leaving." He slipped a couple of bills under his plate, nodded to Johann and Fatima, and left the restaurant.

The guy in overalls dogged his every step on the way out. "Don't bother coming back here either. You're not welcome."

Fatima shook her head at Johann, a curt gesture. He understood. Every inch of him wanted to tell the man off, but he held his tongue—for Fatima. They couldn't afford to be involved in a disturbance. Instead, they too left money on the counter and headed for the door. Maybe they could find a trucker in the parking lot who might be willing to take a couple of paying passengers to Turkey.

Exiting the restaurant, Fatima immediately turned to the left, heading toward the parking lot.

"Sorry about that. But don't worry, we'll find a ride." Johann felt bad for both Fatima and the kindly driver.

A little smile curved on her face. "We already have one. Mohammed is headed south, and Istanbul is on his way."

"How much does he want?" He hoped they'd still have some cash left over.

"Nothing. He just wants to help. I told him that I have a relative in need in Istanbul—it's close enough to the truth."

"That's wonderful, Fatima." *Maybe we can pull this off.*

They reached Mohammed's truck, a Peterbilt eighteen-wheeler that looked as if it had seen better days, the royal blue paint on the cab chipped and scratched. Mohammed opened the side door with a wide smile.

"Make yourselves comfortable." He spoke English so they could both understand. "If you're tired, there's a small bed in the back, behind the seats."

The interior of the cab was meticulously tidy, if a little weathered. A photo of Mohammed's family perched on the dashboard.

"You have three kids?" Johann asked.

"And a fourth on the way. It's a full house." He laughed.

"Beautiful family." Fatima sounded wistful. She must be missing hers. A pang of envy caught Johann off guard. A profound sense of loss vied with the guilt inside.

Chapter 82

Johann woke from a long nap in the back of Mohammed's cab. The undulating of the truck had soothed his frayed nerves, allowing him to sleep. His mind felt clearer, more centered. Fatima had dozed for a few hours earlier but now sat up front with Mohammed. Johann kicked off the blanket and climbed into the front of the cab to join them.

"I was just going to wake you. We're going through border control to Turkey in five minutes." Fatima's voice quavered; she was obviously worried about the crossing. Mohammed had no idea what his two teenaged passengers were transporting.

Johann felt the same trepidation but didn't want to let it show. "Thanks again for letting us ride with you, Mohammed."

"It's been wonderful having company. The late-night radio shows get a little boring." The truck driver laughed, something he seemed to do easily and often.

"How long are you usually away from your family?" Fatima asked.

"At least two weeks every month, sometimes more."

"It must get lonely." She touched the photo of his family sitting on the dashboard.

"Definitely. In Yemen, I trained as a mechanical engineer, but they wouldn't accept my credentials here, so I accepted this job to help pay for my children's university."

"You're a good man." Fatima said.

Johann's face reddened. The Dietrich family had been wealthy for generations, especially now, and he'd never had to consider what he could or couldn't afford.

Mohammed geared down the eighteen-wheeler. "Two kilometers to the border."

Johann reached into the back and covered the two backpacks with a blanket. "What product are you transporting?"

"Fertilizer. Turkey imports a lot of it."

An uncomfortable feeling roiled in Johann's gut. Maybe they'd chosen the wrong ride. He wondered if Mohammed had ever been hassled at the border. The son of an arms manufacturer, Johann knew that fertilizer was often used to make bombs.

"I'd be delighted to buy you a meal after we go through customs." Mohammed decelerated the truck to join the lineup of vehicles preparing for the crossing.

"That'd be great," Johann said. "But we're treating."

"Then I promise not to order the filet mignon." Mohammed smiled.

"Can I ask you something—why didn't you tell off that jerk in the diner?" In the silence that followed his question, Johann wondered if he should have kept his mouth shut.

"Good question," Mohammed finally said with a sigh. "Europe has become a tricky place for people like me. Everyone is scared because of a few horrible events carried out by Muslims, events sensationalized in newspapers and on television without much understanding or sympathy. The anger of people like the man in the café is an expression of that fear."

"But you did nothing wrong," Johann said.

"Yes, but he has been shaped by the society around him. My skin color and my language were enough to provoke him." He paused. "Instead of reacting to the abuse in a negative way—which would make the problem worse—I chose to respond with respect. Maybe next time, remembering our interaction today, that man won't lash out."

Johann thought of the greasy thug in the diner, doubtful he would ever change. Just like his father, he realized. At first Mohammed sounded naïve, but Johann could see how an approach like this might, over time, begin to make a difference in attitudes. He shook his head; time was a luxury they did not have at the moment.

Fatima's eyes were wet. "It's not easy to be judged by your appearance, your religion. Islam promotes peace, helping others. The extremists on both sides feed on each other, and the death and destruction they cause hurt us all."

"What if true Muslims fought the extremists?" Given the relative numbers, Johann figured they'd surely win the fight.

"Through violence? Then we'd be the same as them," Fatima said. "Setting an example of peace is the only way."

But someone has to stamp out terrorism. Johann thought of the innocent people, the kids, killed in the Schönbrunn attack. He believed that Omar Kaleb deserved to be punished. But was he already beginning to think like his father, like the man in greasy overalls?

Mohammed merged into the right lane. Two Turkish police officers toting MP5s stood to one side while the customs representative approached the driver's window of the eighteen-wheeler. The truck driver passed the officer all three of their passports. The customs officer flipped through the pages, studying them intensely. Johann tried to appear calm, even as he was shaking on the inside. In preparing for the trip, he had learned that customs officers looked for physiological signs of stress, like darting eyes, sweating, fidgeting hands. Johann had discussed this with Fatima, and they both managed to mask any obvious tension—until the man asked about their luggage.

Chapter 83

Johann tensed when the officer asked about their belongings. Although he had two pairs of underwear and a fresh shirt stuffed beside one the canisters, it wasn't as if he could show the officer his backpacks. Before he could answer, Fatima did.

"We were robbed on the train. The thief stole everything." Her eyes were downcast.

The customs officer studied their faces. Johann didn't dare breathe.

"It happened in Bucharest. The Gypsies. If this kind man hadn't come along," she said, gesturing to Mohammed, "we'd be stranded."

The officer studied Fatima's face, then his. *Yes, those damn Gypsies.*

"They're visiting her sick aunt in Istanbul," Mohammed said.

Seconds ticked by. Johann felt sick, trapped.

"Go on." The customs guy let them through with a brisk wave.

Relief flooded Johann's body. Mohammed put the truck into gear and drove into Turkey. He probably wondered why Fatima had lied, but he had gone along without question.

After a lively meal together, Mohammed dropped them off near the city center in Istanbul. Johann hated to say goodbye. Meeting this man had been a blessing, and he couldn't be more grateful, especially after their harrowing experience on the train. Best of all, he had never once questioned them about Fatima's declaration at the border.

Johann had been tempted to confide in Mohammed, but he didn't want to involve yet another innocent person. The trucker looked sad as they said their goodbyes. Long-haul driving was a solitary job. Talking to Fatima in Arabic had probably felt like a slice of home.

Now they were alone again, but Johann hoped it wouldn't be for long. They would make contact with Thea Paris, and they'd meet with Fatima's cousin. One important stop first.

While Fatima waited in a nearby coffee shop, Johann entered the all-male Turkish bathhouse, the heady scent of eucalyptus bringing back memories of his last trip to the city, with Uncle Karl. A wave of sadness passed over him as he reminisced about that magical week. They'd spent an entire afternoon at the Grand Bazaar looking for a gift for Father, finally settling on a green hunting coat fit for an aga.

During that trip, he and Uncle Karl had visited many of Istanbul's amazing, exotic attractions, and he remembered being awed by the architecture, the sights and smells of the city's many street bazaars, and especially the multiple daily calls of the muezzin to prayer. The *ezan* chanted from the loudspeakers of the Blue Mosque had mesmerized them as they stood among the benches outside, a call to the faithful that was loud and beautiful and profound. With its enormous tiered domes and soaring minarets, the Blue Mosque was the most beautiful building Johann had ever seen, and that was only from the outside. When they were finally able to venture within, Johann had been amazed at the intricate tiled tessellations, proof that math and art could be one and the same.

Answering the Blue Mosque's call to prayer was the broadcast from the Hagia Sophia, just across the plaza from where they stood. It had originally been built in the sixth century as a Greek Orthodox Christian church but later served as a Catholic church and finally as a mosque. Now it was a museum filled with countless objects of wonder.

Only two years had passed since that visit, but it felt like a lifetime. And now Karl was gone forever.

Shifting the backpacks on his shoulder, he paid the entrance fee for the baths and requested a large locker. Inside the changing room, two men were disrobing. If their hand and foot gestures were any indication, they were engaged in an animated discussion about football. Johann stalled, untying his shoelaces and tying them again, waiting for the men to leave. He wished he could enjoy the healing baths, forget his troubles for a few hours, but that wasn't why he was there.

He and Fatima had both agreed that carrying the plague around the city was a bad idea. If Father knew which train they'd been on, he could easily discover their final destination and track them down. Instead, they would stash the containers inside the changing room—it would be more secure than using the lockers at bus and rail stations, given all the CCTV cameras.

The men finally left, strolling down the hallway into the baths without giving him a second look. Johann shoved the backpacks into a large locker, closed the door, and triple-checked that it was firmly locked.

Slipping the key into his jacket's zippered inside pocket, he left the baths, joining Fatima in the coffeehouse for a quick snack and Turkish coffee. They walked the two kilometers to her cousin's flat, the fresh air and caffeine giving him a lift—or maybe he just felt lighter without the two backpacks.

"What's your cousin like?" Johann was intrigued to meet a member of Fatima's family but also worried about trusting someone he had never met to manage this burden.

"Smart, kind, and righteous." Fatima looked up at him. "Don't worry, Marush will help us."

"Will he call your parents?"

"I'll ask him to hold off until he has taken care of the canisters."

Johann wasn't sure how Marush would react after learning Johann's father wanted to commit genocide against all Arabs. *What would I do in his shoes?*

Fatima led them up a path to a large stone building. Entering the building's foyer, she pressed the button for apartment 4A. Seconds passed. Maybe no one was home. A scratchy buzz sounded, followed by a woman's guttural voice.

"Yamen, it's me, Fatima," she said.

A rush of Arabic followed; then a buzzer sounded, and the door clicked open.

Johann glanced at Fatima. Her face had paled slightly. "My parents called, wondering if they had heard from me. Who knows what Yamen told them. I should have mentioned, my cousin's wife, she's . . . excitable."

"What do you mean?"

"You'll see." Fatima started up the stairs.

Before they could reach the upper flat, the door had already opened. A heavyset, middle-aged woman with weathered skin stepped into the hall and crushed Fatima in a massive hug.

An exchange in Arabic followed. Johann didn't know what had been said, but, judging from the skeptical look on Yamen's face when she looked him up and down, he was already in her bad books.

Yamen dragged Fatima into the apartment. He followed.

"I'd like for you to meet my friend Johann," Fatima said in English.

"Nice to meet you," he said.

"What have you done to my niece, taking her away from her home, her family?"

"Please, Johann is helping me with something important. We need to speak to Marush. Is he at work?" Fatima asked.

Panic clouded Yamen's face.

"What is it?" Fatima asked.

"Marush was taken last week by the Turkish police."

"What? Why didn't you tell Mama and Papa, all of us?" It was Fatima's turn on the offense.

"The police claim he was involved in a failed coup against the president."

Johann's hopes plummeted. The scientist had his own problems. He felt bad for Fatima and her aunt but sick about losing Marush as an adviser.

"I'm so sorry." Fatima placed a hand over Yamen's.

"I'm worried I'll never see him again," she said, tears slipping from her eyes.

"Don't think like that. We'll hire a lawyer, help you. You should have told us—we're your family."

"You mean, like you told your family about your plans to run away?" Yamen asked, wiping her face.

Fatima blushed, and Yamen pressed on. "What did you need from Marush?"

"Just his advice in a scientific matter."

"I won't be much help, then."

"It's okay. It's still good to see you, even under such terrible circumstances." Fatima squeezed Yamen's fingers.

"Your parents are really worried. You shouldn't have run off like that."

"Are you going to tell them you've seen me?"

"I should."

"But you won't?" Fatima asked, pleading. "We need a little more time."

Yamen hesitated. "I will give you a day, but then you must contact them—or I will."

"Thank you, thank you!" Fatima hugged the thickset woman. "I'm very sorry about Marush. He's a good man."

"He spoke out against the government—a brave and stupid thing to do."

Derailed as it was by anxiety, Johann's mind was only half on the conversation. They had but one hope now.

Thea Paris.

Chapter 84

After crossing the humpbacked stone arch bridge over the river Neretva, Prospero directed Bassam's drivers to Vedad's home in the Bosnian countryside. While Prospero supervised the shepherding of the hostages into their new quarters, Luciano and two guards headed to the local market to purchase groceries and other supplies.

Bassam's team had immediately fallen in line after hearing about their leader's death, barely a whisper of sorrow among them. After all, Prospero Salvatore was funding this operation, and they fully intended to get paid for it. And it was well known he made it a policy to pay well. His father had instilled that practice in him, explaining that elbow grease and overtime should always be richly rewarded. Especially in their business.

Returning to the villa brought up vivid memories of his last visit. The Glock he now carried had been part of the deal he'd negotiated that night with the gunrunner Mirsad.

Hungry and tired but also afraid, nearly all the passengers were both more irritable and more pliable. They'd been promised food and rest once everyone was safely ensconced in the new location, so they trudged into the mansion in an orderly line, shoulders slumped and scowls on their faces. Ayan and Jabari were the only hostages seemingly unaffected by their ordeal. They poked each other as they climbed out of the van, laughing and joking.

As motivated as he was to get back to Violetta's *cucina*, he had avoided Thea's call, stalling the exchange and delaying his return home. Chances were, *Liberata* was homing in on their Turkish hideout, and he couldn't risk the kidnap negotiator learning anything she could use to track them here. He needed that nuclear material, or his deal with Enzo Spruilli would fall apart—and he wanted Ocean returned to him. Still, Thea could downplay the situation all she liked, but she desperately wanted those boys back. It was impossible to be too tough when the lives of your loved ones were at stake.

He turned to face the massive home. The Bosnian had spared no expense creating this hideaway. An elegant stone wall protected the mansion from prying eyes. Towering oak trees lined the long driveway, like soldiers standing guard. A sculpted lion's head decorated the large fountain, which was framed by lattice-work and inlaid gold leaf.

Vedad was in the middle of a deal in Singapore, so Prospero wouldn't have a chance to catch up with his acquaintance this time around. But he owed his absent host a night out for lending him the mansion.

The kitchen staff had been instructed to prepare a meal large enough for two dozen people, and he hoped it would be ready soon—like the prisoners, he was hungry. Bassam's men marched the hostages into the great room, an enormous area with floor-to-ceiling windows facing the gardens. Vaulted ceilings, a large fireplace, and three separate seating areas welcomed them—including the many animal heads he remembered from his last visit. The taxidermist had created trophies so lifelike that he felt as if the beady eyes were always watching, no matter where in the room he stood.

A massive rectangular area, the great room offered ample space for all the hostages. It was definitely a step up from the outbuilding in Turkey. To avoid any further escape attempts, Prospero stationed a guard at each of the two entrances to the room. No more live feed—he wanted to keep a close eye on everyone. Across the hall, an enormous bathroom allowed the guards to accompany hostages on restroom breaks.

He leaned against the carved wooden bar, seven leather stools perched in front. Once the passengers were settled for the night, he'd savor a single malt. The Bosnian's liquor cabinet was enviable, stocked with rare spirits from around the world, and the journey had left Prospero with a distinct thirst. He removed his cell from his pocket and placed it on the counter. In a couple of hours, he'd call Thea, explain when and where the exchange would take place.

Laverdeen indicated he'd like to speak with Prospero, who waved him over. In a low voice, the pilot said his piece. "Karlsson isn't doing well, constantly talking to himself now in an angry tone. I'm worried he might try to harm himself or someone else. Can you transport him back to London or isolate him? Or maybe have a doctor prescribe a sedative?"

"No one leaves, and we won't be here long enough to pick up a prescription." Prospero thought for a moment, then grabbed a bottle of the least expensive scotch he could find and thrust it into Laverdeen's hands. "A few belts will cheer him up."

"I'm not sure alcohol is the best solution." Laverdeen remained rooted in front of him.

"Then drink it yourself. If Karlsson needs restraining, let one of the guards know. They'll be happy to tie him up."

"Don't you have any compassion? The man is mentally ill."

Prospero gave Laverdeen a hard stare. "You're not his keeper."

"No, just an empathetic person. Haven't you ever craved comfort in your suffering?"

Before Prospero could respond, three loud bangs sounded from the front hall. He reached for his Glock, but it was too late. Four men in black balaclavas armed with AK-47s burst into the great room.

Che diavolo! The men he had posted outside must have been neutralized, and they hadn't heard a thing.

One of the black-clad intruders—a short, stocky guy—held a SIG Sauer against one of the guard's heads. Prospero's men raised their weapons. Several hostages screamed; others huddled behind the couches. Karlsson dropped to the ground and hugged himself, rolling back and forth.

"Call them off, or your man dies," the stocky intruder said.

Prospero indicated for his men to lower their weapons. A firefight in close quarters would result in massive bloodshed. The hostages' lives, especially the boys', had to come first.

"What can I do for you gentlemen?" Prospero asked, using the term loosely. Tattoos—mostly stars—crawled up the necks of the Bosnian hoods. One star per kill. His organization would never tolerate such a public display. A killer had no business advertising.

The short guy removed his balaclava.

Prospero recognized the man's face—and the dent in his head. *Fucking Mirsad.*

"We meet again," the Bosnian said.

"Yes." Prospero studied the relative positions of his men and Mirsad's, hostages scattered around the room. His men couldn't engage the intruders without risking lives. "And here I thought we were friends."

"We are. Turn over the hostages, and you and your men can go."

Someone's mouth had been running. Not Vedad; he was far too cautious a businessman to betray Prospero, especially for money he didn't need. More likely someone in his organization had shared the news about the unexpected stay at Vedad's villa.

"Let's have a drink, talk this out," Prospero said.

"There's nothing to negotiate." Mirsad closed the gap between them.

No way could he surrender the hostages, not with this much at stake. He reached into his jacket and surreptitiously pressed a button on his cell.

Chapter 85

"My dear Mirsad, there's always time for a drink." Prospero reached for a unique bottle of vodka that was probably worth several cases of M4s. Vedad would be annoyed that he'd opened it, but Prospero wasn't worried about that right now. He poured two healthy shots, motioning for the Bosnian to join him.

"Have your men drop their weapons." Mirsad edged closer.

Prospero nodded. Reluctantly, his team placed their firearms on the floor and kicked them into the middle of the room.

"All of you, over there." Mirsad pointed to the far side of the room, with the largest seating area. The hostages and Prospero's guards moved into a corner, wariness in their eyes. Ayan and Jabari stood behind an armchair, quiet and serious.

Karlsson remained on the rug near Prospero, muttering to himself.

"Do what you're told." One of the Bosnians gave Karlsson a kick, but he just moaned louder, becoming more agitated. Laverdeen was right: the guy needed serious help.

Mirsad looked irritated by the commotion. Prospero remembered how twitchy the Bosnian had been the last time they'd met.

This could go sideways in a hurry.

"Let me talk to him." Prospero raised his hands, so the Bosnians knew he wasn't making a play. He walked over to Karlsson, the man beyond distraught. Prospero leaned down and wrapped his right arm around the hostage's head, right at the jawline. He tightened his hold and tucked his left arm behind Karlsson's head, then jerked his arms in a quarter turn. After a loud snap, silence reigned.

"Now, let's have that drink," Prospero said, standing back and ignoring the pain in his hip and the horrified stares from the other hostages. *Fuck them.* He had just saved all their lives by sacrificing Karlsson's.

Prospero returned to the bar and lifted his glass. "*Živjeli,*" he said, using the Bosnian toast.

Mirsad slipped onto the stool beside him, placing his AK on the counter out of Prospero's reach. "I'll have that drink, but we have nothing to discuss. The hostages are mine."

Prospero slugged back his shot of vodka. "Don't rush to judgment. Information can be useful."

"What information?"

"The total worth of the hostages' K&R policies."

"How would you know that?"

"I've been planning this for a while." Which was true, just not for the reason the Bosnian assumed. Prospero had no interest in ransoming anyone for cash. He had a much bigger prize in mind. "I know the net worth of all the passengers, which ones have liquid assets . . ."

Mirsad wasn't a gifted thinker, but he had the cunning of a fox. You didn't survive in his business without it. Still, greed was often the weakness that brought even the savviest men down.

"I could beat the information out of you." The bald man tossed down the shot of vodka and slammed his glass onto the bar.

"You could try." Prospero poured him another round. "But how experienced are you at dealing with kidnap negotiators? I have history with the consultant on this case, Thea Paris. We can call her now. It's just . . . I can't imagine she'll want to deal with someone new. We've built trust."

"I'll sell the hostages for cash in the Ukraine."

"Your choice, of course, but you won't make a tenth as much." Prospero paused. "Consider: I have wire transfers set up to untraceable bank accounts in the Caymans. In ten minutes, my banker can create an account for you, making you a very rich man. We've done business before, you and I, and I would be happy to partner with you in this venture."

The wheels inside Mirsad's head were grinding.

Prospero lowered his voice. "Dump those goons over there, come in with me, and you won't have to share your portion. You could be on a beach next week with ten of the best-looking hookers money can buy, waiting for all this to blow over."

Mirsad's eyelids flickered. *Predictable.* Prospero wondered if it was the money or the prostitutes that were getting to the Bosnian.

"How much, total?"

"Thirty percent of the take. Upward of six million American dollars."

"I should get seventy percent." The Bosnian grabbed a cigarette and lighter from his front pocket, lit it, and inhaled.

"Without my information and connections, you wouldn't see a fraction of that money. Let me finalize the details with the negotiator—you'll make six million while sitting here drinking vodka."

"Fifty percent." Mirsad blew out a lungful of smoke.

"Sorry. I have a huge investment here . . ."

A slight tightening of the man's mouth. "Forty-five percent."

"Forty." Prospero topped up Mirsad's vodka. Nice as it was, he would much rather be drinking scotch.

"How long?"

"Less than twenty-four hours."

"You could cheat me." Mirsad leaned closer, his hot breath emitting vodka fumes.

"As soon as we create the account, you can transfer the money to your own bank."

Prospero waited, knowing when to stop selling. Mirsad had wanted a quick snatch and grab so he could sell the hostages to a local terrorist organization. But serious money beckoned.

"Call this kidnap negotiator. Tell her you want the money now, or someone dies."

"Don't be hasty. Hostages are only worth something if they're alive."

"You just killed one." Mirsad downed another shot of vodka. "Phone her. For all she knows, he's still alive."

"You are absolutely right." Sunlight glinting off something shiny caught Prospero's eye through the expanse of windows facing the garden. *About fucking time.* "One more drink, and then I'll call her. And why don't we say forty-three percent for you."

The bald man smiled, revealing his crooked incisors. Prospero leaned back on his stool and patiently waited for Luciano to make his move.

Chapter 86

Prospero poured another round of vodka and raised his glass. "To our partnership."

"You'd better not be fucking with me." Mirsad's voice was gravelly.

The passengers huddled in the far corner, the Bosnians' AK-47s trained in their direction. *Perfect.*

With Mirsad's permission, Prospero pulled out his cell so he could share a screenshot with Mirsad before calling Thea. He actually did have an account in the Caymans, with a healthy bottom line. "This is what I made on the last hijacking." A total fabrication, but the Bosnian had no way of knowing better. He typed some more on the phone, looking up when he was done. "My banker is creating an account for you."

Prospero caught a flash of movement just outside the great room's windows. Mirsad was so absorbed by the phone, he didn't notice.

A loud shot rang out, fired through the window overlooking the gardens. One of Mirsad's men slumped onto the floor. Broken glass cascaded through the air as Luciano fired again from outside. The commotion, the angle, the glass—they weren't clean shots. The Bosnians cracked off several rounds in response, the wall of windows dissolving into shards.

Hostages dove behind furniture, seeking cover. Screams peppered the air. Prospero's guards scrambled to retrieve their weapons.

Luciano and the two men he had taken with him stormed inside. The Bosnians were hardened fighters, responding instinctively to the attack. Round after round was destroying the great room and its contents. One of Bassam's men collapsed, followed by two of the Bosnians.

When the attack began, Prospero had lunged for Mirsad's gun, but the Bosnian was too fast—and closer to the AK-47. Mirsad grabbed the stock and raised the weapon. Prospero was able to catch the end of the rifle and tried to twist the gun away.

The two men toppled together from the barstools onto the floor. Prospero landed on his bad hip, the pain lancing down to his marrow. He battled Mirsad for control of the weapon, the acrid smell of gunpowder flooding his sinuses. Prospero head-butted the Bosnian, but the blow barely registered. Enormously strong, his center of gravity low, Mirsad was slowly gaining the edge.

Another Bosnian entered the fray from the front door, spraying bullets across the room. But Prospero kept his focus on Mirsad, wrestling for control of the gun. Pure grit kept him in the fight, but the Bosnian was gaining ground, the barrel of the AK inching closer to Prospero's face. Sweat dripped from his brow, and he struggled for breath.

A shot sounded, impossibly close. His ears rang from the explosion.

Mirsad collapsed on top of him, releasing his hold on the AK-47. The bald man's eyes were empty, lifeless. Prospero sucked in a deep breath, pushing the body off him.

Jabari stood over him, one of the guards' AK-47s in his hands. A look of determination shadowed his face.

Prospero blinked, then shook his head. "Nice work, *bambino*. Glad you're on our team."

"You'll bring us back to Thea. He wouldn't."

His second-youngest hostage had just saved his life. One of the kids Luciano hated had stepped up and assumed a massive risk, calculating that the odds would be better for him and his younger brother if Prospero triumphed. He understood why Thea loved these boys. He suddenly felt like a bastard for what he'd put them through.

But Jabari didn't lower the rifle.

Instead, he kept it pointed straight at him.

Prospero scanned the great room. Mirsad's men had all been neutralized. Two of Prospero's guards secured the shell-shocked passengers in one corner while Luciano sent the others to search the property for any more invaders.

Turning back to the kid, Prospero said, "You can put the gun down now."

Jabari shook his head. "Take us to Thea."

"I will, but it'll take time for her to come. Why don't we all have some dinner first."

"You never keep your promises."

The boy had a point. The whole operation had been one misfire after another. "Thea is bringing me something I want. When she does, you can go to London, and all the other passengers can go to their homes too."

Luciano walked over. "The guy moved before I could shoot—" Agitated, his nephew pointed his MP5 at Jabari.

"Lower the gun, Luciano." Prospero kept his eyes on the boy.

"Shoot him, and you die." Luciano kept his rifle trained on Jabari.

Luciano. "Everyone calm down. We are friends here. Family."

Ayan hurried over to them and touched his brother on the arm. "No more war."

Jabari looked back and forth between Prospero and Ayan. Seconds passed. He placed the AK on the ground. "You'd better not be lying. And you are not our friend."

"I'll call Thea now." The sooner, the better, as far as Prospero was concerned. Kidnapping was not worth the trouble. Not at all.

Chapter 87

Johann and Fatima strode along the Bosporus, navigating back to the Turkish bathhouse, but the stunning vistas the river offered did little to revive their spirits. What were they going to do now? Marush could do nothing to help them from jail.

The air was quite brisk, the chilly breeze more pronounced near the water, and few people were out on the streets. Cheeks numb from the cold, Johann looked at Fatima and saw that her shoulders were hunched up around her ears.

Seeing the look on his face, Fatima squeezed his fingers. "I'm so sorry. I should have called ahead, made sure Marush could help."

"I'm the one who should be sorry, involving you in this mess." A tram passed by, but it felt good to walk, despite the cold. "I hope Yamen can do something to get Marush out of jail."

"It won't be easy, and it won't happen quickly—he's so vocal about his political views. I don't know, sometimes it's best to stay silent."

Johann was about to say that it was always right to fight injustice, but then he thought better of it. "Even Austria has changed in that way."

They walked in silence for a few moments.

"What drove your father to do this . . . this awful thing? Does despair over losing your mother really explain it?"

Johann wished it were that simple. Maybe then he could understand, help Father find a better way to channel his pain. "His hatred began long before *Mutti* was killed, but it deepened. Because of his business dealings, he had developed a warped view of many nationalities." He thought for a moment. "In general, he's never been very tolerant of people who don't share his views."

"But you're not like that at all."

"Guess I defy both the nature and nurture argument." He brought their clasped hands to his chest. "Maybe having an illness that made me so different helped me accept people who aren't like me."

She smiled. "It's one of your best qualities."

They turned a corner, headed toward the baths. He felt tired. "Different is good. I already know about my own culture," he said, sweeping a hand to indicate the skyline of Istanbul. "Why not explore someone else's? There's so much to learn about the world!"

Fatima laughed. "Politics or diplomacy would be a good career for you. The world could use more open minds."

"We'll see." The future seemed far away. When Johann had stolen the canisters, he'd known it would change his relationship with his father forever. Without the support of his family, the future also seemed uncertain. *But if* Vater's *love is conditional on me hurting others, I'll find a way to live without his fortune—or his love.* He had Fatima now, who cared about him for who he was, not who she wanted him to be.

Anyway, none of that mattered if they couldn't put the canisters of plague into safe hands. He really hoped Thea Paris would come through; she was their last chance to make this right. He looked up. They were near the bathhouse.

"You're cold. Why don't you have another coffee while I go into the bathhouse?" He indicated a restaurant across the street.

Fatima shivered. "Think I'll have a tea."

"Perfect. I won't be long."

He kissed Fatima on the cheek. She made him feel as if anything was possible. He stepped inside the bathhouse, the thick, humid air claustrophobic after the clear coldness outside. The manager gave him a curt nod. Entering the changing room, Johann made straight for locker number 101.

His chilly fingers fumbled as he tried sticking the key into the lock. He tried again. A quick twist, and it clicked. Removing the lock, he opened the door and peered inside the locker.

He blinked in confusion and looked again.

He checked the number: *101*. He stared down at the key and could see it had the same number on the fob.

But the locker was empty, the canisters gone.

Chapter 88

Thea hung up from a call with the Hungarian team guarding the bombs. The nukes would be safe in the warehouse until the exchange. She paced the plush carpet of her hotel suite at the Four Seasons at Sultanahmet, waiting for a knock on the door. Johann Dietrich was due to arrive in fifteen minutes. The sitting room's large window faced a manicured courtyard showcasing an herb garden that in warmer weather was usually alive with birdsong.

She was grateful that the team had been able to book the last four rooms available, but the expense would be immense. Hakan would have something to say about that. Still, they had been lucky to get the rooms: a massive cultural event was taking place in Istanbul today, so all nearby hotels were totally booked.

Waiting was usually Thea's strong suit, a necessity in the world of kidnap negotiations. But now she was in a tug of war, two imminent crises pulling at her at once. She had called Prospero an hour ago, but he hadn't answered. He knew she had the truck, so why not set up the exchange? Had something happened to the passengers, the boys?

Rif was on the phone with Hakan in the next room. She forced herself to sit down and reread the file on Gernot Dietrich that had come through. Widowed, he had one son, Johann. President of Dietrich Arms Manufacturing, he managed the company that had been in the family for four generations. The world of arms manufacturing and dealing was often a shadowy one, as she knew all too well from her brother's involvement in it. But Dietrich checked out as legit, contracting with everyone from the CIA to world leaders across the globe. Insanely wealthy, Dietrich had substantial real estate holdings in five different countries.

Dietrich's wife had died in a car accident five years ago. The odd dalliance with a socialite or two was reported in the Austrian gossip columns, but otherwise the fellow seemed to be a hardworking businessman who traveled extensively selling weapons of all descriptions, from small arms to custom-built systems. Now, according to his son, he was involved in a plot to infect millions with a bioweapon. *Bizarre.*

Speaking of family, she needed to talk to her father. Brown hadn't been able to access the records from Prospero's phone from all those years ago—they simply didn't exist anymore. But that wasn't going to stop her from digging. She pressed the button on her smartphone to FaceTime with Christos.

He answered on the first ring. "Any news?"

"Nothing yet. But maybe I could ask you the same question."

His forehead wrinkled. "I don't understand."

"Well, you seem to have the inside track when it comes to Prospero. I've learned that your recent call to him wasn't a one-time thing. You were also in contact during the *Liberata* case."

Papa had an impressive poker face, but his left hand came up, and he stroked his neck in a way that was unusual for him. He knew he'd been caught out and was in trouble. A seasoned pro like her father—a veteran of countless tense oil and land-lease negotiations around the world—could, with practice, mask facial expressions, but the body had many ways to betray itself.

"What makes you think that?" He was trying for indignant but landing somewhere closer to petulant.

"Your phone records." *Let him try to squirm out of that one.*

Papa sucked in a deep breath. She could almost hear the gears of his brain grinding. "The bastard wanted me to invest in a real-estate project he was working on. I said no."

"So he called a complete stranger, asking for money?" Prospero had several other wealthy associates he could have turned to for investment.

"He wanted *legit* money, and I'm a well-known international businessman. But I wasn't about to get involved in what was probably a money-laundering scheme."

"And he calls you at the exact moment he and I were tangling?" She didn't believe in coincidences.

"Maybe that's how he got the idea to approach me—our relationship is public record."

"You expect me to believe this?"

"He wouldn't take no for an answer."

That, she believed. But Prospero hadn't been asking for investment funds—there had to be something else.

She heard stirring from the other room; Rif had finished his call. "I have to go, but this is not over. No matter what it is, I'd prefer the truth. Our 'relationship,' as you call it, depends on a level of trust that we are failing to achieve."

"Don't you think I'd come up with a better story if I were lying?"

"Take this opportunity to do the right thing, Papa. If there's something else going on here, I need to know. The boys' lives could depend on it." She pressed the end button.

Rif walked in, grabbed a bottle of water from the supplies they'd brought, and plunked down onto one of the velvet couches. "Christos?"

"He claims that Prospero wanted him to invest in a real-estate project."

Rif shook his head. "What, the Brooklyn Bridge?"

"Exactly." She sighed. "Any updates from your lovely father?"

"Hakan confirmed that the hostages were being held in Rize, Turkey, but they're gone now."

They'd been so close to locating the passengers, but the boys had changed all that with their breakout.

"You should have heard Ayan and Jabari, so proud they'd escaped. I could throttle Prospero for putting them through this."

"Get in line," Rif said. She knew rescuing the boys was as important to him as it was to her; he had volunteered to help her run the orphanage when Nikos died. It was the most generous thing he'd done for her, and their relationship had changed in positive ways as a result.

She smiled. "Mama bear and papa bear, protecting the cubs."

"Damn right," he said. "Anyway, the nearest airport to where they were being held is in Trabzon, the second closest, Batumi. Hakan is tracking all private flights that departed both airports in the last few days. Maybe we'll get lucky—"

A tentative knock at the door interrupted them. She walked through the foyer and stared through the peephole. Two teenagers stood outside, a tall, lanky young man with blond hair and a petite girl wearing a head scarf. Both of them looked very nervous.

She opened the door. "Johann?"

"Yes, and this is Fatima." The way he looked at the girl, Thea could tell they were more than friends.

"Come in." Thea spoke to Fatima in Arabic, and her pretty face lit up at hearing her native language. She led them down the hall into the sitting room. "I'd like to introduce you to Rif Asker, who works with me at Quantum. You can trust him completely."

Rif shook their hands, and they gathered around the table by the big picture window overlooking the garden.

"We have a serious problem." Johann's face was drawn, his intelligent eyes radiating concern. "The canisters are gone. I stored them in a locker in a bathhouse, and when I went back to retrieve them, they weren't there."

Thea's stomach lurched, but she kept her voice calm. "Start from the beginning. Tell me everything."

Twenty minutes later, the details of Johann's story divulged, Thea wondered if her face was as pale as his. "You're sure no one followed you to the bathhouse?"

"They couldn't have—we were so careful after leaving the train. All I have is this burner phone"—he held it up for her to see—"and my father couldn't have found this number."

"Empty your pockets. Rif will give you a change of clothes. Your father must have some way of tracking you."

Johann removed his jacket, then reached into his jeans pocket, dumping some change, his wallet, a few tissues.

"Anything else?" Was it possible Dietrich had implanted a tracking device under his son's skin? Certain clients who traveled regularly to trouble spots elected to use subdermal implants so that Quantum could find them wherever they were. Could Johann's father really be that paranoid?

"How about you, Fatima? Did you ditch your cell?" Rif asked.

"I left everything at home."

Johann reached into his shirt pocket and pulled out a medallion on a chain. "I have this—it's what the *Freiheitswächter* wear." He placed the necklace on the table.

Rif picked it up and studied the medallion. He then walked to his duffel and pulled out a bug-sweeping device. A soft beeping noise sounded. "It's GPS-enabled."

"I had no idea." Johann looked down at the floor, shoulders slumped.

"You couldn't have known." She felt for him. All his impressive efforts to be elusive, and his father had been tracking him all along.

"The man on the train, the bathhouse. I led *Vater* right to the canisters." He reached over and squeezed Fatima's hand.

"Does your father wear one of these?" Rif asked.

"All the members do."

"Let's count on that." Rif dialed his cell. "Brown, can you join us in Thea's suite?" He pressed the end button.

"Time for the mouse to chase the cat?" Thea asked.

"Precisely."

Johann and Fatima looked confused.

"We have an electronics genius on our team. Using this tracker, he might be able to find your father and his men through the same satellite link."

Johann's face brightened. "So we can hunt them down."

"We'll also need to work up a list of potential targets for an attack."

"They want to infect the refugee camps," Fatima said.

"That was then, but Johann's father won't follow through on the original plan now that he's been exposed. Instead, he'll probably release the plague here in Istanbul."

Fatima blanched. "Where?"

"Most likely a famous landmark or transportation hub," Rif suggested. "Any site that draws big crowds."

"Like the terrorists did when they chose Schönbrunn," Johann said.

"Yes, exactly. The Metro system, the Grand Bazaar, the Blue Mosque—they would all be excellent choices." Rif's expression was intense. "A city the size of Istanbul offers countless targets."

A knock sounded at the door. *Brown*. Hopefully he could work his electronic mojo—and fast.

Chapter 89

Rif spent the next two hours with Brown trying to reverse engineer the GPS connection between the transponder in the Freedom Guardians medallion and the source. As suspected, the medallions were linked on one network as a way of monitoring everyone from a single node. It made sense if Dietrich was the only person with access to the information, because the network would be relatively small, but the setup also made the system vulnerable. Gernot Dietrich was about to have his organization's nervous system turned on itself.

Thea had ordered food for everyone, and now the two teenagers were resting in one of the bedrooms. They'd had a long trip from Salzburg, and they were devastated about losing the canisters. It was remarkable that they'd managed to safely transport them all the way from Salzburg. From Rif's perspective, what they had accomplished was heroic.

Rif battled with Hakan sometimes, but his father always wanted the best for him and for the world at large. Even Thea had a better relationship with her father than this kid. At seventeen, Johann had to cope with a father who had planned genocide and insisted on his son's active participation. *Dysfunctional* didn't even begin to describe it.

"Any updates?" Thea broke into his thoughts.

"Brown's close to cracking the encryption."

"Very close," Brown piped up from the table, two laptops in front of him.

"The team members are scattered throughout the city, sent to the likeliest targets. We're ready to move," Thea said.

"As long as Dietrich and his fellow cultists are wearing their medallions, we'll be able to find them." Rif's confidence belied the tension in the room. "Any news on the hostages?"

"Three private planes left the Rize area in the right time frame," Thea said. "None is registered in Italy, but that doesn't necessarily mean anything. Anyway, Hakan should have the flight plans for each of them ready shortly."

"Got it!" Brown's triumphant yell boomed across the room. "Cracked that sucker."

Thea and Rif joined Brown by the table where he had set up two linked laptops. His fingers glided over the keys like those of a concert pianist. A radar-like image overlaid on a map of Europe and Asia was displayed on the screen. Red dots were scattered across the image.

The door to the bedroom burst open, the teenagers probably woken by Brown's outburst.

Johann walked in, looking rumpled. "Are those dots the Freedom Guardians?"

"Yup." Brown zoomed in on Istanbul, the only city in the world to straddle two continents. "Six members are here. All look like they're headed toward the Blue Mosque. Wait, they seem to be bypassing it."

"The event that caused the run on hotel rooms—what was it again?" Rif asked.

"Oh, yeah, right." Brown tapped a search into Google. "Something about a rally in support of women's rights in Arab countries, in the Hagia Sophia."

Rif glanced at Thea, the implication hitting them at the same time. People from all over the Middle East were here for the event. The release of the bioweapon in the Hagia Sophia could affect thousands—millions when the visitors traveled back to their homelands, not knowing they carried the plague.

"You can see the event on Facebook Live," Fatima said. "It's the Arab version of the Women's March."

Brown tapped a few keys. A live feed from inside the Hagia Sophia popped up on one of the screens. Rif recognized the Byzantine mosaics. A muezzin chanting the call to worship drowned out most of the crowd noise. The camera scanned the scene: thousands of people packed the massive interior of the Hagia Sofia, which at one point in its history had been the largest freestanding structure in the world. Most of the people in the crowd were women, many in head scarves, buzzing with excitement.

"That's got to be it." Rif's mind raced as he considered their options. "Brown, Thea, let's go. Contact the others, have them join us at the Hagia Sophia as soon as they can."

"I'm coming," Johann said.

"Absolutely not," Thea said. "It's too dangerous."

"But I know what they look like. Most of them, anyway."

"Sorry, Johann." Rif respected the kid's bravery, but no way could they put him in harm's way. "You are just as likely to be recognized by them. And anyway, keeping you safe will be one more distraction."

"I want to help. My father created this crisis."

"Watch the Facebook Live feed from here," Thea said. "Let us know if you spot one of the Watchers. We need Brown with us, but someone's got to monitor the live feed and keep us informed."

Johann seemed eager to keep arguing, but Fatima put a hand on his arm, and something passed between them, communicated silently. The lanky teenager nodded to Thea.

Rif's phone buzzed. *Hakan.*

"On my way from Rize." The familiar sound of rotor blades buzzed in the background.

"Via copter?"

"Yes."

"Tell the pilot to hang tight. Text me your exact location."

"What's going on?"

"I'll fill you in on the ride over." He ended the call.

Brown grabbed his cell and punched in a few keys. "I set up the comms for everyone, including Hakan, and looped in Johann so we can all communicate. The tracking grid will be up on your phones shortly."

Rif double-checked that the two M110 SASS sniper rifles were in his duffel, one for him and the other for Jean-Luc. Thea handed him smoke grenades, extra ammunition, and a few other items from her new SINK bag. Only Rif and Jean-Luc could be armed for this mission, since they would be entering the building from the roof.

Rif and Jean-Luc headed for the door. A group text chirped on everyone's phone. Johansson, Neil, and Stewart were en route to the Hagia Sophia.

At the door, Rif looked back at the team one last time. They would pretty much be improvising on this mission, in pursuit of six red blinking dots in a massive crowd, the comms center manned by a teenaged civilian, and fielding a skeleton crew with limited supplies. What could possibly go wrong?

Chapter 90

Johann plugged in an earbud so he could communicate with Thea and her team. Fatima joined him in watching the Facebook Live feed inside the Hagia Sophia. Memories of touring the iconic building with Uncle Karl made him sad. Karl had explained that when the Hagia Sophia had been a mosque, all the earlier decorations and mosaics depicting people had been covered over with plaster. This was because the Muslim faithful frowned on the depiction of human forms in places of worship. The idea was to not distract the devout from the contemplation of Allah. In the end, though, the plaster ended up helping preserve the precious Christian artwork.

Fatima interrupted his musings. "It's incredible. So many people from all over the world, here to promote women's rights in Muslim nations."

"Have you ever attended an event like this before?"

"No," she said, "but I've always wanted to."

The live feed showcased two women beaming into the camera, holding up infants. Johann felt sick. "Kids . . ."

"Do you recognize anyone?" Fatima had met his father, but she'd never seen any of the other *Freiheitswächter*.

"It's too soon—they're not there yet." He glanced at the screen and saw that the red dots were converging on the Hagia Sophia. The main entrance had to be clogged with crowds. He hoped that would buy Thea and her team enough time to reach the site before his father's men could release the plague. Working against them was the fact that the *Freiheitswächter* could unleash it at any time without worrying about being infected themselves. *Cowards.* Hot anger bubbled inside him—anger at himself. He'd stolen the canisters to protect others, only to lose them again. If the plague was released, he'd hold himself responsible.

The live feed showed a panoramic view of the Hagia Sofia's main floor—a sea of people facing the mihrab showing the direction of Mecca. A flash of hunter green caught Johann's eye, the same shade as the jacket he and Karl had given his father two years ago. He leaned closer for a better look. Yes, it was *Vater.* He stood out in the crowd with his height and blond hair.

"Is that your father?" Fatima had seen him too.

His body flushed with disgust. "I'm going."

"What? Where are you going?"

"To the Hagia Sophia. Maybe I can talk sense into *Vater.* This isn't who he is. I don't understand what's happened to him, but I have to stop this." Johann kissed Fatima on the cheek.

"I'm coming with you."

"No."

"You can't stop me," she said.

"If they release the pathogen, you'll die."

"Then we'd better get going."

"Please, Fatima. I'm begging you, don't come." He couldn't bear the thought of something happening to this beautiful, kind girl. "Please stay here and monitor the live feed. Watch where my father goes."

She hesitated. "Okay, but I'll be close by if you need me."

He'd always need her.

Chapter 91

Rif parked the rented Audi A3 outside the helipad and walked around to the back, where Hakan waited with the helicopter. Jean-Luc leaned out the door and gave him a wave. The chopper, a Hughes 500, was painted in an eye-poppingly bright color scheme. The good news was that the Hughes was a dependable aircraft, with a track record of excellent performance and safety. The bad news was that insane paint job, which featured the words TURKEY TOURS: ISTANBUL'S NUMBER ONE TOUR COMPANY splashed along the sides.

His father saw him eying the chopper and shrugged. "It's all I could get at a moment's notice. The helicopter I chartered in Rize had to return."

"This one will be fine." *On second thought, maybe it can work to our advantage.* The Freedom Guardians wouldn't think twice if they saw this innocuous chopper in the sky.

Seconds later, the pilot walked toward them, coffee in hand. He looked like the Turkish version of an American bush pilot, wearing a red baseball cap, ratty T-shirt, and beat-up jeans. Rif hoped the guy could fly.

"You have a steady hand?" Rif asked him in Turkish.

"I'm the best," the pilot boasted, free hand over his heart.

Confident worked for Rif. And it was probably justified: if the guy flew tourists around the city year-round, he must have thousands of hours under his belt.

Rif and Jean-Luc worked quickly to attach descent ropes to the skids while the pilot fired up the Hughes. The Quantum team kept safety belts, harnesses, tethers, and L4 nylon rope in their duffel bags, always prepared for everything and anything. Improvisation in the field was part of their life.

The blades spun with a *thwapping* sound. After a final check of the hookup, rappel seat, and other equipment, Rif pulled on the rope to test the anchor point connections, the rotor wash doing its best to flatten him against the asphalt. He and Jean-Luc adjusted their helmets, secured their eye protection, and slipped on leather gloves with double-reinforced palms and fingers, the extra padding to protect their hands from the friction when they descended the ropes.

Jumping into the Hughes, Rif gave Hakan a quick wave, and the chopper leapt into the air, the smooth liftoff ratifying the pilot's confidence in his own abilities.

The views of Istanbul from above were breathtaking. Ships needled down the Bosporus Strait, their sleek lines cutting through the twinkling sapphire waters. The Golden Horn divided the new town from the old. Historical buildings with multicolored rooftops created a quiltlike effect. The slender, pencil-shaped minarets of the city's many mosques jutted up to meet the crisp blue skies. The view was serene, the people of Istanbul unaware of the threat lurking below.

He glanced at his phone. The red dots had arrived at the Hagia Sophia. He texted Thea, letting her know they were near the Blue Mosque and beginning their descent. They flew over Sultan Ahmet Square. Next up: the drop zone.

Jean-Luc nodded to Rif, yelling to be heard above the engine. "After you, my friend."

The pilot maneuvered the Hughes over the east side of the massive central dome of the Hagia Sophia, avoiding the four minarets that projected two hundred feet into the air. Dropping onto the lower rooftops from there would allow Rif and Jean-Luc access to the upper level of the museum. They would position themselves above the main space of the building, with a view of the crowd below.

A quick signal to the pilot and Rif dropped his deployment bag, the weight of the duffel helping to hold the line steady. His guide hand ensured that the rope had clearance from the helicopter.

When the untethered end of the rope reached the rooftop, Rif was already facing outward, legs hanging from the cabin. Pivoting 180 degrees on the skid, he turned to face the helicopter, bent at the waist, feet shoulder-width apart, knees locked, the balls of his feet touching the skid. His brake hand rested in the small of his back.

Jean-Luc gave him the thumbs-up. Rif flexed his knees and thrust himself away from the skid gear, allowing the rope to pass through his hands. Traveling at eight feet per second, he initiated the braking process halfway down the rope. He released the tension and moved his brake hand out at a forty-five-degree angle to slow his rate of descent.

Rif's feet connected with the rooftop with a gentle thud. Clearing the rope through the rappel ring, he scanned the area. All quiet. Jean-Luc landed behind him a few seconds later.

They grabbed their gear and hurried toward the closest entrance. Rif removed his pick and worked on the lock while Jean-Luc watched for trouble.

After a soft click, he nodded to Jean-Luc and turned the roof door's knob slowly. A rush of hot air greeted them as they entered the building. Searching the interior, he discovered a few mops, cleaning supplies, and an industrial floor cleaner. It was a maintenance room with another door on the opposite end leading into the main building.

Moving silently, he and Jean-Luc closed the door behind them and crouched on the ground so they could assemble their sniper rifles. Weapons in hand, they stood up for a last equipment check. Rif zipped the duffel bag up and secured it to his back before texting Thea.

We're inside. Waiting for your signal.

Chapter 92

Thea had skirted the swelling crowd waiting to enter the Hagia Sophia and cut into the line near the front. Some people grumbled, but everyone was so excited to be there that even the presence of a pushy Westerner couldn't dampen the mood. She hurried through the metal detector and security line, which wasn't all that stringent. She could envision how the Freedom Guardians could have smuggled the ceramic canisters inside—they could almost pass for thermoses.

She'd wrapped a scarf around her head in a hijab style so she blended into the crowd. Passing the donation mosaic featuring Mary and baby Jesus, she threaded through the throngs into the interior narthex. Crowds of people surged around her.

She glanced at the flashing red dots on her phone. All six members of the Freedom Guardians were already inside.

The Imperial Gate loomed ahead. She entered the Hagia Sophia's breathtaking nave, the 180-foot ceilings soaring high above, the mosaics reflecting a golden light inside the building. Shouldering her way through the bustling attendees, she headed toward the Sultan's Lodge, as one of the Freedom Guardians lurked in that area.

Brown, Johansson, Neil, and Stewart were all inside the Hagia Sophia too. They'd considered alerting the Turkish police about the imminent threat but decided against it. Seconds counted, and explaining the situation would devour time better spent tracking the Freedom Guardians. And if the police appeared and started evacuating the building, Dietrich would likely order his men to release the plague immediately.

Glittering mosaics and rare marble set the tone beneath the magnificent dome. The cavernous space buzzed with excited murmurs, everyone's head tilted upward to take in the view. A knot of attendees edged closer and closer to the minbar, an unusual pulpit with a stairway located at the center of the nave. The imam would stand halfway up the staircase when delivering his sermon, as standing any higher would be considered disrespectful toward the Prophet Muhammad.

Well-respected and popular, Imam Mayali was to address the crowd today, and everyone wanted an opportunity to hear him or, better yet, to meet him in person. Thea moved closer to the wall, finding it easier to navigate the horde as she made her way deeper inside.

The forty arched windows along the top of the dome allowed sunlight—and perhaps God or Allah—into the Hagia Sophia. Her gaze drifted to the upper balcony, which had been cordoned off for the event. All quiet, even though she knew Rif and Jean-Luc were up there somewhere in the shadows, waiting for their signal.

She spoke quietly, knowing the earpiece would pick it up. "I've got nothing. Brown, do you have a visual?"

Chapter 93

To minimize the window of time they'd be exposed in the open-air gallery that looped around the Hagia Sophia's second story, Rif and Jean-Luc waited inside the maintenance room for the team to locate the targets. With the swarming mob downstairs, security was tight, and two men holding rifles wouldn't go unnoticed for long.

Historically, upper-class citizens would sit on the higher floor while the masses gathered below. Today, the ramp to reach the balcony area was cordoned off because of ongoing construction, which worked in their favor.

A vent pumped hot air into the small space, leaving Rif's skin coated in sweat. Jean-Luc sat beside him, perspiration dripping down his face. Rif glanced at his watch. The imam would start his welcome speech shortly, then introduce the various speakers, feminist activists from across the Middle East.

They had loaded subsonic rounds into their M110 SASS rifles. Instead of traditional 7.62mm NATO bullets, they were using hollow-point, 180-gram rounds, which would slow down after entering a target, spreading and shredding rather than passing straight through and possibly injuring somebody else. They wanted to avoid accidental casualties at all costs. He'd trained as a sniper in Delta Force, and Jean-Luc had been a sharpshooter in the French Foreign Legion, so there was no question they were qualified for this mission, but firing into a mob carried collateral risks even for the most experienced marksman.

At all costs Rif wanted to avoid causing a panic, which was where the subsonic rounds came in: when fired, they made a noise about as loud as a human clap. In this noisy environment, the shots should go unnoticed. *Whether or not a body or two dropping to the ground from a head wound goes unnoticed is another question altogether.*

Rif logged into the Facebook Live feed. On the screen, the crowd inside swelled, people packed shoulder to shoulder as they gathered for the historic event.

Three minutes until the imam spoke.

"Should have worn my fucking tropical gear," the Frenchman said.

"I'm just hoping you wore deodorant." Rif wiped sweat off his neck.

The older man laughed, his salt-and-pepper stubble at least three days old. "You fancy me, then?"

"Nah, you're not my type."

"Right, you have someone else in mind."

"What's that supposed to mean?"

"You don't reach my age without noticing a thing or two," Jean-Luc said. "The question is, what are you going to do about it?"

Thea's voice sounded in his earpiece, asking Brown if he'd found a target. Her timing was impeccable, saving him from having to deal with Jean-Luc's prying question.

Before Brown answered, footsteps sounded on the hard marble floors outside the maintenance room. Rif raised his index finger to his lips and nodded to Jean-Luc.

They edged to either side of the door, pressed their backs against the wall, and waited. Maybe a security guard doing rounds before the imam spoke?

The footsteps paused on the other side of the inner door.

Chapter 94

Johann sprinted to the Hagia Sophia, his long legs making quick work of the short distance. After bullying his way to the front of the line and passing through security, he searched for the towering form of his father. In the live feed, *Vater* had been close to the apse, but he could be anywhere by now. Johann paused by the ramp leading to the second level and looked out on a heaving sea of humanity. Thousands of people gathered at the nave, their faces alight with joy. He felt overwhelmed, discouraged—and furious. How dare his father plan an attack on people because of their ethnicity, their culture?

Fatima's culture.

He called her burner cell.

She answered right away, her voice tense. "You okay?"

"It's so crowded. I can't see Father anywhere."

"I lost him on the feed too. Maybe you should try calling him?"

"Good idea." He paused for a beat. "I'm so sorry about all this."

"Don't be. It's not your fault." She sounded worried. "Wish I were there with you."

"I like knowing you're safe." People knocked into him as the crowd surged. "Fatima?"

"Yes, I'm here."

"Fatima . . . I love you." It was the first time he'd said the words aloud, but they felt so right.

"I love you too. Now, call me back as soon as you can."

"I promise."

He pressed the end button and dialed his father's number.

The phone rang and rang.

Finally, Father picked up.

"Dietrich."

"Vater."

A long silence.

"Where are you?" Father asked.

"Near the ramp."

"You're here?" His father's tone was incredulous. "I hope you've come to your senses."

"I hope you've come to yours." A flash of that memorable green caught Johann's eye. Looking across the nave, he spotted his father's unmistakable form. Johann couldn't make out his expression over this distance, but he could easily imagine the disapproving stare.

"Don't hurt these innocent people," Johann pleaded.

"That girlfriend of yours has warped your thinking. You're one of us."

"No, I'm not."

"These people are terrorizing us; they're not even human. We are in a war for civilization."

"Can't you hear how paranoid that sounds?"

Thea's voice sounded in his earpiece, asking Brown if he'd seen his father's men.

"You've been duped by the enemy, Johann, as a way of getting to me. Thank God I'm always vigilant."

"Please, *Vater*, call off the attack."

"In time, you'll thank me."

A man spoke heatedly with a security officer near the stanchion blocking off the ramp to the upper level. Someone jostled

Johann from behind, ducking under the rope to access the ramp. Something about his form struck Johann as familiar. The man turned slightly, and cold fear shot through Johann's veins. Leopold—and he was carrying a black nylon bag.

"*Mutti* would never want this for you." It was the one thing that might change his father's mind. Johann pressed the end button. Noticing the security guard was still distracted, Johann stepped over the barrier, sprinting up the ramp behind Leopold.

Chapter 95

Thea waited for Brown's response, her ears straining to hear over the noise of the crowd. The red dots would guide them to Dietrich's men, but in such congested conditions, they'd need to be cautious that they had located the right targets.

"Eyes on a hostile. Negative on the football." Brown's voice rumbled in her earpiece.

The first Freedom Guardian had been located but no sign of a canister.

"Stay on him. Johansson, anything?"

"Still on the hunt," Johansson said.

She moved toward the apse, but the incoming swarms weren't making it easy. For maximum effect, the Freedom Guardians would probably wait until the Hagia Sophia was completely full before releasing the plague.

"Hostile located." Neil's voice buzzed in her earpiece. "No luggage. I'm on him."

She could feel panic rising. "Keep at it."

Two down, four to go.

An older woman wearing a head scarf climbed the steps on the minbar and raised the microphone to her lips. She spoke in Arabic, thanking the crowd for coming, stressing the importance of this event and letting them know that the imam would be with them shortly.

The crowd cheered, anticipating the imam's speech.

"Hostile located. Positive." Stewart's voice was raspy.

The roar of the crowd overwhelmed Stewart's voice in her ear. "Repeat. Did you say positive?"

"Affirmative. He has Johann's backpack with the Red Bull Salzburg patch."

Lots of bags inside the Hagia Sophia today—diaper bags, backpacks, totes, but this one stood out.

"Photo."

"On its way."

Her phone buzzed, a group text with an image file.

She stared at the pic. "Johann, you recognize him?"

No response.

"Johann, you there?"

"Yes, looking now." He sounded out of breath.

"You okay?" she asked.

"That's Hencler Raab, one of my father's men."

A jolt of electricity buzzed through her. "Rif, you and Jean-Luc ready?"

She waited what felt like a lifetime, but there was no response.

Chapter 96

Thea's question ringing in his earpiece, Rif remained perfectly silent and still. The doorknob turned. Jean-Luc stood on the hinge side, Rif on the other. Slowly, the door swung open. A man stepped over the threshold.

Rif snaked an arm around the man's neck, placing a hand across his mouth, and shoved the intruder to the floor while Jean-Luc quietly closed the door. A quick analysis of the man's garb: a uniform but not security—maintenance.

In Turkish, Rif explained they were there to stop something terrible from happening. Just in case their new friend wasn't in a believing mood, they would err on the side of caution. Jean-Luc wrapped duct tape around the man's hands and ankles. A strip on his mouth, and their captive was immobilized. Rif told him not to worry, but judging by the terrified look on the man's face, the message didn't sink in.

"Rif, you there?" Thea in his earpiece again, an edge to her voice.

"Sorry for the delay. Unexpected visitor. Green light now." Rif edged open the door of the maintenance room. The roar of the crowd greeted him. He searched for guards on the upper level. Nothing. Probably all downstairs handling the crowd.

"One target confirmed. Get into position."

"On it." He signaled to Jean-Luc.

They eased out of the small room, leaving the maintenance man trussed up inside. He might dehydrate from sweating, but he'd survive. Jean-Luc took point on the south side of the galley near the enormous Deësis mosaic while Rif headed to the opposite side. Hugging the wall, he scanned for intruders, the soft soles of his boots silent on the marble floor. Moving quickly, he was now in position.

Low-crawling to the balcony, he hid himself behind a partition. Slow, steady breaths, in and out. Cradling the rifle in his arms, he stared at the mass of people below. At first sight, the idea of identifying a target was overwhelming, but Stewart was pointing a laser upward so Rif could easily locate the Freedom Guardian.

Neil's voice buzzed. "Hostile in view, positive."

Another laser in the crowd caught his eye.

"Photo?" Thea asked.

"Already sent."

"Johann, can you confirm?"

No answer.

"Hostile is opening the bag," Neil said.

"Everyone in position. We need to move now." Thea's voice was firm, in control. "Jean-Luc, please confirm eyes on target."

"Red baseball cap, canvas bag." Jean-Luc's gravelly voice filled his ear.

"Correct. Clear shot?" Thea asked.

"Green light." If anything changed, Jean-Luc would let them know. Otherwise, the operation was a go.

Rif's world shrank to a small bubble, all the background noise and activity fading away. It was just him and the target. He stared through the scope at his quarry: a middle-aged man with sandy hair and a prominent nose, dressed in a crisp button-down shirt.

He looked like an office worker, not a terrorist about to unleash a deadly biological weapon.

Another man in the crowd shifted, obstructing his view of the target.

"Not clear." *Shit.* "Man in brown jacket obstructing."

"Stewart, take care of it," Thea directed.

As Rif watched through the scope, Stewart gently touched the man's arm and asked him a question. The man pointed to the door. Was Stewart asking for directions to the nearest pub or what? *Just get him out of the way.*

Jean-Luc's voice cut through his focus. "Target has the canister in hand. Immediate shot required."

"Hold for tandem. Rif?" Thea asked.

They had to coordinate the shots, but he didn't have a clear view. Jean-Luc's quarry was about to release the bioweapon—would he have to take out the man in the jacket, then immediately fire a second shot at his target?

Seconds passed with agonizing slowness.

The man wearing the brown jacket smiled at Stewart and stepped aside. Rif exhaled. He had a clear view. His target was also opening his backpack.

"Ready." Rif settled the crosshairs on the man's face.

"Operation is a go. Three, two, one . . ." Thea set the countdown.

A deep breath. *Hold.*

Rif's finger squeezed the trigger.

Chapter 97

The imam stood halfway up the minbar, addressing the enthusiastic crowd, speaking about the sanctity of peace, the importance of women. Meanwhile, Thea held her breath, waiting for the rounds to take out the targets. Given the tightly packed crowd, any slight movement could result in a miss. But she believed in Rif and Jean-Luc, both crack shots and resolute under pressure.

Two soft claps sounded, hardly audible over the throng.

"Confirmed." Rif's voice was tight, focused.

"Done," Jean-Luc said.

"Package secure." Neil's voice sounded in her earpiece. He'd been able to grab the first canister from Jean-Luc's target.

Less than twenty yards away from Stewart, she moved closer to help secure the second canister. The Freedom Guardian Rif had targeted collapsed to the floor.

Stewart leaned down to grab the second canister when a woman dressed in a hijab coldcocked him over the head with a cane. The interloper scooped up the backpack and sped off toward the minbar. A few people standing nearby seemed startled by the commotion, but most of the crowd barely noticed, intent on the imam's speech.

Thea sprinted forward, chasing the woman. "Stewart is down." Her gaze locked on the slim form. "Woman in a blue hijab has the canister. On it."

Neil and Brown would check on Stewart while she pursued the woman. She couldn't risk losing the woman in the crowd. Thea shoved and jostled after her, dodging between clusters of attendees, pushing others aside. As she closed the distance between them, the crowd began to slow her down. She glanced up. Cold fear seeped into her bones. The woman was headed straight for the minbar, where the imam was speaking.

A security guard tried to block the woman from climbing onto the minbar, but she neutralized him somehow. The cane? A knife? Thea couldn't tell. The guard buckled near the stairs.

The woman powered up the steps, taking them two at a time. At first the imam smiled, perhaps used to overexuberant celebrants, but his smile quickly faded. The intruder pushed him aside and scaled the rest of the stairs, shocking the crowd, as only the Prophet Mohammed belonged at the top.

Thea reached the base of the minbar. The woman faced the crowd and pulled the canister out of the backpack. When she looked up, Thea's mind recoiled in shock.

Wait a minute.

She recognized the woman's face.

Ocean.

The enigmatic passenger from the plane. The real reason Prospero had hijacked the 737. *The woman who'd left Ayan and Jabari alone in a snowstorm while she escaped.*

White fury pulsed through Thea's veins as she sprinted up the stairs.

Chapter 98

Johann rocketed up the ramp that led to the upper galley, trying to catch Leopold. Breaths short and shallow, Johann increased his pace. At the crest of the ramp, he searched for Leopold. The scientist rushed toward the balcony and slid the bag from his shoulder.

Johann tried to see what was in the black nylon bag, but his vision blurred. He shook his head, cursing his Marfan syndrome. Did Leopold have one of the canisters? He called out to the man, "Thea Paris and her team have stopped the others."

Leopold lifted the bag. "That's okay. The batch I used to infect Kaleb—remember how effective it was?"

Johann ran forward. "These people have done nothing to you."

Leopold reached into the nylon sack, revealing a third canister that Johann hadn't known existed. "That's exactly the kind of attitude that led to the Schönbrunn massacre."

"Hate breeds hate. You'll just unleash another backlash." Johann slowed to a walk, only a few feet from the shorter man.

Leopold gestured to the crowd below. "The number of Muslims in the world has reached one billion—but we can change that."

Johann froze in place at the threat.

Sunlight from the dome's arched windows reflected off the lenses of Leopold's wire-rimmed glasses, snapping Johann out of his trance.

Johann spoke to the Quantum team over the comms link. "Leopold has more plague. Upper level."

Chapter 99

Thea sprinted up the minbar's steps. Ocean was poised higher on the stairs, giving her an advantage. Preparing for contact, Thea crouched, keeping her center of gravity low and making herself into a smaller target.

Ocean placed the canister on the top step, freeing her hands. Turning with whiplash speed, she snapped her right leg in a kick. Thea caught Ocean's calf in midair, trapping the limb against the minbar's railing, preventing her from breaking loose to kick again.

Using those precious seconds to scramble up two more steps, Thea was now only a foot lower than her opponent. But Ocean was flexible and fast, bending her leg to lower herself and grabbing a fistful of Thea's hair.

Pain seared Thea's scalp; her vision blurred.

Extending her neck to move with the pull, Thea jabbed Ocean's solar plexus. A wheezing sound, and the other woman's grip on her hair faltered.

Seizing the opportunity, Thea ensnared Ocean's right wrist with her left, twisting it toward the center of her body, then shoved her opponent's elbow upward, thrusting her into an arm lock. A sharp cry, and Ocean released her grip on Thea's hair. Before Thea could force her down, Ocean hammered a swift kick into her face. The copper taste of blood filled her mouth, and Thea stumbled backward. Her hands clung to the railing as she slid down a couple of stairs.

Thea raced back up the steps, but Ocean had already lifted the canister in both hands and was struggling to open the seal. Thea dove forward, tackling the other woman. Ocean landed hard on her back. Still clutching the canister, she swung it at Thea's head.

Thea ducked to one side, delivering a hard punch to the woman's temple. Reeling from the shot to the head, Ocean kicked and twisted. Thea slammed her fist into the woman's throat. A crunching sound followed. Ocean dropped the canister and reached up to her neck, gasping for air. Thea fished two cable ties out of her pocket and deftly bound the woman's arms and legs.

Thea grabbed the canister, inspecting it closely. The seal had not been broken. Sucking in a few deep breaths, she said, "Second package secure. Stewart okay?"

"He'll have a nasty lump but will continue to annoy us with his questionable sense of humor," Brown said.

They had secured both canisters.

Johann's voice in her earpiece set her nerves jangling: "Leopold has more plague. Upper level."

Chapter 100

Johann could see Rif sprinting toward him, but he was too far away to get there in time. He turned back to Leopold. "Don't do this. Please."

"You are a child and naïve." Leopold stepped backward, the canister in his hands. Johann lunged for the scientist, but the man twisted away, leaving him grasping at air.

Father appeared at the top of the ramp behind him and called his name. Johann's gaze connected with his father's for what seemed like a long, heavy moment. Johann searched for the man who'd attended his football matches, the man who had been there when he was ill, the man who knew right from wrong.

But all he saw was madness, fanaticism, determination.

Johann returned his focus to Leopold. He charged the scientist, grabbing him in an awkward and effective bear hug. Leopold writhed, banging against the balcony's banister, managing to stomp on Johann's left foot. He faltered for a moment and stumbled backward, his foot in agony.

Ignoring the pain, he took one step, then two and three, accelerating, propelling his body toward Leopold with every ounce of energy he could muster. He collided with the scientist and again wrapped his arms around Leopold's arms and body, the force of the assault slamming them both against the railing.

Johann felt his center of balance shifting across the railing, his upper body hanging over the edge. Leopold thrashed against his grip, but Johann refused to let go. The canister slipped to the balcony's floor, still unopened.

Johann arched his back in an effort to return to the safety of the balcony floor, but Leopold's writhing thwarted him. Johann's feet rose off the floor, his weight shifting farther out over the railing. He still clung to Leopold, unwilling to let the shorter man escape, and they toppled off the gallery together.

Time slowed, every second frozen in a clear snapshot. Johann hung in the air for a long moment, taking in the beauty of the Hagia Sophia as it spun around him. From his midair perspective, the architecture and design appeared otherworldly. A kaleidoscope of memories played in his mind as he tumbled: Uncle Karl, *Mutti*, happier times, his newfound love.

The crowd buzzed below him. So many hopeful faces. He wanted to see Fatima's face one more time, bathe in the kindness and love shimmering in her eyes. But it wasn't to be. Gravity kicked in. He hurtled downward, terror warring with absolution as the floor closed in on him.

Chapter 101

Commotion sounded from above. Thea glanced up at the gallery, doing a double take as two figures cartwheeled off the balcony. The sight of the blue-checked shirt Johann had been wearing made her stomach roil. *Oh, no, what was he doing here?* The other man hurtling over the edge must be Leopold. A spine-tingling scream from the scientist cut through the buzz of the crowd and was answered with cries from below. She watched helplessly as they plummeted to the nave, people below them scrambling to get out of the way. The two bodies hit the floor with a heavy, wet-sounding *thunk*.

The crowd immediately below panicked, surging for the exits. Thea looked back up at the balcony. A tall man who could only be Gernot Dietrich stood beside the railing, arms fully outreached, as if he were trying to pull his son back through space. She couldn't read his expression from this distance but could imagine his distress. He had come here to hurt others but hadn't expected his son to be a victim.

A tall figure appeared beside Gernot: Rif, his handgun trained on the Freedom Guardian.

"Third package secure." Rif's voice was flat.

Johann Dietrich had just saved countless lives.

The imam stood below her on the stairs, speaking in Arabic. "It's Allah's will that we go outside to celebrate this monumental day. Come, join me."

A sage man, he was trying to clear the Hagia Sophia without initiating panic. The crowd slowly filed out of the structure while security personnel fought their way in.

Numb inside, Thea strained to see if Johann was moving after the fall. Too many people were in her way.

She sensed movement on the stairs below her. Brown and Johansson had arrived to lend a hand. Ocean was awake but subdued, clearly in pain from the blow to her windpipe. Thea handed the canister to Brown. "Let's get this cleaned up."

Sprinting down the steps with rubbery legs, she pushed through the crowd, heading to the area where Johann and Leopold had landed. Hope warred with the facts: the drop had to be almost two hundred feet, and the hard floor beneath her boots was unforgiving. She threaded past one group rushing out, then another, trying to reach Johann.

She found Leopold first. The Freedom Guardian lay facedown, his head twisted at a horrific angle, face smashed beyond recognition. She didn't have to turn him over to know he was gone.

A few feet away was the teenager's body.

At first glance, Johann almost looked unharmed, as if he were napping on the floor. But blood leaked from his ears, pooling on the marble, and one arm was bent under his body at an unnatural angle.

She leaned close, hoping she might feel a breath. Not a whisper. She wanted to shake him, wake him up, but nothing and no one ever would. Johann had been so brave, defying his own father and finally sacrificing his life to save others.

Why didn't he stay at the hotel?

But she understood. He'd felt responsible for losing the canisters. But it hadn't been his fault. It had been his father's. Rage filled her. All the planning, all the hatred, and now the leader of the Freedom Guardians had failed, in the process losing his son, the last of his family. *What a fool.*

A voice sounded in her earpiece. "Johann, talk to me. Are you okay?" Soft, feminine, concerned. Fatima. "I'm coming there now."

Neil appeared beside Thea, his face mirroring her horror. "Go," he said.

Her body drained of all energy, she nonetheless staggered to her feet. The masses swelled toward the door, some having witnessed the horror of the fall, others realizing something was amiss, but the bulk of the crowd simply following the imam's suggestion.

"Fatima, where are you?"

Thea stayed close to the wall and hurried toward the exit. She had to intercept the teenager. There were some things young people should not see. Johann had witnessed too much and been haunted by images of the terrorist's horrific death.

"Almost at the Hagia Sophia. What happened—did they release the plague?" Fatima's voice sounded small and afraid.

Thea hurried forward. "No, the team secured the canisters." The words coming out of her mouth were heavy, thick. "Meet you at the entrance."

"Thank goodness. I'm here now. Where's Johann?"

Thea stepped into the sunlight, the brilliant rays a stark contrast to the sadness inside her. Shielding her eyes from the glare with one hand, she found Fatima standing to the left of the entrance, her hands clasped together near her heart.

Fatima's face lit up for a moment when she first saw Thea, but then dread clouded her face at the sight of the blood on Thea's clothes, her expression.

"No . . ." Fatima said.

"He was a hero." The words barely made it out of her mouth. Her arms circled around the shaking girl.

"No, no, no." Fatima pounded her fists against Thea's chest, tears running down her face. The boy she loved was gone.

Thea held Fatima while she sobbed. Johann had died for the sins of his father, in a pattern that was all too familiar to Thea.

She thought of Nikos and Christos, of families forged in love that still self-destructed, destroyed by forces that, after millennia of existence, humans just couldn't defeat.

Now another man had died too young.

She closed her eyes and held Fatima tight.

Chapter 102

The call from Prospero setting up the exchange came in immediately after the events at the Hagia Sophia. Thea thought
the timing was nothing short of uncanny.

The Quantum team flew to Italy to scout the location before
dawn. Prospero had chosen the thirteenth-century Scaliger Castle at Lake Garda for the hostage exchange, a medieval stronghold
strategically positioned at the tip of a long, skinny peninsula jutting north into the waters of the lake.

The castle was a stunning example of medieval fortification,
with thrusting crenelated towers jutting out above the water and
a high wall around the connected port to dissuade water-borne
attackers. Scanning the grounds through binoculars, Jean-Luc said
the structure looked like a predatory stone frog squatting on the
spit of land. It did look forbidding: strategically positioned at the tip
of the peninsula, the castle was surrounded by a moat, accessible
only via two drawbridges. Today it housed a small museum showcasing the history of the region and was surrounded by brightly
painted buildings. Prospero clearly wanted to be on his home turf
so he could have the upper hand, though Thea was surprised he
hadn't chosen a location in the south, closer to his home base.

Still reeling from the nightmare in Istanbul, Thea struggled with the pivot to Italy, which wasn't like her at all. But Johann Dietrich's death had affected her personally, in ways she hadn't expected. The irony of hearing from Prospero before she heard from Christos was not lost on her, and she said as much to Rif during the trip from Istanbul.

Rif's voice in her earpiece jolted Thea back to the present. "Two boats approaching from one o'clock."

She lifted her binoculars and focused the lenses northward, the rising sun lighting the waters with an orange hue. Sure enough, two vessels came into view—a racing sloop with a deep hull and a medium-sized ferry.

Thea had called Gabrielle while en route to Lake Garda. The Hostage Recovery Fusion Cell agent had discovered that the nuclear cores were earmarked for the CIA in a backdoor deal Prospero had negotiated, so she'd given Thea the green light to hand over the capsules. It didn't feel right to hand nukes to a mobster, but the choice wasn't hers. Prospero Salvatore's machinations never ceased to amaze her. He had his fingers in many pies and always seemed to profit without incurring so much as a parking ticket.

That said, Prospero had proven himself a formidable enemy, both in the past and recently. It would be unwise to underestimate him, even though this exchange seemed cut-and-dried. She studied the incoming vessels through her binoculars. Arriving by water gave Prospero the opportunity to abort if the situation became compromised.

She squinted, trying to spot the boys on the deck of the ferry, but the boats were still too far away to discern any details. Neil and Stewart were in a Nor-Tech racer moored up the shore of Lake Garda, where they would remain unless it became necessary to give chase. No point unsettling Prospero when they were so close to securing the hostages.

Thea stood at the northern end of the castle's battlements. Rif was on the southern wall, staring through his binoculars at the shimmering waters, the Grand Hotel Terme perched directly behind him.

"A mile out." Rif's deep voice on the comms was a comfort to her, especially given all the turmoil of the past few days.

Nine hostages, including Ayan and Jabari, should be on board, given that Ocean now sat in a Turkish jail and Mike Dillman was dead. The woman hadn't been willing, or able, to reveal much about the Freedom Guardians. She had been so consumed with notions of revenge for the loss of her family's honor that she had jumped at the chance to be a part of the genocide, myopic in her fury instead of pursuing her flourishing career in science.

Thea's shoulders tensed as she waited for a view of Ayan and Jabari. She felt bad about Dillman—according to Ocean, he had taken good care of the boys, as promised.

Her phone buzzed. Prospero.

"Ready, *bella donna*?" he asked.

"The passengers are to be freed first." *Worth a try*.

Prospero laughed. "Should I just turn the boats around now?"

"I want everyone on deck where I can see them. Nonnegotiable."

Silence.

She waited.

"You can see the boys."

"All the hostages."

"I'll call you back."

Rif's voice buzzed in her earpiece again. "Half a mile out."

She stared through the binoculars. The two boats knifed through the water toward the castle, the smaller, faster one manned by a driver and lone passenger, both armed. The larger vessel had an upper deck, but from what she could tell, only one figure was visible up top—Prospero's man, carrying a rifle.

In preparation for the exchange, the Quantum team had discussed every potential scenario. They'd considered having divers positioned in the water, but the logistics were challenging on such short notice, and they didn't want to spook Prospero by rising out of Lake Garda like aquatic avengers. In negotiations, response consultants had to live by their word, be straightforward and honest; any hint of betrayal or tricks and the hostages could suffer—or die.

The racing boat slowed, lagging behind the ferry. Jean-Luc joined her on the parapet, passenger manifest and pen in hand, his M5 in a shoulder harness. Thea's phone vibrated.

Prospero now stood on the ferry's deck, in the shadows of the overhanging roof. "I'll show you the hostages; then my men pick up the nuclear material. After the racing boat leaves, we'll unload the passengers."

The muscles in her neck tightened. The situation was far from ideal, but she had to trust he'd abide by his word. With Ocean gone, he had no real investment in the other passengers.

The ferry slowed to an idle less than a hundred yards away, Luciano shepherding the passengers onto the deck. She pressed the mute button on her phone, raised the binoculars, and worked from left to right. "Laverdeen, Rivers, Matthias . . ." she called out to Jean-Luc, as he ticked each one off the list. She had seen the boys right away—they had climbed onto a deck chair and were waving their arms like lunatics. She waved back.

She finished calling out the names of the visible passengers. From her count, it had been only eight. "Jean-Luc?"

"Karlsson is missing."

She pressed the mute button again so she could speak to Prospero.

"I need to see Karlsson."

"Not possible."

"What do you mean?"

"We had a couple of unavoidable incidents. One proved fatal for Karlsson."

That made it two hostages killed: Karlsson, the mentally fragile former MI6 agent, and Dillman. The Texan had been one of the good guys, a real loss. She forced herself to stay calm. The team's responsibility now was to make sure the eight remaining hostages made it back safely.

But she wanted Prospero to pay.

"You there?" His voice cut through her thoughts.

"Bring the racing boat to the southern pier. My teammates will give the cores to your men while we unload the ferry passengers."

"That's not what I agreed to."

"You're two hostages short—Ocean told me what happened to Dillman. I'm fresh out of goodwill." Her voice was polite but firm. Speaking softly often had more impact than yelling.

No answer. Seconds ticked by.

"The boys are the last to leave, after my men confirm the cargo is loaded."

She set her phone to mute. "Rif?"

"I'll make it work."

She pressed the button to reconnect with Prospero. "Agreed. Pull both boats up now."

The ferry lurched forward, turning slightly so the port side faced the castle wall. Prospero was on deck, the guard standing beside him, AK-47 in hand. As the ferry closed the distance, she could see how determined he was, how he wanted this exchange to work as much as she did.

But something isn't right.

She scanned the clear waters of Lake Garda. A high-pitched sound in the distance suggested more boats approaching. Who would be out this early besides more of Prospero's men?

She spoke to her team over the radio. "Incoming?"

Neil and Stewart chimed in from their location up the shore. "Checking it out now." Before the exchange, the Quantum team had combed the coast looking for anything unusual, but there were a million places to hide a boat along the lake's shoreline.

Movement in the water near the outer wall of the port drew her attention. Bubbles. *What the heck?* A dark form in scuba gear broke the surface.

"Diver at three o'clock." She grabbed her M4 and headed for the dock with Jean-Luc behind her.

The ferry was only a few meters away from the castle walls when the scuba diver tossed a small object in their direction. It landed on a rocky outcrop near her position. She immediately identified the small metal object.

"Grenade!" She ran toward the metal sphere and kicked it with her boot back toward the lake.

The grenade spiraled off the rocks back into the water near the diver. Seconds passed. An underwater explosion shuddered beneath the surface, then rippled through the lake and burst into the air. Seconds later, the diver's limp body surfaced.

Thea sprinted down the dock to where the ferry floated, within arm's reach now. By the look on his face, Prospero was every bit as surprised by the attack as she was.

The throaty sound of high-powered boat engines became louder.

"Three incoming units, armed," Neil's voice warned in her earpiece.

She turned and called out to Jean-Luc. "With me—on board."

With a running start, she lunged onto the ferry, Jean-Luc right behind her. Their priority was protecting the hostages.

"Were you expecting company?" she asked Prospero.

"Absolutely not."

"Everyone back inside." Thea marshaled the passengers into the enclosed cabin while Jean-Luc headed for the upper deck.

"I knew you'd come for us." Jabari smiled.

"You bet, buddy. But we're not home free yet. Take Ayan inside and hide under the bulkhead."

"We can help fight," Ayan said.

"Not this time. Go on."

The boys hurried through the doors to join the other hostages.

She leaned close to Prospero. "Keep them safe. I'll be on the upper deck."

Prospero directed his man to follow Thea's orders, then headed inside, pausing before ducking in behind the passengers to look back at her. "*Buona fortuna, Liberata.*"

"*Grazie mille,* Prospero. Now get inside."

Chapter 103

Gunfire erupted as two of the incoming Glasstreams headed for Rif's position on the southern parapet. The angler's platform on the bow of a vessel traditionally used as a fishing boat made an ideal shooting stand. And the boats had serious firepower, each sporting a .50 cal machine gun. Prospero's men aboard the racing boat hurried to secure the two nuclear cores to the rear bench seat while chaos exploded around them.

"Take cover," Rif told Johansson and Brown, who stood next to him. "The nuclear material is our priority."

The two men ducked behind the ramparts, waiting for the opportunity to fire on the attackers.

Prospero's two men were below them so they could load the cores; with their boat moored to the dock, they were sitting ducks. The passenger tossed off the line, and the driver scrambled to fire up the engines, but the Glasstreams cut off the angle of escape. Dozens of the antiaircraft rounds ripped into the Italians and their fiberglass-hulled boat, shredding both with deadly efficiency.

Rif peered out from behind the slits in the merlons along the wall. The boats were within range now. "Let 'em rip!"

The Quantum team opened fire on the Glasstreams with their machine pistols. The 9mm slugs sprayed the two boats, tearing up the hulls and shattering the windshields. A few rounds went wide and sprayed into the water, but at least one hit the machine gunner on the first vessel. He collapsed, and another crew member hurried to take his place.

Rif, Johansson, and Brown ducked low behind the ramparts again, shielding themselves from the incoming fire smashing into the ancient stonework around them. The men on the vessels blasted away, not caring about damage to the castle. The Glasstreams cruised past the shoreline and then turned back out into the lake, giving the three Quantum members a brief reprieve.

Rif shoved a new magazine into his M4, Brown and Johansson following suit. He glanced down at the racing boat still moored to the dock below. Blood pooled inside, both bodies riddled with bullets. The nuclear cores sat intact on the rear bench, untouched by the gunfire.

"Ready for round two?" Rif inhaled a deep breath.

The Glasstreams turned in a tight arc, throwing up a wall of water, then powered straight back toward them.

Chapter 104

Thea scrambled up the metal stairs of the ferry. The wind was gusting, brisk. She crawled along the upper deck to join Jean-Luc and Prospero's guard at the aft edge, the vantage point offering them an unobstructed view of the Glasstream on their trail.

The ferry driver thrust the throttle to full, but the vessel was not built for speed; behind them the attackers were closing fast. Prospero's man fired a few premature rounds into the water, misjudging the range.

"Two boats are targeting the nukes." Jean-Luc lay flat on the deck beside her.

"Rif and team will handle that end." Thea scrambled next to Jean-Luc, her M4 at the ready.

They waited patiently for the vessel to come closer. Timing was critical. Even though the ferry was a sitting duck, the larger boat provided more protection and a stable platform for a fire-fight. That said, the slight chop on the lake didn't deter the Glasstream. The deep-V hull sliced through the water, the .50 cal machine gun on the bow a genuine concern.

Bullets ripped into the ferry, punching holes in the steel and shattering windows on the main deck. Screams filtered through the din of the firefight.

"I'll take the pilot, you two take the gunner." Thea said. "Now!"

Chapter 105

Rif studied the two boats as they came in for a second pass. No way could they break cover and retrieve the nukes from the speedboat below, which was beginning to drift. They'd have to endure the siege, picking the enemy off one by one. The attackers might have more substantial firepower, but the Quantum team had the twin advantages of superior cover and higher ground.

And they had a little surprise up their sleeves.

"Incoming," Stewart said over the radio.

"We're all set," Rif replied.

Neil and Stewart had edged closer in the Nor-Tech, sandwiching the enemy between their boat and the castle. The howl of the Glasstreams' engines and the tenacious defenders along the castle's walls had so far prevented the attackers from hearing the throaty roar of the approaching racer.

Rif, Brown, and Johansson fired at the two boats, the occasional expelled shell casing burning Rif's cheek as it was ejected. His ears buzzed from the continuous blasts, and all three men were being peppered with stone fragments ripped out of the castle walls by the .50 caliber bullets. The racing sloop below absorbed countless rounds, the aft sinking as it took on water; at least it had stopped drifting. Anyway, the cores would actually be safer underwater.

The Glassstreams slowed as they approached, the gunners firing round after round into the ramparts. The bullets that soared high sounded like angry bees as they flew overhead.

Rif pulled back for a moment, allowed Johansson and Brown to continue the answering fire.

"Now!" he shouted into the radio.

The men in the Glassstreams were so intent on their targets that they didn't see what was coming up behind them—until it was too late.

Rif loaded a fresh magazine into the M4 and started blasting at the boats again while Neil and Stewart opened fire from behind. One Glassstream turned abruptly, almost capsizing, then righted itself, bobbing in the water. The pilot and the two men aboard had been killed.

The machine gunner from the second vessel targeted them, even as the pilot realized they were under attack from the rear and banked sharply, trying to evade the fire from the Nor-Tech.

A groan sounded behind Rif. He turned. Brown slid to the floor of the parapet, having taken a round to the chest. *Fuck.* No way his body armor could fully withstand the .50 cal ammunition.

"I'm on it." Johansson grabbed a QuikClot from his kit and started ripping away Brown's vest in order to stabilize the wound.

Rif kept firing, one of his bullets thumping into the driver. The Glassstream accelerated toward the castle. The machine gunner kept firing, not realizing his driver had been neutralized and was leaning on the throttle. *Closer, closer.*

Rif threw himself down on the rampart as the boat slammed into the dock and flew over it and into the castle's wall with a deafening crash. The rampart vibrated, but the Glassstream lost the battle against the ancient stone. Rif poked his head over the edge. Two bloody smudges marked the wall below him where the gunner and driver had been thrown into the wall. The boat was shattered and leaking iridescent fluid into the lake.

Neil and Stewart pulled up to the dock nearby and jumped out to inspect the crash.

"Clear," Stewart said.

"Brown took a round," Rif called down. "We'll get him to a hospital on the mainland. Go help Thea," Rif said.

"Roger that." Wheeling the boat around, the two Scots headed back out as the sound of the local police response kicked up along the shore.

Chapter 106

Prospero's ears buzzed from the cacophony of metal smacking metal and glass as bullets peppered the ferry. Aiming from the empty window frames of the lower deck, Luciano and the remainder of Bassam's men fired back while Thea, Jean-Luc, and the guard did their best from above. The sulfuric stench of gunpowder flooded the vessel, but all Prospero could smell was a rat. Only three people knew the exchange would take place at Lake Garda: Prospero, Bassam's top lieutenant, and Luciano.

Bassam's man had nothing to gain by foiling the exchange; he'd never be able to fence the nuclear material.

Luciano, on the other hand, stood to gain plenty.

Of course.

His nephew's insolence, his defiant behavior, the surprise attack by Mirsad in Bosnia—it all made perfect sense. But then another thought occurred: Luciano couldn't have organized all this himself. He didn't have the resources or the savvy to pull off an attack like this. He had to be working with someone.

Enzo Spruilli.

It had to be revenge for Marco's death. The CIA agent had waited years to pay back the Salvatore family for his father's killing, an impressive display of patience and cunning. And this was the perfect opportunity: steal the nukes, squash the deal, and finish Stefano's son off so Luciano could take over the business. Then again, the men in the Glasstream were firing at the ferry with his nephew on board. Had Luciano been duped? Did Enzo play him too? It didn't really matter: Enzo knew as well as Prospero did that there were a dozen people who would be more than happy to take his place if Luciano didn't survive.

Prospero looked across the passenger deck of the ferry and located Luciano taking cover behind one of the doors to the hold. As the barrage continued, the old man edged his way closer to his nephew's position.

The machine gun operator finished another pass at the ferry, the driver veering away before Thea and crew could take them out. Prospero climbed to his feet and bolted the last few meters to Luciano, ignoring the throbbing in his hip. Realization passed between them. His nephew swung his SIG Sauer toward him.

But Prospero was too close. He grabbed his nephew's gun hand and twisted two fingers back with a vicious jerk. *Snap.* The gun clattered to the deck.

Luciano yelped in pain, then nailed Prospero's bad hip with a ferocious kick. Prospero staggered backward, waves of agony ripping through him. The joint didn't just hurt; it felt loose, unstable. Vertigo setting in, he stumbled forward, grabbing the lapel of Luciano's jacket with his right hand. If the little rat fucker wanted to play dirty, he was all in, fucked up hip or not.

Luciano tried to pull away, but Prospero yanked him tighter, slightly off to one side. A collar choke would halt any more stuttering. Ensnaring the back of his nephew's suit, he grabbed a handful of the *superfino* material with his left hand. Prospero's right hand slipped underneath his other arm, grabbing the left collar of Luciano's jacket. A little tug to tighten his grip, and he had control.

He pushed his head into Luciano's for counterpressure while twisting his wrists as if accelerating a motorcycle. His nephew struggled against the choke hold, swinging his elbows and punching his uncle in the rib cage, but at this distance the blows lacked power. Prospero thought of his father, who valued family above all, and then his sister, Luciano's mother. Should he back off?

He lifted his head to stare into his nephew's bloodshot eyes.

The man was a sociopath, loyal to no one. *Fuck it.* He'd be doing the world a favor. Prospero turned up the pressure on his wrists, compressing the artery in Luciano's neck. Seconds ticked by, and Luciano slumped to the ground, unconscious. Prospero sank with him, his hip screaming in pain, and kept up the hold until his nephew's body shuddered and then lay still.

He looked up. The hostages and hired men stared at the two of them, entwined in a deadly embrace on the floor. One of Prospero's foot soldiers nodded and said, "*Bene*," before turning away to face the incoming Glasstream. Nobody else said a word. As he'd suspected, Luciano wouldn't be missed.

Chapter 107

Thea prepared for the next pass. The machine gun on the Glassman cycled over and over, a steady stream of large-caliber bullets hitting the ferry. She fired back, hitting one of the men in the leg.

She low-crawled across the deck for a better position as the boat veered to the aft end, Jean-Luc right beside her. The noise was overwhelming, bullets smashing into metal and glass. More screams came from below.

She heard a solid *thunk*. Blood sprayed across her cheek. Prospero's man had been hit, the bullet shattering his skull.

Rif's voice in her earpiece moments before had unsettled her. Brown had taken one of the big rounds to the chest, and they were trying to get him to a hospital. But then she got a bit of good news.

"We're on our way," Stewart said, his Scottish burr never sounding better.

In the distance, she spotted the Nor-Tech closing fast. The reinforcements were most welcome, given the pounding they were taking. She shoved in a fresh magazine while Jean-Luc continued firing. One of his bullets connected with the machine gunner, and the man slumped on the platform.

The driver panicked, his main protection gone. He turned away from the ferry, but he was still within range of their M4s. Thea and Jean-Luc fired on full auto, spraying the boat until the driver collapsed. The Glasstream stalled in the water as the ferry chugged along.

She inhaled a deep breath, scanning the water for any other attackers.

Neil and Stewart circled the Glasstream. "Neutralized," Stewart said over the radio from the Nor-Tech. Thea and Jean-Luc gave each other a look, and he knew what was on her mind.

"Go ahead and check on the boys," Jean-Luc said with a nod. "But before you go, take this—from what I can tell, you've been running on empty for a while now and that can't be good."

She gave him a look of pure gratitude as she took the energy bar that had materialized in his hand, wondering why she had hidden her diabetes from the team for so long. Her worry had been that they would think less of her, but those fears had been unfounded; they just thought of it as part of who she was, like the color of her hair. And instead of thinking of it as a weakness, they just made sure to pack extra snacks.

She wolfed down the nut bar as she rushed downstairs, her boots crunching on the shattered glass scattered all over the deck.

"Nice shooting." Prospero sat on the floor with one leg out in front of him at an awkward angle.

"Lucky for you," she said, blowing past him.

All the hostages were facedown on the floor, hidden behind the ferry's large bulkhead. The fortified steel had provided plenty of protection.

"Anyone hurt?"

People climbed to their feet, looking unsteady and shell-shocked. The only person who didn't move was Luciano. She did a quick head count. All accounted for, two of whom ran straight into her arms during her census-taking. Ayan and Jabari clung to her like shipwreck victims holding on to a life raft. She kneeled, hugging them both.

"You guys okay?"

They shrugged. "We're hungry. They didn't give us any breakfast," Ayan said.

She laughed. "We can fix that."

Prospero, limping and clearly in pain, joined them inside. "Everyone okay?"

"Everyone except your nephew." Prospero looked down at Luciano's body and shook his head, taking the news remarkably well. "Who were these guys, Prospero?"

"You wouldn't believe me if I told you."

"Try me."

"The CIA."

Chapter 108

A few weeks had passed since the hijacking and aftermath. Thankfully, Brown's Kevlar vest had saved his life. He'd spent ten days in the hospital but was back in the office as a desk jockey until he fully recuperated.

Some circumstances could be fixed; others couldn't.

Johann Dietrich's death haunted Thea every day. Gernot Dietrich and the surviving members of the Freedom Guardians who had participated in the attack on the Hagia Sophia were in jail, awaiting trial in Turkey. The punishment would be severe, and she wouldn't be surprised if the case figured into the ongoing debate about capital punishment in the country. No matter what happened in the sentencing phase, of course, Dietrich had already lost the most meaningful thing in his life. Just ask her own father.

Papa's scheming had only led to disaster for his family, her brother and stepmother paying the ultimate price for his machinations. Thea burned to discover the real reason Papa had spoken to Prospero Salvatore all those years ago, but he was sticking to the story about the real-estate deal. She knew that was a lie and promised herself she'd uncover the truth one day.

Thea had spoken to Fatima Abboud several times, impressed by the young woman's courage and resilience. Although heartbroken over Johann, she hadn't let the horrific events drain the light from her life. Instead, she was more committed than ever to becoming a doctor and saving lives. Johann would have been proud.

Identifying the attackers at Lake Garda had led to a few interesting revelations. Enzo Spruilli had been working with Luciano to steal the nukes and eliminate Prospero in a double cross. The rumor was that Prospero's father had engineered Enzo's father's disappearance many years ago, but the CIA agent could never prove it. Apparently, Enzo had struck up a business partnership with Prospero years ago so he could get close enough to the mobster to exact revenge. The association through Gladio, and the group's rivalry with the Freedom Guardians, had only helped mask Enzo's true goal. His mistake had been picking Luciano, hotheaded and impulsive at the best of times, as his accomplice.

After Prospero related the bulk of this history to Thea, the ferry had docked back at Scaliger Castle, and the plane's passengers were freed at last. Prospero, true to form, had melted away before he could be questioned by the local police. And by the time Thea had informed Gabrielle Farrah and, through her, the CIA, Enzo, too, had disappeared into the ether. If Thea were Enzo, she would stay in the ether—Prospero would not be forgiving if he ever caught up with him.

Even the Broken Arrow had its own mysterious history. Back in 1956, the CIA had conspired to "disappear" two nuclear cores en route to Morocco so that Gernot Dietrich's father, the original leader of the *Freiheitswächter*, could store them in his cellar—in case the communists invaded Europe again. The nukes had been stored down there for years until Gernot hatched his insane plan to turn the world against the Arabs by faking a nuclear attack on Hungary's Parliament Building. He figured that would make the public more sympathetic to the release of a targeted bioweapon aimed at ethnic Arabs. And at Leopold's encouragement he'd co-opted Ocean to help him. As it turned out, she not only held a degree in nuclear physics but biogenetics as well—and an ax to grind against the Middle East. She'd abandoned her career in Japan to work in an African lab developing genetically targeted medications two years ago, and when Gernot Dietrich came calling, the temptation for payback had proved too much to resist.

She thought of Earl Johnson, the pilot who had never stopped looking for his missing friend, "Slow Joe," feeling he had somehow failed to keep his team together. And how tough it must have been for Joe and the others who had crewed on the missing plane to leave their loved ones behind, sacrificing everything for the sake of their country's secret plans to embed militia cells across Europe. Apparently, the men had been given new identities and were forbidden to ever contact their former friends, family, or associates.

But enough of that—tonight was a night of celebration. Papa was hosting a surprise party for Ayan and Jabari, to celebrate their new life in the UK. Thea, Rif, Hakan, and Christos clustered around the restaurant's entrance, waiting for the boys to arrive with the Wavertons.

The maître d' and restaurant staff rushed to and fro, finalizing the preparations. Most of the partygoers milled around the bar, waiting for the guests of honor to arrive. The entire Quantum tactical team was there too, of course.

Her father had been trying to reconnect with her since the kidnapping, but she had kept him at arm's length, sick of the labyrinth of secrets and lies he still refused to give up. It seemed that he was making an effort to change, delegating the daily responsibility of running Paris Industries to his CEO, Ahmed Khan, so he could focus on his charitable efforts. But that also could just be for show. She hated to be cynical, but she suspected things would never be right between her and Papa—certainly not until he came clean about Prospero and whatever other skeletons were in his walk-in closet.

Christos peered out the window, as eager as she was to see the boys. That much, at least, was genuine, and something they could share.

"Are they close?" Hakan asked.

"Any minute now," Christos said. "Mrs. Waverton just texted me. She asked who was on the guest list."

"We should have invited Prospero Salvatore," Rif said with a big grin.

"Ayan and Jabari did seem to have a connection with him," Thea said, smiling at Rif, handsome in a dark blue suit. "I'd love to know what that's about."

"Stockholm syndrome," Rif said.

She laughed out loud. "I don't think so. Prospero seemed genuinely tender with the boys; did you know he asked me on the ferry about starting scholarships for them?"

"Well, we won't be hearing from him again until he's good and ready to be heard from," Rif snorted.

"We don't need his help anyway," Christos said. "Everything is taken care of."

Thea looked at her father—why was his nose out of joint? Was it just that he wanted credit for all the support he'd given the boys, or did this have something to do with whatever was going on between him and Prospero? She shook her head, trying to clear it. *Not tonight.*

"I still can't believe the bastard got off scot-free," Hakan said.

"Helps to have dirt on the CIA." Thea too was irritated that Prospero had walked away from it all. Dillman and Karlsson had both died on his watch, whoever else it was he wanted to blame. And he had definitely murdered Luciano—there were witnesses to that one. But he knew where the metaphorical bodies were buried and, according to Gabrielle, the CIA was only too happy to help Prospero once they had cleaned up the Italian field office using the information he had provided.

Then again, Prospero had taken care of the boys, and not just because they had given him leverage over Thea; he had genuinely liked them, and besides, hurting children was not in his playbook. Just ask Captain Rivers—his daughters had been returned to him unharmed, as promised. She shook her head: mostly unharmed was more like it; being kidnapped always left a scar, no matter the outcome. Still, for all his sins—and there were many—Prospero had his charms.

"They're here." Papa signaled to the maître d', and the lights dimmed. The room quieted, everyone gathering at the door in anticipation of the boys' arrival. They had been told they and the Wavertons were having dinner with Christos alone.

Ayan and Jabari piled out of the car and sprinted for the door, the Wavertons allowing them to rush ahead.

A hush fell over the crowd.

The doors opened.

"Surprise!" the group yelled.

Ayan and Jabari burst into the restaurant. The boys were beaming, high-fiving everyone. They both hugged Thea hard.

Jabari tugged at Christos's jacket. "Thank you so much. The Wavertons are very nice people." The joy in Papa's eyes melted a layer of the ice around Thea's heart, but there were many more layers to go.

Jabari turned to Thea and Rif, bouncing with excitement. "We love the Wavertons and their horses. We're going to learn how to ride."

"You know," Thea said, "Rif is a talented rider. I'm sure he'd be happy to teach you."

"Will you?" Jabari glanced up at the soldier.

"We can start as soon as you like—tomorrow, even." Rif touched the boy's shoulder, then looked up at Thea. "I believe I've earned a little time off."

"You certainly have, Rif." Thea leaned down and hugged Jabari. "Why don't you go ask the Wavertons when they would like to start your lessons."

Jabari ran off to find his brother and talk to his new family.

Rif nodded to her. "You've earned some time off too, come to think of it."

"You're right. Maybe we should go get that dinner we've been talking about for, oh, the last couple of months." Thea had rushed off to handle a case in Bolivia shortly after returning from Istanbul, so they hadn't had a chance to enjoy a dinner they'd discussed.

"What an excellent idea. How about Italian?"

"Do you know a place?" She didn't go out for dinner much in London.

"I do—in Venice."

Venice. She blushed, then laughed to mask her surprise that she was so excited by the very idea of it. "They ought to have some nice Italian restaurants there."

"One would hope." Rif smiled.

ACKNOWLEDGMENTS

If I were going to be skyjacked, I'd stack the plane with people who have mad skills—asking for the help of those friends who could *write* me out of trouble, or those that could literally *take on* the hijackers kinetically and triumph. Thanks to all of these talented individuals who helped settle any turbulence during the making of *Skyjack*:

This book would be a shadow of itself without the brilliance of two people who have aviation running through their veins. Flight test engineer Bill Scott, the former Rocky Mountain bureau chief for *Aviation Week & Space Technology*, was instrumental in helping me understand aerobatic stunts, disabling a plane's electrical system, and landing a jet in extreme circumstances, among other misadventures. Former stealth bomber pilot and commercial airline captain James Hannibal taught me about thunderstorm penetration speed, the dramatic display of static electricity on a windscreen, the deafening noise created by hail hitting a fuselage, and other key details about flight dynamics. These gurus shared their knowledge, advice, and enthusiasm, and I can't thank them enough. Any errors are mine alone.

Thea Paris has type 1 diabetes, and I'd like to encourage people with diabetes—and those with other illnesses—to remain unstoppable, inspired to reach for the stars. Our grit and determination can take us to amazing places. Thanks to Bethanne Strasser, a dynamic mother of six, author, and runner—your patience and care with my endless questions is deeply appreciated, and your feedback on the diabetes scenes was brilliant. Dr. Hertzel Gerstein, thanks for all that you do for people with diabetes. I appreciate you sharing your knowledge, time, and creative ideas. Thea is lucky to have a doc like you on her team! Bekah Hata from TD1 Mod Squad and Devin Abraham from Once Upon a Crime, thank you for your warm support.

As an action heroine, Thea handles various weapons, uses explosives from time to time, needs jury-rigged solutions, engages in hand-to-hand combat, and thrives on everything tactical. To accurately represent these skills, I need badass help. Christopher Schneider from 5.11 Tactical, you've made learning an absolute riot with your personal how-to videos on edgy exploits. Your support and charm always lift me up. Rigo Durazo, acting out those fight scenes on the stairs was incredibly helpful—and Thea lives by your wise philosophy. Adam Hamon, Mr. SAS, I appreciate you sharing tactical suggestions over Tito's as your stories held me spellbound. Ken Perry, you're such a positive force in my life, full of sage advice, and the very best photographer of my cover in foreign locales—totally excited about book three, but Killian better prepare to drown his disappointment in Guinness!

A crisis response consultant, Thea travels to hot spots around the world to bring hostages home. I've had the honor of meeting several of these real-life heroes, and I only hope Thea can illustrate their bravery. Thanks to Dr. Francis Grimm for his perpetual education and advice—and the best steak dinners. Mark Harris, it's tempting to have Thea kidnap you so I could hear more of your experiences and brilliant suggestions. Gary Noesner, you bring a unique perspective to Thea's world, working in hostage negotiation with the FBI and privately—and many scenes are stronger thanks to your insights. And kudos to Sue Williams, my favorite female freedom broker, someone I greatly admire. It has been an absolute honor to know Peter Moore, a wonderful friend who has shared his experiences in captivity after being held in Iraq for almost one thousand days. Nothing makes me happier than shopping for cheese with him in Harrods. And thank you to the brilliant Lieutenant Colonel Dave Grossman for taking the time to read *Skyjack* and giving it such an enthusiastic review.

The crime fiction community is a supportive one. It amazes me how many people go out of their way to help others, and I'm deeply appreciative that so many individuals have offered me advice and support. ITW has truly become my family. The Great One, Steve Berry, recommended me for the position of executive director of ThrillerFest, and I'm grateful for this honor, as it's introduced me into a community like no other. Steve has also been there every step of the way to advise me in this new career. I'd also like to thank Liz Berry for her sensational support with ThrillerFest. It's an absolute honor to work with such a talented mentor and friend. Jessica Johns, your steadfast support and dedication are inspiring.

Karin Slaughter, thank you for connecting me with VSA, a life-changing moment. Peter James, you and Lara are very special to me. Simon Gervais, let's do a book tour in the Bahamas! A.J. Tata, thanks for creating Kim

Jung Howe. Thank you to Lee Child, Jenny Milchman, Dawn Ius, Bryan Robinson (love those cookies!), Nancy Bilyeau, James Rollins, Linwood Barclay, Neal Griffin, Joseph Finder, Linda Stasi, Anthony Franze, Jennifer Hughes, Barry Lancet, Karen Dionne, Chris Graham, Heather Graham, Amanda Kelly, Kathleen Antrim, Terry Rodgers, Dennis Kennett, Shirley Kennett, Taylor Antrim, Jillian Stein, Roan Chapin, Shannon and John Raab, Lisa Gardner, Lissa Price, and so many more. You know who you are—as you make my day brighter with your kindness. Raising a glass to the Rogue Women Writers who are trailblazing a path for future heroines: Gayle Lynds, Francine Mathews, Jamie Freveletti, Karna Bodman, Sonja Stone, Chris Goff, and S.L. Manning. And to my friends at the Grand Hyatt in NYC: K.J. number one, the super special K.J. Birch, Alison Wied, Wan Yi Tang, and all the other incredible folks who help make the Hyatt my second home. And cheers to Peter Hildick-Smith, one of the smartest and kindest people I know.

Crime writers depend on reviewers and aficionados to spread the word to readers. Jeff Ayers, Jon Land, Mystery Mike Bursaw, George Easter, Don Longmuir, Barbara Peters, Jacques Filippi, Ali Karim, Mike Stotter, Noelle Holten, Sarah Hardy, Pam Stack, Fran Lewis, Dave Simms, Keith Katsikas, thanks for being so supportive—consider Thea on speed dial for you. Michael Dillman, I loved "killing" you using your signature moustache! And the Real Book Spy, Ryan Steck, his lovely wife Melissa (my number-one Thea-ologist), and their phenomenal kids, including little "Mitch Rapp"—you have been beyond generous. I'm touched by your genuine enthusiasm for Thea Paris and her adventures.

Receiving honest feedback from critical minds is a gift, and I'm indebted to Larry Gandle for his contributions in that regard. His analysis of both *The Freedom*

Broker and *Skyjack* led to significant changes that have made both books stronger. One thing for sure—if Larry offers a compliment, you can truly celebrate, as every word out of his mouth is direct and honest.

Warmest thanks to Donna Scher whose brilliant psychological analysis and eagle eyes helped shape the book from draft to finished manuscript. And Wendy Chan, who is such an ardent cheerleader. Susan Jenkins, Empress of All Things Literary, you're an inspiration (and a heck of an editor), always working hard and striving for more. Gabi Fockter, your support has been truly amazing. Thanks to Marsha Mann, Angela Trevivian, Suzanna Zeigler, Linda Crank, Robyn Strassguertl, and my phenomenal tennis friends who help clear my mind of sinister plots. Cheers to Russ and Pauline Howe for their lovely support. And thanks to Anne and Chuck Jones for fostering my love of travel and adventure. I'm grateful for Frank Gomberg's keen eyes and the generous support of Jim Vigmond, Sharon Vigmond, Tim Boland, and Erin Farrell. And warmest thanks to Janet Zucker, Katie Zucker, and Jamie Napoli for believing Thea Paris has film potential.

My team at Quercus is simply remarkable. Each and every member goes above and beyond to offer their support and expertise. Amanda Harkness and Elyse Gregov, thank you for brainstorming with me, dreaming up innovative and fun ideas to spread the word about Thea. Your hard work preparing for the tours is deeply appreciated. Jason Bartholomew, thanks for giving me this wonderful opportunity to share Thea's adventures. Amelia Ayrelan Iuvino, your brilliant editing, insightful questions, and remarkable attention to detail are so appreciated. A *very* special thank you to my publisher Nathaniel Marunas for his tireless efforts to delve deeper into character, background, and the recesses of the web to find the most fascinating details. *Skyjack* is richer and smoother than I could have ever made it alone. And we'll always have Robbie, with two *b*'s, the British way.

It's truly a privilege to be published in the U.K., and I'd like to thank my brilliant team at Headline for their efforts to build an audience for Thea near Quantum International Security headquarters. Led by the intrepid Jennifer Doyle, my sincerest thanks to the Sachertorte and Pimm's dream team, Jo Liddiard, Millie Seaward, and Kitty Stogdon. And thanks to Emma Horton for the keen editing. You all brighten my day. I appreciate the efforts of the Midas team, who always go the golden mile: Tony Mulliken, Sophie Ransom, Fiona Marsh, and Rachel Kennedy. I'd also like to thank Donna Nopper from Hachette Canada for her kind efforts, Mickey Mikkelson from Creative Edge for his unflagging gusto, and Kim Dower of Kim-from-L.A. for her positivity.

Thea has Quantum International Security backing her up, and I'm proud to have the dynamic Victoria Sanders Agency on my side. Victoria Sanders, thanks for believing in me and Thea. I'll join you for potato chips and champagne in your pool any day of the week. Bernadette Baker-Vaughn, your warm support and wonderful sense of humor is deeply appreciated. Jessica Spivey, you are so upbeat and helpful, it's always a pleasure to hear from you.

I'd like to give special thanks to David Morrell, to whom this book is dedicated. When I read his spy trilogy years ago, I was inspired to become a thriller author—took a little while, but here I am. Imagine how excited I was to first meet David at Seton Hill while I was doing my Masters in Creative Writing. His sage advice stayed with me, and I kept working diligently on my craft. When I reconnected with him at

ThrillerFest, I had the pleasure of writing a profile of him that's now featured on his website. The day he offered to mentor me, it felt like my life had come full circle. I'm honored to call David a friend, and I have the deepest respect for his incredible drive and body of work. Since creating Rambo in *First Blood*, he has been a trailblazer in our field, constantly reinventing himself and striving for excellence while still finding time to help others.

A profound thank you to RJH, who is always there, commiserating during the tough times, celebrating the good times, and helping me maintain a sense of humor at all times. My life is so much better with you in it.

About the Type

Typeset in Swift EF, 10.75/15 pt.

Named for an acrobatic city bird native to Holland, Swift was designed by Gerard Unger in 1985 to meet the need for a typeface that could remain crisp and clear after coming off the high-speed newspaper presses of the day. For its original distribution as a PostScript font, it was leased to German foundry Elsner+Flake.

Typeset by Scribe Inc., Philadelphia, Pennsylvania